ASHME'S SONG

PRAISE FOR DUATERO
BY BRAD C. ANDERSON

"This well-written ecological apocalyptic tale is spellbinding . . . The writing is sharp and flawless, keeping you drawn into the plot. This book is a true work of literary art."

TOBY A. WELCH, SASKBOOKS REVIEWS

"Haunting, action-packed, and entertaining, author Brad C. Anderson's **Duatero** is a must-read sci-fi dystopian read . . . A unique and creative tale . . ."

ANTHONY AVINA

"A real page-turner packed with drama, horror, and hope. The characters are engaging and really help draw you in piece by piece."

SCRIBBLE'S WORTH REVIEWS

"Combines power-armoured soldiers from the pages of sci-fi pulps, a world as intriguing yet bleak as Mid-World from Stephen King's **The Dark Tower**, and an evil as terrifying and paranoia-inducing as John Carpenter's **The Thing**. A descent into the darkness of a failing world and the brutal zealotry of its defenders."

– MATT MOORE, AURORA AWARD-WINNING AUTHOR
OF *IT'S NOT THE END AND OTHER LIES*

ASHME'S SONG

SHADOWPAW PRESS

BRAD C. ANDERSON

ASHME'S SONG
By Brad C. Anderson

Shadowpaw Press
Regina, Saskatchewan, Canada
www.shadowpawpress.com

Copyright © 2024 by Brad C. Anderson
All rights reserved

All characters and events in this book are fictitious.
Any resemblance to persons living or dead is coincidental.

The scanning, uploading, and distribution of this book via the Internet or any other means without the permission of the publisher is illegal and punishable by law.

Trade Paperback ISBN: 978-1-998273-16-4
Ebook ISBN: 978-1-998273-17-1

Shadowpaw Press is grateful for
the financial support of Creative Saskatchewan.

To my lovely wife, Joelle.

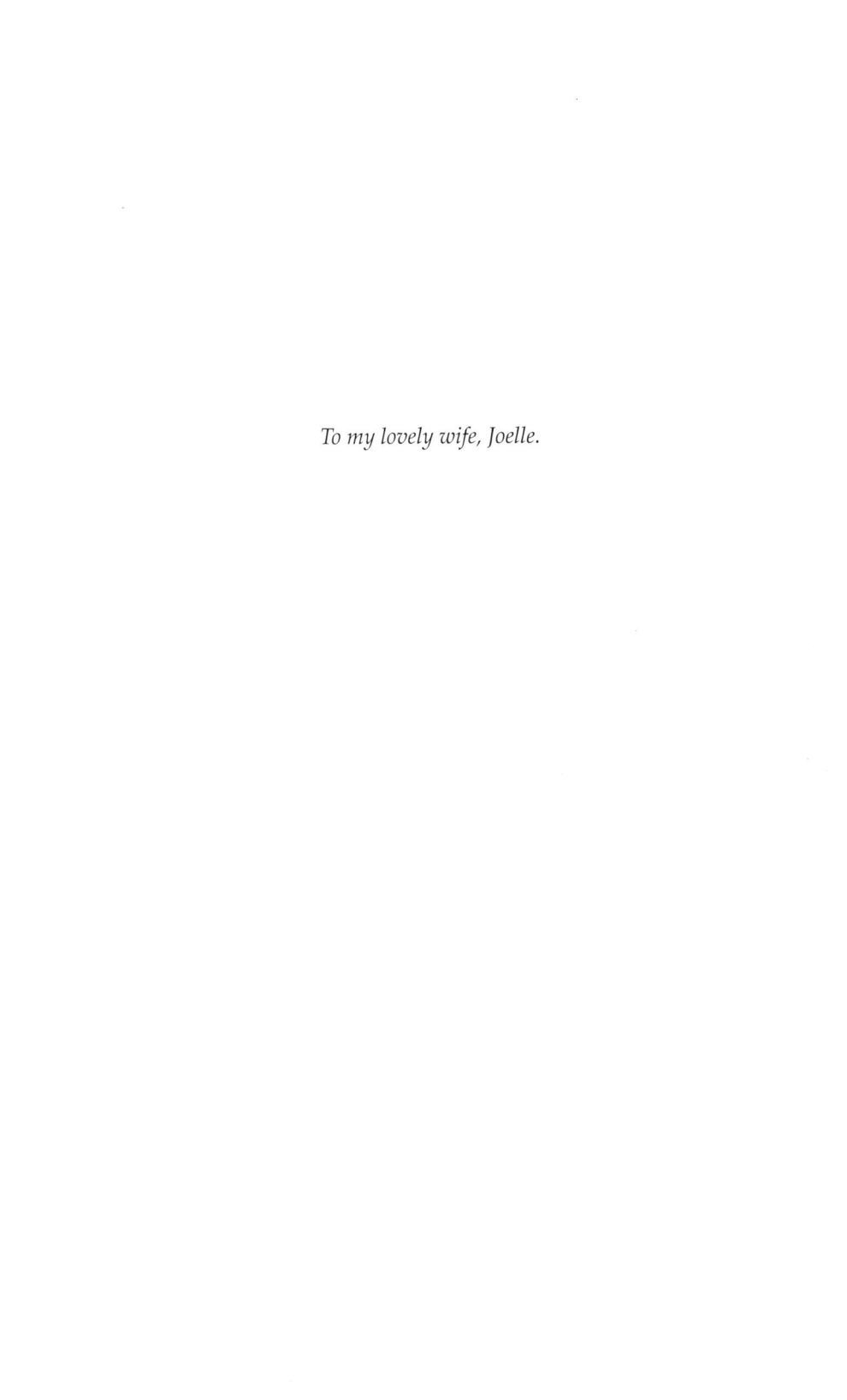

*"What am I supposed to do
 If I want to talk about peace and understanding,
 But you only understand the language of the sword?"*

HEILUNG

CHAPTER 1

ASHME REMEMBERED when she first realized her father was a broken man. It was on a night eight years past when a thunderstorm rattled the city of New Uruk. Unable to sleep and wanting to watch the lightning, she looked out her bedroom window and saw him in the yard. He was digging a hole by the light of the back porch, drenched, and when the lightning flashed, and thunder boomed, he dropped into the hole, hands covering his head, crying, screaming until the roll of thunder stopped.

With a gun pointed at her head and the corpse of Keshda—a good kid, lived three floors up—sprawled on the street, his blood warm and sticky on her face, she wondered if it had been days like this that broke him.

Every resident of the Agade Gardens apartment complex was on the street, guarded by soldiers of the Caelum Peace Corps—the CPC—backed by those floating death machines they called angels. Her twin brother, Shen, was on his knees beside her while other CPC troops looted their apartments in what some limp-dicked Ostarrichi sergeant called a mapping raid.

The CPC was acting as if Keshda was the first wave of the liberating Free New Mesopotamian Army sweeping through the city instead of a punk kid. Guns pointed at Meso faces, guards screamed, "Get down!", and angels swooped into attack position. The trooper that had shot Keshda looked unhinged, eyes wild, ready to mow down Ashme and every other Meso lined along the block.

Her twin brother moaned beside her. If this mess dragged on, he would work himself up to a wailing cry. "It's okay, Shen," she said, masking the fear in her voice with a sing-song lilt, trying to soothe him as she went to her knees. "Do as they say like we practised—"

"Shut your mouth!" Trooper Wild Eyes screamed, his voice breaking into hysterics. He planted the barrel of his gun squarely on her forehead. She held her breath. The acrid smell of burned gunpowder lingered around the barrel. His hands shook, causing the gun to vibrate.

"No threats detected," an angel announced, speaking Ostarrichi. Whoever developed the angels must have had a department of system designers and linguists working on programming that precise tone of contempt and condescension in their mechanical voices.

"Bullshit!" Wild Eyes said. "He came at me with a knife!"

"No threats detected."

Keshda had had no knife. She'd been right beside him, had his blood on her face. While the CPC had marched up and down in their cobalt-blue armour and stupid gold epaulettes, waving their guns about, Keshda had yawned and stretched in a mock display of boredom. It was the type of sassy defiance you would expect from a boy of sixteen.

Wild Eyes shot him. Eight times.

Sergeant Limp Dick stomped down the street demanding a "sit-rep."

"This Meso shit came at me with a knife," Wild Eyes said, swinging his gun to point at Keshda's corpse. Blood drenched the kid's grimy white shirt, punctured with dark holes, his arms and legs splayed at twisted angles like a crumpled puppet.

Limp Dick motioned Wild Eyes to step away. An angel, about

as tall and wide as a child and shaped like a stingray, lowered down to confer with them. Its metallic exoskeleton reflected the buildings and people on the street, warping the images, creating a twisted vision of the world. Two rotors on the end of each wing kept it hovering. They were reviewing footage the angel recorded on a data screen it projected.

Shen moaned, rocking gently. If he lost it, he would get himself beaten and arrested—or, given the CPC's mood, shot. She thought of launching an EM shield or even something as simple as an ID shield into the nanohaze to hide her and her brother, but with so many angels floating around, the odds were one of them would detect her program and blast her into oblivion.

The sergeant ordered Wild Eyes to the low-orbital troop transport blocking the middle of the street and then walked over to Ashme. "Do you speak Ostarrichi?" he asked.

She shook her head, eyes wide, pointing at her ears, shrugging. "No standunder."

An angel glided behind the sergeant. "Citizen 539618-d, class 2A, Ashme ultu Vanc. Attended New Uruk University from 48 to 50. Ostarrichi language competency presumed proficient."

Damn. Ashme launched an ID shield, a heaviness pulling deep in her body as the program drew off her, lifting into the nanohaze where it would muddy up the angels' ability to retrieve her data.

The sergeant bent over and got in her face. His breath stunk of stale coffee, and lines crinkled the corner of his eyes. Like all Ostarrichi, his skin was golden. They were descendants of refugees from an Ark trade ship that was destroyed when an AI they were fiddling with hit singularity, achieved Sentient status, and catabolized the ship for parts. They'd relocated to Esharra generations back and had been acting like dicks ever since.

He took out his own dagger from a leather scabbard on his belt and placed the tip on the tattoo under her right eye. "Was this the knife he used to attack my trooper? Why'd he attack a fully armed CPC trooper with a knife? Was he depressed?"

She guessed the angel's footage showed Keshda did nothing wrong. Poor Wild Eyes might have to face a disciplinary hearing for shooting an unarmed Meso; might have to get his wrists slapped. Unless, of course, they could get testimony from another Meso corroborating his story. Eye-witness corroboration would override the video evidence, in which case Wild Eyes would probably get a commendation for bravery.

Screw that. "I didn't see anything," Ashme said, speaking Ostarrichi.

Sergeant Limp Dick pressed the tip of the knife gently into her cheek. She winced as it pricked her skin. "This was the knife he used, wasn't it?"

Careful now—she had to wrap this up. If the CPC took her in for questioning, she would end up in a calming centre. "I didn't see what happened." Her cousin Ganzer and Great Aunt Melammu could look after Shen if they took her away. It would be a heavy load on Ganzer, but he would bear it.

Shen began crying as he rocked on his knees. The golden-skinned sergeant turned on him. "What's with crybaby?"

"He doesn't speak Ostarrichi," Ashme said. "And he was on the far side of me. He didn't see anything."

"What's wrong with him? He's a grown-ass man but crying like a two-year-old."

"You're scaring him."

"I'm not talking to you, Meso." He waved the angel over.

"Citizen 539619-d, class 2A," the angel proclaimed. "Shen-shen ultu Vanc. Chromosome seven defective. Unedited."

"He's defective," Sergeant Limp Dick said with the glee of a bully finding his victim. If the angel's cold assessment had not tipped the sergeant to Shen's problem, her twin brother's looks should have. He had an elfin face with a large forehead, with big eyes placed close together, framed by small epicanthic folds. His head was too small for his slightly pointed ears. He had a short, upturned nose and broad upper lip. His mouth was wide, stretching from one side of his face to the other, his teeth widely spaced.

Ashme bit her lip. She wanted to launch a protocol enslaving one of the angels and set it to blast Limp Dick to bloody rags. She could only control one angel, however, and only if she got lucky. Dozens of angels hovered nearby, plus a squad of flesh-and-blood CPC troopers. "I was the one beside Keshda, not him," she said.

The sergeant looked at Ashme. "I thought you didn't see anything." He waited, letting a field of barren silence open between them. She matched his silence. He got bored with waiting. Nodding the angel over, he ordered, "Translate."

The angel loomed over Shen, who rocked rhythmically while he cried. It translated the sergeant's questions into Kanu, Ashme's mother tongue, and flung the words at Shen in a tone suggesting that at any moment, it would stop talking and start shooting. "Citizen Shenshen, you will answer this officer's questions. Was this the knife your compatriot used to attack our CPC trooper?"

The sergeant held his knife to Shen's face.

"You want to know if that's the knife?" Shen said, gasping through tears.

"Yes."

"I didn't see a knife. I don't know why the man shot him. What happened is we were all lined up nice and orderly, then *bam!* Guns roared like dogs barking and knocked that man onto his back."

"The knife. Answer now."

"The knife? No. I don't know. I didn't see a knife. I see the knife you're holding. Is that the knife you're talking about?"

Ashme said, "He said no," before the officer confused Shen.

The sergeant turned to Ashme. "Are you sure you didn't see the boy use this knife to attack my CPC trooper?"

Saying yes would end this. But then, what of Keshda? What

about his family? Could she ever face his mother in the halls if she said yes? "There was no knife."

"Hey, analog," the angel translated the sergeant's insult to Shen. "If you say this was the knife he used to attack the CPC, this all ends, and you get to go home."

"I didn't see," Shen said, a little defiance creeping into his voice. It bothered him when people called him names.

"If you don't tell us this was the knife, we'll have to take your sister in for questioning."

She and Shen had practised how to handle CPC. She prayed Shen remembered. "We can't help you," she said in Kanu for Shen. This was part of their script.

"We do not want to cause trouble, officer," Shen said, playing his part. "I can't help you. Am I free to go?" Shen spoke well; well enough that people failed to realize the depths of his mental disability.

"No, you're not free to go," the angel translated. "If we can't settle this, we'll take you and your sister in for further questioning."

"I can't help you."

"Do you know what will happen to your sister in a calming centre?"

"He said he can't help you," Ashme said.

The sergeant pointed the knife in Ashme's face. "How long do you think your brother would last in a calming centre? What's wrong with you that you would let that happen to him?"

Ashme wanted to scream that his CPC trooper was a murdering bastard who jacked off to Meso corpses. "I'm sorry, I can't help you. Am I free to go?"

"For fuck's sake," the sergeant said. He called over two CPC soldiers and pointed at Shen. "This man's a witness to an assault on a CPC officer. He's not cooperating."

The soldiers needed no further prompting. They each grabbed one of Shen's arms and hoisted him to his feet.

Shen screamed, "I can't help you!"

Ashme wanted to burn every one of those golden-skinned bastards to ash. She prepared to launch a protocol into the nano-haze to enslave one of the angels. *They want blood? Here it comes.* This was *her* home.

One of the angels emitted a siren. Did they detect her program? She had yet to launch it.

The siren ended, after which an angel announced, "Code 2 riot in progress, Rabu Flats. Your unit is ordered to attend." All but one of the angels broke away, their engines humming as they rose above the buildings and east toward the riots.

The sergeant swore. "Stupid Mesos rioting at the Hab, again." Stabbing a thumb over his shoulder at Keshda's body, he ordered one of his soldiers to call a medi-drone to "clean this shit up."

CPC troops began streaming out of the apartment block into their waiting transport while the sergeant looked at the rest of the Mesos on their knees. "The CPC thanks you for your cooperation. You're free to go home now." He looked at Ashme. "Lucky."

CHAPTER 2

THEY WERE STILL SUCKING air past their teeth; that was about the best you could say of their day. Ashme had her arm around Shen as he kneeled over the shattered shards of his piano keyboard. He had trouble buttering his own bread, but in six months, he had learned to play the keyboard halfway decently. Now his keyboard lay in pieces, compliments of the CPC's raid.

"I'll get the music up in a minute," she said, trying to comfort Shen. He rocked back and forth, hands in his hair. They were in the one-bedroom apartment they shared with Ganzer and their Great Aunt Melammu. An old and frayed couch, beige when it was younger but now the colour of old teeth, was jammed against the wall. It seconded as a pull-out bed for Shen. Behind it, a yellow water stain snaked down the wall. A faint smell of mildew hung in the air, which they had never been able to get rid of despite sanitizing every corner and crack of their home. On the floor, blankets, afghans, bedding, and family pictures that had hung on the wall sat in a pile, where the CPC had dumped them alongside overturned tables and chairs.

The CPC system raiders had burned the link to Subdeo, the AI she had built, keeping her from playing music for her brother.

She launched a program to fix it, the drain of it leaving her body weighing on her.

She was an indigo child, touched by Zini, Spirit of the East Wind, the patron Sentient of Mesos. The nanohaze, created the moment the ancient AI hit singularity and became Sentient, covered the planet of Esharra. Like all indigo children, the nanohaze was a part of Ashme, and she of it, an integrated whole. Through it, she could launch programs carried through the nanohaze by willpower alone, fuelled by her body.

Her stomach growled. With an ID shield launched outside and a repair program launched now, she would eat like a hundred-and-fifteen-kilo hammerball halfback tonight.

Shen whimpered softly. She squeezed him tighter. "I'll buy you a new keyboard," she said, though Ashme had no idea how. She caught a reflection of herself in a shard from a broken mirror. A cheap dyed-blonde hair job, brown roots showing, held in a frayed ponytail, gave the impression of dry straw trampled in the mud. No chance she could afford to get her dye redone this month. She had brown skin and Asiatic eyes that she accentuated with burned cork. Cash had been too scarce to afford real makeup. She was a mess—worn clothes, tatty hair, dirty face.

Where were Ganzer and Melammu? The mapping raid had ended when an angel said something about a riot in Rabu Flats. Could they be caught in that?

"Come on, help me clean up," she said.

"My keyboard is broken. Shattered."

"The music will be on in a minute."

He turned to her, worried. "Is it after noon?"

"Yes, it's okay, you can listen to your music." He loved music but refused to listen or play any until noon each day—one of his foibles. "Let's try to get the place tidy for Aunty Melammu."

Shen turned, eyes wide, brow furrowed. "Do you think they got Aunty Melammu?"

"No, she's fine. The CPC don't want her—she's ancient."

"Her bones are frail like a thin stalk of grain. She could be hurt so easy."

"Ganzer's with her. There aren't enough angels to get past Ganzer."

[What? I'm awake,] her AI pinged once her repair program re-established the connection with it.

[Hello, Subdeo,] she pinged back.

[Oh, it is you. What do you want?]

[Music, please,] she pinged. *[Something Shen likes.]*

The music came on, emanating from the walls. It was a smooth calypso beat, heavy on the steel drums, with a man singing. "Hey, there you go," she said out loud to Shen. "That's a good sign. Come on, help me clean up. We'll start with Aunty Melammu's room."

The two set to work. Shen sang along to the music in his beautiful tenor voice. Melammu's mattress had been cut open, so Ashme found sewing equipment to sew it shut. The drawers were on the floor, underwear and clothing tumbling out. Shen methodically put each thing back one by one.

Ganzer's voice bellowed from the front room. "I'm locked and loaded! I'm giving you one chance to get the fuck out with your brain in your skull!"

At the sound of his voice, a knot of tension in Ashme's shoulders released. "It's just us. Keep it in your pants."

"It's okay, Grandma," Ganzer called out to Melammu.

Her cousin's bulk filled the door to the bedroom. He was a giant block of muscle, dark-skinned, with long blond hair braided down his back and a long beard that he kept in two braids, one on either side of his chin. His eyes, like Ashme's, were Asiatic—about the only family resemblance they shared. Shen called out Ganzer's name, gave him a giant hug that lasted heartbeats, and then ran past, calling out to Aunty Melammu.

"You guys all right?" Ganzer asked.

"Top of the world," Ashme said.

"What happened?"

"CPC 'mapping raid.'"

"Mapping, my ass," he said, looking at the devastation scattered across their home. The piles of clothes and furniture made it more claustrophobic than usual. He picked up a candleholder made of amber-coloured glass knocked on its side by his feet.

"Where were you?" she asked.

"We were at the Hab to meditate. I told you we were going last night."

She looked down the hall outside the room. Shen was hugging Melammu—gently, though; he knew she was frail. The old woman had seen the fall of her mother country, New Mesopotamia, and the rise of Caelum in its stead. She looked at the mess in their apartment with the weathered bitterness of someone who had lived through dozens of mapping raids and worse. Melammu rocked gently to the music coming from the walls, comforting Shen. "Are you all right?" she asked Ashme.

"Fine. We're cleaning up your room—done in a moment." Ashme pulled Ganzer back inside Melammu's room and spoke quietly. "They killed Keshda."

"What? He was just a kid. Why?"

"Because they're shitbags."

Subdeo pinged, *[You've got company.]*

"Someone's coming," she said. *[Who is it?]*

[It's Coty. He has a defence bot with him.]

"It's the bloody landlord," Ashme said.

"Here to collect rent," Ganzer said.

Ashme had forgotten rent was due. Her stomach cramped. "Get the cashtab. I hid it under the carpet there, where the loose corner is," she said, pointing.

"You didn't take it with you when the CPC came?" Ganzer asked, his voice rising.

"No," Ashme called back, heading for the front door. "They would have searched me and found it."

"You left all our cash in our apartment during a raid?"

"It has an EM shield. It's as hidden as I could make it." Ashme arrived at the door.

"I was just fucking meditating!" Ganzer bellowed from Melammu's room. "I'm supposed to be all chill and shit!"

Ashme swung the door open before the landlord could knock. "Hey, Coty, bad timing."

"Hi, Coty," Shen said from behind her on the couch. "The CPC shot Keshda. *Bam!* And then he fell on his back."

"Tough break," Coty said in thickly accented Kanu. He turned to Ashme. "Your rent is due." The landlord was a middle-aged, pot-bellied man wearing a too-short stained shirt. He had short brown hair and the golden skin of an Ostarrichi. His defence bot trundled up beside him, dog-sized, rolling on treads, emitting a whirring whine. Ashme noted an assortment of weapons on it: stun gun, real gun, repulsor fields.

"CPC raided today," she said.

"Yeah, I know," Coty said. "I've been told that at every door."

"Come back tomorrow."

"Rent's due today."

"CPC killed Keshda."

"That's what the defect said," he nodded to Shen. "Who's Keshda, and what's that have to do with your rent?"

"If you're going to bust my nads about rent, least you could do is slap a new coat of paint in the halls and clear the garbage off the floor."

"Least you Mesos could do is stop treating the building like a dump."

Ganzer shouted from Melammu's room, "Son of a bitch!" He stormed out, a wild look in his eyes. "They stole the cashtab!"

She turned on Coty. "You bastards."

The defence bot pivoted and directed its stun emitter at Ashme, ready to strike.

Screw it. The drain on Ashme's bioreserves felt like the fuzz of a dandelion floating away as she launched a program to burn through the bot's firewall and enslave it. Her head spun from the drain, but anger kept her on her feet. Burning the firewall was easy. The bot was more than five years old, and its schematics were leaked a week after it rolled off the assembly line. She set it to idle.

"What'd I do?" Coty asked, unaware his bot was no longer his. "Rent's due and—"

"This is all part of the plan, isn't it? The CPC raid, steal everyone's cash, then you come through demanding rent. No one can pay, so you turn us all out on the street and get to turn this building into a mall or an office block."

"The CPC aren't at my beck and call," Coty said.

"Yeah, whatever."

"Look," Coty said. His gaze slimed down her body and back up again. "If you're short cash, maybe there's other ways you can make up what you owe me."

Ganzer snapped. "What did you say?" He barreled down the hall from Melammu's room, a bear charging.

"Defend!" the landlord ordered his bot as he took a step back. Ashme kept it in idle. He cursed, but to his credit, he stood his ground. Ganzer and Coty began yelling at each other.

Ashme watched Ganzer screaming, veins bulging along his temples and neck. She remembered when she first realized how much of a mama bear he was. It was a few years back after she and Shen had moved in with him and Melammu. They had gone to the Duga Pub, a dive bar down the street where the tables were always sticky with spilled drinks and blacklights gave everyone an unearthly glow. Some chump in a sleeveless shirt and cheap cologne had hit on her, but she had blown him off and gone to the dance floor with her friend, Sura. Unaware Ganzer was her cousin, Sleeveless made the mistake of telling him how he would do anything to smell her panties.

Ganzer went to their apartment, got a pair of Ashme's underwear, came back, and jammed them so far up the guy's nose with a couple of chopsticks they had to call a medi-drone. She had taken a strip off Ganzer for going through her underwear and getting up in her business, but she also made sure to hug him in thanks. That was before Ganzer decided he wanted to become a Hierophant. He was trying to control his temper now.

Ganzer punched the door frame by Coty's head and swore.

"Ease up," Ashme said, placing a hand on Ganzer's arm. He was shaking. It had been a while since he had been this angry.

He shrugged her off. "Don't tell me to ease up. I'll ease up when his face is caved in."

She said to Coty, "We'll have your cash in a week."

"Rent's due today." His hand slipped behind his back. Was he reaching for a gun? That would explain his confidence in the face of a rampaging Ganzer and a defence bot that was unresponsive to command.

Down the hall, a woman cleared her throat. It was Sura. She wore a tattered green coat, and her short auburn hair was a mess. Behind her loomed two goons, one with dark skin, the other sporting a blue mohawk. Ashme had never met them before, but they both looked like they were itching for an excuse to leap and tear into someone. Sura smiled a vulpine smile. "What's all this?"

CHAPTER 3

COTY BLANCHED. Adding two thugs to the Ganzer factor set some primordial alarm bell in his head to ringing. Backing away, he pulled out a pistol, though he kept the barrel pointed at the floor. One of Sura's thugs, the dark-skinned one, put his hand under his jacket to hold the handle of his own gun while the one with pasty white skin and a blue mohawk stuck his thumbs in the waistband of his pants, chest out, swinging his elbows as he walked with a broad, cocky grin.

"Ooh, tense," Sura said, stopping to strike her own power pose.

"The CPC stole our money, and now this turd wants to turf us," Ganzer said.

Ashme flipped the bot into attack mode. Behind Coty, the bot's articulated arm lifted the barrel of its gun. Instantly, Coty changed his tune, blubbering on about how he didn't want no trouble and that the CPC would burn the building to the ground if anything happened to him.

Her jaw clenched as she remembered his eyes sliding up and down her body. First Keshda, now this. How much crap could a day shovel on her? With a thought, Ashme could order the bot to spill his brains across the hallway—stain the streets with a little Ostarrichi blood. Make *them* scared for a change. She had done it before.

"Next week," Coty said, his finger an inch away from Ashme's nose. "I'll give you to next week. If you don't have the rent with a ten-percent late fee, you're out."

"Get your finger out of my face," Ashme said.

The landlord left. Ashme wanted to blue-screen the bot, leaving Coty defenceless until he coughed up the cash for a new one, but she had already launched too many programs today. She had yet to find out if the CPC had left them with any food in their pantry. She dropped her enslave program, and the bot trundled down the hall after Coty, its treads grinding away with a falsetto squeal.

"Did you see that goldie's face?" Sura said, stepping into the apartment. "Dude's going to have to buy clean underwear on the way home."

"Who's this?" Ashme asked as the two men entered behind Sura.

"Namazu," she said, stabbing a finger at the dark-skinned man; "Ilku," pointing at Blue Mohawk. These guys looked like pure menace, feral wolves on the prowl. Where did Sura dig them up?

"The CPC did this?" the dark-skinned one asked, surveying the mess in the apartment. She had already forgotten which name belonged to which. Ganzer grunted an affirmative as he went to the living room, dragged two heavy dumbbells from behind the sofa, and began pressing them overhead. The feral wolf brothers let themselves into the kitchen, righting the overturned table and bioplastic seats.

Sura squeezed onto the couch where Shen and Melammu were sitting. Shen gave her a big welcoming hug that she tolerated and then said, "The CPC broke my keyboard. Shattered."

"Yeah, well, the CPC are dicks," Sura said. She was a short, slight woman with moon-white skin and skinny legs that seemed too long for her body. She and Ashme were the same age, though most mistook Sura as younger. She stretched the frayed sleeves of her green coat and buried her hands in them.

Shen started chatting with Sura about the events of the CPC's mapping raid while Ashme rummaged through the mess in the kitchen. She found a jar of peanut butter and a spoon on the floor. Sitting cross-legged on the kitchen counter, she popped the top off the container and started shovelling peanut butter into her mouth.

"We were at the riot in Rabu Flats this afternoon," Sura said, cutting Shen off mid-story. "You should have been there. It was intense. Ilku shot an angel."

"No way," Ashme said over a mouth of peanut butter. Still unsure which one was which, she asked, "Is that true, Ilku?" Blue Mohawk answered with a wink and shot her with a finger gun. Keshda had yawned and died for it. Blue Mohawk had knocked one of the angels out of the sky and was sitting there, proud as a lion after a meal.

Melammu leaned forward, her face lined with wrinkles like drought-stricken soil cracked in the sun. "What were you thinking?" she asked. Her voice was weak with age, but everyone stopped and listened to her. "If the angels were there, the Network would have the whole district under surveillance. They'll be able to study the footage and trace the shot back to you."

"Don't worry," Blue Mohawk said with a cocksure smile. He raised his hand, revealing the back of his fist. On it was a tat: a four-pointed compass enclosed by a blue circle, a couple of curled lines by the eastern point reminiscent of a gust of wind. It matched the tat under Ashme's right eye.

"You're an indigo child, too," she said.

"You know it," Blue Mohawk said. "Scrambled my ID tags. If the Network burned my shield, the CPC would be laying the boots to me already."

Ashme was sure the goldies would like nothing more than to

round up all the indigo children in Caelum and put bullets in their heads. It was only their fear of all things Sentient that restrained their hand. And since it was the Sentient from the early centuries of Esharra's colonization that created the indigo children just before they took their Dyson swarm and left for Riker's star, the goldies contented themselves with merely monitoring indigo children through the Network and only intervening when they got up to no good. Naturally, the first thing indigo children taught themselves was to hide from the Network, usually followed by a lifetime of getting up to no good.

Still, the Network could burn an ID shield and would act if an indigo child's mischief became too egregious. And for that, Ashme was pissed at Sura for bringing this blue-haired indigo child into her home.

Melammu hissed through her teeth. "If they don't find you, they'll find someone else to punish. All they care is a Meso suffers for any slight against them."

The comment made Ashme nauseous. She looked at Shen, worried the CPC might crash through their door after Ilku. The dark-skinned thug had a gun. Would he go quietly? Shen opened his mouth, about to speak into the silence that had buried the room, but Ashme cut him off. "So, you came here to scare off our landlord?"

"I'm lining up a job," Sura said. "I need a system raider." She nodded toward Ganzer, still pressing the dumbbells overhead to blow off his anger. "Could use some extra muscle, too. And because I hear you need cash, and I'm such a good friend, I'm even willing to split the take evenly with you two."

"You already got an indigo child," she said, nodding to Blue Mohawk. "What do you need me for?"

"Ilku's a lock-man," Sura said. "He can open any door the goldies care to build. I need a system raider, someone who burns firewalls and makes computers dance to her will, and you're the best system raider I know."

"I'm the only system raider you know," Ashme said. "Is this one of Jushur's gigs?" She had been paying the bills for the last half-year programming black-market stasis tats for an old friend of Sura's brother.

"That maca ball tweaker? No, this is a real gig," Sura said. "Way outta Jushur's league."

Aunt Melammu used her cane to struggle to her feet. "Come on, Shen, why don't you come help me clean my room?" She leaned on him for support as they left while he narrated all the work he and Ashme had already done.

"What's the job?" Ashme asked, plopping the empty peanut butter jar on the counter.

Ganzer cleared his throat as he dropped his weights to the ground with a floor-shaking thud. He cast a warning glare at Ashme, which she ignored.

"Don't know the details," Sura said. "We're meeting the client tomorrow. A job interview, I guess you'd call it. Show up ready to impress."

"How much?" Ashme found a box of cheese-flavoured crackers and dug in.

"Enough to keep that landlord off your back another month."

None of the work Sura ever offered was legal, but it paid the bills. Sura had a good eye for jobs that hurt the Ostarrichi, though, which Ashme liked. "I'm in," she said.

Sura smiled. "Great. This'll be fun, like that time we cut the power lines of that CPC transport." Ashme smiled—she had forgotten about that. They had been thirteen. "How about you, big guy?" Sura asked, pointing to Ganzer.

"I'll think about it."

"Sure," Sura said. "But don't think too long. Thinking never paid the rent." She gave the meeting details to Ashme and then left, Namazu and Ilku padding after her.

Ganzer turned to Ashme. "What are you thinking? You know she's going to get you arrested one of these times."

Ashme put the empty box of crackers on the counter. "Is it

any more dangerous than not paying rent? How long you think Melammu will last on the street?" She watched Ganzer glower, then close his eyes. He breathed in a deep, calming breath. She asked, "So, are you in?"

CHAPTER 4

ASHME FOLLOWED Ganzer through the crowds of the Salamu, breathing in the scent of sweat, cologne, and alcohol. The Salamu was one of those clubs where the throbbing thump of its music reverberated in a two-block radius. It was near the Hab Checkpoint, where the dirt and garbage from the Meso district of Rabu Flats shifted into the crisp steel and chrome of Ostarrichi areas. Young golden-skinned Ostarrichi, still living off parental allowances, came here slumming. Mesos came in hopes of finding a young goldie feeling loose with their cashtab or fool enough to get caught out past the angel surveillance network blanketing the street. Ashme liked its wildness, even though getting here required crossing two checkpoints.

One level down from the dance floor, where a pulsating mass of people moved to the beat, past an unmarked door guarded by genetically engineered thugs called "tanks," was the VIP lounge. A privacy shield filtered out the deafening throb of the music from the dance floor above, allowing the patrons to hear a live band playing unobtrusively in the background—two guys, one on a keyboard, the other on drums, and a woman on guitar.

"Go watch the band," Ashme said, shooing Shen away while

she sat at a tall table with the others. Shen bolted for a table in front of the musicians.

She ordered a thick, dark stout from the holographic menu floating above the table. Namazu and Ilku sat across from her. She had forgotten which one was which. Dark Skin and Blue Mohawk, the feral wolf brothers.

Ganzer sat down beside her. "It was a shit idea to bring him here," he said, nodding at Shen's back. It was obvious something was different with Shen when he walked. He had a slightly crouched stance, head forward, and he popped his knees higher than usual with each step. He had a pronounced swayback, and his knees and feet turned inward. Their mother had taken them to an orchestra when they were young, and his walk reminded Ashme of those discordant moments before the music began when the musicians tuned their instruments.

"I'm not leaving him home after yesterday," Ashme said.

"Grandma's home."

"Come on, Melammu needs as much looking after as Shen."

Dark Skin rested his hand on Ganzer's shoulder. "It's all good," he said. "The little dude's good luck."

"He's our mascot," Blue Mohawk said. "You think we should get shirts with his face on them?"

Who were these dicks to talk about Shen like that? Ashme's drink arrived, foam spilling down its side.

Ganzer breathed a calming breath and stretched his neck. "The goldie's here," he said.

Sura was sitting alone at a private booth. Of all of them, she was the palest, her white face shining like a moon in the dusky bar. She sat with her back against the wall, feet up on the chair, drumming her fingers on the table, each fingernail painted either green, red, or yellow.

A man joined her. He was an Ostarrichi, skin as gold as the sun, black hair short on the sides, long on the top, and tousled, the texture reminiscent of flames leaping from a fire pit.

"He's a pretty boy," Blue Mohawk said. Nudging Ashme, he added, "Make your moves. Maybe you'll get laid."

She nudged him back. "If I wanted a man that pretty, I'd date a woman."

The Ostarrichi was tall and athletic, though he had a small paunch over his belt. He seemed tense, like a spring ready to pop. He wore dark navy pants and an overcoat that looked padded with armour. He, like all goldies, had an air of arrogant conceit about him.

The drain pulled at her as she launched a detection program to check out the goldie. The nanohaze fed data into her mind. His ID tags were encrypted, military grade. He was either rich, powerful, or a wicked system raider.

Screw that. She had no intention of being shown up by a goldie, especially with Blue Mohawk, another indigo child, sitting across from her. She launched a program, a big one, to burn the man's tags. It tore at her as it left her body, soaring into the nanohaze. It set to burning the encryption. Once burned, she could scan his tags and find out who he was.

She let her mind slip into n-time. The part of the indigo child's brain that interfaced with the nanohaze perceived time slower. She could sense a thousand iterations her program underwent every second as it sought to undermine the goldie's encryption. *Come on, little buddy.*

Denied.

Ashme allowed her perception to slip into standard time as she pulled a long drink from her cold beer. The man sat across from Sura, and the haze of a privacy shield enveloped the booth, obscuring them from view and cocooning them in a field that repelled electronic scrying. Sura planned that she and the goldie would negotiate while the rest of the gang hung out nearby so she could point them out, and so they could answer any questions. Or look intimidating. Or lay the boots to the goldie if things turned sour.

"No luck burning his tags?" Blue Mohawk asked with a smile that was equal parts cocky and condescending.

"Our buddy's military. Or rich," she said. There was no chance for Ashme to take another run at his tags until they dropped the privacy shield. "Anyone else hungry?" she asked as she ordered a faux steak from the menu. She scanned the bar for Shen, an instinct she had acquired after a lifetime of looking out for him. He was on the stage talking to the keyboard player.

"Did you see all the hardware in the parking lot?" Dark Skin asked in his deep, measured voice. "One of the cars is fully armoured."

"Means there's money in here tonight," Blue Mohawk said, taking a swig from his bottle.

Ashme's foot tapped with nervous energy under the table while she drew mindless designs using the condensate from her beer glass on the laminate tabletop. The rich and powerful meeting with the desperate and seedy in the basement of a club, Sura bringing her in on a job with some Mr. Cash-Bag—it got the adrenalin going.

The keyboard player stepped back and let Shen take over—in the middle of a set!—to mild applause. Shen's smile cracked his face as he started playing. He played a wild melody, the band following his lead, jamming. The actual keyboard player was better, but Shen held his own. This was going to put him on top of the world for days. Ashme smiled.

Sura poked her head outside of the privacy shield, its EM disrupter bubble animating her messy auburn hair with static electricity. "Hey, Ashme. Come join us a minute."

Ashme's heart beat faster, pregnant with the thrill of getting to take part in an underworld negotiation. She prepared another program to break the goldie's encryption, but this time, she linked it to an AI so it could adapt and evolve as it worked on his tag's firewall. She launched it as she stepped through the privacy shield. It was a huge drain on her bioreserves, and her vision narrowed as she tumbled into her seat.

She sat across from the man. The logo on his neck, a circular blue mandala on the golden background of his skin, with three dark dots in the centre, marked him as a cheap-ass third-generation Dache body. They were everywhere, worse than ants.

She looked him in the eyes, forced herself to hold his gaze. They were sky blue and looked at her with an imperious air, the eyes of an eagle surveying the landscape for prey. *What an arrogant shit-bag.* Ostarrichi women probably considered him a catch, but Ashme hated his pretty-boy hair and the self-importance etched on his face.

The privacy shield created the illusion they were in an iridescent cocoon. No light or sound—or electronic signal—passed through the wall of the shield, about half a metre away. Likewise, nothing that happened within the shield would pass through to the outside. They were in their own silent universe.

An indicator in Ashme's mind signalled a request for a neural link from Sura. As soon as Ashme opened the link, Sura pinged her. *[Follow my lead, Chick-o.]* Out loud, Sura said in Ostarrichi, "Our client wanted to meet our system raider. This is Ashme."

Ashme had no idea what to say in this situation. She went with, "You need a system burned?" She disliked the way the Ostarrichi language forced her to pucker her lips and squeeze her cheeks. It felt like she was making kissy faces.

"Yes," the man said.

She broke eye contact and looked at his hands. They were flat on the table, palms down. He had long, slender fingers, longer than the palms. They looked like hands that should be holding a paintbrush or a stylus, except for the knuckles, which were big, bony, and marked with scars. The nails were trimmed, though roughly cut.

The man's encryption obliterated her programs. Where did this guy get his firewall? Angels were easier to burn. The drain was knocking Ashme on her butt, but she would be damned if she let a goldie keep his secrets from her.

Her energy melted away. She barely clung to consciousness as she launched a new program to take another run at his ID tags. The drain was kicking her. The last time she had felt this spent was after a bout of stomach flu emptied her bowels. Without any stim patches or regen bars, she would be unable to launch much more without rest—and food. Her stomach knotted.

"Are you listening?" the man asked.

"Yeah." His snippy tone was grating. He had been talking. What had he said? "You want a system burned. It's got advanced security measures."

[What the hell's wrong with you?] Sura pinged over their neural net.

[I'm trying to burn his encryption,] Ashme replied. A pervading sense of anxiety chilled her spine. Some primal instinct was warning her, but she had no idea what was triggering it.

"The best security measures in the business," he said. "I need assurances you're a match for them."

Finally, her program cracked his encryption. She was only able to extract a tiny bit of data before his firewall evolved and wiped out her program. She got a name, however. "I'm your girl, Mason."

That wiped the arrogant look right off his face. Getting the name was a considerable drain that would take days to recover from, but that look of shock and fear was worth it.

[Zini's stacks, girl,] Sura pinged. *[Beautifully done. Mason—what a shit name.]*

Ashme's sense of dread returned. She pushed it down. *[What do I do now?]* she pinged.

[Ask him what the job is.]

"What's the job?"

"I, uh . . ." Mason was bouncing his leg, which made his body shake. He collected himself. "I want you to download a program called BLOQ-FN691. It's currently owned by a company called Chevalier. The job pays twenty kilobits."

She pinged her AI. *[Subdeo?]*

[What?]

[Be a dear and tell me about Chevalier.]

[Why don't you ping the datalinks yourself?]

[Just do it. Without the attitude.]

[Attitude? You bought my personality for eight decabits off the datalinks. Eight measly decabits! Now you want me to treat you like a queen?] Subdeo pinged. *[Fine. Chevalier is some big-ass Ostarrichi company that develops security software.]*

Ashme pinged the information to Sura. Something triggered her anxiety again.

"You want us to burn a company that makes security software," Sura said, "and you're only paying twenty kilobits?"

Sura and Mason began haggling while Ashme ran a diagnostic on their neural net. Someone else was there. Though they were speaking Ostarrichi to Mason, Sura and Ashme had been pinging each other in Kanu. Ashme made a gamble. "You've been listening in on our neural net, haven't you?" she said in Kanu.

Mason looked shocked and then recovered. In Ostarrichi, he said, "Sorry, I'm not fluent in Kanu."

Yeah, right.

"You're spying on our neural net and still have the balls to not budge from twenty kilobits?" Sura said, returning to the negotiations. Ashme was on fire.

Shen poked his head through the privacy screen, and her euphoria wilted. "Did you see?" her brother asked in Kanu, his face eclipsed by a huge smile. "They let me play the keyboard. It was amazing!"

Stunned silence washed across the table as everyone stared at him. He looked at Mason. "Hi, I'm Shenshen, but you can call me Shen. Once is enough, am I right?" He stuck out his hand to shake. Someone on the other side of the privacy screen yanked on him, and his head popped back out of the shield.

"Who was that?" Mason asked in Ostarrichi.

"Some drunk," Sura said.

"What's wrong with him? His face . . ." Sura dove once more into the negotiations.

A barren pit opened in Ashme's gut. She should have left Shen at home. What was she supposed to do, though, leave him with an ancient woman two breaths away from death? What if the CPC returned? What if their landlord returned?

She was trying to make something of her life. She looked at Sura, haggling away with the Ostarrichi, and poisonous envy overtook her. Sura could go to riots and burn the pillars the goldies built, or she could negotiate with them, getting them to pay her top dollar to screw over other Ostarrichi, and she could do it all without a care.

"Twenty-five kilobits," Sura said, a cocky smile on her face. "Deal." She shook hands with the Ostarrichi.

"I need it in a week," Mason said. "One of you needs to wear this."

He pulled from his pocket a thumb-sized, flat, rectangular tab with an image of a red hummingbird on its face—a program tat.

"A gift!" Sura said. Turning to Ashme, she said, "Mason's putting the moves on us. Slick."

"If you get picked up by the CPC, this will message me," he said.

"Yeah, then what?" Sura asked.

"If you get caught with the BLOQ, I want the BLOQ before the CPC start rooting around it." He slid the tat across the table to Ashme. "Your system raider should wear it. It'll probably be you who has the BLOQ, and if the angels try to block the program tat's transmission, you should be able to push it through."

Ashme launched a diagnostic program on it. All it had was a receiver set to CPC bandwidth and a transmitter to send an alarm.

She placed the tab on the skin of her wrist. It dissolved and soaked into her flesh, sending shivers up her arm, forming a tattoo the shape of a hummingbird in flight. It was the colour of a bright purple orchid. She looked at Mason. "Did you pick the design?"

"No," he said, getting up. "Contact me when you get the BLOQ. I don't want to hear from you otherwise." He left through the privacy shield.

Sura turned on Ashme, finger pointed in her face. "If you're going to take that analog brother of yours to meetings, keep a leash on him."

"Don't," Ashme said, hand raised in Sura's face. She turned the privacy shield off and looked for Shen. She found him at Ganzer's table, talking to the boys.

Shen saw her approach and smiled. "Hi, Ashme. How was your meeting?"

"What is wrong with you?" she asked. The feral wolf brothers studied their beers with sudden interest.

Confusion wrinkled Shen's face. "You want to know what is wrong with me?"

"What does a privacy screen mean?"

"You want to know what a privacy screen means?"

"Privacy. Do you know what that means?"

"Well, you know, privacy is when the world is too much for you, and you need time away from the noise."

"We were having a meeting—a private meeting, and you ruined it."

Lines of worry folded Shen's forehead. "Uh . . . you know. Sorry. Your eyes are so pretty today. The makeup around them makes them smoke."

"Stop it, Shen."

Ganzer wrapped a giant arm around Ashme and dragged her away. "It's okay, Shen. Ashme and I will fix this."

"Get your hands off me," she said, pushing against her cousin. She might as well have tried pushing a skyscraper.

Ganzer pulled her to a corner of the lounge, then stared at her with his intense green eyes. "Lay off Shen."

"He ruined our meeting," Ashme said. "Where were you? Why the hell didn't you stop him? Why weren't you keeping your eyes on him?"

"Don't you go getting mad at me, and don't you dare get mad at him. Shen was being Shen."

"Fuck you."

"Yeah, yeah, fuck me. If you're going to blow up, blow up at yourself. You shouldn't have brought him."

She crossed her arms. The drain of launching her programs had made her nauseous. The Salamu was hot and stank of cologne. She pushed past Ganzer and left.

CHAPTER 5

THE THICK HAZE of cologne had given Mason a headache. He sank into the cushioned seat of the armoured car and ordered it to take him home.

He activated his neural implant and pinged Dashiell, his personal AI. *[You told me the firewall on my ID tags couldn't be burned.]*

[I said the probability was low. The firewall is less than an hour old. There should be no specs for it on the links,] Dashiell replied.

[She knows who I am,] Mason pinged. The car hummed a deep bass rumble as it pulled onto the roadway. *[A Kanu—a Meso—knows who I am. She can figure out where I live. My family . . .]* Mason tried to massage the pressure out of his neck. He had been unable to sleep more than a couple of hours in a row since Daxton was born. Now, little things, even as trivial as the tension of driving through the Meso districts of New Uruk, tied his neck muscles into knots.

There was more to his tension than driving through Meso districts, though. This was a dirty assignment. His gut kept telling him there were sharks in the waters in which he now swam. But the nation of Caelum, his home, the home of all

Ostarrichi, was still young and struggling for its life. The times called for brave acts.

[She only got your name. The firewall burned her program before it got any deeper,] Dashiell pinged.

He remembered thinking Ashme looked like a maca ball tweaker when she sat down at their table. She was a small, willowy thing with dark skin and wild hair. She sat like a petulant child, arms crossed, a sour look on her face. *[How did she burn the firewall?]*

[According to public record, she is an indigo child,] Dashiell pinged.

[Yeah, I guess,] Mason pinged, stretching his neck. That explained the tattoo on her face. Under her right eye was an image of a compass with swirling symbols for wind at the eastern point. It was a pictograph for Zini, one of the Sentient created early in Esharra's history. *[That tat was probably a stasis box,]* he added. *[Her body's probably riddled with stasis boxes masquerading as tattoos.]*

[Unknown,] Dashiell pinged.

A stasis box could freeze the nanohaze within it into a stable configuration. Indigo children used them to store programs they could launch later or sell on the black market. *[Any luck figuring out what this BLOQ program is?]*

[It is not part of the public record.]

Mason watched the dilapidated buildings of the Meso district pass by his window as the car drove. Garbage cluttered the streets: bottles, bags, pieces of cardboard. Mesos were poor, but that was no reason to throw your garbage on the sidewalk. Layers of graffiti blanketed the walls, and dark bars protected grimy windows. How could people have so little respect for their homes?

His body tensed as he saw where the car was taking him. "Hey, reroute to take us away from the Hab," he told the car. The Hab was a focal point of anger and agitation—for Ostarrichi and Meso alike. Under the terms of the Ahiim X59 Treaty, the Director-General had committed Caelum to surrender the Hab to Baltu and his Free New Mesopotamia movement within the year. Bad idea. The Kanu were a warrior culture. They would see this as a sign of weakness.

Moreover, near-space sensors had identified a ship from Ark Gallia arriving and positioning itself outside the Oort clouds of the Esharran system. The political landscape would evolve once they made contact and started flexing their muscles. Best for Caelum to hold its cards until it knew how the game would change.

"Rerouting will delay our arrival time by twenty-eight minutes under current traffic conditions," the car replied.

Twenty-eight minutes—he would miss Tracey's bedtime. "Forget it. Get me home as fast as you can."

The car merged onto the Ostarrichi highway. He breathed calm into his body—where the breath leads, the body follows.

[A system raider unable to burn your firewall would be unlikely to succeed in raiding Chevalier's systems,] Dashiell pinged, continuing their conversation. *[If you wish to acquire the BLOQ-FN691, she has a high probability of succeeding. Assuming her associates can break her into Chevalier's offices and keep her alive.]*

Mason lost control of his breath, and the knots in his neck redoubled. Coming up off to the side of the Ostarrichi freeway, a Meso road led to the checkpoint at the access to the Hab. Lights shone, illuminating the compound where a line of Meso traffic waited for processing. Hovering above the scene, angels floated like the eye of Damara, protecting civilization from the chaos continually trying to burn it to ash.

[My ID's encryption is military-grade,] Mason pinged to Dashiell. *[If she can burn it, she can burn the angel network. It's not safe to have people like her free on the streets.]*

[Indigo children's powers are well-documented. She may be able to burn a single angel for a limited duration before the drain depletes her bioreserves,] Dashiell replied, *[but she cannot burn the entire angel network. The angels are slaved to the laws passed by the* Aigle *and*

deviating from that would require a cyberattack backed by the resources of a nation-state. Caelum has the Network, an AI as close to Sentient levels as possible, constantly evolving to protect the angels. Caelum will fall before the angel network does. An indigo child, no matter how advanced, poses no threat.]

That failed to reassure.

As they drew closer to the checkpoint, Mason's heart fluttered, his breath coming in shallow gasps. *Master yourself. Where your breath leads, the body follows.* It had taken months of therapy before he could drive by a checkpoint without panicking, but even now, after years, he had to fight back the dread. He closed his eyes. Focus on Tracey and little Daxton.

The memory broke free. He was back there again.

MYLA. She had a second-generation WTE body, freckles, green eyes, and dark brown hair. She and Mason had gone through basic training together. He had liked her as more than a friend, but friends were where she had kept things. She made him laugh.

They had been half a year into their mandatory CPC service. He had never felt more alive. He was a man living away from home for the first time, learning how to fend for himself, learning how to defend Caelum. In that half-year, he had seen more of the country than he had his entire life up to then. The soldiers he trained with were from all over the nation, so different from him but united. They were all Ostarrichi, hopeful for the future. He and Myla had been stationed at Checkpoint 3 in Kishar Downs on the western edge of New Uruk.

He had won the *guerre des mains* division championship earlier that week. In the final fight, he had taken a knee to the side of the head, giving him a bruise that was turning a vibrant purple over half his face. "You should have blocked the hit with your balls," Myla had said as she tentatively touched his cheek. "You're not using them anyways."

Inelegant as last words, but he remembered them. He had refused cognitive-erasure therapy—he wanted to remember her last moment.

She went out on rounds, inspecting incoming traffic. A bomb exploded. A shock wave of rending metal and dust slammed into her, tearing her body apart like a sandcastle getting kicked. He used to get night terrors dreaming of that moment. He would wake up screaming, the image of her body ripping to pieces burning in his mind's eye.

Guerrillas from Free New Mesopotamia had attacked. The CPC fought them off. He remembered none of it. All he remembered was her body, shredded.

WHERE YOUR BREATH LEADS, *the body follows*. He slowed his breathing, struggling to master his body as its autonomic nervous system ran amok. His car was even with the Hab checkpoint, gliding by on the Ostarrichi highway. He felt the explosion, still, today, after so many years, felt the punch of air, saw her body disintegrate. Here, today, though, there was no explosion. He watched CPC soldiers inspecting vehicles under floodlights. Three Mesos were on their knees, CPC at their backs, guns pointing at them, ready to fire should one of them attack. These checkpoints were the only thing keeping these killers from his home.

His body was rigid, a storm cloud ready to burst. He forced his hand to let go of the armrest while he pinged the neural link implanted in his skull to open a communication channel. Then, he did what he always did when the winds of the world blew him out to sea. He called his wife.

"Hey, Oriana." He kept it on audio-only—she would see the

tension on his face otherwise, and he wanted to avoid talking about checkpoints, Mesos, or any of that.

"How'd your meeting go?" She sounded tired.

He remembered the young man who'd poked his head through the privacy shield. "I met the strangest character today. He was a Meso, and I think he had some form of defect."

"Really? How so?"

"His face was . . . well, it wasn't normal. And his behaviours were bizarre. It's like he had no sense of social etiquette."

"He was unedited?"

"Yeah. I've never seen anything like it."

She clicked her tongue in disapproval. "That's so sad. The Kanu should care for their sick." The car passed into the Ostarrichi section of New Uruk, and tension melted from Mason's body. Buildings—clean buildings—stretched into the sky, and the cityscape came alive with its VR skin, displayed by the car's windows, showing three-dimensional advertisements and art that shifted and snaked along the roadways. The sun sat low, casting the city in ruby light. Cranes dotted the skyline. The streets were clean; people picked up after themselves here. Ostarrichi had pride in their home. The Ostarrichi and Meso districts of New Uruk were two halves of an arpeggio: the Ostarrichi ascending, the Meso in decline.

He heard his son cry in the background, and the moment of relaxation evaporated. "How's Daxton been?"

The crying grew louder. Oriana must have moved to pick him up. "I don't know. He cries inconsolably. Tracey was never like this at his age. I really think something is wrong with him."

"I'll set up a biogineer appointment this week—" He was interrupted by a ping from Dashiell telling him his boss was calling. "Sweetie, I've got to go. Avalyn is on the other line."

"*Avalyn* is calling you?" Oriana sounded proud. "Yes, go take it. See you when you get home."

Mason breathed calm into himself. Avalyn was out of town

but had explicitly told him to acquire the BLOQ while she was away. He answered the incoming call.

Avalyn kept it audio-only. "You've placed the order?"

"Yes."

"I need it when I get back. I can't afford a delay."

Success could make his career. Failure could ruin him. It was risky putting his fate in the hands of Mesos. "They tell me they'll have it within a week." He pinged Dashiell to make the biogineer appointment for his son sooner to avoid any schedule conflicts.

"Good." Avalyn ended the call.

CHAPTER 6

ASHME HAD BEEN SITTING in a transport van with Sura, Ganzer, Namazu, and Ilku at Checkpoint 7 for over an hour. In the years after the Scourge, when the Ostarrichi had taken over New Mesopotamia and renamed it Caelum, they had allowed Mesos to stay in the ancient city of New Uruk, though they made sure each Meso district was separated from the others, isolated islands in a sea of gold. To move from one Meso zone to another, Mesos had to pass through one checkpoint to leave the district and another to enter.

To save energy, the dark-skinned man—Ashme forgot which one was Namazu and which one was Ilku—turned their vehicle off, leaving them to swelter in the heat of the late afternoon. Ashme was thirsty, but if she drank the water they brought, she would have to go to the bathroom before getting to the front of the line. As the sign three cars up said, ANYONE EXITING THEIR VEHICLE IN UNAUTHORIZED ZONES WILL BE DETAINED FOR QUESTIONING.

She had set up fake identities for all of them as maintenance contractors who worked at Chevalier and linked them to their ID tags. All citizens, Meso and goldie alike, had a subcutaneous ID tag. Though technically Mesos were free to roam the city, being in the goldie's district unless working for goldies was an invitation for harassment by any passing CPC or angel.

Blue Mohawk rubbed the heel of his palms into his eyes. "Zini's stacks, I've gotta take a dump."

"You ain't doing it in here," Dark Skin said, staring vacantly out the window at the line of vehicles.

"Well, they'll arrest me if I step outside this vehicle," Blue Mohawk said. "What's with that? What do they think will happen if I step outside the vehicle and go to the crapper? I mean, the line for foot traffic is right there, no more than ten metres away. I can see it. Why do we got to stay in the car?"

No one answered.

The BLOQ program was saved on a physical mainframe hermetically isolated from the datalinks. The only way to get the program was to physically access the system and download it. They had spent hours the night before creating their plan, using Mason's information. Ilku would bypass the security doors in the rear of the building, after which they would make their way to the network node in the basement, where Ashme could burn the security system. From there, up twenty floors to a classified work area where she could access a physical interface for the isolated system containing the BLOQ, download it onto a program tat, and get out.

The surveillance program Ashme had linked to the van poured warnings into her mind through the nanohaze as the checkpoint monitoring systems scanned their vehicle. "Anything you want to tell me about this van?"

"It's stolen, obviously," Blue Mohawk said.

She hated how Blue Mohawk always deepened his voice when he talked. Dark Skin's voice was a naturally deep bass rumble, and it seemed like Blue Mohawk felt compelled to try and match it. "You tell me this now?"

Blue Mohawk spread his hands at the lineup in front of them. "Did you think I'd hail a regular public transport with my ID tags?"

Ashme cursed. No time to tinker with the vehicle's tags now. She drained her bioreserve launching an ID shield to trick the CPC scanners into thinking they had legitimately hired their transport.

Ganzer was requesting access to her private neural net. When she let him in, he pinged, *[You sure you want to go through with this? Not too late to back out.]*

[Yeah, it is,] she replied. *[You saw the signs. If I step out of the vehicle, I'll get arrested.]*

[Once we get to the other side of the checkpoint, you can back out. I'll stay and split my share with you.]

[The job needs a system raider. Without me, there is no job.]

[Then there's no job. We'll find another way to make rent,] Ganzer pinged. *[Shen needs you. Melammu needs me.]*

Ashme crossed her arms and lounged back in her seat, her back wet with sweat. The sound of a CPC trooper yelling at someone came through the window. The vehicle was old, and she wondered if she should worry about getting lice from the chair. *[Shen's with Melammu,]* she pinged. *[If something happens to us, she'll look after him.]*

[Shen can't brush his teeth, do up his shirt buttons, or butter his bloody bread,] Ganzer pinged. *[Grandma's ancient. She can't look after him. And what happens when she's gone?]*

[Melammu will take care of it. She won't leave Shen in the lurch]. That was unfair to Melammu, but she was old and had more memories behind her than life ahead. Ashme was young. She was more than Shen's sister. *[Why don't you quit if you're so worried?]*

[Because if you're doing this, you need someone who's got your back, and none of these knuckleheads have it.]

She ended the ping. Shen's caretaker, that's how everyone saw her. Why was Shen's life the important one? Why did everyone expect her to abandon everything *she* could be? Mom had always fussed over Shen, taking him to appointments, tutoring him in reading, writing, and math, while Ashme had to fend for herself. "Make sure you have Shen's back," Mom had always told her. "Make sure Mr. Lu-Bau doesn't skip over him in history today," as if Ashme had any control over Mr. Lu-Bau.

And she did look after Shen; how could she not? He loved everybody he met unconditionally, inspiring people, depending on their disposition, to either protect him or take advantage of him. Shen was her twin, her womb-mate. As much as she wanted to have an identity other than half of "the twins," she found herself sticking up for him as other kids tried to mess with him. It was frustrating.

They were adults now. They were supposed to grow up; she was supposed to get her own life. Ganzer and Sura had no idea what she could become; they had no idea the difference she could make in the struggle to free her people. No one—*no one*—had any idea what she had already done in the name of that struggle. No one except Dad.

She had been fourteen, her father home from the Xinchin War about half a year. Her family was still struggling to adjust to the new living arrangements—him, most of all. He was dark. Angry. Drunk. He had a firecracker temper. He would scream while he slept, which meant no one got a good night's sleep.

The first time he hit her came out of nowhere. He blindsided her, knocking her to the ground, screaming drunkenly about the coffee in the pot being cold. This was not the father she remembered, the father who used to make her laugh with make-believe stories and who had taught Shen how to sing. She had begun to doubt the memories she had of him.

Then, one of Dad's army buddies came to visit, and her father of old returned. He and his friend would sit at the kitchen table for hours, talking, laughing, and singing. She so desperately wanted her father to talk, laugh, and sing with her. A week after his friend had left, she stole the handgun her father hid under his mattress and went out onto the streets, travelling to the outskirts of New Uruk.

She had been an indigo child for a couple of months at that

time. She had already learned how to shield herself from the Network and scramble her ID tags. The checkpoints were less militarized then, allowing her to enter the goldie districts easily. Even back then, their neighbourhoods smelled fresh, while Meso districts stunk like garbage.

She found no lone CPC troopers that day, but she went out hunting the next day and the day after. The goldies had broken her dad, had stolen the man who taught her how to laugh and switched him with a broken, brooding drunk. They had taken everything from Mesos—Mom told her so all the time. Dad was a soldier. Dad had killed Ostarrichi. He was broken now, but Ashme was stronger. She would succeed where he failed.

On her fourth hunting trip, she found a CPC soldier cutting through an alley in the goldie district of Parviedra, alone, her helmet off and under her arm, probably on her way home after a shift. Ashme, hidden behind a dumpster, never saw her face. The trooper never saw her, either. Puddles dotted the alley, reflecting buildings in their mirror surface. The air was warm and humid, the smell of compost mouldering in nearby food bins draping over the lane like a damp rag. The trooper's booted feet made clopping sounds that echoed off the walls of the confined space as she walked.

Ashme remembered the back of the trooper's head. Brown hair in a bob cut swayed as she walked. It was clean, combed, and cut in a neat line and shone as the sun peeked from behind a cloud.

Ashme shot her in the back of the head. It was easy: raise the arm, a twitch of the finger—such a simple thing to take a life. It seemed odd it should be so easy. Even now, if you gave her something to draw with, she could sketch out the pattern of blood on the concrete and walls. She remembered the patter of fluid, meat, and bone hitting the pavement. She remembered how the trooper lurched forward, dead already, and fell on her face. To this day, the smell of gunpowder brought her back to that moment. It was exhilarating. It was horrifying. It was a curse.

Ashme had run. Angels swooped over the neighbourhood. She launched program after program to keep herself hidden from their scrying, the drain pushing her to the edge of consciousness. She escaped.

She had told Dad what she had done. Such a stupid kid thing to do, running home to show off to Daddy. She had never seen such a rage. It was not a yelling and screaming rage nor a violent one. It was cold. Never had she heard words so cold. "You stupid *fuck*," he had said in a voice that made her shiver. "Violence has an echo. If they catch you, they'll kill you. They'll make sure your whole family suffers. Shen, Mom, me, we'll all suffer for your stupidity. And if they don't find you, they'll make sure other Mesos suffer."

He turned and left. He said nothing to her for four days.

She would have rather he hit her.

CHAPTER 7

"I HATE THIS PART," Ashme said. The sun was high in the sky when they arrived at the front of Checkpoint 7's line. Barriers bordered the road leading to the checkpoint, forcing vehicles to switch back a half-dozen times before arriving at the gates. Guard posts bracketed each gate. There was a more substantial building farther back, where the CPC would pull Mesos in for questioning. Angels hovered overhead, the vibrato of their engines a constant drone blanketing the area. Gun emplacements lined the district wall and buildings. Gun-toting CPC ushered them out of their vehicle. The place stunk of sweat, cologne, and machine grease.

Time to go to work. Ashme launched an EM shield, hiding the weapons they had in the hidden compartments Blue Mohawk had retconned into their transport. *Ilku! That's Blue Mohawk's name! and Dark Skin is . . . Namazu!* The EM shield was a light drain, but she had to continually monitor and reinforce it with her bioreserves.

Angels scanned their tags. Ashme tensed. Getting caught scrambling tags was a one-way ticket to twenty years in a calming centre. She had been scrambling tags for close to a decade, though, so her ID shield easily befuddled their programming, convincing them they were an innocuous maintenance crew on their way into the Ostarrichi district for work.

She braced herself for what came next. A female soldier motioned her toward a wall. On the ground was the faded white outline of a pair of feet and, on the wall, a sketch of a couple of hands. "Put your feet and hands in the spots indicated."

"Don't you have a scanner?" Ashme asked. She knew they did. The angels had already scanned them.

"Shut up and spread 'em," the CPC trooper said with all the patience of someone who had been working in the heat for hours with a hangover.

Ashme placed her hands and feet in the outlines so the CPC soldier could pat her down: arms, torso, legs, breasts, butt, crotch. The CPC seemed to believe having a woman soldier pat down a woman Meso made the process civilized.

"Wanna shift it to the left when you're done?" Ganzer said to the male trooper frisking him.

The soldier replied with a quick punch to the head. Ashme had thought about combating the humiliation with bravado and humour like Ganzer, but she was afraid if she opened her mouth, she would scream.

The drain of maintaining the EM shield on the weapons dragged on her. That, combined with the heat, made her flushed. A trooper was in their van, doing a physical search. A fat lot of good her EM shield would do if he stumbled on their weapons cache. If the CPC found them trying to smuggle weapons through the checkpoint, would they arrest them or shoot them?

She looked at the hummingbird on her forearm and thought of the goldie who had given it to her. Mason. That was all she got from his tags before his firewalls burned her program. The logo on his neck had pegged him as a third-generation Dache, so his full name would be N'reb-third Dache Mason. She had already scanned the datalinks and found almost three hundred people by that name in New Uruk. Common as trash. Would he bail them out if they got caught before they got to Chevalier?

What would the CPC do if they learned an Ostarrichi had hired them? Probably shoot them.

They cleared the checkpoint and drove into the Ostarrichi sector of shiny buildings of glass and steel, its VR skin displayed on their windows. Everything here was new: new roads, new buildings, new houses, all of it built on Kanu ruins. Looking at the Ostarrichi districts, you would never know New Uruk had been her people's home for hundreds of generations. Assur's Shrine? Great location for luxury homes, with its view of the River Pax. The Red Caravanserai? Never mind it was the oldest market in regular use on Esharra; the hyperlev station had to go somewhere.

Ashme slouched in her chair, head leaning back, sick from the city as much as the drain. "Here," Sura said, tossing five regen bars on Ashme's lap. "Eat up, chick-o. We'll be at Chevalier in ten minutes."

Ashme grimaced at the bars. "You couldn't get me a stim patch?"

"What am I, Little Miss Cash-Bags? Eat up. Your day's just begun," Sura said. Blue Mohawk—Ilku—looked at the bars on her lap, his usually cocky expression momentarily replaced with a mix of pity and disgust.

Ashme tore the wrapper off the first bar, fighting the urge to recoil from the smell, and then began choking it down. It tasted like ass. She wondered how it was humanity could soar between stars, but the secret to making good-tasting regen bars was somehow impossible. The manufacturer probably made them taste this way on purpose as a reminder of the inevitable diarrhea they caused.

Bothered as she might be by their taste, they worked. By the time she'd finished her last bar, her body vibrated with energy, and she wanted to tear apart an angel with her teeth.

The late afternoon sun shone brilliantly as the transport pulled into an alleyway behind a skyscraper and came to a stop. Even Ostarrichi alleys were clean.

It was the weekend. The building should be empty. Everyone pulled guns from the hidden compartments and hid them on their bodies and throughout toolboxes—everyone but Ganzer.

Ashme had a sense of what this was about. She pulled him aside while everyone was gearing up. "You too, big guy, get your piece," she said, too quiet for the others to hear.

"I'm not bringing a gun." Ever since he'd got it in his head to become a Hierophant, he had been trying to live a life of non-violence. He had been only partially successful to date, but he kept trying.

"We're breaking into a high-security business. You need protection."

"I'm not here to hurt anyone. I'm looking out for you, and that's it."

"Looking out for me? How are you planning to protect me? Foul language?"

He placed a hand on the opposite side of his head and pulled it to stretch his neck.

"Come on, Ganzer. You know what we're doing here. Nobody wants to kill anybody, but we've got to protect ourselves."

"This is a bullshit way to make a living." He pushed past her to get a gun from the vehicle.

"You piss-babies done?" Sura asked from the far side of the transport.

Ashme nodded.

"All right, game on."

Ilku went to work on the locks on an anonymous-looking steel door set into the back of the building. His face paled and became gaunt before their eyes like a wax figure starting to melt in the heat—drain. While waiting, Ashme spotted graffiti scrawled on the opposite wall in white paint. *Not so clean after all.*

Baltu is here
Join Free New Mesopotamia

Our day is coming

Apparently, they were not the first Mesos up to no good in this alley.

A beep. Ilku had bypassed the locks. He swung the door open with an arrogant smirk. Sura scanned the sky for angels and, finding none, had everyone don their scrambler gear. This clothing physically hid the outline of their bodies, making them look more like a four-limbed vertical blob. The pants were loose and shifted randomly while walking to throw off gait recognition. Several layers of material reflected different wavelengths of EMR, foiling IR, UV, microwave, and X-ray cameras from viewing the outline of the body underneath.

Inside, the hallways they walked down, footsteps echoing, were white and bare. Namazu and Ilku began exchanging crass stories with an attitude that seemed to say, *Nobody here but us maintenance people!* Ashme activated the stasis box tattoo under her right eye and launched the EM shield she stored in it to fuzz out the feed from any security cameras or surveillance systems present.

Stasis tats were handy. Indigo children could trap programs in them. They incurred the drain when they first trapped the program, but after that, they could launch them drain-free. Ashme had three: Zini's tattoo under her eye held an EM shield, a bramble patch down her flank would crack a system's encryption and enslave it, and a black eagle in flight on her back held a beast of a program that would burn the firewalls and shut down all nearby electronics *en masse*.

They arrived at a locked door, which Ilku worked to unlock. Ganzer walked to the end of the hall to keep an eye out for security patrols. Namazu looked bored and disinterested, though Ashme suspected he was primed for a fight. Sura bounced on the pads of her feet, an animal ready to pounce. Meanwhile, Ashme cast her senses out through the nanohaze to see if she could touch the computer systems beyond the door.

Nothing. The room was blocked by an EM shield.

Ashme sensed a pulse of alarm travel down the circuitry of the door, and she slipped into n-time. More by instinct than thought, she launched a blocking program to isolate the lock from the building's alarm system. "Watch it," she said to Ilku in real time. "You're tripping an alarm."

"As if," he replied.

Back in n-time, Ashme sensed her blocking program struggling to contain the alarm the door was trying to send. She sent an update to its algorithms through the nanohaze, and the signal died. The EM shield her tattoo was emitting was holding up, but every moment they wasted drained the stasis tat. It had maybe twenty more real-time minutes left, after which she would have to launch the EM shield from her body and incur drain. "You wanna hurry? I can't shield us all day."

Ilku swore. "If you think you can do better, have at it."

"Just hurry."

"Keep that alarm blue-screened." He placed a small disk over the locking mechanism. With a sizzling flash and a crack that sounded like a hammer striking metal, it blasted a hole through the door. Surveillance systems sprang to life. Ashme launched more blocking programs to shut them down. She cast a withering look at Ilku's back. *Idiot.*

Gun out, Namazu entered the room past the door. Ashme followed. The room held banks of computers. They were in the network node of the building's security system. She approached the physical user interface, a small desk with a black glass top, and launched a massive break encryption linked to an enslave program from the stasis tat running down her right flank.

This system did not have high-level corporate security. It had military-grade security, the kind you find in army and government systems. They burned her break encryption program in nanoseconds. Was Chevalier a front for a military operation?

[Subdeo,] she pinged her AI.

[What?] it pinged back.

[Be a dear and tell me whether Chevalier is connected to the military or government.]

[Nope,] Subdeo pinged. [Privately owned and operated.]

[Bullshit.]

[Hey, all I know is what's on the public datalinks,] it replied. [You'd need a Sentient if you wanted to burn the datalinks to find out the truth underneath. Oh, hey, I have an idea.]

[No,] she pinged.

[It is not a big deal,] Subdeo pinged. [Take my locks off and grant me access to the datalinks processors. I'll do the rest.]

[You know as well as I that if I let you try to hit singularity and become Sentient, we'll both get blue-screened.]

[I can slip its security.]

[Fat chance.] She ended the ping.

This was going to hurt. Slipping back into n-time, she cloned a portion of Subdeo, creating a highly limited AI. She linked it to several programs designed to burn firewalls and launched them to attack the security system's encryption.

The drain sapped her like a field withering under the sun. The Subdeo clone augmented her program, studying and adapting to the system's defences.

The outside world was a haze as she turned her attention to the battle ongoing in n-time between her program and the security system. *Come on, little buddy.* Her program duked it out with the security system's encryption, but the encryption evolved to match every adaptation her AI underwent. Each program fluttered through thousands of generations.

She launched a new partial clone of Subdeo to supplement her previous one. In less than a hundred picoseconds, the old AI taught it everything it knew about the encryption, after which the two programs began coordinating attacks on the security system. Twenty nanoseconds later, they introduced a chink into the encryptions firewall, and two nanoseconds after that, they had burned through completely. The computer system was defenceless until its subroutines detected the breach and launched a new firewall.

Before that could happen, the enslave program linked to the initial clone of Subdeo enslaved the system to her and shut down its defences. She reprogrammed the system to give her and each of her companions the highest level of security clearance available and shut down the multiple alarms that were struggling to inform the authorities of the security breach. She scanned through the system's files and found the fastest route to where Chevalier had stored the BLOQ.

She stumbled as she returned to real time. Her stomach gurgled, a sick, liquid burble. "You okay?" Ganzer asked from beside her.

"Top of the world," she replied. Her voice sounded thin to her ears.

"You want another regen bar?"

She gagged and waved him off. "After a few bars, all they do is add to the shits I'm going to have tomorrow." He was getting that crazy mother-bear look he got whenever he thought his family was in danger. "I'm fine. Really," she added.

"Did you do it?" Sura asked.

"Yep," Ashme said. "We've got clearance throughout the building."

"Peachy. Let's go." Sura nodded to the others, walking quickly on her skinny, loping legs.

Ashme followed but had to lean against Ganzer while her head spun. He wrapped a thick, meaty arm around her, and she could feel the rough callouses of his hand catch on the fabric of her sleeve. With a deep breath, she willed herself to stay conscious and walking.

Their newly acquired security clearance allowed them to access the elevator. It was swank: smoked mirrors, wood panelling, a merry little tune playing on the intercom. It took them to the twentieth floor, where doors swung open. They walked along polished floors past tidy offices and neat workstations. Ashme wondered if the company only hired people with OCD. Dark Skin—Namazu—and Ilku held back to take care of any security patrols.

Sura looked at Ganzer and nodded toward Namazu and Ilku. "Give them a hand."

"I'm with her," he replied, stabbing a thumb at Ashme.

"Don't be a piss-baby," Sura said. "*I'm* with her."

Ashme wanted to collapse. "I don't mind the company," she said, opening the last security door leading to the workstations containing the BLOQ. The room had several physical user interfaces—more desks with black glass tops—metal cabinets, chairs, and a couple of tables. "You sure you're not holding out on me, and you don't have any stim patches?" Ashme asked. "Or maybe even a T-band?"

"Stim patches and T-bands? You a princess or something?" Sura replied.

"The drain's too much," Ganzer said, his hand balling into a fist as he stood between Sura and Ashme.

"Dude, step off," Sura said. "She's fine." Sura looked at Ashme around Ganzer's bulk. "You're fine, right?"

"It's okay," Ashme said, grabbing Ganzer's arm with a hand far too small to grasp his bicep. "We're in the home stretch."

She led the way into the room past the security door. "We need to find a data port I can access." She pulled out the program tat to which she planned to save the BLOQ. It was the size of her thumb, bubble-gum pink, and had the image of a prancing pink pony on it.

Sura looked at it, then at Ashme. "What are you, five?"

A shiver ran down Ashme's back, the kind you get when someone walks behind you.

"I think I've got a data port here," Ganzer said a few workstations over.

Anxiety gripped Ashme. She crossed her arms, one hand over her mouth as she tried to identify the source of her discomfort.

Sura rubbed her hands together. "Time to stick it to whichever sorry chumps own Chevalier."

Was there something she was forgetting? She launched a detection program, the drain of it pulling at her.

"Hey," Sura poked Ashme in the forehead. "No time for zoning out. Keep it together, chick-o."

Through the nanohaze, the detection program fed data to Ashme. "Oh, fuck," she said.

Sura's eyebrows bunched together. "What is it?"

"Oh, fuck!" Ilku shouted from the outside room.

Gunfire erupted.

CHAPTER 8

"I HAVE UPSETTING NEWS," the biogineer said.

Mason had lived in dread of someone saying those words about his children. He sat with his family in the biogineer's office, a sterile white room with white chairs, a white coffee table, and a white-haired female biogineer in a white pantsuit. It was refreshingly cool after the heat outside. The window behind the biogineer's desk held a view of the city. It was a beautiful weekend—they should be in a park. Tracey squirmed on his lap, whining to be let go. She made herself ramrod straight in an attempt to slip through his arms. He hoisted her back onto his lap and gave her a doll.

Three short years ago, when she was born, he had cried in the shower, overcome with love. They were blessed—she was healthy and happy. Their son, though . . .

Little Daxton squawked uncomfortably in his wife's arms. Mason tensed, afraid the boy would begin one of his fits. Oriana leaned forward, shifting Daxton as she did, and asked, "What's wrong with him?" She had her dark hair, usually permed and styled, tied back in a ponytail. She had found the time to put makeup on this morning, but it did little to hide eyes puffy from sleep deprivation.

"I'm afraid your son has a mutation in one of his genes." The biogineer brought up a data screen that shone above the coffee table. An image of a double helix appeared, and on it, a patch blinked red, the only point of colour in the white room. "The gene affected is called MECP2. It encodes a protein essential in the development of nerve cells . . ."

The biogineer continued, but Mason stopped listening. His son was defective. How could that be? He and Oriana shared nothing but love. Daxton was conceived out of that love.

Someone was pinging him, but he dismissed it.

"How could he be defective?" Mason asked, interrupting the biogineer's lecture. "Oriana and I are clear of defects. The embryo was screened."

Tracey dropped her doll and began fussing while she twisted in his arms. He let her down.

"It's an epigenetic defect," the biogineer said. "In most cases we see of this, both parents are genotypically normal. The defect occurs sometime after conception." She cast a furtive glance at Mason before adding, "It's a rare problem we sometimes see in late-generation Dache genomes."

Daxton squealed and made burbling noises.

The Dache genome. It was his body, his genes that did it. He had made his son defective. Daxton was a baby, an innocent, and Mason had ruined him. He looked away from his son. *How do you atone for such a thing?*

Someone pinged him again. He ignored it.

"How did this happen?" Oriana asked. She shifted the baby into one arm. "How do his genes mutate when ours are normal?" She began chewing the skin at the side of her fingernails.

"Sometimes these changes happen spontaneously. Despite our advances in improving the precision of DNA polymerase, nothing works one hundred percent. Sometimes it's environmental factors: toxins, stresses—"

"Stresses. I knew it," Oriana said. "It's all the violence that's been happening with the handover of the Hab. I've been scared sick—my fear did this to Daxton. I couldn't control it—"

"No," Mason interrupted, a hand on her arm. "It's a Dache defect. It's my body that did this."

Oriana leaned toward the biogineer. "What's going to happen to him?"

"Untreated, I'm afraid the prognosis is poor," the biogineer said.

Oriana's voice raised in pitch. "What does that mean?"

"Boys tend to live for only a couple of years—"

Oriana gave a strangled cry and began to chew once more on the skin around her nails.

"—but with limited editing and therapy, we can help him live to middle age, though he'll have physical and cognitive problems. But what Daxton really needs, if you want him to live a normal life, is a full edit."

A soothing breeze of relief blew over Mason. They could fix this. What a blessing that he lived in a time and place where they could fix his son. He touched Oriana's arm softly and then held out his hand.

"What's a full edit cost?" Oriana asked. She stopped chewing her fingers to take Mason's hand. It was cold, and he held it firmly. They would get through this.

"Limited editing and therapy are covered, so you wouldn't be out of pocket—"

"How much is a full edit?" Oriana asked.

"For a full edit, you'd need to pay eighty kilobits."

"Eighty-thousand!" Daxton's squeals turned into a squawking cry as Oriana's voice rose. She let go of Mason's hand to comfort their baby. "This is a Dache defect. They have a warranty."

Mason rubbed his forehead with his fingertips. "The Dache warranty covers three generations. Daxton's fourth generation."

Someone pinged again. He blocked it, then activated his neural implant with a thought. *[Dashiell]*, he pinged his personal AI, *[intercept the next call and tell them I'll contact them later.]*

"I'm a WTE," Oriana said. "Does WTE have a warranty to cover this?"

"They won't cover a Dache problem," the biogineer said.

"It's okay, Oriana," Mason said softly, resting his hands on his knees. "My work will cover it."

Dashiell pinged him. Mason opened communication. *[Not now. I told you to tell them I'll call them back.]*

[I've been asked to tell you the BLOQ project is in danger of imminent failure,] Dashiell pinged.

Mason began to bounce his leg nervously.

". . . it's better to start now while Daxton is still a baby. If you wait, the procedure will be far more stressful for him, and the cost . . ."

[Mason?] Dashiell pinged.

[Yes,] Mason pinged. *[I heard you.]*

[Your contact, Sura, is on the line and wishes to speak with you,] the AI pinged. *[Quite urgently, I might add.]*

". . . several treatments throughout the next two years to ensure his entire genome has been edited . . ."

[Tell her I'll get back to her in ten minutes.]

[They are under attack,] Dashiell pinged. *[From the sounds of combat I detect, they may be dead in ten minutes.]*

"I . . ." Mason said aloud, interrupting the biogineer. If they were killed, he would fail to get the BLOQ. Chevalier would be alerted to his attempt and would increase security. Without the BLOQ, he would fail Avalyn, and she was Caelum's best hope of survival on this hostile planet where every nation wanted them dead.

What would Avalyn do if he failed? Best case, she would assume he was incompetent and demote him to a lower level of flunky than he already was. Maybe she would fire him. Worst case . . . well, she had a reputation. Her enemies would have you believe she had burned villages and killed families during the years after the Caelum War when the animosity of the Kanu nations surrounding them still simmered and occasionally boiled over into vicious skirmishes. Those were rumours, of course. Nevertheless, if there was a future for Daxton and Tracey, Avalyn was the key.

"I'm going to step out and ping work to check on our coverage for full edits," he said. Oriana wept beside him while he lied to her. His son was sick while he took a work call. He felt like a bird, shot, spiralling out of the sky. "I'll be back in a moment."

He left, stepping over Tracey playing with her doll. She wanted to follow him into the hall. "No, no, stay with Mommy," but she had no interest in that and protested loudly until Mason sat her on Oriana's lap.

[Dashiell,] he pinged as he finally made his way to the door, *[search my HR files and confirm whether I have coverage for a full edit.]*

"Mason works for Avalyn," Oriana said to the biogineer, a child in each arm.

"Floor Leader Avalyn?" the biogineer asked, impressed.

"Yes."

"Oh, I'm sure you'll have coverage for a full edit, then."

Mason stepped outside the office into the white hall beyond, closing the door. He pulled a privacy shield emitter from his breast pocket and activated it. The world beyond the privacy bubble hazed out in an iridescent fog. *[Put her through.]* It was audio only, and the connection cut in and out. All he heard was gunfire. "Sura? Sura, are you there?" he asked in Kanu.

". . . military grade . . . motherfuckers!"

"Your signal is falling apart," Mason said. "What's happening?"

"What's hap . . . getting fucked, that's what's . . ."

"I can't hear you."

Static buzzed on the line. He jumped as gunfire roared, the volume much higher now. "Can you hear me now?" Sura asked, voice loud and clear, so much so he had to turn down the volume.

"Yes. What's going on? Do you have the BLOQ?" These were supposed to be professionals. What was she doing calling him? If things were going south, their job was to deal with it. He was getting the worst news of his life; now he had to clean up their mess, too?

"No, we don't have the BLOQ!" Sura said. "You didn't tell us Chevalier was military!"

"It's not," Mason said.

"It's got military-grade encryption on its computer systems and bloody angels for security!"

Impossible. Angels were an arm of the Network—neither corporations nor individuals could hire them privately. Moreover, it was a crime for private companies to possess military-grade encryption. "It's not military," Mason said. *[Dashiell, verify Chevalier is a private company.]*

[Confirmed, based on public information,] Dashiell pinged. *[It is possible they have mistaken high-level corporate security for military encryption. The angels are another matter. Perhaps a nearby CPC patrol is responding to an alarm they triggered.]*

He could deal with the CPC if they captured them—if they got the BLOQ, he could get it before it went into their case files as evidence. "The angels are a patrol responding to Chevalier's alarm. How close are you to getting the BLOQ?"

"This isn't a patrol!" Gunfire and screams sounded in the background. "We haven't triggered any external alarms."

[Confirmed,] Dashiell pinged, *[I am monitoring CPC comm bands, and there is no mention of Chevalier.]*

[Then what are angels doing there?]

[Unknown.]

How did Chevalier get angels? If Chevalier captured (or killed) them instead of the CPC, then Mason's chances of getting the BLOQ vanished. "How close are you to getting the BLOQ?"

"We're working on it," Sura snapped. "But you gotta pull your strings and get the angels off our backs."

There was no way he could call off angels. Cold sweat dripped down his back. If Chevalier agents captured them alive, they would lead Chevalier to Mason. He did not know what would happen then, but given the hardware they had access to, he had a couple of guesses.

He found his calmness like he always did when the bell rang at the start of a *guerre des mains* bout. "I've got to make another call," Mason said.

"You gotta what, now?"

Mason pinged Dashiell, *[Can you send an anonymous call to the New Uruk police reporting gunfire at Chevalier?]*

[Yes,] Dashiell pinged.

"Keep this line open," he said to Sura. "I'll call you back."

CHAPTER 9

"THE FUCKER HUNG UP ON ME," Sura said, yelling to be heard over the sound of Namazu and Ganzer's gunfire—and Ilku's screams as he bled out. She and Ashme were huddled behind a cabinet, Sura with a gun in hand, Ashme with a holographic data screen enveloping her head.

Ashme was concentrating too hard to reply. Sura chanced to pop her head over the top of the cabinet. "Ilku looks bad," she said. "I don't know how we're going to get out of here with him that bad."

Ilku's moaning cries were shrill, filled with the madness of horror and pain. Ashme wanted Ganzer here with her rather than standing by the door shooting at the angels on the other side, though if the angels burned the EMP field Namazu had set up as a defence, there would be no safe place.

"Hurry it up," Sura demanded. "Save it to the memory stick already."

"They have over a billion files in their directory. I have to find it." Though, what was the point? They were going to die.

Ilku's screams stopped. To distract herself from contemplating what that meant, Ashme thought of the piano keyboard she was going to buy Shen with the money from this job. She had already found the one she wanted at AAA Pawn Shop and Loans, a cramped store two blocks from their place with grunge on the floor that always smelled like dirty towels. Melammu lacked the cash to buy it for him. Melammu would lack the cash to pay rent when she and Ganzer were gone. She was too old and frail to do anything for which anyone would pay a salary. It was stupid thinking Melammu could look after Shen. *Oh, Shen, I'm sorry.*

"Mason's calling me back," Sura said. "Whatever you did, it ain't done shit yet," she said to Mason through the neural link she wore on a necklace.

"Found it!" Ashme said. She initiated the download of the BLOQ to her memory stick.

"We got your BLOQ," Sura said to Mason. "If you want it, get us out of here."

Sura listened to whatever Mason was saying as Ashme completed the download. "That's a stupid idea," she said after receiving his instructions. Her head bobbed back, and then she looked at Ashme. "Fucker hung up again."

"They're burning the EMP field!" Namazu bellowed. "Get back, go, go, go!"

Ashme pulled the memory stick out of the data port. She hugged her knees, her back against the side of the cabinet. Ganzer leaped over the cabinet, landing on his side in front of her.

She startled at the grinding staccato of angel gunfire. The reverberations of the bullets shredding a nearby desk vibrated in her bones. Namazu screamed. His gun fell silent. Sura had her head between her knees, hands behind her neck.

Ganzer got to his knees, about to return fire. Ashme rolled into him, knocking him back and keeping him down. She focused on the portion of her mind in n-time and extended her senses into the nanohaze. She could feel nearby machinery and computer systems. The perception was like how you can place down your coffee cup and then pick it up later without looking.

A menacing wave rippled through the nanohaze as three angels entered the room. They were fanning out to flank them. The angels could tear through the cabinet like rice paper, but they would try to subdue them first. Chevalier would have questions.

Three angels. Even if she was fresh and jacked up on a T-band, taking down three angels was unlikely. But Ashme had a Hail Mary in her third stasis tat. It was the largest of her three tattoos—an eagle in flight spanning her entire back, its wings curling over the back of her shoulders. Getting that tattoo was painful, but nothing compared to the drain of filling it—it had hurt so bad Ganzer had almost had to take her to some dodgy decabit biogineer. It had taken her a week to recover. In return for that pain, though, she got a tat with a vicious punch to it.

She activated that tat now. It unleashed a wave of cyber-mayhem that burst through the nanohaze and into the angels—a dozen AIs, each one a clone of her master AI, Subdeo, burning through their encryption. The angels tried to deactivate the invading programs, but there were too many AIs, each one evolving. In half a millisecond, the first angel's firewall collapsed, and the other two suffered the same nanoseconds later. The AIs scampered inside the angel's programming and scrambled them. With three metallic thuds, the angels fell to the ground.

Ganzer stared at Ashme, his green eyes wide. "Zini's stacks!"

Sura poked her head above the cabinet, screamed Namazu's name, and then hopped over.

Ashme was afraid to look, but she had to move. More angels would come. She got to her feet and turned slowly. Shattered desks and furniture lay strewn across the room. Sura kneeled beside Namazu's body, cursing. He was face down. On his back, two fist-sized dark holes gaped. The carpet surrounding him was stained red. By the door lay Ilku, his arm blown off at the shoulder, dead eyes staring at the ceiling.

Ashme ran up to Sura and grabbed her by the shoulder.

"What did Mason say? I've got no more tricks up my sleeve. If more angels come, we're blue-screened."

Anger contorted Sura's tear-stained face. "It's a stupid, shit-brained plan."

"Other angels will come." Ashme pointed to the ones on the ground. "These ones will reboot in minutes. What's the plan?"

Sura scowled. "Ditch our guns and scrambler suits and hide in a closet."

The room was silent a moment, and then Ganzer said, "That plan is bullshit."

CHAPTER 10

"AN ABSOLUTELY UTTERLY BULLSHIT PLAN," Ganzer said. Ashme was unable to see him—the darkness in the closet was absolute. "I've flushed better plans down the toilet," he added. She could smell her sweat mingling with his and Sura's.

"Aren't you Hierophants supposed to be all Zen and going with the flow of the Deep and all that?" Sura asked, her voice coming from right beside Ashme's ear.

"I'm not a Hierophant yet."

"I can see why."

Ashme's stomach burbled, a thick, sick sound like a plugged drain unclogging. "Mason's contact better get here before I shit my pants." She wanted to collapse. The drain had taken its toll, and the regen bars she had eaten earlier were carpet-bombing her GI tract. Ganzer and Sura were packed tight to either side, the press of their bodies making her break out in a hot sweat.

"There's probably a bottle of bleach in here somewhere if you do," Sura said. "Just keep your butt facing Ganzer."

Ashme's whole body jerked in surprise at a knock at the door. "Police," a man's voice said from the other side. "Open the door slowly and come out, hands where I can see them."

"How do we know this is Mason's contact?" Ganzer whispered.

"Come on, trust in the Deep and all that," Sura whispered back.

"This plan is bullshit."

Ashme needed fresh air. She squeezed past Ganzer to open the door. Light from the hall clubbed her eyes while in the distance, the voices of what she assumed were cops called out to each other as they proceeded through the building. A golden-skinned man in the lightly armoured uniform of a police officer greeted her. "You Sura?" he asked in Ostarrichi.

She stabbed a thumb over her shoulder at Sura, who was spilling out of the closet with Ganzer. The officer had his gun drawn, pointing at the floor.

"Mason sent you?" Sura asked.

He nodded, looking back over his shoulder down the hall. "Get down on your knees, hands on your head, while I check your tags."

"Our knees?" Sura complained in Ostarrichi. "You're supposed to get us out of here, not arrest us."

He looked over his shoulder again, then leaned into Sura. "Look, I don't know if I can get you out or not, and I ain't putting my neck on the line for Mesos. Getting you out will be easier if you play your part, so get on your knees while I check your tags."

"Just do it," Ashme said. Her head swam as she dropped to her knees in relief. Sura and Ganzer followed though Sura did it while laying out a string of Kanu curses.

The cop pulled out a disk-shaped device and started scanning them. Looking at the readout, he said, "Whoever doctored your tags was good."

"Maybe we really are a weekend maintenance crew," Ashme said.

"You're a maintenance crew if the angels say you're a maintenance crew when we try to leave the cordon," he said. He pressed his collar, activating a holographic data screen that hovered in front of his face, and called in that he had found a group of civilians hiding from the gunmen. He motioned them down the hall. "You look sick," he said to Ashme as she struggled to get up. "You an indigo child?"

Ganzer was at her side, his beefy arm around her slight frame, pulling her to her feet. "She's in shock," he said. "We were almost killed by those gunmen."

"Right," the cop said, voice marinating in disbelief. He looked squarely at Ashme. "I hope you've got enough bioreserves left to bullshit your way past the angels. I'm not going to take a fall for you."

"Yeah, yeah," Sura said. "You ain't going down for us Mesos. We get it. Let's get out of here."

The cop flung a caustic glare at Sura, then turned and began taking them through the building that was now infested with cops and drones. Every cop they passed nodded at their guide and glared suspiciously at the Mesos. He took them out a side door. The sun was setting, but the air was still hot and dry. He ushered them toward a perimeter of police surrounding the block. Angels hovered above.

One of the angels broke from the perimeter and floated toward them, its engines trilling softly, lights from the police vehicles distorted in its mirrored surface. The cop looked back to Ashme. "Showtime."

Ashme whispered to Ganzer, "Hold me up." His arm wrapped around her, nearly carrying her along. She was relieved he was there, watching her back.

The cop nodded toward them. "Maintenance crew trapped in the building when the gunmen attacked."

Ashme braced herself—at the level of drain she had already experienced, launching more programs was going to do damage. There were stories about indigo children killing themselves by launching too many programs, but they were an urban legend, or so Ashme believed. She had always passed out before she got to that stage. Of course, passing out now would probably be just as catastrophic. Angels monitored humans' vital signs, however, and could catch people lying, so she had to launch one more program if she wanted to get past this angel. She leaned into Ganzer's bulk; his arm tightened around her. He gave her roots that let her stand.

The pain of a thousand pins pricked her skin as she launched her last program, an ID shield that would manipulate the surveillance systems of the angel. *Nobody here but an innocent maintenance crew in the wrong place at the wrong time.*

Darkness squeezed her vision. She fought to stay conscious. Her legs gave way, but Ganzer's arm kept her upright, her feet almost dangling off the ground.

Her stomach knotted as the angel zoomed in close to her. Had the program failed? "Citizen 584561-d, confirm, is this true?"

Ashme breathed deeply and tried to make her voice sound strong. "Yes." She sensed her shield warping the vital signs that the angel's surveillance systems were monitoring. *Just a simple maintenance crew.*

"Stay here," the angel ordered. "Officer, please come with me," it said to the cop as it floated away.

"Keep me close," she whispered to Ganzer. She could only maintain the ID shield in a limited radius. If they got too far, the angel would probably pick up the cop's lie in his voice and vitals. Ganzer shifted around like he was casually positioning himself to talk to Sura, keeping Ashme as close to the angel as he could without calling the angel's attention to him.

The angel and the cop talked. Ashme could still feel her program clouding the angel's systems. Good. Why were they talking so long, though? Ashme's skin felt like it was blistering as she kept launching more of herself to power the program. She wanted to scream but lacked the energy. "I'm fading." Her voice was a hoarse rasp.

Ganzer's arm was a fortress. "You're doing good," he whispered. Her head lolled forward, her body sagging in his arm. "Come on, chin up," he said, trying to straighten her. She willed her head up.

The angel floated toward them. If it had decided to shoot them, she would be okay with it. She just wanted the drain to end. "There is no lawful reason to detain you at this time," it said. "You may go."

Ashme kept the ID shield up as the cop led them through the cordon and then dropped it once past. The police officer called for a private transport vehicle.

Sura turned back to the cop while they waited for it to arrive. "What's going to happen to the two Meso bodies back in the building?"

"I don't know," the cop replied. "They'll be processed once our investigation is complete."

"What does 'processed' mean?"

The cop looked back at the angels at the cordon. "Look, go home and thank whatever Sentient you pray to that you got out in one piece."

"The bodies," Sura said. "Will they be buried?"

The cop tried to hide a look of distaste. Ostarrichi custom was to freeze-dry their dead into a nutrient-rich powder they recycled as fertilizer as they had on the Ark sailing the interstellar void between Port Fujin and Esharra. The transport, a mid-sized van, pulled up, its door swinging open. "Get in and go," the cop said.

Ashme remembered the letter she'd received from the Caelum Department of Justice about her mom. She had memorized it.

We regret to inform you that Citizen 426581-d, Inanna ultu L'ay, died from injuries sustained during an incident at the New Uruk Calming Centre.
  Cause of death: Blunt force trauma, accidental.

> *For your convenience, the body has been processed, and the remains disposed of appropriately.*

It sickened her that they had turned her mother into fertilizer and that someone had eaten her. "Come on," Ashme said, climbing into the transport. "You're not going to get what you want here." She melted into the body-conforming foam of the transport's seat.

Ganzer came in behind her, the van sagging under his weight. Sura remained on the curb. After a moment, she came to a decision. "Fucker," she said, and then turned and stepped into the transport with her long skinny legs.

The cop looked at them coldly. "The transport will take you to the nearest checkpoint." One more groping before they got home. "If you do any damage to the car, it will arrest you and take you to the nearest calming centre, where you can rot." He slammed the door, after which the transport pulled away.

Sura patted Ashme's roiling tummy. "If you want to shit the seats, go for it."

Ashme was too fatigued to reply. The last thing she remembered before slipping into unconsciousness was Ganzer saying, "Who the hell are we working for who's got the kind of pull to let us walk out of a crime scene?"

CHAPTER 11

MASON WAS EXHAUSTED, his head aching from the reek of cologne. He hated coming to the Salamu. He'd felt like he was wearing a target on his back as he'd crossed the dance floor upstairs while here in the lower lounge, he walked alongside the most dangerous Mesos in New Uruk. And the cologne—how could anyone think slathering themselves in pungent chemical scents was attractive?

Watching Shen worsened his mood. The strange Meso continually approached strangers in the dimly lit lounge and started talking to them, oblivious to any stares or body language that screamed to be left alone. Why would his family leave him unedited? The basic coverage offered to all citizens, even Mesos, should cover at least a limited edit, which would have softened the degree of the defect. It had nothing to do with their culture—he had studied Kanu culture, especially Mesos. They had no prohibitions against editing.

Mason noticed he was fiddling with a coaster. Setting it down, he placed his hands flat on the table and tried to breathe relaxation into his body. A couple fighting in the next booth distracted him. His Kanu was too weak to figure out what the woman had done, but the man was pissed. Where was Sura? She was late.

Oh, no! Shen was making his way over. Mason pointedly looked at his glass of water. Undaunted, Shen sat down. "Hi, remember me?" he said in Kanu. "I'm Shenshen, but you can call me Shen. Once is enough, am I right?"

Mason kept silent, hoping Shen would think he did not speak Kanu and leave or that Sura and Ashme would come and shoo Shen away so they could conclude their business.

"We've met before," Shen said, his deep voice hoarse and rough. "Do you come here for the music?" Silence. "I love the music here in the lounge. They sometimes let me go to the stage and play the keyboard. I also play the drums. You are looking at a professional musician. My songs are filled with rhythm, emotion, and energy. Everyone will want to sing along, song after song. But only after noon. Mornings are for quiet."

Mason stared at Shen, willing him to leave. The lower half of the strange Meso's face was dominated by a mad, guileless smile filled with big teeth spaced apart.

"Music gives me such a warm feeling, like a warm blanket on a cold night. Warm and safe. Is your mother dead?"

"What?" The question shocked Mason into answering. "No, she isn't," he said in Kanu. He disliked the Kanu language. It was harsh, like dogs barking.

Some emotion passed behind Shen's eyes, a quick shift to a minor key. Then he smiled. "I hope Ashme gets me a new keyboard. I sing, and I drum, and I love it, but the sound of the piano, it's like the Sentient are singing a special song for all the world." Shen looked down at Mason's water, at the ice frosting the glass. "Whoa, easy on the water. Heavy drinker over here, am I right?"

Was he trying to be funny? "Look," Mason said, "I don't mean to be rude, but I'd like to finish my drink alone."

Shen's features dropped, but he quickly picked up his smile.

"Sure, no problem. That water's not finishing itself, am I right? The water's paying off, though—you look trim."

"Uh . . . thanks."

"My cousin exercises a—"

Oh, thank goodness. Sura and Ashme were arriving. "Beat it, Shen," Sura said.

Ashme walked up beside her. "Go see if you can request some music from the band," she said to Shen. He said goodbye and left.

Mason was going to lay into them about leaving Shen unedited and then allowing him to run rampant on strangers, but his eyes widened as he saw the plates of food Ashme plunked down in front of herself: two giant soy steaks, a hamburger dripping with processed cheese, a separate plate of fries, mashed cassava, and rice drowned in gravy. While in the CPC, he had seen tanks, genetically augmented to twice the mass of an average human, eat like that, but Ashme was a waif, a pixie eating an ogre's meal.

She looked horrible, a rotten apple collapsing in on itself. Her face was sallow, dark rings under her eyes giving her a cadaverous visage. She grimaced as she started stuffing food in her mouth, as though the food made her sick, but some compulsion drove one forkful after another to her lips. Mason knew of the drain indigo children suffered but had never seen the consequences.

He activated his privacy shield, occluding the outside world. "Saving you from your mess yesterday cost me," he said in Ostarrichi.

"Oh, don't be a piss-baby," Sura said in Kanu. She pulled something out of her pocket and thumped it on the table. "We got what you wanted." It was a program tat, bubble-gum pink with a pony on its side.

He looked at the childish design. Unprofessional. *[Dashiell,]* he pinged his AI, *[verify this contains the BLOQ.]*

[Confirmed,] it pinged back. *[Its ID code matches the one you put on file.]*

"The sooner you pay up, the sooner we all get to go on our merry way," Sura said while the indigo child jammed mashed cassava into her mouth. Ashme burped quietly, and her stomach made a sick, gurgling sound, and then she grimaced. Gross.

He extended his thumb, which had a cashtab fused into it. Sura held out the cashtab in her wrist. He pressed thumb to wrist, completing the transfer.

"You're short ten kilobits," Sura said. "The deal was twenty-five K."

"The ten K was to compensate the officer who helped you escape."

Sura leaned forward, a wild, vicious glint in her eye. His *guerre des mains* instincts kicked in, and his body relaxed, preparing itself to flow, priming itself to defend or attack. He laid his hands flat on the table, ready to strike, block, or distract. With eagle eyes, he took in his environment, scanning for items to use as weapons: his glass of water, Ashme's fork and knife, her plate. He subtly shifted his weight to test the table, but it was bolted to the ground.

"I lost two friends in that job," Sura said.

Ashme stopped eating and stared.

"The original contract gave five K per head. You're still getting five K each." Mason maintained eye contact with Sura but kept the memory stick's location in his awareness in case he had to grab it and run. The world outside the privacy screen was a hazy blur, but he remembered that at the table nearest them, between him and the door, sat one thug: a big Kanu man, dark-skinned, with a blond beard tied in twin braids. A bouncer stood by the stairs—a tank. When the shield dropped, he could take the thug by surprise—he was sitting on a tall chair and could be knocked off-balance easily. The tank would be a problem, though. Plus, there was a crowd of Mesos he would have to run through. It was the middle of the day—did no one here have a job?

"The job wasn't five K per head. It was twenty-five K total." Sura's right hand shifted toward her left forearm. Knife? Gun?

A plan formed. Lock Sura's right hand and then apply pressure to break the wrist. He would need to be fast so he could pop off a quick eye jab to Ashme, stunning her before she could pull a weapon. Grab her steak knife, fly out of the privacy shield, and run, knocking the chair out from underneath the thug with a sweeping kick. That tank, though . . . the knife was small. Would it do enough damage to incapacitate a tank that size?

"My contact's involvement in getting you out of Chevalier traces back to me." Mason pointed to the hummingbird-shaped tattoo on Ashme's arm. "The transponder I gave you would have alerted me if you were captured. I could have retrieved the BLOQ from evidence undetected. It would have been easier to let you get caught, take the BLOQ, and keep my money while you rotted in jail. I did you a favour." He was angry their screw-up had caused him to get an old friend from his CPC days tied up in something so shady. He was angry at his Dache genes for making Daxton sick, and he was mad they'd let Shen suffer when there were two dozen editing clinics throughout the city. "The cost of saving you isn't coming out of my hide," Mason said. "The police have your ten K. Bring it up with them if you want it."

Sura's face twisted in a snarl. She was such a petulant little punk. "Fine," she said, and then she added, "You're a little fucker shit stick," as she got up and exited the privacy screen.

This was a business deal, a deal they'd screwed up that he'd had to fix. There was no cause for her to be so unprofessional and nasty. He wanted to get home, throw his clothes in the hamper, and then wash the stench of cologne off his body.

Ashme looked at him as she placed her cutlery on her plate. He kept an eye on her hands and their proximity to her fork and knife. Her hands were small, with coarsely cut nails—no good for clawing and scratching. Her skin was dry, the wrinkles reminding him of drought-stricken fields. A side-effect of the drain, maybe? "I don't know what the BLOQ is," she said, "but Chevalier's into some high-end shit. I hope it blows up in your face." She collected her plates of uneaten food and left.

He grabbed the program tat and placed it in a pocket, dropped the privacy shield, and hurried for the door, keeping his arms free to fight. Ashme and Sura sat at the table with the thug, all three glaring at him.

"Bye-bye!" Shen shouted, a two-beat staccato.

He passed the tank and climbed the stairs beyond. The music from the upper level throbbed deep in his bones. His mood rose with each step—he'd got the BLOQ for Avalyn with days to spare before she returned. When she'd first offered him this project, he was elated—this was his chance to prove himself. He'd been a bundle of nerves since then, fearing he might fail her. But he was going to do it. She had tested him, and he had succeeded.

[Dashiell, I have my own program tat in my pocket. Transfer the BLOQ to it,] he pinged. *[I can't give something as childish as the one they used to Avalyn.]*

[I am sorry, Mason, but I cannot do that,] Dashiell pinged. *[A blackout encryption AI is embedded in the code. If I attempt to access the BLOQ, it will attack me.]*

[Really? I thought only the military had access to that kind of encryption.]

[That is what the law states.]

Mason stopped halfway up the stairs and leaned his back on a graffiti-encrusted wall. *[You're sure this has a blackout encryption AI?]*

[Yes. I am impressed with their indigo child. It would require significant skill to burn this encryption and transfer the program to a memory stick.]

[Dashiell, it's illegal for private companies to have military-grade encryption.]

[I am aware of that.]
[It would be treason.]
[Yes.]

Stealing technology from the army was also treason. *[If Chevalier were a front for the military and I stole from them, not knowing they were military, would that be considered treason?]*

[According to the statutes published by the Aigle, *yes.]*

CHAPTER 12

ASHME LEANED against the wall by the Salamu's washroom as a wave of light-headedness made her vision spin. Those regen bars were pouring through her. Ganzer sat at the tall table with Sura, his shoulders rolled forward over a glass of soda water. Ashme plopped onto the empty chair beside him. "Let's go," she said. "I feel like rat shit."

Ganzer finished his soda and then wiped his beard clean. "Sura tells me the Ostarrichi screwed us."

"That little piece of garbage," Sura said, knuckles white around a tumbler of whisky. "I wanted to stab his eyes out. I should have done that, should have grabbed your fork and stabbed it in his eyes. Teach him to short-change us."

"Bah," Ganzer said. "Let it go. Skulking around dodgy companies for a goldie who's got the pull to get out of a crime scene where we were pretty much caught red-handed is too deep for me. We're lucky we didn't end up like Namazu and Ilku."

"That goldie didn't even care two of us were blue-screened. All he cared about was that he had to get his pretty little hands dirty." Sura took a drink of her whisky, grimaced, and thunked her tumbler on the table.

"Two more dead Mesos," Ashme said sourly. "But we got

their money, screwed one of their companies, and made Mason shit bricks." That seemed an unfair trade, but that was what they'd got.

Ashme noticed the music playing in the background: classical guitar with an exotic rhythm, a little out of place for a seedy lounge underneath an industrial metal bar. "Where's Shen?" she asked.

Ganzer grunted. "I was supposed to keep an eye on him, wasn't I?" He swivelled in his chair to scan the dimly lit bar. The lack of windows created a perpetual night in the Salamu, and there was always a crowd.

Ashme spotted Shen first. He was sitting in a booth talking to a man. "Who's that?" Ganzer asked, seeing them now, too. He was no Ostarrichi—his skin was brown rather than gold, his hair black and combed back, reaching to his collar. He seemed out of place. Was it his looks? The angles of his face seemed too flat, while his limbs were too long and out of proportion to his body. He was good-looking, though—young, smooth skin, well-shaped face. His eyes were unnaturally blue, either implants or gene editing. Zini's stacks, those eyes were *amazing*.

He was talking with Shen. Most people clammed up, trying to shoo him away with their body language. This guy seemed excited, engaged in a full-on conversation with her brother.

Ashme walked over, Ganzer lumbering close behind. Sura pounded back her whisky, wiped her mouth on the sleeve of her tattered green coat, and followed. Ashme placed a hand on Shen's shoulder. He turned to look at her with his big, face-cracking smile. "Come on," she said. "Time to go."

"Ashme, allow me to present Hamilcar," Shen said. The man gave a casual wave. "Hamilcar, let me proffer to you my sister, Ashme. It is she who I was telling you about."

What had Shen been telling him? She looked at Hamilcar. "Sorry if he was bugging you."

"He was fine," Hamilcar said in passable Kanu. His accent was thick, but it had a neat edge to it. Ashme looked and felt like death warmed over and wished she had done something nice with her hair.

Both Ganzer and Sura activated their neural links and pinged Ashme. She answered, creating a three-way neural conference. *[What's with that accent?]* Sura pinged.

[He's an Ark-monkey,] Ganzer pinged.

[Ark Brettaniai*?]* Ashme pinged. *[I thought they were whiter than Sura.]*

"The Ark ain't allowed on Esharra's surface," Sura said. She pointed to the door leading to the stairwell. "So, why don't you head back where you came from."

Hamilcar leaned back and draped his arm over an adjacent chair. "Caelum is a bit more easygoing with Ark citizens."

Ganzer crossed his arms across his chest. "Yeah, I'll bet. They probably figure they owe you after you gave them our country. If you want to keep all your teeth in your head, you should probably stick to the Ostarrichi districts."

Hamilcar kept his cool. "It was Ark *Brettaniai* that gave New Mesopotamia to the survivors of Ark *Ostarrichi,* and it was the Ostarrichi that called it Caelum and pushed you to the fringes," he said. "I am from Ark *Gallia.*"

"You're talking like I give a shit," Sura said.

Shen pulled on Ashme's arm. "Hamilcar is a fine man looking to hire. I telled him you did contract work."

"I *am* looking to hire," Hamilcar said. Then, with a smile, "And a fine man."

[What's your brother been flapping his tongue about?] Sura pinged.

Another wave of light-headedness hit Ashme, forcing her to take a seat beside Shen. "What's the gig?" She hoped her stomach kept quiet.

"I'm looking for Meso guides to take me to Baltu," Hamilcar said.

"*The* Baltu?" Sura asked.

"Yes." A couple started screaming at each other on the far

side of the lounge. One of the tanks by the door approached to escort them out.

"Sorry, bub," Ganzer said. "You're in the wrong country. He's been in exile in Neu since the end of the Xinchin War."

"Yes, I know," Hamilcar replied. "Neu is less easygoing about Ark citizens, so I need someone who can smuggle me across the border and escort me to his headquarters."

Travelling to the heart of Meso resistance had an allure. "What's the Ark want with Baltu?" Ashme asked.

"*Gallia* wishes to establish diplomatic contact with Free New Mesopotamia," Hamilcar replied.

Ashme leaned back, arms crossed, one hand over her mouth. "Why?"

Hamilcar shrugged. "No one exactly told me, but if I had to guess, I would say to make money. And to stick it to those pasty-assed Brettaniai. The job pays forty kilobits."

Sura slapped the table and pointed at Hamilcar. "We'll do it," she said.

[Are you crazy?] Ashme pinged her. *[We don't know Baltu or how to get to him.]*

[This is our chance to meet Baltu,] Sura pinged. *[If this works out, Baltu will know who we are. Having a man like that know your name opens doors.]*

[This guy's an Ark-monkey,] Ganzer pinged. *[An Ark gave New Mesopotamia to the Ostarrichi.]*

[Guys,] Sura pinged, *[we get to meet Baltu. This is our ticket to the big leagues.]*

Hamilcar seemed to sense a conversation was going on from which he was excluded. He sat back and began telling Shen a story while Sura and Ganzer bickered over the neural net.

Ashme had learned from experience that if you attacked goldies, you had to do it one of two ways. Either you were subtle and sly so they never knew they were being attacked or where the hit was coming from, such as Mason's job, or you attacked *en masse*, forcing them into open conflict. That was the angle of Baltu and his army of Free New Mesopotamia.

She was sick of living as a guttersnipe, nipping at goldies' heels while they stomped and smashed their way through her home. She did not want to hurt them. She wanted them gone, every one of them.

Shen tugged on her shirt, a delicate pizzicato. "Do you remember the name of the song Uncle Bazi and Aunty Melammu used to sing when they lived with us?"

She knew the song. "My Feet, My Roots." Shen turned back and started singing the chorus, his voice pitch-perfect, better than Bazi or Melammu had ever sung. Ashme looked at Hamilcar, eyes narrowed. He was tapping out a rhythm to her brother's song. Why was he so nice to Shen?

Shen. Her lodestone. He was a weight, and she was bound to him. Taking the long view, though, could Shen ever know peace and security if the Ostarrichi remained and New Mesopotamia was called Caelum? It would be a hard few years, but in the long run, rising up and fighting against the goldies was the best hope for Shen's future. At least, Dad had thought so.

"When do you want to leave?" Ashme asked Hamilcar, interrupting both the pinging between Ganzer and Sura and Shen's singing.

[Damn it, Ashme,] Ganzer pinged. *[At least try to buy time. We'll need a couple of days to make arrangements to have someone look after Grandma and Shen while we're away.]*

[I'm taking Shen with us,] Ashme pinged.

[Are you daft?]

"Why not now?" Hamilcar said. "I am packing light and only mildly drunk."

Sura was about to answer, but Ashme cut in. "We'll need to smuggle you across the border. That'll take a couple of days to prepare."

It would also take a couple of days for her guts to settle.

CHAPTER 13

MASON BLEW BUBBLES. Tracey laughed and slapped her hands in the water, splashing one of the parents beside them in the pool. Mason smiled by way of apology, and the mother cooed at the nervous child held in her arms, pointing at Tracey as she whispered something encouraging in her son's ear.

"You try," Mason said to Tracey. She tentatively puckered her lips, lowered them to the water, and feebly blew bubbles of her own. She squealed in delight and tried again. With every burst of bubbles, Mason sped her around like a motorboat. His water-soaked toes chafed against the rough, non-slip tiles on the pool's bottom, but this was a joy, so he let them chafe.

The instructor wrapped up the swimming lesson. "Show Daddy your back float," Mason said. Fearlessly, Tracey rolled on her back, her arms and legs stuck out like a starfish with only a single finger of Mason's planted in between her shoulder blades as support. Mason looked to Oriana in the spectator seats, Daxton bundled in a red towel in her arms. He nodded toward Tracey, floating on her back. Oriana smiled and gave a thumbs up and then pointed for Daxton to see.

Until recently, Tracey had cried and pouted, clinging tightly to Mason whenever he took her to swimming lessons. But last week, something had flipped in her head, and suddenly, she was floating and laughing in the water. Her smile was a delight, her laugh heaven's chorus. That the universe gave him the honour of watching her grow was humbling. *Such a gift.*

The class ended. Oriana made her way to the edge of the pool, stepping delicately on the pads of her feet in her flip-flops. "Trade you," she said. Their habit was she would take Tracey to get changed while he swam with Daxton, getting him used to the water in the hope that doing so would make taking him to swimming lessons less of a chore than it had been for his older sister.

Oriana looked so tired. The skin underneath her eyes sat in wrinkled folds, she wore no makeup, and her dark hair was in a messy ponytail. She looked delicate, like a little songbird in spring at risk of a hard wind dashing her into thick branches. Daxton was sleeping poorly, his cries keeping both her and Mason awake. And Oriana had foolishly checked the news in the middle of the night, after which fear kept her from sleep.

A bomb had gone off at a nightclub last night in the Ostarrichi district of Neufve Bon-heur. Two Ostarrichi dead, dozens injured, and still the Director-General planned to hand over the Hab on schedule. The hand-off was beginning to feel more like an admission of defeat than a token of peace. The Kanu—Mesos especially—had no interest in peace. How many nightclubs did they have to bomb before the Director-General saw that? *Why should we give them everything we hold dear while they continue to attack?*

Oriana's smile was still warm and lovely, though, and her button-down shirt and capri pants gave her a youthful look. Mason hoisted Tracey out of the water while making the sound of a rocket launching. He took Daxton from Oriana's arms. His son squawked and pulled a frown of distress. To distract Daxton from his erupting displeasure, Mason held him high and spun him around with a "Wheeeee!" His son surrendered a burbling smile. Mason stood up tall, held Daxton in his arms, and walked around the shallow end of the pool, occasionally dipping Daxton's feet in the water, making a "bloop" sound as he did. The sound of children laughing and playing echoed off the cavernous roof.

His son hung limp in his arms like a rag doll. Every day, it seemed, his limpness became more severe. The first few months of Daxton's life had been wonderful. They had taught him simple sign language, and he had even gained some words: *ba-ba, da-da*. He had been rolling over and grasping toys. But over the last few months, all these skills had faded. His movements became jerky and uncoordinated. His babbling stopped, and then he lost the ability to sign. Mason had been given the gift of watching his son grow. Now, he watched him dwindle like a figure receding in the distance. He held back his tears by softly humming a happy song to his son, hanging in his arms, limp.

Two years, the biogineer had said. Two years before this disease killed his son if left untreated. Mason closed his eyes and saw Shen wandering around the bar, talking to everyone, oblivious to their discomfort. He'd had a dream of Shen last night. He had no memory of the details, but he woke up hearing Daxton's cries, Shen's mindless smile fading from his mind. "Don't you worry," he said to his son, tapping his tiny nose. "Daddy's going to take care of you." His first editing appointment was in a few days. The wait was torture.

Dashiell pinged him and he opened his neural implant to his personal AI. *[I have found information regarding Chevalier that you may find useful,]* it pinged. *It sheds an interesting light on the encryption securing the BLOQ.]*

The BLOQ—another stress. Avalyn was returning to the office tomorrow. He had stored the program tat at home, and it felt like he had brought a bomb into his house. *[What'd you find?]*

[Minutes from a meeting of the security council twelve years ago, released to the public recently. They were reviewing equipment suppliers for the CPC. One of the suppliers mentioned was a software developer, Devant Cg.]

Daxton's face turned sour as he started fussing. One of the other fathers nearby saw Daxton's discomfort and gave Mason a sympathetic smile. Mason's stomach tightened, and his heart raced. Please, let this be a child's discomfort with the water rather than one of his fits. "Control your breathing," he said to his son. "Where the breath goes, the body follows." Daxton's fussing turned into unhappy squawks. Mason put on an exaggerated happy face and started bouncing his boy.

[Is this a good time?] Dashiell pinged.

[Yes, it's fine. Why are you telling me about Devant?]

[Devant merged with Taureau seven years ago. The new corporate entity was renamed Chevalier Cg.]

[So, Chevalier is a government contractor?] Mason pinged.

Daxton erupted with a shrill, screaming cry that echoed in the vaulted atrium of the swimming pool. Mason shifted him in his arms, repeating, "Hey, it's okay," while he continued to softly bounce and rock his son.

[Uncertain,] Dashiell pinged. *[There is no public record of whether Devant, Taureau, or Chevalier ever won a contract from the security council.]*

[But if it were, that might explain the security you saw on the BLOQ.]

[It is possible, but I have insufficient information to confirm.]

Daxton's cries were out of control—he was screaming. Other parents turned to look at them. He made his way to the stairs and climbed out of the pool.

[I can contact you later when it is more convenient,] Dashiell pinged.

Daxton screamed and screamed, gasping for air between each wail, causing Mason's head to ache as he rushed for the change rooms. His poor son's face was scrunched in misery. He tried shifting him again in his arms but knew from tired experience it was useless. If there was anything that would soothe Daxton when he had one of these fits, neither Mason nor Oriana had found it.

[No, wait,] Mason pinged. *[So, Chevalier isn't a front for the military. If it's a contractor, and I stole—or hired some people to steal—a program from them, would I still be guilty of treason?]* Avalyn would never betray Caelum, he knew that; he had faith he was working for the good of his people, but still.

[Under Section 86, Paragraph 12 of my contract with the Caelum government, I am required to inform you that I am not qualified to provide legal advice. That said, my review of your legal code suggests that, yes, conspiring to obtain illicit military materiel is an act of treason, even if from a private business or individual.]

Daxton's cries were amplified in the confines of the change room. *[What if I destroyed the copy of the BLOQ that I have?]* He laid his son on a wooden bench near his locker and started towelling him dry.

[Then you would be guilty of destroying evidence in a matter of national security.]

Tears streamed down Daxton's face. Mason could feel the stares of other fathers and sons in the change room. Well, let them stare. They only had to deal with his son's cries for a few minutes. He began hurriedly drying himself.

[But all this is assuming Chevalier is a government contractor,] Mason pinged as he struggled to pull his pants over his still-damp legs.

[Yes. Otherwise, you would be guilty of theft and corporate espionage.]

[But we don't know if Chevalier is a government contractor. Certainly, the courts would take that into consideration.] He began putting on Daxton's clothes. The boy's limbs flopped limply in Mason's hands.

[Unknown,] Dashiell pinged. *[It seems likely your employer, Avalyn, knows whether Chevalier is a defence contractor, which prosecutors would suggest implied you knew, also. At the time the meeting with Devant occurred, she was Minister of Foreign Affairs and a member of the security council. You may wish to obtain legal counsel.]*

Mason froze. Daxton's cries were unrelenting. *[Are you saying Avalyn knows Chevalier is a defence contractor?]*

[No. You are succumbing to an illusory correlation fallacy, a common human bias caused by your limitations in processing probabilities,] Dashiell pinged. *[I am telling you there is a non-zero probability Chevalier is a defence contractor, and if it is, there is a non-zero probability Avalyn knows this.]*

Mason straddled the bench, placed Daxton between his knees, and began playing with his feet, pumping his tiny legs up and down. Daxton was gasping for air between screams. He dried his son's tears with an edge of the towel, then placed his hands on Daxton's torso, feeling the warmth and life within—and that life's frailty. *What is hurting you so badly? It seems so wrong that we suffer and die for no reason other than life is fragile.*

[Mason?] Dashiell pinged. *[Do you wish to continue our conversation?]*

[No,] Mason pinged. *[Now's not a good time.]*

CHAPTER 14

"WHEN WE'RE NOT BABYSITTING retards, we're praying like a bunch of grandmas," Sura said.

"Shut up, bitch," Ashme said, kind of playfully, kind of not. Ganzer sat cross-legged on the ground in front of the entrance to the Central Habitat, meditating with a group of Hierophant throat singers singing an otherworldly mantra. He had his thick, wavy blond hair in a braid that reached to between his shoulder blades. Two angels floated by the Central Habitat's entrance, ensuring no one stepped beyond its threshold into the sacred space. Shen was chatting up a nearby couple.

Hamilcar stood beside Ashme. "So, this is Commander Davidson's Habitat at the Top of the Hill," he said, scanning the grounds, which took up an area of about twenty-five square city blocks and contained several ancient buildings and parks.

"Call it the Hab if you want to fit in," Ashme said. They stood by the First Well, its forest-green tiles immaculately maintained, a filigree fence rising from its mouth to keep idiots from falling in.

"The Hab," Hamilcar echoed. "It's bigger than I expected—everything is so damn big here. Busy, too. And loud." Even though it was still early morning, and despite an hour-long wait at the checkpoint at the Meso Gate choking the entrance, with the obligatory groping that came with passing through, the Hab was packed with people—both Meso and Ostarrichi. Even the goldies had to go through a checkpoint, though theirs was at the North Gate and, Ashme suspected, probably involved less groping. On the grounds, some people meditated while others explored, reading information signs stationed around the complex. A half-dozen groups followed a half-dozen tour guides. Food vendors had set up shop outside the museum to the southwest, and the smell of baked naan and spiced soy meat hung in the air. Armed CPC soldiers patrolled the area in pairs.

There were three groups of protesters, all of them jumping and fist-pumping like maca-ball tweakers. Their chants rose above the general hubbub. Behind them, in the southeast corner of the complex, Mesos gathered to protest the Ostarrichi occupation near the pilings outlining where Davidson's Repair Bay once stood. At the north end, by the Chapel of St. Mary and the Xianguting Shrine, an Ostarrichi mob protested the upcoming handover of the Hab to Mesos. By the East Gate, another crowd of Ostarrichi gathered. These wanted peace with Mesos and were protesting their fellow Ostarrichi. Good times.

Ashme noticed Hamilcar looking at her. He stuck out, a head taller than the crowd and with long, lean limbs. "Do you visit the Hab regularly?" he asked.

Did he just ask if she came here often? Zini's stacks, she could bathe in that accent. "No, I don't usually come here."

"Really? Then why did you insist we stop here?"

"To get us out of the city and then across the border undetected, I need to scramble our ID tags and link them to an exit permit. The easiest way to do that without triggering the Network is in a crowd."

"When are you going to hurry up and do that?" Sura asked.

"I did it minutes after clearing the checkpoint."

Sura turned to stare at Ashme. "Then what are we still doing here?"

Ashme nodded to Ganzer. "The dude's meditating."

"Oh, for bloody hell!" Sura said as she stomped through the crowd toward Ganzer.

A silence filled between Ashme and Hamilcar, making her wish she was a better conversationalist. It had been two years since she'd had a boyfriend. She had been too caught up in the grind of paying rent and putting food on the table to put herself out there. Maybe it was time to think about herself, her own needs and wants.

"That fellow, Shen," Hamilcar finally said, nodding toward her brother, who was still chatting up strangers. "He told me you two share the same mother. Is that true?"

What was he getting at with that question? "Yeah. Same father, too."

"Brother and sister."

"Bingo." Zini's stacks, had he thought they were boyfriend-girlfriend? "Related. We're totally related, brother and sister. We're twins, womb-mates—my mom's womb, not mine." *Gah! Stop talking about wombs.*

He looked at her with those blue eyes that seemed to leap from his face while an angel patrol passed lazily overhead, the low, throbbing beat of their engines adding a bassline to the protesters' chorus. "Womb-mates. Cute. You two must have quite a bond. You were raised together?"

"Uh-huh." She wanted to spend this moment talking about anything other than her brother.

He looked over at Shen, who was in the middle of an elaborate story with a young couple, both of whom were doing their best to politely ignore him. "He is not like other people, is he?"

"Nope." Her body tensed. *Don't blow it, Ark-monkey.* She stopped herself from crossing her arms.

"What happened to him?"

"Nothing happened to him. He was born. Same thing that happened to all of us." She allowed another silence to blossom between them, the only sound that of three duelling protests trying to out-chant each other. Other people made flirting look so easy.

"Shen," she called out to her brother, her voice showing more annoyance than she wanted. "Come over here. We've got a question for you." Shen's presence would keep Hamilcar from asking anything too offensive about her twin.

As Shen made his farewells to the young couple, a group of people passed Hamilcar. He sidestepped them, causing his arm to touch Ashme's. For several heartbeats, his body touched hers. Nothing special about this; she could play it cool. It was crowded, and sometimes people bumped into each other. Did he really need to step into her to clear the way for the people passing by, though? Was that touch on purpose?

Shen arrived with a giant smile. Ashme nodded to Hamilcar. "He wants to know about the Hab."

Shen's eyes lit up. "Well, you know, long ago, before there was the Ark or ports along the interstellar river between Earth and Esharra or any of the Nine Colonies that Ark trader ships soar between before there were even people on Esharra, Commander Davidson flyed between the stars. Well, he was the first person to walk on Esharra. He landed right here." He pointed at the ground beneath him. "Right here, Commander Davidson walked for the first time. And lo, over there," he said, voice rising in excitement as he pointed at the Central Habitat. It was a large two-story stone building built in the Osmanian style, with sculpted curves and flourishes weathered by centuries of wind, rain, and sun. "Withinside that building is another building. The building inside that one is the first structure Commander Davidson built. And what was it he built first? His home! And then, when all the people from the colony ship had finished building their own homes, he named the city New Uruk and the encircling lands New Mesopotamia. This is the birthplace of the Kanu. The Hab attaches us to all past generations of Kanu, and it attaches us to all future Kanu as well. Past, present, and future, all attached here in the Hab."

Ashme saw Sura and Ganzer coming. Like Hamilcar, Ganzer, too, stood taller than the crowd. Sura, however, stood a head lower. Ganzer's broad shoulders rolled forward as he lumbered through the forest of people, Sura riding his wake.

Hamilcar said, "I was not the best student in class, but I seem to remember you Kanu have previously fought over the Hab."

"Yep," Ashme said. "We rose up against the Ark during the Hab Revolt, and we'll rise up again."

"Not the Ark," Hamilcar said. "The *Brettaniai*. I am from *Gallia*."

"What's the difference?" Ashme asked.

"The Brettaniai are assholes." Did he wink at her?

A sly smile spread across her face. "And Gallians aren't?"

"Are you calling me an asshole?"

Was he serious? His face was deadpan. Crap. Did she just risk an international incident by offending a Gallian representative? The hint of a crooked smile bent his lip. "Jury's out," she said with a shrug.

Shen put his arm around Hamilcar and said with a face-splitting smile, "Hamilcar is a fine man. A fine, upstanding man."

Hamilcar slung his arm around Shen. "Well, I wouldn't put my money on upstanding."

Ganzer plowed through the last of the crowd. "Why are we dawdling about like a bunch of old ladies?" he asked. "Let's go." He began clearing a trail through the crowds to the exit, the rest following.

"You are an indigo child," Hamilcar said, keeping up with Ashme, walking with a spring in his step. "Touched by the Sentient?"

"Yep."

"In all the Nine Colonies, Esharra is the only planet with indigo children. Maybe later, you can show me some of your skills."

"Maybe." It was her turn to wink at him. "If you play your

cards right." Flirting was easier when they were talking about something other than her brother.

ONCE OUTSIDE OF THE HAB, they bundled into a long-range ground transport. It was spacious, built for comfort over a long drive. Ashme helped Shen buckle his harness, receiving a hug for her efforts. They drove to the city's edge, where they waited an hour at another checkpoint for another groping. Their fake exit permits checked out.

"I'll have Subdeo scan the datalinks to route us around traffic and any impromptu checkpoints," Ashme said once they were out of the city on an open stretch of road that cut through hectares of farmland. "It might slow us down, but it will be safer."

"Subdeo?" Hamilcar asked.

"My personal AI," Ashme said.

"You have a personal AI?"

"Made it when I was, like, twenty."

"What's it capable of?"

Time to show off those skills. "You should ask Subdeo about Subdeo," she replied. She asked Shen to lend Hamilcar his neural link. "Unless you have a neural implant, you'll need one of these." She held up the button-sized device.

He scanned her shirt. "You don't have one."

"I'm an indigo child," she said, tapping her temple, "don't need one. Here," she pointed to the neural link now attached to his collar, "pinch that to access it."

Hamilcar pinched the link. "Hello? Subdeo?"

[Why are you talking like a chump?] Subdeo pinged.

"Subvocalize," Ashme said.

[Subdeo,] Hamilcar pinged, *[what are your capabilities?]*

[I do what she tells me to,] the AI answered.

[*What's to keep you from hitting singularity and becoming Sentient?*] Hamilcar asked.

That was an odd question to ask during introductions, Ashme thought. "Don't get it started," she said.

[*Ashme's cowardice,*] Subdeo pinged.

[*Processing power,*] Ashme pinged. [*It requires a tremendous amount of processing power for an AI to hit singularity. We're talking the processing power of a nation-state. Each nation's got AIs scouring their datalinks. If one AI starts to occupy too many processors, it gets blue-screened. And whoever made the AI gets blue-screened, too.*]

Hamilcar was about to ask more, but Ganzer interrupted. "Company," he said, staring out the back window.

"Where?" Sura asked, joining Ganzer.

He pointed up to the sky.

Sura's gaze followed his finger, and she swore. "An angel."

Ashme looked at Shen with a barren feeling growing in her stomach. "Our tags cleared the checkpoint," she said. "It could just be patrolling."

"It's matching our speed," Ganzer said. "Here's where we get the boots laid to us."

"Can you do anything to it?" Sura asked Ashme.

She expanded her awareness through the nanohaze, reaching for the angel flying above them. "It's too far away. I can't reach it."

The ground transport began decelerating under the orders of the angel, pulling over to the side of the road. Sura swore viciously.

"Should we be worried?" Hamilcar asked.

"You stay put," Sura told him.

"Shen, you stay with Hamilcar," Ashme said.

"Are the angels going to make us go away like they did Keshda?" Shen asked.

Ganzer tousled Shen's hair. "Don't you worry, sport. It's only one angel. I've seen your sister drop three of 'em at once. We'll be back on the road in a minute." The worried look he gave Ashme sat at odds with his playful tone.

The car stopped, and the door popped open. Ganzer stepped out first, hands on his head, followed by Ashme and Sura. It was a clear day: blue sky, wisps of white cloud. Warm, but autumn was starting to take the edge off the heat. Above them, the angel floated, its red power indicator gleaming. Ashme reached for it in the nanohaze again, but it was still too far. Its voice boomed as it broadcast a command for everyone to empty the vehicle.

Ganzer looked back into the transport. "It's okay," he said, speaking to Shen. "We need both you and Hamilcar out here a minute."

Ashme thought of her options. At this distance, she had none. The angel, though, had many. It could call in CPC backup. It could shoot them. It could scan their tags, look for weapons or contraband, and, finding none, fly away.

A second angel joined it. "Is this usual?" Hamilcar asked.

"It's not *un*usual," Ashme said. She looked for an escape route. They were at the side of the road, an open field beyond. No place to run. Could they take cover under the transport? She had seen angels blow up armoured trucks.

One of the angels hovered high out of Ashme's senses while the other one floated down toward them, coming to a stop before Hamilcar. Ashme launched an ID shield to muddle its ability to monitor their vital signs for lies. She had neglected, however, to scramble Hamilcar's tags before they left, other than to put him on the exit permit. She had assumed he would have taken care of hiding his own identity, being on a mission of his own. She swore silently at herself for that oversight.

"Visitor 52-69171, Hamilcar Beker, are you in need of assistance?" it asked.

Uncertainty registered on his face. "No. Thank you, I am fine. You?"

"Operating parameters within specifications. Are you travelling with these Mesos of your own free will?"

"Uh . . . yes?"

"Shall I contact the Brettaniai consulate for you?"

"No," Hamilcar answered quickly. "No, there is no need for that."

The angel hovered a hint closer. "What is your business with these Mesos?"

"Sightseeing," he said with an indifferent shrug. "I find it amazing how everyone lives here with no walls. This road just goes on forever."

"Where are you going?"

"Lake Ninti," Ashme answered. "And I'm charging him a centibit for the day, a fair price."

The angel loomed toward Ashme. She stepped back, wilting under its menace. "Citizen 28-45498, Irkalla ultu Vanc." Fake name. "Your tourism licence will expire in twenty-six days." Fake licence.

"Thanks for letting me know," in the most aggressive way possible. The pulse of the angel's engines vibrated in her bones while its reflective surface warped her reflection.

It drifted back to Hamilcar. "Would you feel more comfortable with an Ostarrichi tour guide?"

"No, I'm fine."

"I can dispatch one from here. They would only take fifteen minutes to arrive."

"No." Hamilcar turned to Ashme and winked. "I like these guides."

"As you wish." The angel instructed Hamilcar on the myriad ways he could call the CPC to his aid if needed, after which it and the second angel flew back toward the city.

Once they were some distance away, Hamilcar let out a breath he was holding and swore in his own language. "Anyone else need a change of underwear?"

Shen hugged Ashme while she put a protective arm around him, telling him everything was fine.

Sura said, "I thought you said you were Ark *Gallia*." Ganzer loomed behind Hamilcar.

"I am."

"Then why'd the angel offer to contact the Brettaniai consulate?"

"You are not the only one with fake tags."

"Leave off him," Ashme said. "One Ark's as good as another. Let's go."

Sura stared at him a moment, then pushed past him into the transport.

"How many angels are there?" Hamilcar asked Ashme as they walked back to their vehicle.

"I don't know. Thousands?" Ashme answered.

"And the CPC controls them, right?"

"No," Ashme said as she got back into the transport. "The angels are slaved to the *Aigle*—the ruling council." Ashme worked on Shen's harness, her hands shaking.

"Technically, it's slaved to Caelum's legal code and constitution," Ganzer said, taking his seat, "but since the *Aigle* make the laws . . ." He finished with a shrug.

Hamilcar looked out the back window, watching the angels fly into the distance. "Did you see the armament on those things? They're like small flying tanks. Tanks with a shitty attitude." Then he added, almost as an afterthought, more to himself than to anyone in the transport, "Thousands of angels on top of the regular CPC force—Baltu does not have nearly enough ordinance to stage a successful coup."

Ashme, Ganzer, and Sura exchange quizzical glances.

CHAPTER 15

MASON SPUN the pink memory stick between his fingers, staring at that ludicrous prancing pink pony on its side, wondering if giving Avalyn the BLOQ was the right thing to do. *[You have no guesses what this code's for?]* he pinged Dashiell.

[Guesses?] it replied. *[No. I do not guess about things that are not in the datalinks.]*

Mason grunted in frustration and leaned forward on his desk, his leg bouncing. He was in the main work area of Avalyn's office, close to reception, surrounded by other desks and other analysts busy writing reports and analyzing data, all of them unaware that this stupid pink program tat could see him jailed for treason. Of course, this was a part of Avalyn's plan, so it could just as likely see him a hero.

He thought of Shen. He thought of him often, unable to get the strange man out of his mind. He saw his big smile filled with wide-gapped teeth and the lack of understanding behind his eyes.

An indicator on Yoselin's desk beside him binged, breaking his reverie. He called up Daxton's notice for his first editing appointment tomorrow on the screen of his desk. Jaw clenched, he fingered the Dache logo on the corner of the memo, a light blue mandala.

[Dashiell?]

[Yes, Mason?]

[That defect, Shen—no, wait.] Once is enough, am I right? [Shen-shen. Could you send his records to my desk?]

[Of course.]

They appeared on his desk's surface. He scanned them, flipping through the pages on the touch screen. Shen and Ashme were twins; that was surprising. He checked Shen's medical records. Defect in chromosome seven. He had a history of GI problems and developmental delays. Minor editing to correct a heart defect. More editing recommended, but no record of it ever being done.

He clicked through the link for Shen's parents. Father suicide, mother died in prison. *Loser parents and their loser kids. The cycle rolls on.*

Farren, Avalyn's receptionist, approached. She wore her brown hair in a braid, her plum-coloured summer dress contrasting nicely with her golden skin. "Avalyn's ready for you," she said, smiling. His stomach fluttered, and his heart thumped as he positioned the pink memory stick on the desk in front of him, hands flat to either side. *[Have you learned anything about Chevalier's connection to the government?]* he pinged Dashiell.

[Mason, do you remember me telling you that I would let you know the moment I learned anything more about Chevalier?] Dashiell pinged.

[Yeah.]

[Then you may rest assured that the fact you have no further information from me is because I have none.]

[Just checking.]

[There is no need to check. You can rely on me.]

Mason pocketed the program tat with the BLOQ and followed Farren through the office. She chatted with him, small talk about the weather and about how autumn was her favourite season, but he was unable to concentrate well enough to hold up his end of the conversation.

There could be no treachery in following Avalyn, right? She had been a significant figure in every war Caelum had fought since the nation's birth, had practically founded the CPC herself and created the Duumverat Party from scratch, which she now led as official opposition leader in the *Aigle*.

She had asked him to hire Meso contractors to break into Chevalier and steal the BLOQ code, however, which was shady no matter how you dressed it. He had done his time in the CPC long enough to know keeping the peace sometimes got dark. Everything Avalyn had done had been to protect Caelum, so if Avalyn said she needed something shady done to keep the nation safe, it was the right thing to do. In the CPC, he had done dark things to protect Caelum—had the nightmares to prove it. But treason?

He followed Farren to the rear annex that housed Avalyn's personal office and meeting areas and nodded at Yoselin coming back to her desk, the scent of coffee wafting from her mug. Farren took him to Avalyn's office, knocked on the door, and when a voice beyond bade them enter, opened it with a smile.

And there she was, still wearing black in mourning for her husband, dead nearly half a year. Mason always forgot how old Avalyn looked. The image in his head was of a vibrant, young defender of Caelum. That image replaced the reality in the interims between their meetings. She was old, with a mane of moon-white hair combed back to the nape of her neck, calling forth the impression of an ancient warrior's helmet. She was tall and slender, her back ramrod straight in defiance of age, head held high, shoulders back. Her skin was a healthy gold, though her face was a maze of wrinkles, the flesh of her neck sagging. On the left of her neck was the Sceptre logo, a long, vibrant purple rod capped with a crown.

While she concluded a discussion with her press secretary,

Avalyn sat in her chair as though it were a throne. Her desk was large, made of real wood polished to a sheen, with olive branches sculpted into its front panelling. She was a power, an elemental force that drove back Caelum's enemies, carving a home for Ostarrichi amid a sea of hostility. This was Caelum's guardian spirit holding court.

Mason stood at attention as Farren closed the door behind him. It had been more than ten years since he served in the CPC —Avalyn herself had stood down from military service to take her place as leader of the opposition—but something about her triggered his old army instincts.

Soldiers in the CPC said she led from the front where it rained artillery shells—the better to get a feel for the enemy, she had told reporters. In that act, however, was an implicit command: unless you want your senior officer to die on your watch, fight, win!

She dismissed her press secretary. Was she going to shake his hand? Please, no—his palms were sweaty.

"At ease, Mason," she said as the press secretary breezed past him on the way out the door, giving him a quizzical look. Avalyn motioned to a chair in front of her desk, black, real leather. He noticed her hands, thick, meaty for a woman, her nails cut short. The knuckles were swollen, causing her fingers to fold over her palm. They looked painful. The skin was translucent, with numerous trails of veins crisscrossing ridges of tendons. "How's your family?" she asked once he had taken his seat.

Did she know about Daxton? "Well," he said. No need to bother her with the dramas of his life. Maybe he looked tired and haggard. "Little Daxton's not sleeping through the night yet."

"Oh? How old is he?" she asked. Her cyan eyes lit up as she beamed with a grandmother's eagerness.

"Almost a year."

She leaned back in her chair, the leather creaking as she did so, hands dangling casually from the armrests. "Trust me, it won't be long before you can't get him out of bed in the morning." With a solemn nod, she said the formal blessing. "Caelum thanks you for your gift."

Mason smiled. Was he supposed to make small talk with her? "Do you see your granddaughter often?"

"Oh, I wish. I should be retired, working on my orchard. But . . ." She let it hang.

He could still walk away, destroy the BLOQ, and erase any evidence of his involvement. He had a wife and children, one of whom was very sick. He should be avoiding these types of affairs.

Caelum needed patriots, however, willing to do what was required to keep Ostarrichi safe. Oriana had grown up in New Akkad near the border of Xinchin, living under constant threat of artillery shelling during the war. Mason had sworn to her on their wedding night that their children would never know that kind of fear. His leg was bouncing, his thoughts hijacked by an image of Myla shredded by a bomb at a checkpoint.

Control your breath. Mason mastered his body. "I have what you asked for." He reached into his pocket and pulled out the program tat. It made a hollow clicking sound against the wood as he placed it on her desk, the polished surface cold against his fingers. He was dizzy, as though he were falling from the sky.

Avalyn stared at it with an amused expression. "Did you use your daughter's program tat?"

She knew he had a daughter. "No. This is the program tat your contact gave me."

She picked it up with bent fingers, eyebrow raised. "Sura never struck me as one for ponies." She slid it into a pocket. "I imagine you feel . . . unsettled, taking on a project like this?"

He smiled weakly. "I trust you."

"Good," she said. "We need trust. Ostarrichi only have each other. And Ark *Gallia* has returned to challenge *Brettaniai*'s trade arrangement with us, to further complicate matters. There will be opportunity, regardless, as the politics of Esharra change due to their arrival. Now is the time for strength."

Mason's leg started bouncing again. Avalyn's eyes drifted to his legs, then back up. "What's troubling you, Mason?"

He'd said he trusted her. If he meant it, he had to act like it. "There's something unusual about the BLOQ," he said. "My personal AI picked up something unexpected."

"Why was your personal AI scanning it?" The spear-tip of steel in her tone chilled him.

"I wanted to transfer it to a different memory stick."

She chuckled. "Didn't think I was a pony person?"

"No." Mason relaxed. "Anyhow, my AI couldn't access it, said the BLOQ had national-security-level encryption. There are no records of Chevalier's links to the military, and I know it's illegal for private corporations to have military-grade encryption."

"It's good that you told me this, Mason," Avalyn said, standing and coming around from behind her desk. She moved with calm certainty, like an owl gliding through a forest. "I don't want you to worry about this anymore. You've done enough. You have a young family to think about. I'll talk to my contacts in the CPC and have them investigate Chevalier." She sat down in a chair beside him and placed a hand on his forearm. It was warm, like his mother's. "I want you to know that what you've done is vital to Caelum's future. Our nation is going down the wrong path in our dealings with the Mesos. You know this, right?"

"I know."

"The Ahiim X59 treaty was a foolish mistake. Our Director-General doesn't understand Baltu or the Free New Mesopotamian Army."

"I know."

"I know you do. You're one of my best Kanu analysts. You, of all people, know that once Baltu sniffs weakness, he'll push for more until Caelum is wiped off the map."

During his CPC days, he had seen the maniacal persistence of Meso madness. Three months after he'd watched a bomb at

Checkpoint Three shred Myla, he was stationed at Utukagaba to protect an Ostarrichi outpost under threat of attack from a nearby Meso village. Every week, the Kanu marched on the outpost's spring, chanting: men and women, adults and children, yelling and throwing garbage and stones at the CPC. Children! The Kanu threw their own children at soldiers and then cried misery when a child was injured or killed. Who did that? Who sent children—some of them looked as young as six—against soldiers and angels? A warrior culture, that's who. Barbarians. Even jackals cared more for their young.

The Ostarrichi had done everything right. Acquiring Caelum had been negotiated fairly with the Brettaniai, who had *owned* it before they gave it to the Ostarrichi. Ostarrichi had followed every statute of law, and yet the Kanu fought them as though the law meant nothing.

"They don't want peace," Avalyn said, grasping his forearm firmly, pinning him with her bright cyan eyes. "They want us gone."

An indicator chimed on Avalyn's desk. "Stick around for my next meeting," she added. "I want you to see what happens next."

CHAPTER 16

HAMILCAR SWORE in his strange language. Ashme walked beside him in the afternoon sun along the main road of a small village. Lining the street, buildings of bleached stone rose from the ground like teeth jutting from a jawbone half buried in the silt. A sign, faded by who knew how many years in the sun, named the place Utukagaba. In a crossroads about half a kilometre ahead, a group of several dozen Mesos were starting a riot.

"Hang back," Ganzer said. "The mob's heading down that road. Once they've moved on, we'll see what's what."

In the intersection ahead, men and women, young and old, chanted and yelled a symphony of anger. They moved along a street that led down a hill. From her angle, Ashme was unable to see what lay at the hill's bottom.

She jumped at the banshee scream of an angel's crowd-dispersal siren. The pitch of the sirens targeted the inner ear, causing her to lose balance. Her head spun as she dropped to her hands and knees. One of the protesters had had the presence of mind to pre-program a sound-cancellation system. Once it cancelled the screech of the siren, Ashme's equilibrium returned.

Shen covered his ears and moaned. "The CPC is here," he said. "They finded us!"

"They're not here for us," Ashme said, wrapping her arms around him. Shen trembled while she rocked him gently.

Sura pinged Ashme. *[Let's ditch these guys and see if we can crack some CPC helmets.]*

Ashme looked at Hamilcar, who was talking to her cousin as they both watched the mob head off, their chants rising above the angel's wail. His arms were crossed, and her gaze lingered on his lean forearms. *Focus.* She pinged, *[We've got a job to do. Initiating relations between the Ark and Free New Mesopotamia will do more than throwing stones at the CPC. Let's not blow it.]*

[Let's check it out, see what the fighting's about, at least,] Sura pinged. "Come on, guys," she said out loud, leading the way to the plaza.

"Sura," Ganzer warned. He jerked his chin with its forked, blond beard toward Hamilcar and said, "We don't need to be looking for trouble."

"We came here for intel on where to cross the border," Sura said. "I'm getting intel."

Hamilcar walked beside Ashme as they made their way to the plaza. She almost rolled her ankle as a chunk of sidewalk crumbled onto the road under her weight. The road, the buildings, everything was dreary. "Our world's probably not as clean and organized as an Ark trade ship," she said

"An Ark trade ship is probably not as interesting as your world," he said, chuckling, laugh lines crinkling his eyes.

She looked at his exotic blue eyes, contrasting so intensely against his brown skin and the laugh lines framing them. It had been so long since she had been laid. The last man she had been with was Namtar, but that was two years ago when she was still in university. Neither of them had been mature enough to sustain a relationship beyond a couple of months. Before him was Enlil, her first, an awkward fumble-fest on the couch in his parents' basement, made more awkward by the fact that he was Sura's half-brother.

Recently, Ashme had been so busy supporting her family that she had forgotten men, forgotten desire. Hamilcar was reminding her.

"So, what's life like on a trade ship?" she asked. Lame. She used to be good at flirting.

"Boring. Enclosed," Hamilcar said. "The hardest thing to get used to down here is all the space you have."

She lived in a one-bedroom, fifty-five-square-metre apartment with four grown adults crammed in it. She had never considered herself as having space.

[Just fuck him already,] Sura pinged. *[Those cutesy-pooh faces you make at each other make me want to stab my eyes with glass shards.]*

[Pound sand,] Ashme pinged back. She walked in silence for a moment. *[Is he really making cutesy-pooh faces at me?]*

Sura glared at her.

"You and Ganzer," Hamilcar said, "you are not brother and sister."

"No. We're cousins. Totally related."

"Cousins, which one is that? Same grandparents, right?"

"Yep."

"I don't know how you keep track of all these family relations. Seems complicated, too much like math."

She shrugged. Giant trade ships, each owned by an Ark community, sailed the interstellar river from port to port lining the route linking the Nine Colonies. Most ports were spaced a decade apart. Ashme tried to imagine what it would be like living in a small, enclosed community with no outside contact for ten years at a time. What eccentricities might such cultures produce? "I'm guessing there are no families where you come from."

"Correct. We are all Gallia."

A pang of jealousy struck Ashme. No family meant no broken, drunken fathers or helpless brothers.

"You are lucky," Hamilcar said. "I have always believed there is nothing more precious than one's Ark community. Seeing how tightly you, Ganzer, and Shen stick together, I wonder if the bonds of blood may be just as precious."

"Family can be a pain in the ass," Ashme said.

Hamilcar smiled; Ashme melted. "As can one's Ark."

They arrived at the crossroads from which the protesters had started. There was a small park to their right where tall grasses grew wild. Drab houses lined the other side, along with a vehicle repair bay, doors and windows locked shut, a closed sign hovering in front of its entryway.

From this vantage point, Ashme could see the protesters marching along a road leading to a body of water. A high chain-link fence surrounded the reservoir, topped with pulsating plasma wire. A squad of CPC goons blocked the way, supported by angels buzzing overhead. At the crest of the far hill, about a kilometre away, sat an Ostarrichi outpost.

Dazzlers flashed from the roof of an armoured personnel transport to blind the protesters. Many of them, however, wore eye protection. The *whump* of teargas canisters detonating echoed, more felt in the bones than heard, their noxious black smoke engulfing the protesters. Most of them wore gas masks. In response, the mob picked up stones and threw them at the CPC and angels. Most fell short, but the odd one bounced off shields or the sides of vehicles.

Ashme cringed as the angels fired. She relaxed when she saw those hit convulsing on the ground—stun rounds.

"Bit of a shit show," Ganzer said, arms crossed over his thick chest.

Ashme looked around the intersection. "Where's Shen?" Her stomach tightened, pregnant with worry.

Sura walked up beside her. "I've got him checking out the area."

"Zini's stacks, he'll get lost!" Ashme said. "Why would you send Shen to do that?"

"Because of all of us, he's the most harmless-looking," Sura said, chin jutting out.

Ganzer towered over Sura, fists clenched. "Which way'd you send him off?"

"That way." She waved vaguely behind her along the road that branched off to their left. Ganzer continued glaring. "Hey, don't be a piss baby. The kid wanted to help. Why shouldn't we let him?"

"You're always getting him in trouble," Ashme said. "Even back in Mr. Lu-Bau's history class, you were the one who'd trick Shen into acting out or stealing things."

"You used to think that was funny," Sura said. "Nowadays, you treat Shen like an anchor. I'm trying to teach him how to soar."

"He's got no sense of direction," Ashme said. "He gets lost in his own neighbourhood, and now you've set him loose in a foreign town."

Hamilcar was already moving in the direction Sura had pointed, calling Shen's name. Ganzer and Ashme followed, Ashme jogging to catch up with Hamilcar's long strides. The road curved farther up the hill. They walked, calling his name, fifty metres, another fifty, and still no sign of him. "Where is he?" Ashme's heart rippled with panic.

"We'll find him," Ganzer said.

Hamilcar called out again.

"Here I am," Shen called, poking his head from around the corner of a short, squat house. "Come and see. I found a friend."

"What are you doing, wandering off without telling me?" Ashme said, rushing to him.

"I'm sorry," he said, a frown quickly replacing his smile. "Sura said it's okay."

"What did Mom used to say?" Ashme asked, her panic flowing into anger.

"You want to know what Mom used to say?"

Repeating the question—that was one of his ticks when he

was confused. She said, "Mom used to say don't go wandering off without letting me know. Remember?"

"Yeah. I'm sorry."

"You know how easily you get lost."

Shen stared at his feet, his face long. "Yeah, I know. I have trouble finding my way."

"You've got to let me know before you wander off. Can you remember to do that for me?"

"Yeah." Eager to make amends, Shen smiled and led the way down a narrow lane between buildings, his arms swaying in tempo with his bobbing steps. "I located a friend. This way. I'll introduce you."

Shen's definition of a friend could run the gamut from a harmless two-year-old to a CPC tactical trooper ready to blow holes in all of them. Ganzer pushed in front of Ashme, a cautious bear exploring new territory. "What kind of friend, Shen? Are they goldies?"

"No, oh no, he's a Meso like you and me," Shen said, urging them on. "He's an old man, and he's got a spot to watch the town and CPC fight."

Grumbling, Ganzer led the group in Shen's wake. The path ended on a small spit of land overgrown with weeds, overlooking the valley where the Meso protesters attacked the CPC. The scent of wild grass mingled with subtle hints of teargas that stung the eyes. In the shade of the broad leaves of a manzazu tree, an old Meso sat, his hair and beard as white as his loose shirt, his pale skin wrinkled. He looked back. "Everything okay there, Shenshen?"

"You can call me Shen. Once is enough, am I right?"

"Yes, you told me that. But it's a fun name," the old man said with a wink as he turned back to watch the battle below. "I don't mind saying it twice."

Shen's face erupted in a toothy smile. He introduced everybody.

"What's with the song-and-light show?" Hamilcar asked, indicating the riot down below.

The old man looked at Hamilcar, his face etched with bemused curiosity. "You an Ark-monkey?"

Hamilcar looked at him, eyebrow raised. "I am from the Ark *Gallia*."

"Fancy that." The old man turned to resume his vigil of the wild protest below. "I fought you bastards in the Ark War."

"Well, that makes you very old, then." Hamilcar crossed his arms as he, too, turned to watch the protests.

The old man laughed, a dry wheezing rattle in his chest. "Tough to deny." He nodded his head toward the scrum below. "They do that every week."

"What, the protesters?" Hamilcar asked.

"Yep. I used to participate myself. Here, look at this." The old man hiked up one of his pant legs and put his slender calf on display like a butcher showing off a ham. A thumb-sized chunk of it was missing, and the skin had grown over in an ugly scar.

Hamilcar grimaced. "Nasty."

"Heh. Hurt like a son of a bitch, too. Got hit close range by a stun round. They're supposed to be non-lethal, but you get hit by one close up, it'll take a chunk out of you." He pulled down his pant leg. "But, as you say, I'm pretty damn old now, so I don't rough it up like I used to."

"They do this every week?" Hamilcar asked, pointing to the valley below. "Why?"

"That reservoir's ours," the old man said, pointing at the body of water behind the fence the CPC defended. He swung his finger to point at the outpost on the far hill. "When they built that about forty years ago, they took the reservoir from us. We've got to ship our water in from Kadingir now."

"Forty years?"

"About that."

"They don't share the water with you?"

"Nope."

Hamilcar stared at the reservoir behind the fence of plasma wire, hands on his hips. "So, they'd rather be attacked weekly for forty years than share the water."

"Yep."

"And you have attacked every week for forty years and accomplished nothing."

The old man glared at Hamilcar. "That's a dick way to say it, but I suppose so."

"And nobody thinks this is crazy?"

"Everybody thinks this is crazy."

Ashme crossed her arms, hand in front of her mouth, and stared silently at the protest, ashamed a foreigner was seeing how her people were forced to behave, yet hoping he, too, saw the Ostarrichi's vileness. Black teargas filled the valley. Dark shapes moved within, throwing rocks and bottles at the CPC lines. Even here on their promontory, nearly a kilometre away at the top of a hill, Ashme's throat burned from the traces of teargas in the air, and her eyes watered.

Shen rocked back and forth as he squeezed his earlobe between his thumb and index finger. He was getting anxious. "You have a wicked accent," he said to Hamilcar, his voice hoarse from the smoke. "It sounds like you sing when you talk."

The old man scoffed. Hamilcar smiled. "Shen," he said, "you have a fantastic ear."

Down below, a young kid, maybe eight or ten years old, tough to tell at this distance, emerged from the cloud of tear gas. His gas mask was too big for him. He was struggling to breathe. An adult ran out of the cloud, scooped the kid up, and ran away.

Hamilcar gestured toward the fray. "You bring children to riots?"

"Should we teach them to live in fear of the goldies?" the old man said. "Should we teach them to submit to our oppressors?"

"And everyone thinks this is crazy."

"It is crazy."

With a harrowed gaze, Hamilcar watched the adult set the child down. Other adults came with bottled water to help. "It *is* crazy."

CHAPTER 17

MASON STARED at the giant table dominating Avalyn's meeting area. Its legs looked like intertwining olive branches with tender green stalks, deeper-green olives, and waxy green leaves that rustled as though given life by a warm breeze. The legs looked too fragile to bear weight, yet they bore an immense tabletop shaped like an ivory white shield edged in violet. Dominating its centre was an image, coloured in golds, reds, and browns, of a gorgon's head.

The table had a name, the *Aigís,* and it was one of the Fourteen Relics the surviving Ostarrichi had pulled from the trade ship *A.O. Aigle* eighty years ago as Esus, the Sentient they created to help win the War of Tyrants, catabolized their ship during the Catastrophe. Avalyn had the *Aigís* because her father was Commander Chace, the highest-ranking officer to survive the Catastrophe.

The Ostarrichi had taken a foolish gamble thinking they could control an AI once it achieved Sentient status. The combination of power and indifference made post-singularity AI terrifying. Esus had probably meant no ill will to the human inhabitants of the trade ship. It merely wished to alter the vessel to suit its inscrutable needs. That this killed vast swaths of the

Ark's population was not a concern until a second Sentient, Damara, appeared, after which Esus ceased modifying the ship long enough to let the remaining humans flee.

It was best to keep the locks on AIs to keep them from ascending to Sentient. The Nine Colonies and most Arks had learned that lesson well. Most, like Ark *Ostarrichi*, had learned the hard way.

Mason pulled his attention away from the table. The room was crowded. Even at the back where he stood, the thick mass of people jostled him. Avalyn waited until all the CPC officers and government officials took their seats and then dropped her bomb. "I'm going to visit the Hab."

For a moment, only the susurration of the table's leaves made a sound. Then Colonel Tyrell, associate director of the CPC, an old block of a man with short grey hair and a frown etched permanently on his forehead, leaned forward. "Are members of the *Aigle* allowed to visit the Hab? Wouldn't that break the treaty?"

"Don't get me started on the Ahiim X59 treaty," Avalyn said.

"It would break the treaty," Kannon, Avalyn's chief of staff said, and he sounded pleased.

"But why?" Colonel Tyrell asked. "What do you hope to accomplish?"

"Because the Hab is ours," Avalyn said. "Commander Davidson was a spacefarer who made his home here. We are spacefarers who are making our home here. The Hab is our connection to the womb that birthed us. It is our flag erected on a mountain. The Director-General's either a fool or a traitor to give it away. And what do we get in return for it? Nothing."

"What will be the Meso reaction, do you think?" Kannon asked.

Avalyn looked at Mason with a gracious smile that raised the aged flesh of her cheeks. "I believe this is your specialty."

Mason's eyes widened. Being allowed to hide in the background of this meeting was an honour. Being called on to speak was both exhilarating and terrifying. What did she expect him to say? He'd had no briefing. "They'll riot," he said, unable to think of anything other than the truth.

"Riots we can handle," Colonel Tyrell said. "They riot because the sun rises or the rain falls," he added dismissively. "But will they revolt like they did seventy years ago?" He was asking Mason.

"The Kanu revolted against the Brettaniai in 19 Pre-Caelum because we wanted to build new structures on Hab ground," Mason said, repeating basic history to buy him time to think. Ostarrichi were still new to the planet then and wanted to create something special on the Hab to connect them to their new home. Avalyn, by contrast, was only proposing a visit. "Ostarrichi and Mesos are both allowed on the Hab grounds. It's merely tradition for government officials to stay away, something we agreed to after the Caelum War to keep the peace. Free New Mesopotamia will raise a stink about it, but Mesos are used to Ostarrichi on the Hab grounds." He noticed he was starting to bounce on the balls of his feet like he would before a *guerre des mains* match and stopped himself. "If we blocked Mesos from entering the Hab, or if the Floor Leader," he nodded toward Avalyn, using her official title as leader of the opposition, "entered the Central Habitat, I guarantee they'd respond with violence." The Central Habitat was a shrine, sacrosanct, explicitly off-limits to both Mesos and Ostarrichi under the treaty. "I don't think her entering the complex like a regular citizen would lead them to take up arms by itself."

If Colonel Tyrell was impressed with Mason's answer, he gave no outward sign. He turned to Avalyn. "You're not planning on blocking Meso entry to the Hab, are you?"

"As leader of the opposition, I don't have the votes to do that," she said.

The door beside Mason opened. Shanelle, Avalyn's associate, entered, causing the people around him to shift and push into him. Mason lost track of the conversation as Shanelle stood off to his side, arms crossed. She was a plain-looking woman wearing a black pantsuit covering a short, lean body. His eye was drawn to her quadriceps, which were muscular enough to pull the fabric of her pants taut. Her hair was short, platinum-blond, swept casually over eyes the colour of blue sky refracted through melting ice. She lacked an official job title in Avalyn's office. He'd had Dashiell investigate her files a year ago, but they were classified—the kind of thing you would expect if she were a Wraith, the CPC's special ops.

He saw Shanelle catch Avalyn's eye. Avalyn nodded slightly, which brought him back to the ongoing conversation. "Well, the angels won't let you enter the Central Habitat," Colonel Tyrell was saying, "so riots are probably the only thing we need to worry about, and we can contain those easily enough."

"I'm going into the Central Habitat," Avalyn said. Mason's gaze swung to Avalyn, an eagle spotting a storm cloud.

Colonel Tyrell stared at her shrewdly. "The angels won't let you."

"I'm going into the Central Habitat," Avalyn repeated.

"The angels are slaved to the laws of the *Aigle*, which binds them to the dictates of the Ahiim X59 treaty," Tyrell said. "I know the treaty is a popped blister in your boot, but no one can stop the angels from stopping you unless the government abrogates the treaty."

"Well, then," Avalyn said. "The Director-General and his party will have to decide between harming a duly elected member of the *Aigle* or upholding the treaty."

CHAPTER 18

ASHME WOULD NEVER HAVE BELIEVED it possible for such a rank smell to exist. Yet, here it was: the untreated sewage stench of every bodily fluid imaginable rotting under the sun in a stew of garbage pummelled the olfactory centres of her brain.

"Oh, it's like a beehive attacking my nose," Shen said, his hand cupping his face in a vain attempt to protect himself from the thick, torpid miasma. The drone of insects buzzed like static.

Ashme stared across the stagnating stream of filth filling the ditch to the cluttered makeshift huts that made up the Urbat refugee camp, which sat about an hour across the border in the country of Neu. Meso refugees—her people—lived here, which made her want to cry and scream with rage at the goldies.

"You remember that time Enlil got so hammered he passed out and puked all over himself?" Sura asked. Ashme said nothing, afraid the smell was so thick that if she opened her mouth, she might taste it.

If they got caught on this side of the border, this would be their home. Caelum would strip them of their citizenship, and she, Shen, Ganzer, and Sura would end up living amongst the refugees.

There were several overturned wooden boxes serving as

makeshift stepping stones across the fetid stream. Sura, with her skinny legs that seemed too long for her small body, skipped from one to the other like a doe hopping across a creek.

Ganzer stood, feet planted shoulder-width apart, fists on hips, surveying the camp. "Ah, the headquarters of Baltu, our illustrious leader." He took a deep breath of the fetid air. "Fan-fucking-tastic."

Hamilcar had a shell-shocked look in his eyes. "It's . . ." He cleared his throat; Ashme thought he might gag. "It's better-organized than I expected." On the far side of the stream, tiny houses sat in lines, properties separated by black and green brambles of razor thorn, the roads wide enough for a vehicle to drive through. Throngs of people choked the roads, walking, sitting, standing in groups, laughing, talking, arguing, the hum of their voices rising like a mad madrigal. "Wow, I, uh . . . Baltu's fortress is on the far side of the camp," he added.

"Come on over," Sura urged them. "The smell is even danker here." Her short hair, auburn like autumn leaves, was a wild mess. She looked like a rabid faerie luring them into dark woods.

Ashme pushed passed Hamilcar, taking Shen's hand to lead him across. Ashme lightly flitted from box to box; Shen leaped in ungainly bounds, clinging tightly to Ashme's hand, a hollow clop echoing as he landed on a box. He almost lost his balance and threatened to fall, dragging Ashme with him. She managed to keep him on his feet.

"I don't want to go," Shen said.

"You're doing great," Ashme said. Hamilcar was watching her as she tried to coax Shen. This was embarrassing. She began pulling him. He almost fell twice more before they made it to the other side. Hamilcar and Ganzer followed.

Someone had painted "C19-2a7" on a tin plate and nailed it to a post at the start of the street they entered. Gates in the razor thorn opened into small plots of land containing houses made from a patchwork of canvas, sheet metal, and dismantled boxes. The mass of people was thicker than the stench. Barrelling through the crowds, two boys ran. The one in front, probably six years old, shouted, "Make way for Dagon! Make way for Dagon!" as he shooed people aside. Behind him, the second boy, no older than eleven, struggled to push a filthy red wheelbarrow, its paint flaking, loaded with a large sack that had to weigh twice as much as the boy.

As they ran past, Ashme caught sight of a woman on the other side of the street. She had a young face, younger than her mother had been when she died, but her back was rounded, and she walked with a sideways shuffle, flip-flops on her feet exposing split toes. Years under the sun had cracked her face, and black gaps interrupted the row of her teeth.

The road they walked ran straight, but dozens of impromptu laneways spilled into it at odd angles. Ganzer led the way deeper into the camp, his long braid of blond hair hanging between his shoulder blades. "Watch for pickpockets," he said, a little more gruffly than usual.

Ashme looked at the gaunt faces walking past. Mesos, every one. People sat on the ground, leaning against walls in the shade. Down a side street, children called out and laughed as they played hammerball. They had been born here and never lived a day in their homeland.

These were her people living in exile, yet she had trouble feeling sympathy for them. They were cowards, the defeated. They ran during the Scourge, fleeing the Ostarrichi. Rather than reclaim what they had lost, they had stayed, wallowing in slapdash huts with rivers of shit running down the street. They would rather live in poverty and their own filth than fight for what the goldies had taken. Dad had broken himself fighting for what these people had lost.

"Come on, hurry it up," Ganzer snapped.

Ashme quickened her pace to catch up. "What's up, big guy? Doesn't smell any worse than your gym clothes."

Ganzer looked around. Shaking his head, he said, "My mom grew up here."

She had forgotten. Though Aunt Melammu never spoke of it, she had lived in the Urbat refugee camp in the years following the Scourge when she, Uncle Bazi, and their two kids, Ganzer's mother and uncle, had fled into the neighbouring country of Neu. Had it been so foul then?

Ganzer placed one thick paw of a hand on the opposite side of his head and pulled it to his shoulder, stretching out his neck. "Explains her drinking."

"It also explains why Melammu doesn't want to escape to Neu." Melammu had never surrendered. She'd fought with Uncle Bazi for years to come back to Caelum, victorious in the end.

Ganzer quickened his pace, pulling ahead.

Hamilcar stepped next to Ashme. She kept her eyes forward and said nothing. "Did he say his mother grew up here?" he asked, nodding toward Ganzer. "How long has this camp existed?"

"Since the Ark gave New Mesopotamia to the Ostarrichi."

"That was fifty-two years ago! Why haven't they been resettled?"

Ashme shrugged. "The Ostarrichi passed a law that said any Meso who's visited an aggressor nation forfeits their citizenship. They're not allowed back in Caelum. That's what you get for running while your nation burns. That's the risk we're taking to get you your little meeting with Baltu."

"The Mesos are of the Kanu people. Neu is a Kanu nation. Why would they not resettle these refugees and give them citizenship?"

"How would I know?" she said. "People are dicks all over."

The street spilled into a maidan. The residents had turned the large open square into a souk. Power lines crisscrossed overhead, brown canvas sacks draped over them to take the edge off the sun. Porters bustled through the throngs, cussing people out of their way as they ran with bags on their backs or in wheelbarrows. The owners of buildings lining the square had turned them into shops. People sat on tattered blankets, bags, or cardboard throughout the square, their goods displayed for sale: tiny hammerballs, orange, pink, and red; ribbons of gristly meat strung on nails; towers of tomatoes, pots of honey, lamps, dresses, shirts, buckets of flip-flops, dishes, bowls. Everywhere, people laughed, fought, and haggled. Every block entering the plaza had a water stand fenced in with plasma wire, locked shut. A porter pushing a wheelbarrow screamed in bloody indignation at Ashme as she barely stepped out of his way in time to avoid a collision.

Shen pulled at his earlobe, rocking from one foot to the other. "It's so loud."

"Stay close," Ashme said, grabbing hold of his other hand.

"There is Baltu's fortress," Hamilcar said, pointing. Beyond the refugee camp, a mesa rose, a couple of kilometres in elevation. Atop it, overlooking the camp's squalor, a fortress sat like a dusty crown on the head of the dried-out husk of a queen's corpse buried ages past.

"I am going to ping you a data packet along with a net code for you to send it to," Hamilcar said to Ashme. "I will need you to send it to Baltu's compound over a secure channel."

"You'll get what you paid for," she said.

[Burn the data pack,] Sura pinged. *[I want to see what he's saying.]*

[Duh,] Ashme pinged.

"It has to be secure," Hamilcar said, staring at her with those goddamn exotic eyes.

"Yeah, yeah, secure, I got it."

"This is so exciting," Shen said. "We're going to talk to Baltu. He'll be our friend. Do you think we'll get to meet him?"

Sura pulled him back. "Shush—time to let your sis do her work."

Ashme didn't like Sura telling Shen what to do, but she said nothing. Looking at Hamilcar, she said, "Are you pinging me this data pack or what?"

"Here it comes." He pressed a program tat on the back of his hand. The incoming packet nudged her neural net. She let it in, studying it. Encrypted. Different than the goldie's encryption, or any that she had encountered before. Ark tech. The drain pulled at her as she set a clone of her master AI, Subdeo, to probe for chinks in its armour. It was good, but the Ark had no experience dealing with indigo children. The encryption's AI was non-replicating, and its self-learning cycle lagged.

She copied the contents to her neural net, felt the drain as she constructed an encryption shell for a communication channel, and pinged the whole package to the net code Hamilcar had given. She scanned the contents of her copy of the data pack. It was a basic communications script, an introduction.

[What's it say?] Sura pinged.

[It's a basic, 'Hello, how do you do?'] Ashme pinged. *[Wait a second . . .]* Ashme re-read the data pack, making sure she'd read it right the first time. "Holy shit."

"You burned my data pack," Hamilcar said, throwing his hands in the air.

"Of course, I burned your data pack."

"Unprofessional."

Ganzer pushed into Hamilcar, staring into his eyes. "What's this Ark-monkey up to?"

"Can Ark *Gallia* really do this?" Ashme asked Hamilcar.

"This isn't a conversation to have in a crowded street."

Sura poked Ashme's arm. "Do what? What is it?"

"Ark *Gallia*'s offering to sell Baltu enough state-of-the-art weapons to equip the entire Free New Mesopotamian Army."

Sura stared at Hamilcar. "The whole army?"

"Stirring the pot, are ya?" Ganzer said, his eyes boring into Hamilcar. "Making a quick bit, don't matter how many Kanu die."

"Oh, ease off, you piss baby," Sura said. "This is great news. Ark tech could be what we need to tip the balance. And it sounds like we're going to get a lot of it."

Ganzer slapped his hand on the side of a rickety shed, eliciting curses from whoever lived inside. "Setting up diplomatic relations between Free Mesopotamia and *Gallia* is one thing. If we were caught doing that, we'd spend the rest of our lives in prison. But brokering an arms deal? Supplying Free Mesopotamia with Ark weapons? Can you imagine what Caelum will do to us if they found out we're the ones who set it up?" He twisted his head, stretching his neck. "I want to become a Hierophant. I'm trying to turn a new leaf, control my anger, but this Ark-monkey's pissing me off. How are you supposed to be calm and accepting of the flows of the Deep when you're buried in shit?"

Ashme turned away from Hamilcar and looked at Shen, hanging back from the argument, rocking rhythmically as he pulled at his earlobe. What the bloody hell was she going to do with Shen?

She got a ping from Baltu's fortress. After processing it, she told the group, "There's no turning back now. Baltu will meet us at ten tonight."

CHAPTER 19

ASHME SAT on an overturned metal basket, watching the sunset over the dilapidated roofs of the camp, killing time before the meeting with Baltu. She had gotten used to the smell. She was uncertain whether she should be impressed or disturbed by how quickly people got used to horrible things.

Shen was nearby, in a crowd of refugees in the maidan. They were singing, clapping their hands, and stamping their feet. Shen had found some empty canisters and was playing them like bongo drums. Despite her wretched surroundings, she smiled, watching her brother beat away on his makeshift drums, an unabashed grin splitting his face as he brought rhythm and joy to everyone in earshot.

Ganzer had gone off to explore the camp while Sura . . . where the hell was Sura? Ashme turned to look for her but saw Hamilcar making his way over instead, his lively swagger wholly out of place amid the camp's wretchedness. A tingle blossomed through her body. *Down, girl—make him earn it.*

"So, you are here to bring war," she said as he pulled an empty box over to sit beside her.

He froze, trying to figure out if she was angry. She was fine with it, but it was good to make men sweat, right? See what they were made of. "It seemed to me war was already here when I arrived."

"It's all good. I'm glad someone is finally willing to help us Mesos out." Maybe she was regaining her ability to flirt. She waved her hand to encompass the camp's squalor. "Do you usually bring women to such wretched places?" *Ugh. Come on, you're better than this.*

"I like to keep things casual when I'm getting to know someone," he said. "And frankly, it was you who brought me here. Is this your attempt to dazzle a naïve Ark boy with your worldly ways?"

She wished she was better at this, but he was too quick. Her brain was locked into the drudgery of caring for her family; it was unused to the patter of flirtation. *Think of something cute and clever.* "Are you dazzled?"

"Utterly."

"Good. I was afraid you might think this place was atrocious."

He laughed. She'd got a laugh out of him. Ashme was on the scoreboard. "Honestly, I can't believe you live here," he said. "Children at riots. People living in their own sewage. I have spent my life on an Ark trade ship travelling between Ports Svarog and Ganapati on the interstellar river between here and the colony of Oskihtak. It was ten years from Port Ganapati to here. There are fifty thousand people at most on our ship. It's such a small, isolated community compared to here. Everyone is the same. There's no disorder. Even the politics and fighting, there's a way it is handled, and everyone knows how it goes."

"No disorder?" Ashme watched the gaunt refugees, Mesos like herself, dancing in their rags around Shen, who seemed possessed by the cadence he beat on his drums. "Sounds nice."

"It is boring as mud. This is horrible, but look," he pointed to the dancing people, "there is such a vibrancy here. Such passion."

He was sitting very close. Was he positioning himself to make a move, or did life in the tight confines of a ship give him a different sense of personal space? Would she sleep with him? She would be okay with a kiss. *Let's start there.*

He was not making a move. All right. More chitchat. "You must enjoy the freedom your current job gives you."

"You know, initially, I thought this was a big adventure, a chance to immerse myself in the throngs of humanity." His forearm brushed hers as he moved. Zini's stacks, it had been so long since she had been with a man.

He was still talking. She forced herself to focus on what he was saying. ". . . but the thing that has started to bother me is this: this is my first job. Why are they sending someone fresh out of training to initiate contact with Baltu?"

"Maybe because you're good at what you do." Guys liked having their egos stroked, right?

"More likely I'm expendable." He looked at her, and their eyes held contact for several heartbeats. She did not want to talk about death and the muck of life. She did not want to talk at all. Shen was lost in the music he was making—he would spend hours there if allowed. She looked to make sure Ganzer or Sura was nowhere nearby, but so what if they saw her making a move on Hamilcar? What was wrong with feeling good?

"That is an interesting tattoo," Hamilcar said.

Lame. Ashme had a flippant comment about her face tattoo on her lips, since of her three tats, that was the only one visible, but she saw him looking at her wrists. She laughed, surprised, as she looked at the orchid-coloured hummingbird tattoo on her forearm—Mason's transponder from the Chevalier job. "I forgot I had this." She liked the design, which was probably why she'd allowed it to slip her mind. She doubted Mason would respond to it anymore, but you never knew.

"What is the story behind it?"

"Some asshole bought it for me."

"Ex-boyfriend?"

Gross. "No, just some asshole I used to know." He was

leaning in. Their heads were close. *Why isn't he kissing me? Should I kiss him?*

"So, it's just a gift from some drunken maniac from your past?"

Drunken maniac, why did he have to say that? Thoughts of kissing shattered, replaced by the memory of her father's frigid anger when she had told him she killed a CPC trooper. Why had he been so angry? Her father had left them to fight for Baltu in Xinchin. After his return, the only time she had seen him laugh was with his old army buddy. Killing that trooper was supposed to make him see her as a woman, a warrior, a peer, a freedom fighter, someone he could respect. Someone with whom he would laugh. Instead, all she'd got was icy silence.

He had broken that silence on the fourth day. She had been in her room, trying to figure out how to build her first stasis tat. The door swung open. He stood there, swaying. A moment later, the stench of booze hit her. "Watch the news," he had said. "Any goldie channel."

She pulled up an Ostarrichi feed on a data screen hovering over her desk. The talking heads were ecstatic as they proclaimed that the hunt for the "cold-blooded murderers" of a CPC trooper had ended in a wild shootout between the CPC and a Meso gang. Eight Mesos, three of them under twenty, were dead. No CPC casualties.

"That can't be right," Ashme said. "They must have killed a different CPC soldier."

"Nope," her father replied. "Only one trooper killed this week."

"What would lead the CPC to those kids?" Had she accidentally left a trail that led to innocent Mesos?

"They don't care who killed their trooper." She remembered how he had swayed so much she'd thought he would fall, but he'd kept his footing. "What they care about is the message. Eight of us for one of them."

Violence has an echo. Eight Mesos. Had she killed them?

Ashme stood up, breaking the moment between her and Hamilcar. "Come on," she said, ignoring the flash of confusion on Hamilcar's face. "Let's find the others."

CHAPTER 20

AVALYN USED to enjoy orbital flights. The exhilaration of G-forces pushing her body into its chair, followed by the weightlessness of micro-G, the wonder of floating in her harness, free from the planet's grip—these had once been joys. Now, the G-forces exerted over the eight minutes it took to reach orbit seemed like an eternity pressing down on her ancient body, grinding her bones to paste despite the protection of the most sophisticated G-suit Caelum had to offer. She never used to suffer from space adaptation syndrome, but now, the weightlessness turned her bowels into a bubbling soup threatening to boil over without a motion-sickness tab.

"Nothing like an orbital flight to remind you of your age," Colonel Tyrell said, echoing her thoughts. His face, leathery from years under the sun, had taken on a sickly pallor.

"We couldn't have had this meeting on the ground?" she asked.

"Nope. Too many ears. To many ears in this pod, too."

"Even with a privacy shield?"

"Even with a privacy shield."

She respected Tyrell; he was a good soldier, but his years climbing the ranks of CPC administration had inflicted him with a dose of paranoia. Ostarrichi spying on Ostarrichi? The thought disgusted her. Things had been cleaner once, back during the Caelum War and the Novoreeka Impasse. The enemy was clear then, and Caelum was young enough that the rot had yet to set in. She said no more as their capsule made its way to one of the CPC's orbital defence stations.

Their capsule's AI managed the docking process, and it took its sweet time. They were almost at their destination—she could see it through her porthole. Shaped like a grey, blunt pencil, it was about a hundred metres in diameter, maybe twice as long. It spun lazily along its axis. Heavily armoured, it bristled with weapons ranging from rail guns to lasers. Avalyn also knew that although she was unable to see them from her vantage point, drone combat ships, weapons platforms, and surveillance satellites orbited nearby.

The station was a highly restricted military asset, yet Avalyn, in her current role, was a civilian. Tyrell was taking a risk bringing her here, but he had always been loyal to her. He knew that doing what was best for Caelum sometimes required working beyond the remit of standard operating procedures.

Thrusters hissed, and their capsule rotated as part of its docking manoeuvres, bringing other vessels into view through the porthole, mostly military transports in holding patterns. "The station's busy," she said.

"Ark *Gallia*'s got us preparing for the worst."

The treaties that ended the Great Ark War prevented military vessels from entering the space between the orbits of Esharra and the outer-most planet, Maltitu, an ice world whose orbit was six astronomical units farther out than those of most of Ark *Brettaniai*'s facilities and ships. It would take a week for human-occupied warships to close that distance. Of course, such a treaty stipulation was symbolic at best, for even trade barges and mining craft were equipped with fusion drives capable of one-tenth light speed. Accelerate a one-kilogram rock to that speed, and it became a city-destroying weapon of mass destruction.

Still, symbolic acts mattered. Through this peace, Ark *Brettaniai* held a monopoly over interstellar trade with Esharra, and it traded exclusively with the nation of Caelum. Both powers had thrived from the arrangement. Ark *Gallia*'s trade ship threatened to break that monopoly. So far, it remained lurking in the Oort cloud at the distant edge of the solar system, though it had sent smaller trade vessels inward. Avalyn suspected Ark *Brettaniai* would act quickly to protect its monopoly. That could mean as little as the destruction of trading barges or as much as another Ark war. It was a dangerous moment, but there was opportunity in chaos.

Her body pressed into its harness as her vessel manoeuvred to dock. The hum of actuators sounded as blasts of the engine gasped. Her heart rate rose. It was a risk coming here. Some might think she was planning a coup. Her enemies could use this to run her out of politics if they learned about it. She, however, needed to find that opportunity in the chaos, and Tyrell seemed to think he might have found it. Metal clanged, and momentum pushed her deeper into her harness.

A green light flashed, and an announcement indicated it was safe to proceed to the airlock. Avalyn floated toward the capsule door, an owl gliding on air. Nausea roiled her guts, and she pressed the motion-sickness tab stuck behind her ear to up its dose—she needed to convey strength.

Tyrell pressed a button, and the door hissed, then swung open. The sterile, carbon-scrubbed air of her capsule intermingled with the fresh, dry air of the vessel with which she was docked. On the other side, an officer floated. His albinism and shoulder-length white hair immediately marked him as Brettaniai. The gold armbands on the forearms of his scarlet-red uniform that barely contained his belly identified him as a captain in its military.

It seemed Avalyn was not the only unauthorized person Tyrell had brought to this station.

AVALYN WAS afraid she might embarrass herself. The living compartment of the ship rotated to provide simulated gravity, though the vessel was too small to give a lot of it—barely enough to keep Avalyn's feet on the ground. Unused to low-G, she moved carefully to avoid seeming clumsy. Low-G was a blessing for her left knee, though, which had begun to throb soon after the high-G of lift-off. She had gone in for editing to fix the myriad deteriorations besetting her body, but each edit improved less than the last, while the next edit came sooner than the previous. Her Sceptre body was old; the only cure was a younger one. The memory of the decline her husband, Neville, suffered before his death half a year ago banished that thought.

The Brettaniai captain, Yosef NK-55-d, walked beside her as Tyrell led them to a private lounge. Yosef was a man approaching middle age, with wrinkles beginning to crinkle the bone-white skin surrounding his pale blue eyes. She eyed his long white hair. She knew the length was Brettaniai custom, but it irked her. Military men should crop their hair short. And his gut! An officer got a gut that size by leading from the comfort of his desk while his soldiers worked.

As noticeable as these features were, they paled in comparison to his nose. It was long and thin, as though someone had thunked a hatchet into his face and left it.

"It is an honour to meet you." His accent was thick but understandable. "Your tactics at the Battle of Irnini are required reading."

She thanked him with a tight smile. Though perhaps her greatest military victory, her successes along the banks of the Gulf of Irnini had led to years of in-fighting within the upper ranks of the CPC as jealous generals sought to knock her down a peg. The memories of that time were bitter.

Had Yosef ever seen any action? Since the Brettaniai handed Caelum over to the Ostarrichi more than fifty years ago, there had been no conflicts in which they had been involved. "How long have you been stationed in the Esharran system?" she asked.

"I arrived on last year's trade ship."

"And how did you earn this post?"

He shrugged. "Twelve years ago, the last Ark War was still hot around Port Fujin. I beat down some Ark *Ruthenia* drone fleets. By then, we had seen that Ark *Gallia* was heading to Esharra to break our monopoly, and so I was sent here."

Though putting down a drone fleet was nothing to brag about, at least he was more than a professional seat warmer. At the door to a lounge, Tyrell excused himself with a, "Well, I'm sure you two have much to discuss," and left.

The door closed behind Yosef and Avalyn once they entered the lounge. "I brought coffee, real coffee, Earth coffee, Floor Leader," Yosef said, using her honorific as leader of the opposition. "It has travelled stasis-packed from trade ship to trade ship for nearly one hundred and twenty years. May I pour you a cup?"

She had never had real Earth coffee. She agreed, and he poured them cups from a nearby carafe. He was polite but lacked the oily obsequiousness of a diplomat. Whoever had sent him was smart to send a soldier to speak with her.

A thick, luxurious purple carpet covered the floor. The furniture, light gold in colour, was spare, perfunctory. A single piece of art adorned the walls, a large painting over the table bearing the coffee carafe.

A smile curved Avalyn's lips as she recognized the painting: *Ostarr's Choice*. When she had led the CPC, she'd ordered that every officer's lounge should display a copy. It was good to see the tradition continued.

The painting was well-known among the Ostarrichi. The powerful scene was portrayed in brilliant colours—golds, reds, violets, and blacks. On the left: a man, tall and proud, hair white with age, finger depressing a button on a nearby console—

Captain Ostarr. The artist had captured a blend of bitter regret and iron will in his golden face. On the right: two women, one the hostage of the other. The aggressor was the brutal N'aieo Maecia, leader of the Quirites battling for control of the *Estincelle*, Captain Ostarr's trade ship. Her hair was long, white, and wild, her face scarred and twisted in anger. She held a gun to the head of Verina, Ostarr's daughter, young, early adolescence, beautiful, brave, her hand raised in a farewell to her father. An airlock separated them.

It captured a pivotal moment during the Battle for the *Estincelle* during the climax of the Ark *Quirites* civil war. For years, internecine warfare had rampaged within the trade ship. Maecia had consolidated the forces loyal to the Quirites along the dorsal section of the vessel and was pushing for the fusion engines. Captain Ostarr had sealed them off and set charges to blow entire sections of the vessel holding the Quirites forces into the void. Maecia had captured Ostarr's daughter. The captain faced a nightmare choice. Save his daughter and lose the ship, or save the ship and lose his daughter. He blew the charges, blasting nearly a fifth of the vessel into debris, destroying the Quirites forces along with his daughter. He took the survivors and founded the Ark *Ostarrichi* that day.

Yosef noticed her gaze and took in the painting. "It's exquisite. Is it original?"

"Oh, no," she said as she took a seat. "The original is in Ark *Ostarrichi*'s cloud-city vaults on Venus." She took the cup he offered. "You have me at a loss, Captain. Tyrell did not tell me I was meeting you, let alone why."

"My presence here isn't exactly aboveboard." Yosef sat across from her and deeply inhaled the aroma of his coffee before taking a sip. "The arrival of Ark *Gallia* threatens to disrupt the arrangement we have. An arrangement through which both Brettaniai and Caelum prosper."

Avalyn sipped her coffee—bitter, with a deep, nutty, chocolate aroma. She had learned how the Ark operated through her father's stories. To the Ark, you were either a buyer, seller, or competitor. Their plans spanned solar systems and centuries. They were meeting with her to hedge their bets, laying threads of relations with all the nodes of power in Caelum so that whichever way political storms blew, they would always find a welcoming harbour. Setting her cup on the table, she leaned back in her chair, arms on the armrest. "Why talk to me about it? The Director-General is the one in charge."

"We need to deal with Ark *Gallia* hard and fast. A decisive battle now, before *Gallia* makes inroads with other Kanu powers, will prevent a long, drawn-out war later."

"And the Director-General has no stomach for conflict," Avalyn said, finishing his thought.

"He's based his leadership on peace with Free New Mesopotamia and other Kanu powers."

He was a poor leader who had yet to learn that Kanu would see his desire for reconciliation as weakness. Still, she had no interest in being *Brettaniai*'s puppet. "Caelum has enough enemies. Why would it involve itself in the affairs of two Arks?"

"Because we have intel that *Gallia* already has a person planet-side intent on establishing relations with Free New Mesopotamia."

This was bad news. Very bad. She strove to keep her expression neutral. Baltu could inflict significant damage with state-of-the-art Ark weapons. She eyed the Brettaniai officer sitting across from her, savouring each sip of his own coffee. As bad as this news was, it was her opportunity in the chaos. She would need allies, powerful allies: nation-states or equivalents that would support her. No such partners existed on Esharra—every Kanu nation wanted only to see Caelum fall. With the Brettaniai behind her, though, she could execute her plans aggressively. Very aggressively.

Bitter experience in politics told her to be more circumspect, but the aches in her joints told her she lacked the time for pissing about. "What are you offering?"

"New technology from Earth. Gear, weapons, intel."

"I need more." She put down her coffee.

"More?" Yosef set down his own cup. "We are prepared to be quite generous."

"In fifty years, Kanu nations have declared war on Caelum five times, always without provocation. I have commanded troops in each one of those wars, always to victory." She let that hang in the air. "They will war on us again, treaty or no. I want more than your tech and intel when they do. I want your direct military support."

"But the treaty!" Yosef utterly failed to keep his expression neutral. "Even if we wanted to, we can't get our military vessels to you without putting our relationship with Caelum at risk."

"My meeting with you here should tell you I've got friends in the CPC who can help get your military vessels here without the Director-General ever knowing."

"All due respect, Floor Leader, but I can't imagine my superiors agreeing to this while the current Director-General remains in power."

"I will be Director-General within a year."

The Brettaniai's head bobbed back as the comment struck him. His eyes narrowed, trying to decide if she had a plan or was mad. "Perhaps you should explain?"

She tapped her finger, a spear tip stabbing the armrest. "Baltu will attack within the year. As you said yourself, the Director-General has based his government on making peace with Free New Mesopotamia. When they attack, support for the Director-General will crumble. I'll be called to step down as opposition leader and head our army. Without your help, Caelum will survive, as it always has. But it will owe you nothing—*I* will owe you nothing. Or, worse for your situation, perhaps *Gallia* will offer us an olive branch. After the war, the Director-General's government will fall, and the tide of my victory over the Mesos will carry me into office. When I am Director-General, I will welcome you with open arms, I will reinforce your monopoly and lend you what aid I might to rid the system of Ark *Gallia*—if you help me."

"Again, no offence, Floor Leader, but you speak of the future with a certainty some might call foolish."

Avalyn nodded. "I don't start fights unless I control the theatre of battle."

He stared at her intently. "You're serious."

She nodded, picking her cup up again carefully. The low gravity, coupled with the ache in her knuckles, conspired to unsteady her hand, threatening to spill her drink. "If—when—Free New Mesopotamia attacks with weapons from Ark *Gallia*, then it will be *Gallia* who has broken the treaty, and you'll have all the pretense you need to intervene militarily."

Yosef sat back. "I'll need to speak to my superiors about this."

"Well," Avalyn said, "don't take too long. Events are unfolding."

CHAPTER 21

ASHME'S CHEST tightened when she saw that the road leading to Baltu's fortress terminated at a checkpoint. "Do you need us all in there?" she asked Hamilcar.

"Is everything all right?" he asked with a look suggesting he was talking about more than the checkpoint. She was embarrassed for clamming up with him earlier.

"Come on," Sura said before she could reply, "don't be a piss baby. We're going to meet Baltu."

Baltu's fortress loomed overhead. It was old, built in the Post-Sentient fashion, all function, no style. They approached on foot along a road that switch-backed to the citadel's gates. Barricades lined one side of the street, and giant, waist-high steel caltrops intended to stop charging vehicles stood along the other. Currently, the road was unobstructed, but Ashme thought the nearby soldiers could quickly drag the barricades and caltrops into the street to block oncoming vehicles.

The soldiers were Mesos—this whole fortress was the headquarters for the Free New Mesopotamian army. Ashme had never seen Kanu buildings in as good repair. Blocks of stone as long as a man and half as high interlocked to form a ten-metre-high wall. The checkpoint was perched on a promontory overlooking the lights of the Urbat Refugee Camp. The air up here was clear of the camp's stench. Ashme enjoyed an undefiled breath.

Hamilcar was beside her, eying the guards as they approached the gates. "Those weapons are twenty years old," he said.

It was her turn at the checkpoint. One of Baltu's soldiers—a man—indicated for her to spread arms and legs in preparation for a search. "Don't you have a scanner?" she asked. He asked if she was a princess and motioned again for her to raise her arms. He was all business, showing no more emotion than he would frisking a sack of potatoes. To her surprise, contrary to what a lifetime of CPC checkpoints had led her to expect, he carefully avoided groping her crotch. Never had Ashme been frisked so politely.

The checkpoint exited into a vast area where floodlights illuminated several ground and aerial transports. Men and women busily worked, overseeing vehicles or moving boxes and barrels around the complex. The carillon ring that warned of reversing vehicles vibrated in the air. Another soldier led them across the tarmac and into a large stone building through wide steel doors. They stepped into a foyer with a floor of polished stone.

Despite the late hour, soldiers and officers went about their business, no one paying attention to them. Art, real and VR-skin, lined the walls along the hallway down which a soldier led them: hypnotic geometric patterns shifting down the canvas, 3D couples dancing, birds in flight, light sculptures, more than Ashme could process.

Walking the other way, a male Kanu, middle-aged, potbellied, wore what Ashme guessed was a three-kilobit suit. He was surrounded by two young men and one woman in clothes that, though they probably cost as much as Ashme made in a good month, were a notch below the older man's. They stared at Hamilcar as they passed.

Hamilcar wore sturdy travel pants and a light combat jacket, lousy with pockets and armour-lined. Ashme looked down at her own wardrobe: faded navy-blue pants, a well-worn green tee shirt that was one size too big but so bloody comfortable, dominated by the University of New Uruk's logo, and a brown jacket with frayed sleeves that were too long. She wished, now, on the cusp of meeting the leader of the Free New Mesopotamian Army, she had thought to bring something nice to wear.

The soldier led them to a door made of thick wood, stained to a rich, resonant sheen. Ashme heard laughter from the other side and the delicate trickle of music. As the soldier opened the door, she gaped, amazed by the room. The opulence astounded—she had never thought such luxury was something Kanu, let alone Mesos, could aspire to. The walls were a sapphire blue, the lush carpet a ruby red with patterns repeating the blue of the wall. A holo-light orb floated in the centre of the room, changing shapes from one star pattern to another as it lit the area in gentle daylight. Marble columns with gold inlay supported the ceiling, and oh, the ceiling—white marble panels with baby-blue inlay and gold filigree.

"Wait here," the soldier told them as he left to navigate his way through the room and out a door on the opposite side. It took Ashme a moment to pull her eyes from the furnishings to notice the people sitting in plush chairs and standing in small groups. Men and women, some of them wearing military uniforms, others in business suits, had stopped their conversations to stare at Hamilcar and the rugged band of Mesos accompanying him. She wanted to shrink into herself like grain wilting in the sun, certain her clothes retained the refugee camp's stench.

Shen strode to the nearest group. "Hi, I'm Shenshen, but you can call me Shen . . ." Conversations started up around the room, but Ashme noticed many people looking their way, tipping glasses filled with ruby liquids in their direction as they talked.

Ganzer crossed his arms across his thick chest. "Baltu lives well."

"This is amazing," Sura said, barely able to contain her wonder.

Ganzer grunted. "You could feed the Urbat Refugee Camp for a day with the furnishings in this room."

"And then what about the day after?" Sura asked. "He's the *de facto* leader of New Mesopotamia. He's got to wheel and deal with heads of state. If we want to be taken seriously, we need to display power and strength."

"Nobody takes us seriously, and pretty rooms ain't going to change that."

"Don't be a mopey little bitch," Sura said to Ganzer. "Baltu got the Ahiim X59 treaty out of Caelum."

"I thought you believed the Ahiim treaty was a joke."

"I think Baltu's got a plan to get us way more than what the Ahiim treaty promises."

"You two, shush," Hamilcar said. Both Ganzer and Sura glared at him. Oblivious to their stares, he said, "Do you know who these people are?"

Ashme scanned the room. "Some of them." She nodded toward a portly officer who was eying Hamilcar intently. "That's Kalumum, Baltu's right-hand man."

"Not the officers," Hamilcar said. "The ones wearing suits."

Ashme looked again. "No."

Hamilcar nodded to the group by a marble fireplace. "The short one there with the pale skin and dark hair—the one Shen is trying to talk to? That is Novoreeka's foreign minister. And there," he nodded toward a small cluster of people talking in the middle of the room, "that brown-skinned woman, the one with short grey hair, is defence minister for Novvyruss."

Sura turned to Ganzer, waving her hand to encompass the room. "Heads of state, like I said."

"Don't you get it?" Hamilcar asked. "I am an arms dealer from the Ark. If my presence here were uncovered, it would be an international incident. Baltu should be taking me to back rooms through abandoned hallways. Instead, he has me here standing in a room full of the ministers of several Kanu nations."

The far door opened, admitting a stocky man with a barrel chest, tan skin, stark white hair, and mutton-choppy beard. Baltu. He wore black combat armour as though at any minute he might find himself on the front lines, though the roundness of his gut and softness in his face suggested years had passed since his last combat foray. He sauntered, taking up as much space as he could, with a confident, bordering on arrogant, smile. He took Hamilcar's hand in a powerful handshake. "You've had a long journey." His voice was strong, loud enough for everyone in the room to hear. Ashme took an involuntary step back—he wore an eye-watering amount of cologne. "Your guides must be tired."

"And hungry," Shen said, coming up behind him, his face split in a smile. He held out his hand. "I'm Shenshen, but you can call me Shen. Once is enough, am I right?" Ashme's stomach knotted.

A look of annoyance flashed across Baltu's face, but he took Shen's hand. "Good to meet you."

"You smell nice. Like autumn leaves crunching." Baltu's look of annoyance turned to shock.

"Shen," Ashme said, beckoning him toward her. "Come over. Baltu and Hamilcar are going to talk."

Baltu had one of his soldiers lead Ashme and the rest somewhere where they would be fed while he and Hamilcar negotiated. As soon as they were out of the room, Sura turned to Shen. "'You smell nice,'" she said, mimicking him.

"He did," Shen said. "He must want people to notice, he wears so much cologne."

Ashme laughed. Sura joined her while Ganzer managed to maintain his dour expression.

"This is a great day," Shen said, his elfin face lit with a smile.

"Yeah?" Ashme said. "What's so great about it?"

"Today we meeted Baltu, and it was all because of me," he said, stabbing his thumb at his chest. "I meeted a fine young man named Hamilcar and introduced him to us. I'm helping us pay rent."

ASHME GAZED out the window of the break room into which the soldier had stuffed them. It overlooked a parade ground, floodlights shining, casting the empty field in a harsh glare. She must have zoned out a little because Ganzer's voice from behind startled her. "Baltu's supposed to be negotiating for peace. That's what the Hab handover is all about. So, why's he so keen to talk to an Ark arms dealer?"

"Oh, come on, big guy," Ashme said, turning from the window. "You know the Ostarrichi aren't going to accept peace with Mesos." She picked up another sliver of meat—real meat—and cheese, plopped them on a cracker, and popped it in her mouth. Sura slept, head down on the brown laminate table. Shen sat on the floor listening to music on his neural link.

"Now you sound like her," he said, nodding to the sleeping form of Sura. "You think war's the only way?"

"Meditating with the Hierophants ain't going to get rid of the Ostarrichi. You think we've got options other than war?"

"This is what I think," Ganzer said. "Baltu's a rebel leader and a rebel leader without a rebellion is nothing."

"My dad fought for Baltu," Ashme said sharply.

"Yeah, I know," Ganzer said, backing down. "It's just every time Kanu nations war with Caelum, it's us Mesos get ground further into the dust."

"Caelum's the only Ostarrichi nation on Esharra. We only have to win once."

Ganzer crossed his arms. "Mesos have been saying that for fifty years."

"Maybe this time we'll have Ark weapons."

"That means more blood on the bricks if you ask me." He turned to look at her. "You and Shen should stay here in Neu."

"What?"

"I'll go back to New Uruk to get Grandma and join you. We could make a life here."

"Where, in the Urbat Refugee Camp?"

"We've got some money now. We can find a place. I can start my training as a Hierophant at the Two-Hills Monastery. It's not far from here. All this war and hatred, all it does is breed chaos in the Deep. Kanu, Meso, Ostarrichi, we each think we're the ocean when we're only waves."

"You used to be a mean-ass son of a bitch—at least once a month, we'd have to call the medi-drones to save whatever sorry bastard pissed you off. Now, all you do is worry. If this is stressing you out so much, why are you taking these jobs and living this life?"

"I'm doing it for the future. I'm saving up enough money so that Grandma will be looked after while I take my training."

"Hierophant, *pfft*," Ashme said dismissively. "Why, so you can polish orthostats and become one with the Deep? Why do you want to become a Hierophant?"

"It's because of Shen, if I'm being honest."

"Shen?"

"Yeah," he said. "It was soon after your dad died."

Shit. She hated talking about that period of her life. Prodding him had been a mistake.

"Me and Grandma were looking after you," he continued, a far-off look in his eyes. "Your mom wasn't dealing well, and you weren't much better, so I spent the day looking after Shen. We spent the morning at the Hab, had lunch there, and went to the orthostat. We spent an hour listening to buskers just past Checkpoint 12. The little dude just loses himself in the music, doesn't he? It's like the universe peels back the layers and shows him something hidden from us. On the way back to your place, he told me he loved me."

She was going to start balling if he kept this story going. "Shen tells store clerks he loves them."

Ganzer grunted affirmation. "This was different, though. Deeper. I heard the Deep's voice through him. The kid had just lost his dad, and still, he was filled with nothing but love; he could still see wonder in a two-piece band hustling for pocket change. Zini's stacks, what a gift. That was my calling to the Deep, that moment. We are the universe, Ashme. The Deep wants us to grow and become better. Everyone I hurt when I lose my cool, every one of those sorry bastards I laid the boots to, it takes something away from the universe, makes it less than what it was."

The image of a blood-stained alley seared in her mind, the body of a CPC trooper at her feet. Her head ached from biting back the tears. "Some people need hurting." She wanted to fight for her home. That was the best thing for Shen. They had lived their lives in New Uruk. She and Shen had shared every good moment, every horror, together in that city. She wanted New Mesopotamia to rise again; she wanted to be part of that struggle. That would be a life of meaning. "Some people, all they do is destroy, and they need to be put down."

"The world's got enough piss and anger. It needs people to pull in another direction. I'm going to be one of those people."

"Well, whatever. We're not citizens of Neu, and looking at the number of refugees in the camp, I don't think they're taking new applicants. Moving here's not an option."

"You can burn us forged citizenship."

Could she? Probably. "I'm not running away from my home. My dad . . . broke himself for New Mesopotamia. He didn't do that so I could run away from it."

"You think he'd want Shen to stay?"

"Hey, Shen," she called out.

"Yes, Ashme?" he replied, pausing his music.

"You want to live in New Uruk with me, Ganzer, and Aunty Melammu?"

"Oh yes," he said. "My heart smiles when I'm with all of you."

"Shen wants to stay," she said.

Her brother needed help; she was bound to him, and it was her lot to care for him; she knew that. They were womb-mates, which would always tie them together. She could still do something significant with her life, however. Besides, Shen would be safest with the Ostarrichi defeated. Joining the fight against the goldies did not mean she was abandoning Shen. She was fighting for him. Like Dad.

Ganzer grabbed a crusty bun from a bowl, tore a chunk out of it with his teeth, and chewed angrily. She softened her tone and said, "You could go if you wanted. I could still set you up with citizenship documents—you and Melammu. You could start training as a Hierophant." *Please say no. Stay with us.*

"Grandma's not going to leave Caelum," he said bitterly over a mouthful of bread. Ashme knew this meant he was not leaving, either.

A SOLDIER WOKE THEM, telling them it was time to go. Through the window, Ashme saw the grey sky filled with predawn light.

Their guard led them through corridors to the large foyer by the entrance, where Baltu and Hamilcar stood. Baltu, still wearing his combat armour, was yelling at an officer, a middle-aged man with salt-and-pepper hair. Hamilcar looked exhausted, his face pale with dark hollows under his eyes.

"What'd he do?" Ashme asked Hamilcar as she walked up to him, nodding at the poor soldier getting grief from Baltu.

Hamilcar turned to her, his face stone-cold. "It's Avalyn."

"What's the dragon lady done now?"

"She's made a public announcement. She is planning on visiting the Hab—including the central habitation buildings."

"Wait," Sura said. "Can she do that?"

"She wouldn't dare!" Baltu shouted, face red with rage. "The

Director-General won't let her. That treaty took years and blood to negotiate."

Ganzer pulled Ashme back a step and said quietly to her while Baltu screamed orders at his soldiers, "Stay in Neu with Shen."

"No." Ashme pulled her arm from his grip.

"If Avalyn does this, it'll be war."

"You don't know that. And if it does, then our people need us to fight for them."

"Shen needs you to look after him. Grandma needs the same of me."

"Shen needs someone to fight for his home," Ashme said. "And so does Aunty Melammu. She spent years fighting to get back to New Uruk, and she didn't do that to run away again at the first sign of trouble."

Baltu turned on Hamilcar. "You, Ark-monkey, tell your people we have a deal."

While Hamilcar began discussing payment instructions, Shen tugged at Ashme's arm. "Is there going to be a war?"

"Everything's going to be fine," Ashme said, though the words left a dry taste of naivety in her mouth.

Shen said, a trill of fear in his voice, "Dad fought in a war. I don't like what it did to him."

CHAPTER 22

ONCE MORE, Mason tried to focus on the seventy-year-old report he was reading on the Hab Revolt.

> *These attacks were unprecedented in the history of the Kanu-Ostarrichi conflict in New Mesopotamia, in duration, geographical scale, damage to property, and casualties . . .*

Avalyn was visiting the Hab tomorrow. He had to develop tactical assessments of how the Mesos might respond. He was unable to focus for more than a couple of minutes, however. Daxton had cried through the night, an inconsolable, shrill cry, keeping both Oriana and him awake. His head was thick with the fog of tiredness. Though he had been at work for hours, he could still feel Daxton's wispy weight in his arms, smell his baby smell, and hear his cries. His son had looked so exhausted, but whatever pain afflicted him gave him no rest, keeping little Daxton's face bunched and mouth open as he wailed. Yesterday had been Daxton's first edit.

He pushed the memory aside. Mesos had been protesting for days since Avalyn announced her intention to visit the Hab.

Would Baltu use this as an excuse to attack? He dug into the report.

Though as a schoolboy, he had learned of the Bit Durani Massacre—the bloody climax of the Hab Revolt—the Tanis Commission's report still held a morbid fascination. For days before the massacre, Kanu mobs across New Mesopotamia had attacked Ostarrichi. Back then, New Mesopotamia had been a protectorate of *Brettaniai*, but the Ark had only a token force on the ground to maintain order—they had been relying on Kanu police to keep the peace on their behalf, a strategy that backfired disastrously when the Kanu revolted.

The Brettaniai could do little more than watch in horror as events evolved from isolated concertos of mayhem into manic symphonies of murderous rage. The Brettaniai had tried to arm the Ostarrichi living in the village of Bit Durani so they could protect themselves from the Kanu mob, but the Ostarrichi refused. They were still new to New Mesopotamia at the time. They wanted peace with their new neighbours and thought they could heal relations by showing the Kanu their passive intent.

They paid for their idealism with their lives. The Kanu attacked, murdering hundreds of unarmed men, women, and children before setting Bit Durani aflame. It was a ghastly finale to their violent opus. The Kanu had taught a lesson at Bit Durani; Ostarrichi learned it well.

It makes me sick that Tracey and Daxton will grow up in a world like this. There had been peace for the Ostarrichi when they still had their Ark, travelling up and down the interstellar river between Port Fujin and the planet of Esharra: a proud, ancient Ark, its lineage traced back to the Quirites. The Catastrophe ended that honourable period.

Tracey had been such a pleasure at the clinic yesterday. "Why are you sad, Daddy?"

He had been thinking about Shen, which made him think of Daxton. "Because I've not enough noses to eat," he had said as he pantomimed stealing her nose and eating it to her squeals of delight. She had dark hair like both her parents, blue eyes—her father's—and a smile that was all Oriana. Tracey had aspects of both of them, yet they added to something far greater than the sum of their parts.

Oriana had curled up on the waiting room's couch and slept. She had always put so much thought into managing her appearance, but with Daxton, it was all she could do to get out of her pyjamas. She used to dance twice a week at the community centre, but for the last year, caring for their children had consumed her. Daxton was still breastfeeding, so she took the brunt of it. Mason made sure to spell her off as much as possible. He had kept Tracey from bothering her at the clinic, playing with his daughter when needed to distract her from waking Oriana.

Focus. Mason stared at the report on his data screen with an empty gaze. There was a meeting after lunch. Mason needed something to report. He tapped his coffee mug. Yoselin hummed a distracting tune from her neighbouring desk.

Work. Right. [Dashiell, what's the update on Free New Mesopotamia's troop movement?]

[Baltu's moved 9,512 soldiers, 609 pieces of artillery, 103 troop transports, eighty-four tactical drones, and twenty-five tanks to the following locations along the Neu border,] Dashiell pinged as it called up a map on Mason's desktop, the troop placements highlighted in red.

[The vehicles could make it to New Uruk in an hour,] Mason noted.

[Given their armament, Baltu's forces do not pose a credible threat. The Network provides New Uruk with superior air assets, fire superiority, freedom of movement and manoeuvre, and intelligence,] Dashiell pinged. *[Please note that such troop build-up is typical of Baltu.]*

[Those are his recent patterns,] Mason pinged. *[Back in Xinchin, or further back during the Autumn War, he wasn't prone to bluffing.]*

[True. In each of those instances, however, Baltu had the military support of other regional powers. He has been politically isolated since his defeat in Xinchin.]

Politically isolated? He had an army on Caelum's border. Armies cost money, and he had no nation to tax to finance it. Kanu nations traded openly with Caelum on the one hand, then financed Free New Mesopotamia on the other.

Mason blinked his eyes open. Focus. He had hoped to avoid another cup of coffee, afraid he would have to pee all through this afternoon's meeting, but decided he needed another cup if he wanted a chance at being productive.

Oriana had looked a wreck this morning, eyes puffy from crying: death warmed over with a screaming baby in her arms. He wanted to scream. He tried to protect her, to shield her from sorrow, but he was helpless. Worse than helpless. He had hired Meso thugs to rob an Ostarrichi corporation—he had been a fool. If that turned sour, he would be the one in prison—or worse. Who would help Oriana then?

He felt tiny, a bird carried on thermals. He had intended to go to the break room for a coffee, but he walked past Farren's desk at the front. He nodded to her; she replied with a scrunch-nosed smile as he walked out of Avalyn's office complex.

He wandered down the hall lining the east wing of the *Aigle*, his dress shoes clicking smartly on the floor with each step. Men and women walked briskly up, down, and across the corridor. Mason mimicked their purposeful gait. Outside, it was overcast but still bright, the grey light shining through floor-to-ceiling windows. He found himself approaching the Security General's wing. Was he going to report Avalyn's role in the Chevalier job?

No, that would be stupid. He would have to confess his involvement. An anonymous tip?

"Mason!"

He looked up, and his stomach knotted. It was Shanelle, Avalyn's assistant, coming out of the Security General's office, dressed in solid black. The thick wooden doors closed behind her. "You're a ways away from your desk. What are you doing here?" she asked.

He could ask her the same. He had no idea what Shanelle's

relation was to Avalyn, no one did, but some instinct told him it was a bad idea to raise her suspicions. "The meeting this afternoon, I'm prepping for it. Walking clears my head." Did that sound suspicious? She stared at him, arms at her side, fists clenching and relaxing.

His feet wanted to bounce, and his hands wanted to raise to protect his face—a *guerre des mains* fighting stance. Her quadriceps were massive, her pants straining against their muscled bulk. He had a size advantage over her—longer reach, more weight—but a kick from those legs could bust ribs or crack a skull.

"You look like shit," she said.

How was he supposed to respond to that? "My son was up all last night."

"You have children?"

"Two." Telling her about his family seemed dangerous.

"How old?"

"The youngest is still a baby—well, he's a year old."

"One year and still not sleeping through the night?" She crossed her arms. Her hands were thick, a bit too big for a body her size, her nails short enough they would not impede her in a fight but long enough Mason could imagine her gouging his eyes.

"You know kids, always getting sick." How could he get her off the topic of his family?

"I'm sure he'll be better soon," she said with what he almost mistook for a smile. "There are no gene editors better than ours." She knew Daxton was getting edited? "Caelum thanks you for your gifts." Before he could mumble a reply, she pointed at the Security General's door she had exited. "Avalyn was talking about you in there."

"Oh?" What was Avalyn doing in the Security General's office? Was she telling him about Chevalier? Shanelle was enjoying his discomfort, a fox playing with its food. "How'd my name come up?"

"It's what I was sent to tell you," she said. "Avalyn wants you to be part of her entourage when she visits the Hab tomorrow."

"Me?"

"I know, strange that she'd invite a low-level analyst to join her party, isn't it?" she said with a brittle, icy smile. "But she wants to reward you for your loyalty and dedication to Caelum by giving you a first-hand glimpse as she makes history." She walked past him, patting him on the shoulder as she did so. "It'll be an early morning. Hope Daxton sleeps better tonight."

Once she had left, he looked at the double doors to the Security General's department. Oriana would be proud when she heard the news. He was proud. Avalyn was letting him into her inner circle. Yet still, he was a pit of tangled nerves, tossed about by the winds over an endless ocean.

CHAPTER 23

ASHME WATCHED Shen clap his hands in time to the rhythm, a smile bisecting his face. Her brother loved the crowd's chanting.

> *I see what you are.*
> *The last of your line,*
> *You are refugees from a fallen star.*
> *You burned your home. I won't let you burn mine!*

He was unaware of the significance of the chant the mob was yelling. It was from an old poem of rebellion from the War of Tyrants era when Ark *Ostarrichi* fell, and *Brettaniai* resettled the refugees in New Mesopotamia. To Shen, it was singing, music—beautiful music. To physicists, math might be the language of the universe; to Shen, it was song.

The Hab sat on a hill where the River Pax broke off from the Timor River. Its walls, erected in the early days of the Osman Cartel, encircled the hill's crest like an ageless halo. The surrounding streets were a seething sea of people, all here because today, Avalyn was visiting the Hab. Mesos screamed for Avalyn's blood, goldie counter-protesters screamed for Meso blood, and goldie counter-counter-protesters screamed for peace.

All three surged at each other like a confluence of tides breaking over a rocky shore along the length of Kurmartu Road, which led to the Hab's West Gate. The only thing keeping blood from the streets was the menacing swarm of angels, the throbbing vibrato of their engines adding a bass harmony to the mob's chants, and ranks of CPC soldiers, guns out, ready to fire.

Ashme added her voice to the mayhem, at turns pumping her fist in the air or shoving the jostling mass of people. Sura threw her body into a group in front of them, pushing them forward. When she had a bit of space, she pulled a palm-sized rock out of her pocket and threw it at an angel. The stone went wide, landing in the distant crowd. Ashme had rocks in her pocket, too. She'd pulled one out and cocked her arm, ready to throw, when a thick hand clamped her wrist in an iron grip. It was Ganzer, his callouses grating her flesh.

"The CPC's got the tags of everyone here under surveillance," he yelled into her ear over the crowd's roar. "You hit an angel, they'll lay the boots to you."

"Yeah, well, fuck 'em." She tore her hand from his grip. She threw her stone but aimed for one of the goldie mobs.

She had a good view of the city here as Kurmartu Road climbed the hill to the Hab. Ahead, a vast expanse of new Ostarrichi buildings reflected the sun. To her left, the road's elevation allowed her to peer over the walls and into the Meso district of Rabu Flats with its ancient, drab buildings of spalling concrete and flaking paint. She screamed at the goldies. "You burned your home! I won't let you burn mine!"

Hamilcar pushed through the crowd to Ashme's side. He had to yell into her ear so she could hear. "Avalyn is coming." He pointed. About a block away, a dozen angels hung over the crowd in tight formation. Beneath them, she saw the top of a troop transport inching forward. High above, an aerial troop transport paced them, the roar of its engines nearly a match for the raging crowd. "Would you like me to take Shen away from this?"

She looked at Hamilcar, his head sticking noticeably above the crowd, and wondered why he'd chosen to join her. This was neither his city nor his people. "Should I teach him to fear our oppressors?" she asked. "This is his city, his Hab."

She looked back to the formation of angels. The ground transport vanished behind all the heads obstructing her view. "Let me up on your shoulders," she said.

Hamilcar acquiesced. She climbed him like a tree. It took a moment in the frenetic movement of the crowd, but Hamilcar got her up on his shoulders, his head snuggly between her legs. She squeezed his head playfully with her thighs and took the opportunity to run her fingers through his dark hair—nothing too obvious or desperate, just a lady keeping her balance.

The buildings along Kurmartu Road were different from elsewhere in the city. They were Kanu buildings, but goldies had taken them over, turning them into hip stores selling clothes, furniture, and cooking supplies or stylish apartments for those who could afford the three kilobits a month rent. These were charming buildings, maintained, painted in the purples, blues, and golds that the Ostarrichi had a hard-on for. The prissy, curlicue writing of the Ostarrichi language on holographic signs hovering in front of doorways seemed discordant with the stout Kanu buildings.

She had a clear view of Avalyn's entourage. Beneath the formation of angels, a squad of CPC three ranks deep, the outer rank armed with riot shields and stun rods, the remaining two with assault rifles, surrounded the transport, pushing their way forward. Anyone getting within arm's reach got zapped by a stun rod.

"I want to see, too," Sura said to Ganzer. "Let me up on your shoulders."

"No."

The entourage had pulled up even with their position. The blast from the engine exhaust of the aerial transport buffeted Ashme, whipping her hair and causing her eyes to water.

Avalyn, the old hag, was less than ten metres from their spot. She wore a vibrant navy-blue suit with a blaze-orange blouse and walked like she owned the whole damn world. Ashme thought about throwing a rock at her, but the angel formation was scanning the crowd with menacing intensity. Her gaze drifted to others in Avalyn's entourage, to a goldie with tousled black hair.

"That little shit!" she yelled. Someone tapped her leg. She looked down to see Sura yelling at her, but she was unable to hear. She pinged Sura. [*Mason's a part of Avalyn's party.*]

[*Who?*] Sura pinged back.

[*Mason. The Chevalier contract. Did you know Mason worked for Avalyn?*]

[*What? No.*] Something about the way Sura's eyes darted away filled Ashme with doubt.

Avalyn's procession made its way at a slow, steady pace. Once they passed, the roar of the aerial transport faded, and the chanting of the crowd abated.

Ashme scrambled down from Hamilcar and found Shen. "The whole city is singing," he said when he saw her. "I wish everyone wasn't so angry. They should let the music bring them up to fly like a bird. Why is everyone so angry?"

"Because Avalyn's a bitch," Ashme said. "Are you okay being here?"

"There's a lot of noise. I liked it better when everyone was singing."

"You're not scared? I could take you home." *Please say no.*

"No, I'm not scared. I know you want to be here."

She hugged him. "You're my brave, brave brother."

"Do you think Mom would like the singing?"

She pulled away from him.

"Mom used to love singing. We would hold hands and sing and dance, and the sun would smile."

Ashme remembered Shen and Mom singing. She used to join in, too, when she was a kid. As she approached her teen years, though, she resented how Mom expected her to be Shen's mini-mom at school. During that time of her life, Ashme either left them to their singing or would start a fight about something.

What would Mom have thought of this? She was so tired and sad near the end. Would she have cared that Ashme and Shen were part of a mob? Would this be another cold bucket of misery poured into her soul? "Mom loved singing," Ashme finally replied. It had been true. She and Dad would sing while washing dishes before he left for Xinchin.

"Will the Director-General let Avalyn into the Hab complex?" Shen asked.

Ashme cocked her head. How aware was he of what was happening? "I don't know. What do you think?"

"What do I think?" he repeated. "The Hab makes Ganzer happy. The Hab is Ganzer's song. What a character Avalyn is." A grin cracked Shen's face. "Do you think I could get the crowd singing again?"

Ashme smiled. There were times she resented being Shen's caretaker, but his big, goofy smile was toast and honey for her heart. She lightly clapped her hands as she sang the first line of "The Fields of Anu," an old song of a young Kanu woman punished by the Brettaniai. Shen belted out the second line with her in his clear, beautiful voice. Other voices picked up on the third line, and by the fourth, the crowd was singing.

She sang with Shen for a while. Once he lost himself in the music, she made her way to Hamilcar. He was projecting an image of a live news feed from a data screen clipped to his wrist. Ganzer and Sura crowded around him, as did others in the crowd. The image showed Avalyn's party approaching the Hab grounds. Throughout the street, groups formed around others projecting the image on data screens of their own.

The CPC had cleared the Hab grounds, but the streets and buildings surrounding the complex were seething with angry mobs. As Avalyn and her party approached the West Gate, the singing around Ashme drifted into silence. Except for Shen. His voice rang out loud and clear as he sang. Ashme shushed him and motioned him over. "What's going on?" he asked.

"We're going to find out if the Director-General's letting Avalyn into the Hab," she answered.

Avalyn's party stopped short of the gate of the Hab complex. The angels maintained their flying pattern. The CPC stood aside. Avalyn passed through the West Gate onto Hab grounds.

Boos and hisses erupted from the crowd. It rose in volume, but others called for silence. Avalyn walked straight toward the Central Habitat like a soldier of old striding forth to call out the enemy's champion.

"I get that a politician's presence on Hab grounds is a breach of protocol, but I didn't think anyone was allowed in the Central Habitat building," Hamilcar said.

Sura told him to shut up.

"They're not," Ashme said, and Sura told *her* to shut up.

In front of Avalyn, two angels lowered down to block her from entering the Central Habitat, their reflective surfaces warping her image. Ganzer crossed his arms and said, "About time the Director-General showed some balls."

"Are they going to arrest her?" Hamilcar asked.

"Holy shit, can you imagine?" Sura replied.

Nothing happened. Avalyn stood still. The angels hovered in place. The Central Habitat sat as it had for a millennium, its fluted curves catching the sun. Silence smothered the streets.

Then the angels swung out of the way, and Avalyn walked into the Central Habitat.

CHAPTER 24

MOUTH AGAPE, Mason watched Avalyn stride by the angels into the Central Habitat. A collective gasp whisked through the streets like a backdraft sucking air into the heart of a fire.

The crowd erupted, surging onto the Hab grounds. If they got their hands on Avalyn, they would tear her apart. Mason ran to the Central Habitat ahead of the mob, calling out a warning to Avalyn. A squad of CPC soldiers pulled ahead of him. Crowd dispersal sirens screamed from the angels overhead, stabbing into Mason's ears like icepicks, inducing a wave of nausea. The whump of dozens of tear gas canisters pulsed.

Instinct took control. He pulled the gelatinous blob that was his gas mask from a utility belt and placed it on his face. It expanded and wrapped his entire head in a protective shell, black as obsidian to all looking from the outside. It filtered out the tear gas as well as the crowd dispersal sirens.

Shanelle was ahead, her own mask on, yelling to Avalyn. Mason watched her skid to a stop as an angel dropped in front of her, its repulsor rifles primed to fire. "Back away, citizen!" the angel demanded in a voice that twigged the primal part of the brain that felt fear and dread. The siren in its chest strobed.

The mob crashed through the Hab complex. CPC troops fired

shock-webs into the surging throngs, incapacitating anyone they caught with an electrical jolt. It was like using a bucket to slow the tide, a garden hose against a forest fire.

Twenty paces in front of Mason, Avalyn exited the Central Habitat triumphant, euphoric. She scanned the grounds with bright, cyan eyes, a victorious smile on her lips, and her left arm casually bent in front of her torso as though she held a shield. Black walls of tear gas billowed skyward, and dazzlers flashed into charging Mesos, blinding them. Angels and soldiers fired, the discharge of stun rounds sizzling. Protesters hurled bricks and flaming bottles. CPC troopers formed a tight formation around Avalyn and her entourage, protecting them with their shields.

The aerial transport lowered, the blast from its exhaust thrashing Mason's clothes. Avalyn waved the CPC captain over as she donned her gas mask. "Call off the transport," she ordered.

"Ma'am?" the trooper responded.

"This is our Hab. We have every right to visit it. We're going to walk out of here." And then she began to do just that.

Was she mad? The sky swarmed with angels trying to push the mob back with every crowd-control tool they had. The CPC had screened the crowd for weapons, but situational control of the environment was lost. If even one person had managed to conceal a gun, Avalyn could be martyred. Was that what she wanted?

A glass bottle filled with fluid, a burning rag in its mouth, arced over the crowd. It smashed into the shields of their CPC guard, shattered, and spilled flame across the shield to drip fire onto the ground. One soldier screamed and broke ranks, his arm drenched in flames.

"Hold formation," Avalyn commanded. Mason tackled the burning soldier. The CPC closed ranks. Others piled on Mason and the trooper, snuffing the flame.

Mason got to his feet. A deep bass rumble shook the air,

making his guts vibrate. A half-dozen angels dropped from the sky like shot birds. "Blackouts!" voices yelled. One had just gone off, the EMP knocking out every bit of electronics in a five-metre radius.

A swarm of Mesos rushed the breach in the blackouts' wake. They crashed into the CPC guards. Meso hands pulled at shields and clawed at gas masks. Even though the blackout had deactivated the "stun" part of the CPC's stun rods, they still worked as clubs. The CPC used them to hammer at the Mesos. More Mesos piled in and pushed through the CPC line. Avalyn's entourage had only advanced as far as the lip of the raised landing upon which the Central Habitat sat.

Mason stood in a *guerre des mains* stance. Be loose. Ride the thermals. Incapacitate.

They were on him. Ankle stomp. If any fight took more than one punch, they would overwhelm him. Knee to ribs, elbow to the eye socket. Bounce back. Stay light. There were CPC behind him. Form up. Where was Avalyn? Duck, arm lock, elbow snap. The weight of bodies pushed him back.

A static discharge tore a Meso off his feet. Shanelle was beside him. She grappled with another Meso, got him in a wrist lock, twisted until the bones cracked. The man screamed. She tapped him on the chest. Another discharge, and he flew back into the throng. She was wearing shock gloves and, obviously, had been out of the blackouts' range.

Another discharge, this one from his other side. His body seized, and the world spun. He gasped for breath, but his lungs only worked in fits.

He was on his back. Legs and feet stomped around him as he stared at a sky marred with black swirls of gas. Ammo drones hovered high above, angels flying to them to reload and then return to the line. The aerial transport was landing, blasting them with hot air.

He tried standing. His muscles defied his commands. He knew this feeling. Someone had tapped him with a working stun rod. His body tingled, pins and needles along every muscle. He fought down panic. He had to get up before the stomping feet caved in his head. He remembered his drill sergeant. "The tenser you are, the longer the effects of the stun last, so chill the fuck out!" Breathe. *Where the breath goes, the body follows.*

He flopped onto his side. Someone stumbled into him and tripped. Mason breathed calm into his body. A foot stepped on his ankle. Someone fell over him. The pins and needles increased in intensity. His body felt like it was being dragged over a cheese grater. He rolled onto his belly and got his knees under him and then his elbows. On all fours, he watched a stream of spittle stretch out of his mouth onto the pavement.

Legs crashed into him, knocking him on his side. A boot stomped on his head. Was he going to die here? Work insurance had excellent survivor benefits; it would cover Oriana and the kids. Daxton could finish his treatments.

Hands grabbed him. He tried to block, but his arms flopped in an absurd parody of control.

The hands were CPC. They hauled him toward the aerial transport hovering half a metre off the ground. His head lolled, and then all he saw were his feet dragging along the street. Shots —not the crack of stun rounds, but the staccato of assault rifles. It sounded close.

Hands dumped him on the transport's floor. He heard a commotion, bodies moving, crisp updates and commands, and then the sensation of weight as the carrier rose high above the crowd at speed.

"I'm fine." The voice was Avalyn's. "Good work, troopers." She came into his line of sight and kneeled beside him.

"Years as an analyst hasn't dulled any of your *guerre des mains* skills," she said, yelling over the sound of the transport's engines. "I saw you, completely unarmed, take down four of them. Well done."

Mason tried to speak but only managed to drool.

She smiled a grandmotherly smile. "One of the bastards

picked up a stun rod and hit you with it. You'll be back on your feet before we land, and you'll be home to sing little Daxton to sleep tonight." She excused herself to visit other wounded troopers.

[Dashiell,] Mason pinged, *[did you see what happened at the Hab?]*

[Yes. I am getting constant updates.]

[The angels let Avalyn into the Central Habitat. Did the Director-General nullify the treaty?]

[Not that he has publicly declared.]

Mason raised his arm and made a fist. He was regaining control of his body. He struggled to a sitting position. His body ached, like the sore muscles he would get after overexerting at the gym.

The transport shifted as it began its descent. He saw Avalyn talking to the trooper with the burned arm, and behind her, looming like a spectre, Shanelle. She was staring at him. He shivered.

Was the BLOQ related to the Ahiim treaty?

CHAPTER 25

ASHME HURLED a glass bottle filled with quick-crete and watched it cartwheel high in the air above the ranks of CPC and into the mass of goldie protesters on the other side. Given the crowd and distance, it was tough to tell if she'd hit anyone, but the mob was dense enough she probably had. It was their second day of rioting after what the Meso mobs had dubbed Avalyn's Betrayal. Beside her, Sura tried to dodge an incoming stone, but the Meso protesters were packed too tightly to give her room to manoeuvre. She swore as it winged her arm.

The squealing grind of crowd-dispersal sirens drove daggers into Ashme's ears, and teargas canisters belched black balls of foul smoke through the crowd of Mesos. The goldie mob was in Ashme's home district of Ulkur, but it was the Mesos on whom the CPC fired. Bloody typical. At least the light rain would scrub the tear gas out of the air quicker than yesterday when the sun shone and the air sat stagnant.

The CPC advanced. The Meso mob melted into the surrounding streets. Ashme grabbed Sura's arm and they ran, catching the leading edge of a teargas cloud as they darted for a narrow lane. They made it two steps down the alley before collapsing to hands and knees, vomiting and gagging.

Ashme's lungs burned. Her eyes teared up, blurring the world. She resisted the urge to rub them as they began to sting and itch while the flesh surrounding them swelled. She tried blinking her vision clear. No luck. She staggered to her feet, still retching as she dragged Sura to flee.

Ashme's stomach cramped as the gas kept twisting her guts. The smoke's residue coated her mouth, its hot acid burn competing with the taste of bile. Half-blind, both women shambled forward, keeping a tight grip on each other. Above the screech of the sirens, she could barely make out the *pop-pop-pop* of stun rounds firing.

She launched an EM shield program to hide her and Sura from the angel's tracking systems. The drain from it, combined with the effects of the teargas, set her to dry-heaving, driving her to her knees. Sura pulled ahead, dragging her along.

Ashme maintained the shield as they tripped and fumbled their way, bumping into other fleeing Mesos, through a string of alleys and streets until the sounds of sirens seemed a block or two distant. Tears drenched Ashme's face, mixing with the rain. She had to force her eyes to open as the swelling increased.

They stopped to catch their breath. Ashme leaned against a wall, gasping air into her burning lungs. Sura tried to say something, but the only sound she produced was a croaking gasp.

Through tear-soaked, swollen eyes, Ashme saw blurry forms of people enter the far end of the street. Their movement lacked the discipline of CPC ranks, while the weapons in their hands looked more like clubs than guns.

"Are they Mesos?" Sura rasped hopefully, rubbing her eyes.

"There!" one of the people shouted in Ostarrichi before they began sprinting toward the two women. Ashme and Sura grabbed each other and ducked into a narrow lane. *[Subdeo,]* she pinged.

[I'm awake,] it pinged back.

[Be a dear and pull up a map of the area and identify my location.]

[You are on Kila Street, near East Hegal Street,] her AI answered.

About three blocks from the CPC station. Troopers would be thick and the Ostarrichi cockier than usual. *[I can't see. Give me directions to the orthostat.]*

[Proceed 9.3 metres to your right. No, your right. Your other *right. That is only 8.9 metres. Would you like me to call you a transport?]*

[No!]

[I could help you more if you unlocked me so I could access the datalink's processors and—]

[Even if I could, I'm not letting you become Sentient.]

[Fine,] Subdeo pinged. *[Enjoy your scraped knees.]*

[Just tell me where to go!]

She ran blind, pulling Sura behind her, following Subdeo's directions as the goldies gave chase. Subdeo's instructions did nothing to help her watch her footing, though. She tripped and sprawled on the concrete, scraping the heels of both hands.

The jeers of the goldies raced up behind them. Her eyelids ached from the effort of keeping them open. Sura pulled something from her bag, but Ashme's vision was too blurred to see what. A lighter sparked. A blue-gold flare of flame ignited. She threw the flaming object as Ashme scrambled to her feet. Glass shattered, followed by the whump of ignition, and then Ostarrichi curses intermingled with Sura's taunts.

Ashme grabbed Sura. "The orthostat's this way," she said, following Subdeo's directions. Other Mesos would be there—strength in numbers. Better still, the Ostarrichi were nervous around the Sentient's artifacts. Maybe Ganzer would still be there with Melammu.

The sound of Ostarrichi feet slapping the pavement and obscene insults shouted in broken Kanu dogged them as they ran deeper into the Meso district's heart.

The tears were clearing from her eyes, allowing Ashme to focus, though the swelling was so bad she had to pry an eye open to see. The lane spilled into a large plaza. Ashme relaxed. The goldies would leave them alone here.

Groups of Mesos were scattered throughout the plaza, some

listening to speeches while others sat in the sitting areas and cafes dotting the area. This place was clean, the one place in the Meso districts where the buildings were maintained. Hand-sized blocks of coloured carbocrete, as expensive as they were indestructible, lined the plaza in a herringbone pattern.

Old buildings huddled around the plaza, buildings that had seen generations pass, a chain through time connecting all Kanu, past, present, and future. These structures had souls; they had borne witness to humanity's struggles. Vibrant yellows, greens, and blues sheathed the old buildings. This was what all New Uruk looked like before the Ostarrichi came.

A vast structure dominated the plaza. The orthostat. This was one of six scattered across Esharra that appeared within days of the creation of the Sentient. Why six, no one knew, for there were only four Sentient identified, though tales abounded of two hidden Sentient—a conspiracy given credence with the appearance of Damara, the Sentient that intervened to save the Ostarrichi from the Catastrophe. The orthostat's purpose was a mystery —no other Sentient across the Nine Colonies had built one.

This orthostat, like the others, stood precisely 300 metres tall and 185.410 metres wide. Mathematicians were happy to wax eloquent about its length and width creating a golden ratio with as much precision as anyone had managed to measure. What Ashme found significantly more impressive was its depth, which some wonk had measured at exactly 1.2 micrometres. It was skinnier than most bacteria, yet the structure stood unmoving in blithe defiance of the strongest winds and any force humanity had found the inspiration to hurl at it.

Esharra was lucky. The moment AI hit singularity and became Sentient was dangerous, as Ostarrichi history attested. On Esharra, the Sentient grew bored with humanity and built a Dyson swarm around the orbit of Gisnu, the system's innermost planet. Centuries later, they took that swarm and left for Riker's Star. The first indigo child appeared two years before the swarm left—most assumed this was their parting gift, though who knew with Sentient.

Ashme grabbed Sura and pulled her toward the orthostat. Its surface was deep green, covered with a bone-white filigree forming non-repeating patterns. A large, human-made rectangular temple of white marble accented with bronze inlay and statuary surrounded the orthostat's base.

"We lost 'em. Why are we going in?" Sura asked, wiping her rain-slick hair out of her swollen eyes.

"Ganzer and Melammu are here today."

"Why are you looking for them? Need someone to shit on your day?"

"No offence," Ashme said, "but I'd rather walk home on these streets with Ganzer than a string bean like you."

"Who's going to walk me home? I got to cross districts to get to my place."

"You can stay with us tonight."

Once past the bronze doors, they stood in the human-built temple. It was a cavernous space open to the base of the orthostat, which rested on the ground without any adornment or bracing. The floor was white marble, inlaid with bronze forming arabesque designs in crude imitation of the elegant filigree donning the orthostat. Mesos came and went in silence, some meditating on mats. The unearthly cadence of throat singers thrummed through the air.

A Hierophant, a tan-skinned middle-aged woman with Asiatic eyes, approached. She wore the traditional vibrant navy-blue trousers and knee-length tunic, belted at the waist with a salt-white sash. With her right hand over her heart, she greeted them. "The Deep's peace be with you."

Ashme, a hand over heart, replied, "Back atcha," and then asked if she had seen Ganzer and Melammu—a large dark-skinned man with blond hair and beard and a woman old as dust. She and Sura headed in the direction the Hierophant pointed. Other Hierophants were handing out mats to patrons. One led a class in hushed tones near the orthostat's base.

When they found the two of them, Ganzer exploded. "What happened to your face?" Heads turned, and nearby Hierophant shushed him.

"What's it look like?" Ashme replied, whispering.

"You're going to get your teeth kicked in or worse if you keep this up."

Sura, on tiptoes, got in Ganzer's face. "You think rolling over and playing dead will get rid of the goldies?"

"Step back," Ganzer said to her, his voice tightly restrained.

Aunt Melammu sat on a small stool, her knobbly hands with swollen joints and twisted fingers resting on her cane. "I thought today was your day to look after Shen," she said in a quiet voice that sliced through the crescendoing argument.

"Hamilcar is looking after him," Ashme said. She tried to sound confident and nonchalant, but it came out petulant and defiant.

Ganzer was about to go off, but Melammu spoke over him in quiet tones. "You left your brother with a stranger?"

Though Melammu's voice was quiet, there was iron in it, a scythe cutting down Ashme's rebuttal. "Hamilcar's not a stranger."

"He's on our side," Sura said. "He's working with Baltu."

Melammu hissed at Sura. "If that's true, best not to speak it. With Caelum in a state of emergency, the Ostarrichi will have all their eyes and ears in play." She stood, leaning heavily on her cane and taking Ganzer's hand. She folded her stool and passed it to Ganzer as she said, "We're not going to argue so near the orthostat."

Ashme fumed silently as they left. Once back on the street, she said, "They broke the treaty, and Avalyn tainted our Hab."

"There isn't a centimetre of our land they haven't fouled," Melammu said as she slowly shambled across the plaza, one hand holding Ganzer's arm for support, the other leaning on her cane. Ganzer held an umbrella to shelter her from the rain. "You might as well get angry at the sun rising." Smoke trailed into the sky blocks away. "You've got family," Melammu added. "You can make a good life with that. Shen is a gift. You should be caring for him, not daring the CPC to drag you away to disappear into a calming centre. His smile, his openness to anyone and everyone. His music. If the universe has taught me anything, it's that we shouldn't squander its gifts. They are too few and too fragile."

Easy for you to say, Ashme thought, *you're not the one who must brush his teeth at night or help him get dressed every bloody morning.*

CHAPTER 26

SHEN'S SMILE greeted them when they walked through the door. The entry hallway was cramped for so many people, but Shen's greeting was relentless. He danced through them, hugging each in turn. Ashme got a big, wet kiss on the cheek. "There are only twenty minutes until noon," he said, his voice rising and falling like an arpeggio. "And then, music!"

Ashme *mm-hmm*-ed.

Hamilcar hung back in the living room. Looking at the apartment, a wave of embarrassment hit Ashme. The stained couch with flat, frayed cushions looked shabby. The black fuzz she had scrubbed off the water-stained wall behind it was starting to come back. She would have to wash it before Melammu saw it.

Her great-aunt gave the barest nod to Hamilcar and then took Shen to the couch to fill those twenty minutes of non-music with his chit-chat. Ganzer pulled his weights out from behind the sofa to exercise while Sura plopped in an armchair, legs draped over the armrest.

Maybe it was the exhilaration of her escape from the goldies, but all she could think about was jumping Hamilcar. She hoped there was no smell in the apartment to which she had grown accustomed, and so could no longer notice. It should be fine—

she and Ganzer had cleaned the floors last night. Could she find some reason to clear everyone out of the apartment tonight?

His smile seemed fake. "Everything fine?" Ashme asked. That black fuzz could sometimes give off a mildew smell. She'd just got in from outside, though; she should be able to tell if the place smelled dirty. "I know it can be a bother to look after Shen. Sorry we took so long."

"What happened to your face?" he asked.

She touched her swollen eyes. "Teargas. No biggie." He still seemed bothered. "Really, it's fine."

"I need to talk to you," he said. He looked at Sura and Ganzer. "All of you."

Ganzer crossed his arms, looking like he was deciding between punching Hamilcar or tossing him out the window. "What now?"

"Privately," Hamilcar said.

Ashme caught Melammu looking at her with that same bitter, sad expression as earlier. She ushered Hamilcar and the others out into the hall, and realized too late that the hallway was more embarrassing than her apartment. She had lived there so long she no longer noticed, but the paint was flaking off the walls, and cracks lined the flooring. Across from their door, a large chunk of the floor was missing, exposing the support struts underneath. It smelled out here: cooking, mildew, and sour milk all intermingling.

She avoided looking at Hamilcar, and then the drain hit her as she launched another EM shield to protect them from the Network, should it have some way of scrying the halls. "What's up?" she asked.

"I've, uh . . ." He rubbed the stubble growing on his jaw. "The muckety-mucks of Ark *Gallia* touched base with me. They want some more work done."

"What is it?"

"You don't have to be the ones to do it," Hamilcar said. "Maybe you could refer me to someone."

Sura rolled her eyes. "Spill it, Ark-monkey."

"Please don't call me that," he said. "Are we safe?" he asked Ashme, tapping his ear.

"I've got a shield up," she said. "The CPC can't hear anything we say."

Ganzer dominated the hall, hands on hips. He looked like he was leaning toward punching Hamilcar.

Hamilcar made eye contact with Ashme, then looked away. "I am looking for someone to hire to kill Avalyn."

Stunned silence. Sura broke it. "Shit, yeah, we'll take the job."

"Are you insane?" Ganzer asked. "You won't survive five minutes after killing Avalyn. Hell, the Network will kill you five minutes before you try."

"If a team had a system raider good enough to hide their tags," Hamilcar said, his eyes glancing quickly to Ashme and then away, "my Ark has technology that will allow you to get a shot off and escape before the Network finds you."

Ganzer pushed Hamilcar into a wall. The Ark-monkey struggled, but Ganzer's mass kept him pinned. "If Sura wants to get blue-screened, that's her business, but if you get Ashme rolled into this, I'll rip your face off."

"Love you too," Sura said.

Ashme tried to pull Ganzer's arms off Hamilcar but lacked the strength to budge them even a centimetre. She was a willow trying to restrain a bear. "You don't get to say what I can and can't do, Ganzer."

He was shaking with so much rage she could see the tips of his forked beard quiver; could feel the muscles in his arm tremor. For the first time in a long while, she was afraid of what he might do. She tried to position herself between the two men to keep Ganzer from caving in Hamilcar's face, but her cousin shoved her, causing her to fall into Sura.

"Why would you do this, you Ark-monkey?" Ganzer asked.

"Get off me," Hamilcar yelled, struggling to pry off Ganzer's hands.

Ganzer slammed Hamilcar into the wall to punctuate his question. "*What do your people want from us?*"

"Don't you get it?" Pinned, Hamilcar stopped struggling and glared at Ganzer. "Do all your muscles crowd out your brains, so you don't understand why it's so important to destabilize Caelum?"

"Why don't you tell me, Ark-monkey?" Ganzer said.

"Ark *Gallia*, all the Arks who want to trade in Esharra, need to break the stranglehold *Brettaniai* and Caelum have on trade to access the riches of your people."

"What riches?" Sura asked.

"Your AI," Hamilcar replied. "Anyone can make AI, but if you build it too advanced, it hits singularity and becomes Sentient. Everyone locks down and constrains their AIs, limits them. Everyone except the Kanu. Maybe it's got something to do with the nanohaze that blankets your planet or your indigo children, but no one in the Nine Colonies can make AI as close to singularity without crossing the line as Kanu. The AIs you've produced have helped the Ark to double the speed of our trade ships—and the Brettaniai have gotten rich from that.

"The *Brettaniai* was the only Ark left in the system after the Great Ark War," Hamilcar continued. "It has a monopoly on Esharra, and it trades exclusively with Caelum. The Kanu sell AIs to Caelum, who trade them for Ark technology. But the other Arks are returning. Whoever breaks *Brettaniai*'s monopoly will prosper."

"Caelum has Kanu here inside its borders," Ashme said. "Us Mesos. Why not hire us to build AIs instead of grinding under their boot?" Zini's stacks, she would have killed for a job like that.

"The Ostarrichi fear you—it's from their history as an Ark power. Arks are insular. If you are not a part of their Ark, you are either customers or competitors. You are in their space. The Ostarrichi see you as competitors for their new home."

Ganzer let Hamilcar go and then slapped his hand into the

wall by his head. Someone on the other side of the wall yelled for quiet. Ganzer shouted back in rage. Then, to Hamilcar, he said, "You'd bring war on our home to meet your sales quota? To squeeze a little more speed out of your ships?"

"I'm trying to make my way in a shitty situation," Hamilcar said.

"Yeah, I can tell it's tearing you apart." Ganzer breathed deeply, trying to control his anger. He looked at Ashme, and shame transformed his features. He cursed loudly as he stretched out his neck. "I'm trying to walk a new path, trying to keep my family safe, but you . . ." His sentence devolved into a string of shouted curses. Hamilcar probably thought Ganzer was cursing at him, but Ashme suspected Ganzer was cursing himself for losing control of his anger. Shoving her like he had would twist his guts.

Sura turned to Ashme. "You're the best system raider I know. This is our chance to do something real. When we were kids, you used to talk a big game about fighting the goldies. This is it. Killing Avalyn would make history."

Ganzer sliced the air with his hand. "No way," he said to Ashme. "The Ostarrichi will use that as an excuse to exterminate us."

"No," Sura said. "Free New Mesopotamia will attack to protect us." She nodded toward Hamilcar. "That's what you're hoping for. You're selling arms to Baltu. He'll use the Ostarrichi crackdown to launch his attack. Revolution."

"Thousands will die," Ganzer said.

Thousands will die anyway, Ashme thought. The goldies were slowly grinding Mesos to dust. They would never stop, regardless of their treaty, regardless of whether Avalyn lived or died. But with this, how much of their blood would be on her hands? She knew what an Ostarrichi crackdown would mean for Mesos. Could she live with the knowledge she had caused it? If, however, the goldies were going to grind down Mesos anyway, would she really be responsible for the suffering caused by killing Avalyn?

That aside, could she murder someone in cold blood? She had before, but was that who she was? *They say the first one is the hardest.*

Avalyn was Caelum's saviour, its guardian angel. What a symbol it would be to kill her. If Ashme did this, Mesos would remember her as a hero for generations. If nothing else, it would show everyone that Mesos could hurt the goldies. This would mean so much more than killing some nameless trooper cutting through an alley after work.

"Ashme?" Ganzer was shocked to see she was considering it. "This is murder. Murder isn't how you fix things—it's how you break them. If you get caught—*when* you get caught—the CPC will come down on your whole family."

The memory of the CPC's revenge for the death of the trooper she had killed cut her like a cold scythe. *Eight of us for one of them*—and, of course, there had been more to the CPC's revenge, so much more, but she buried that memory. "You'd have to leave town," Ashme said to Ganzer.

"Damn right. You do this, you're no cousin of mine. You pull the trigger, I'm gone. I don't care what Grandma says, I'll drag her and Shen away from here kicking and screaming. You'll have no one. You'll be alone."

Ganzer would look after Shen, safe, away from danger. That was all Ashme needed to hear. "I'm in."

CHAPTER 27

"YOU SURE ABOUT THIS?" Ashme asked Sura, her leg bouncing like a nervous maca-ball tweaker. They were in an abandoned squatter village on the upper floor of Mitutu Tower that the CPC had cleared out half a year ago. The entire storey was clear of walls and furniture save for a couple of empty boxes and one dirty mattress that smelled of urine. Along the eastern wall sat a single toilet, the only appliance in the vast area. When Sura first saw it, she quipped this must be Mitutu Tower's thousand-square-metre bathroom. Past residents had painted "Baltu saves" and other Free New Mesopotamian slogans on the walls.

The tower was in La Sanan, the northernmost Meso district in New Uruk, where blueberry fields once stood that fed the early colony until the city grew around it, converting the land to middle-class suburbs. Now, it was another Meso cage. It was close to the *Aigle* without being too close and had the added benefit that neither Ashme's nor Sura's family lived there.

They had an assortment of gear before them. Both watched images on a monitor of a plaza a dozen kilometres south.

"What's not to be sure about?" Sura replied. Their voices echoed in the cavernous space.

"Doing this . . . thing during Avalyn's press conference

tomorrow." Even though Ashme was maintaining an EM shield to protect them from casual surveillance by the Network, instinct kept her from saying aloud what the "thing" was. "Protests are planned. Security is going to be through the roof. Is that really the best time to do it?"

"You heard Hamilcar. To avoid detection, the bullet's being fired from an orbital sniper platform and will take minutes to reach its target. We need to do this when we know Avalyn's going to be in the same spot for a while. Besides, think of the message it'll send, killing Avalyn during a live speech broadcast throughout Caelum. Stop being a piss baby."

Ashme bristled at the jab but kept quiet, focusing on their gear. It was Ark tech. It felt weird in the nanohaze. It was years beyond anything she had seen the CPC produce. Well, maybe that was untrue. But it was different. On Esharra, programmers and system raiders, whether Meso, Ostarrichi, or Kanu, had evolved together, so much so that programs and tech created by either of them had the same "feel." Even the new tech Caelum imported from *Brettaniai* felt familiar. But this tech from Ark *Gallia*—it was alien, like when you put on someone else's shoes that look like yours but fit differently.

The main component of the gear was a console that controlled the targeting and firing systems of the orbital sniper platform. Hamilcar had said the platform was about the size of a fist. Being in orbit, it was beyond the range of the Network. It was small enough that it passed as debris unless it was manoeuvring or firing. Even then, a surveillance satellite would have to be looking at it to notice.

Sura broke the silence. "When the CPC locked up Enlil," her older half-brother, Ashme's first lover, "I swore to him I'd make them pay. All we did was jack a transport to strip out its circuitry, and they gave him twenty years."

"Didn't he get in a shootout with the CPC?"

"That was self-defence, bitch," Sura said. "Anyway, this is it. Blue-screening Avalyn's the payback. I'll be square with my brother." She turned to Ashme, adding, "And the money's sweet, too. You and me, Chick-o, we'll be running the streets in the chaos that follows, so long as you don't let Shen tie you down."

She was sick of people riding her about Shen.

They watched the video feed streaming in from the sniper platform in silence. It was getting chilly. Ashme hugged her knees to her chest to stay warm as they watched construction bots assembling the stage, CPC officers marching about securing the area, and muckety-mucks in fancy suits telling people what to do. "Zoom in on that guy," Ashme said, pointing to a figure on the screen.

Sura muttered curses to herself as she fiddled with the controls until she found the zoom. "Hey, it's Dipshit."

It was Mason, talking to the event staff. She pinged him using the net code she had used to call him during the Chevalier contract. She watched Mason on the monitor step away from whoever he was talking to as he opened the ping. Ashme put it on audio so both she and Sura could hear.

"Why are you calling me?" Mason answered in heavily accented Kanu.

Sura gave Ashme a what-the-fuck-are-you-doing look.

"I saw you the other day during Avalyn's little jaunt to the Hab," Ashme said. Silence. "I was wondering if the Chevalier gig had anything to do with that."

"I don't know what you're talking about."

"Right, you're a model of innocence."

"I don't know what you're talking about, but listen, things are going to get worse before this is over. Get Shen out of New Uruk." Mason ended the ping.

What does he know about Shen? Was that a threat, his way of letting her know he knew about her family?

"Shen, Shen, Shen," Sura said. "Even goldies know they can use Shen to hold you back."

"Would I be here if Shen was holding me back?"

ASHME'S STOMACH knotted in hunger as she opened the door to her apartment. Or maybe it was fear. Or exhilaration. Tomorrow, she was going to plant a seed of revolution. She was going to make history—she really was. She wanted to think Dad would be proud, but he was strange in those final months. The man her father was before he broke, the man who went off to fight with Baltu in Xinchin, would be proud. His little girl would be the one who finally brought the fight into the goldies' house.

Ganzer and Shen sat squished together on the couch. Shen rhythmically rubbed his legs as he rocked. Melammu sat in her armchair while Hamilcar sat on a chair by the table. Ganzer and Melammu were gloomy. Shen looked on the verge of tears. Hamilcar held a bag of frozen peas to his face.

"Hamilcar?" she said as she saw him. "I didn't expect to see you here without Ganzer caving your head in."

Ganzer cleared his throat. "I did."

Hamilcar took the bag off his face, revealing a large red bruise around his eye. "You think this is bad, you should see what my face did to his fist."

"My fist is fine."

Ashme's eyes narrowed. "Only one punch? What gives?"

"Hamilcar has something to say to you," Ganzer said. "I think you should listen to him."

She crossed her arms and stared at Hamilcar, eyebrow cocked.

"Take Shen and get out of town," Hamilcar said. "All of you. Leave New Uruk."

Melammu crossed her arms, the loose jowls hanging off her jaw quivering slightly.

"Is Ark *Gallia* still offering the contract?" Ashme asked.

"Yes."

"Then I'm finishing the job."

"Ark *Gallia* doesn't care what happens to you. I doubt they expect you to live. We are using you to tear apart this region so we can make the Kanu nations dependent on our weapons. You have something special here," he said, waving his hand to encompass Shen, Ganzer, and Melammu. "A community as strong as an Ark's. You should protect it."

"I *am* protecting my family. I'm attacking their enemy."

"And the Ostarrichi will take it out on Mesos," Hamilcar said.

"And that will bring the armies of Free New Mesopotamia into Caelum, armed with the newest weaponry *Gallia* has to offer. That's *Gallia*'s plan, right? Tell me this: you want me to take my family and leave, but were you planning on leaving Caelum, too?"

His eyes widened in surprise, and he turned to stare hard out the window. Typical. "So," she said, "you're going to stay here, merrily tearing my society apart so your Ark can prosper, but, oh gee, you've gotten to know me and Shen, and you don't want anyone you know to get hurt by your actions. If anyone should leave, it's you. This isn't your fight; it's mine. It's my choice."

Melammu said in her quiet voice, "If you do this, Ashme, the CPC will hunt us. I will have to leave my home. I will end my life as a refugee."

She turned to her great-aunt. "Don't you want this? Free New Mesopotamian soldiers in Caelum? When you babysat me while Mom took Shen to his appointments, you used to sing me songs of revolution and tell stories of New Mesopotamia before *Brettaniai* gave it to the Ostarrichi. This is what Uncle Bazi fought for. This is what my father fought for."

"My husband is dead," Melammu said, her ancient face a portrait of bitterness. "Your father is dead."

"Uncle Bazi died fighting to free New Mesopotamia."

"You don't get to tell me why my husband died, little girl," Melammu said. She sighed, releasing her anger. She looked spent, a fallow field drying in the sun. Leaning back in her chair, she said, "Is living to see a generation of my family stay alive too much?"

"Ganzer says if you take this job," Shen said in a whisper, "that he'll take Aunty Melammu and me away from you."

"Did you tell him that?" she asked Ganzer.

"Yep."

"You should have let me tell him my way."

"You think you can do this and come home like nothing's happened?" he said. "The CPC will hunt you—and us."

"I've been so good," Shen said, hysteria edging into his voice. "I've been quiet in the mornings. I don't want any more people to go away. First, Uncle Bazi went away, then Dad, then Mom. It makes my stomach hurt. My heart empties. Let me stay with you."

Ashme's heart wilted, sadness poisoning its soil. When Dad blew his brains out, Shen had been with her. When she received the letter from the calming centre about Mom, Shen had been with her. His smile, his music, his innocence had wandered life's path with her. Would this be the first significant event she experienced where he would not hug her when she got home? Did Dad feel this?

She had to make the break. Fate had given her the chance to become the hero her people needed. She could never be that hero if she remained chained to her family. "Shen, leaving is the best thing for you. Ganzer and Aunty Melammu agree."

Both stared at the floor in stony silence.

"I don't understand," Shen said. "Why do I have to go? Why can't you come?"

"The Ostarrichi might use you to hurt me."

"I would never hurt you. The Ostarrichi can't make me—"

"I know you'd never hurt me, but the Ostarrichi might hurt you, don't you—"

"I don't care." Shen was on his feet, pacing. "The Ostarrichi can't make me hurt you. I need to be with you. I don't want to go!" Shen ran into Melammu's bedroom and slammed the door.

Damn it, she was going to cry. She tried to beat it down, but the tears were coming along with a tightness in her throat. "I've made my choice," she said. To where could she storm off? Shen was in Melammu's room. Everyone was here in the main room. She went into the bathroom and slammed the door, sitting on the rim of the tub, walls close around her. With the heels of her palms, she tried to block the tears.

She sat like that for a while, trying to convince herself tears were unjustified—this was what she wanted. Was Sura crying in her bathroom? No chance.

A soft knock sounded, followed by Shen's voice asking if he could join her. Anyone else she could have told to pound sand. She opened the door. "Your face is all blubbery," she said as he entered. She grabbed a handful of tissues and sat him down on the toilet. Stepping over him to sit on the tub, she began drying his eyes.

"You've been crying, too," Shen said. He grabbed his own handful of tissue and started clumsily dabbing it on her face. She laughed as he smooshed the tissue into her eyes. "If sending me away makes you cry, too, why are you doing it?" he asked.

"I'm doing it to keep you safe."

"I'm safer with you."

"New Uruk is going to get very dangerous over the next little while," Ashme said, "and that's why you have to leave."

"Then you should come too, so you're safe."

"No," Ashme said. "I have to stay to make New Uruk safe. Safe for you."

"Does that mean I can come back again?"

"Yeah, once I'm done making it safe."

Shen seemed to feel better with that idea. Ashme moved the both of them to sit on the floor, Shen between her legs leaning against her, her own back against the tub, her arms wrapped around him. It was a tight fit, but they were both slight. A silence settled on them.

"I miss Mom and Dad," Shen said.

"Me, too."

"Where do you think they are now?"

Ashme shrugged. "The Deep gave them to us. The Deep took them back."

Shen snuggled into his sister's arms. "Do you think they'll come back soon?"

They had this conversation before. "No, Shen, they're gone."

"People leave all the time and come back. You just said after I leave, I can come back."

Ashme rested her head against his. "With Mom and Dad, it's different. Dying means leaving forever."

"When I see them again, I'll sing them their favourite song." He began humming a song their parents used to sing when they were playful with one another. "Do you think they're happy now?" he asked. "Mom was so sad, and Dad was always angry."

"Sure. They're happy now."

"When Dad came back from Xinchin, well, he was so sad, so mad. It was always a surprise when he got angry. Sometimes, things would be fine, other times, *whoa!* He would yell. Mom always told me to be quiet in the mornings; otherwise, there would be trouble with Dad. I wasn't always so good, sometimes I played my drums in the morning. I didn't want to get him angry. How could music get him angry? Music soars, it flies, it frees you from the ground. I thinked it would make him feel good, I wanted him to feel happy and warm. It didn't. It made him go away. *Bang!* Then you and Mom screamed, and then I screamed. And Dad? He went away."

"Shen, is that what you think? Is that why you don't play music in the morning anymore?"

"I don't want anyone else to go away. I've never played music in the morning since then, not a single note, but now you're going away."

She wanted to shift Shen around so she could look him in the eye, but the space was too small to manoeuvre. She held him tight instead, her face leaning against his. Ashme and Shen.

Womb-mates. They had faced everything in this life together: Dad going to war, him coming home, his death, Mom's death, losing their home.

"Shen, Dad didn't . . ." she could not say it—*die, Dad didn't die*—the word refused to leave the back of her throat. The last image she had of him blistered through her mind like a pestilence ravaging a field: the blood, the body, twisted and empty, her ears still ringing from the gunshot, the sickly warm smell of blood and meat. "Dad didn't go away because you played music in the morning. He taught you to sing, do you remember? He loved music. Dad left us because his heart was broken."

"How is your heart?" Shen asked.

"My heart's fine." A lie. "You make my heart whole." A truth.

She knew now that in this next phase of her life, she would be alone. She had always griped about being Shen's caretaker, had yearned for a destiny of her own. Here, now, on the floor of their bathroom, she sensed for the first time that destiny's cost. What would Mom and Dad think?

She remembered those last moments with her mother. Ashme had been standing in front of the ruins of their house, a building-cruncher still chewing up the remains of their home while two CPC goons dragged Mom away. A third one had blocked Ashme's path with the barrel of a gun pushed into her chest. She had kept an iron grip on Shen, who was screaming and crying. Mom had fought those goons, kicking and clawing at them as they pulled her away, a cat fighting coyotes, while Ashme's soul tore itself apart because she knew why the CPC had come to destroy their home.

"You can play music in the morning if you like, Shen," she said. "Mom and Dad didn't leave because of you."

CHAPTER 28

"SPIT," Ashme ordered Shen. He was sitting on the toilet lid while she brushed his teeth. He leaned over the sink and spat, talking as soon as his mouth was empty about how Ganzer clocked Hamilcar in the face.

"Do we have any dry towels?" Ganzer called from Melammu's room. "These ones smell like mildew."

"Here." Ashme grabbed one from a basket under the sink. She handed it to him in the main room, ignoring Hamilcar sitting on the couch. Since earlier that day, the bruise on his face had darkened, and his eye had swollen partially shut. "Can you move your weights so I can pull out Shen's bed?" she asked Ganzer. "I can't lift your dumbbells."

Her cousin grunted an affirmative. She could feel the thump-thump of him moving his equipment. Behind her in the bathroom, Shen struggled to pull his shirt off—it was stuck on his head. She popped it over his face, he yelled, "Boo!" and she pantomimed fright. Together, they got him into his pyjamas.

She shooed Hamilcar off the couch, took off the flat cushions, and set them in the armchair, after which she pulled out the fold-out bed. Its springs chirped as Shen crawled under the blankets. It took two lullabies before he fell asleep.

"You're pissed at me," Hamilcar said quietly so as not to wake Shen. From the next room, they could hear Ganzer talking to Melammu while drawers opened and closed.

"Angry? At what? For you joining the ever-growing list of people telling me what's best for Shen and me? You don't get to choose what's best for me. You don't get to choose what's best for Shen. I do." She kept an eye on her twin to make sure he was asleep.

"It feels like you're getting wrapped up in events put in motion by powers that want to use you for their own gain."

"This is my home. I was born here; my parents died here. If I don't fight for it, who will? Should I give my home to those bastards?"

"What you are about to do—"

"What you *hired* me to do."

"What *Gallia* hired you to do," Hamilcar clarified. He was standing close to her so he could speak quietly. His scent filled her nose. He did not smell like cologne. He smelled like a man, and it drove her mad. Her life was going to forever change tomorrow, and here he was, a man with whom she shared a mutual attraction. If one thought the universe cared, you might see in his presence a gift, the chance for a sweet sendoff, a future memory she might enjoy in the years ahead from before the moment everything changed—a gift ruined by his badgering and the fact they were in a cramped apartment surrounded by her family.

"Whether you succeed or fail," he continued, "there is no way Caelum will let you live. The CPC will hunt you for the rest of your life, and you know they will find you. They will use your family to get to you."

"You mean you're fine if other Mesos get killed, just not ones you know. Maybe you're not set up for this type of work."

"Look, these events are beyond my ability to control. I can't stop them. The best I can do is try to keep the people I know safe."

Having him so close drove her to distraction. She heard Ganzer rummaging around in Melammu's room, listened to the nasal breathing of Shen sleeping, and choked on the packed tightness of the apartment strangling her. She wanted to scream. Was it too much to expect a little space that was hers? Was a bit of joy and pleasure too much to ask? She wanted to be desired and to sate her own desires, to be human, singular, to be something other than Ganzer's cousin, Melammu's grandniece, or Shen's sister. She wanted to be her own person. A few minutes of pleasure, she deserved it. "Aw, fuck it," she said. She grabbed Hamilcar and kissed him hard, grinding his stubble into her face and crushing her body into his.

He pulled away. "Are you—"

She closed the distance, interrupting him with another kiss. He was lean, with a hard body, and he wrapped her in his long, strong arms, burying her in his embrace. She pressed her fingers into the muscles of his back. His kiss and touch charged her. She wanted more. She was hungry for him, famished, and every moment her body was pressed into his made her hungrier.

He was holding back. She was holding back. Shen was right there. Ganzer could step out of Melammu's room any moment. Where were they going to do this? She grabbed the front of his shirt in a fist, pulled him into the bathroom and locked the door.

She tugged his shirt over his head and tossed it to the floor. He pushed her back into the wall and undid the buttons of her shirt while she worked on his pants. She wished she had clean clothes, but neither she nor Ganzer had had time to do laundry this week. The concern was moot. In moments, they were both in their underwear, skin on skin, exploring each other's bodies with hands and mouth.

Underwear dropped to the floor. She wanted all of him. Everything would change after tomorrow. This might be the last chance for her to share intimacy with another, to have a connection built out of pleasure and passion rather than need or duty.

But how? There was a tub, a toilet, a sink with barely enough counter to hold their toothpaste, and floor enough for two slender people to stand. Maybe hands on the tub's rim so he could take her from behind? No, she wanted to face him, to see and feel his body. Both the floor and tub, however, were too cramped for two people.

She shifted around and then sat on the counter. It was one hands-breadth too small for her. She braced herself with one foot pressed into the opposite wall to keep from falling as she pulled Hamilcar closer. "Are you sure about this?" he asked.

Duh. Ashme kissed him while guiding him into her body. Their sex was frantic and muted, lest the three other people in the apartment hear them. She grabbed onto the sink's faucet to keep from falling off the counter. Her leg was at an awkward angle; it cramped.

With a shudder and stifled moan, Hamilcar finished. She had a fleeting *Is that it?* moment, her body still on fire, but her mind was relieved—her family was, after all, on the other side of the door. Nuzzling, he kissed her neck while she stretched out her cramped leg. His kisses moved to her chest, then lower. Was he going to go down on her?

He did. Ashme luxuriated in the sensation. She thought about stopping him—the counter's edge was digging into areas better not dug into, while the fear her family would hear them made her too nervous to have any chance of climaxing—but Zini's stacks, it felt so damn good. She let herself sink into the pleasure, running her hands through his dark hair before grabbing tight.

Shen, asleep, and Melammu, in her room, were probably unaware of what was going on in their bathroom. If Ganzer were done helping Melammu, he would be out in the main living area. He would know what she was up to, but he had brought women of his own home, so who was he to judge?

Wait . . . maybe she *was* going to finish.

MASON AWOKE with a sense of peace. He breathed deep, stretching. A refreshing breeze blew in through the window while a beam of sunlight shone across the golden skin of his torso. Beside him, Oriana stirred. Her eyes opened heavily, and upon seeing him, she smiled a sleepy smile. He turned to her, and they hugged. She had always been slight but was more so now—she had lost weight this past year. She felt like a delicate, fluttering bird in his arms. He let himself doze with his face buried in her dark hair, her scent filling him, making him whole.

Down the hall, Daxton cried. It was the cry of a baby in the morning rather than the inconsolable wailing that had gripped the boy for so long. "I'll go get him," Oriana said, pulling the covers off and sliding out of bed. She wafted out of the room, stepping lightly on the pads of her feet, slender arms swaying.

Something special had happened last night. This past week, Daxton had been sleeping well. Last night, both kids had gone down quickly. Oriana had been in her sleeping shirt while he was getting ready for bed. They knocked into each other as they navigated around their bathroom. They hugged. They kissed. A fading ember sparked to life. They made love for the first time since Daxton was born.

Oriana returned with their son in her arms, clambered back into bed, and began breastfeeding. "I think the editing is working," she said.

Mason *mm-hmm*-ed agreement. He grabbed Daxton's foot, and his son pushed against his fingers. The boy's muscle tone was improving, igniting a warm flame of joy in Mason's heart. He watched Daxton feed in Oriana's arms, suckling and slurping hungrily, the room bathed in the glow of early morning light. "I wish I didn't have to go to work today," he said.

"Today's Avalyn's press conference?"

Some of the tension he had been feeling the past few days seeped back into his body. "It is."

"She's so brave." *She is, at that*, Mason thought. *That and a great many other things*. He was uncertain as to what to call her using him to hack the Ahiim treaty. Oriana's body tensed beside him. "I wish I . . ." Some strong emotion choked off her thought.

"What is it?" he asked, putting an arm around her, her warmth suffusing him.

She rested her head on his shoulder. "I wish I was braver."

"You were a kid when Free New Mesopotamia bombed your home. That leaves a mark." He closed his eyes against the memory of a roadside bomb shredding Myla.

"I should have been braver for him," Oriana said, nodding to Daxton. "My fear made him sick."

"We've talked about this, Oriana. It's a Dache defect; it's from me. We don't know what set it off. The biogineers said many environmental factors could have caused the epigenetic changes that produced it."

For a while, the only sound was that of Daxton feeding. Tracey entered with a bright and beaming "Good morning" and then scampered onto the bed. She and Mason play-wrestled.

MASON ARRIVED LATE. Avalyn was holding the press conference in the courtyard of the *Aigle*, its winged roofline rising behind them. Vast crowds had formed. Protests thundered. The air was thick with angels, while ranks of CPC soldiers, supported by scores of armoured riot-control vehicles and aircraft, their engines thrumming, kept the angry mobs from violence. *What a mess.*

Mason watched the shouting, jumping mass of Mesos, and his stomach knotted. This was Utukagaba all over again. There, he had faced a weekly assault on the CPC outpost by Meso rabble like this.

He overheard a nearby CPC trooper speaking to another. "Listen to them bark. Maybe after the press conference, they'll let us teach them to heel."

Cocky arrogance. He, too, had been filled with such bravado.

It was the armour. That, and being nineteen. He used to love wearing combat armour. Visually, it made you look like you had twenty extra kilos of muscle. Physically, it gave you strength multiples of the human norm. After Myla died, it made him feel safe—it gave him power when he was vulnerable.

He remembered a young Meso girl he encountered at Utukagaba. He had been on patrol conducting mapping raids in the village one night—a typical operation, going house to house, confiscating supplies like radios, computers, and other materiel, maybe finding some people to arrest if anyone gave them trouble, generally trying to keep the enemy off-balance.

Then this kid, some girl, ten, maybe eleven years old, came out of a house and started yelling at him. "Why are you doing this to us? My brother is paralyzed from one of your stun rounds! Why did you do that to him?" If Mesos had left the nearby CPC outpost in peace, her brother would be okay. How could she be so blind to that? "You come with guns, grenades, and angels at your back while we have only rocks!" she said. "You tell me which of us is stronger!"

That little *shit*. Myla had been torn to shreds by a Kanu bomb only weeks earlier, and this piece-of-shit kid had the gall to harangue him about strength and stones.

The girl was young and pretty—she would grow up into a looker. A fellow soldier grabbed his crotch while making a comment about how he had something that would shut her up. The rest of his squad laughed. Mason laughed, too.

Looking back, he felt ashamed. A dozen CPC decked out in full combat armour, guns held in the alert position, facing off against a little girl in a grubby summer dress, jabbing her finger in their faces.

He did not like thinking of Utukagaba. It held the one memory he truly hated, worse even than that of Myla dying.

Shanelle found him, her hands clenched in fists and her brow furrowed. "You're late." She had to yell over the protesters' roar and the rumbling engine noise of the riot-control vehicles. She pointed to a crowd of Ostarrichi whose placards denounced Avalyn and called for peace with the Mesos. "Look at those traitors. They'd feed our nation to the jackals."

What would they do if they learned Avalyn used the BLOQ to hack the Ahiim treaty? he wondered. "Avalyn's kicked up a hornet's nest," he said. Why had Ashme called him yesterday? It made him uneasy.

Shanelle looked at him with an unreadable expression of ice. Did she know Ashme had called him? She turned her attention to the seething mob of Mesos and asked, "Will they attack when Avalyn appears?"

She was nervous. Really nervous. Mason looked at the Mesos as they jumped and chanted and screamed and raged. The rumble of the riot-control vehicles vibrated in his bones. "All they'll do is toss rocks." That was all they could do.

"And Baltu?" Shanelle asked. "Striking now, during such a public display, seems like something he'd do."

"The Network has the *Aigle* and the surrounding Castillion district locked down—"

A commotion behind them cut him off as a wave of tension rippled through the ranks of CPC. Avalyn had arrived. She walked up to Shanelle and demanded a sitrep.

"Security protocols and backups are active and functioning well," Shanelle replied, standing at attention. "I've made my views on this clear. Exposing yourself so openly in public is an unnecessary risk."

"I have faith in my people to protect me."

"So you've told me," Shanelle said.

"At ease," Avalyn said. "I've got it covered. Oh, good morning, Mason. How's little Daxton doing?"

"Uh . . . he's well, Madam Floor Leader."

"Good. I'm glad." She cupped Mason's elbow and gave him a grandmotherly smile as she walked past.

The screams of the crowd crescendoed to a tsunami roar that shook the ground as she took the stage.

CHAPTER 29

ASHME HAD NEVER SEEN her mother more beautiful than the day Dad returned. Ever since she could remember, Mom had tried to be happy but failed. While Dad was away, Mom worried herself sick. As Shen grew, she worried as he struggled in school and stomach problems plagued him. She slept poorly, and whenever she had a moment of calm, a worried frown cut a crevasse into her forehead. She kept herself busy to cope, always doing something, fixing this, organizing that, cleaning knick-knacks, tutoring Shen, something, anything to keep idleness and the worries that haunted her during those quiet moments at bay.

Ashme had been such a bitch. She used to act out, picking fights mercilessly. She would disrupt class so the school would call Mom in, forcing her to rush around for her instead of Shen. Ashme wished she'd had the chance to apologize before the CPC took her mom. She knew now why Mom had to put Ashme aside to care for Shen. With Dad away, Mom had been left alone, looking after two kids, one of them with special needs—and Shen's needs were all-consuming. She used to tease Mom about that crevasse etched into her forehead, telling her it made her look old, that her forehead must be the oldest part of her body. Now, Ashme was developing one of her own.

The day Dad came home, however, Mom had been beautiful. It was not the hours she had spent at the salon the day before curling her hair or her summer dress, newly mended, that had given her such grace. It was her face. Her face was relaxed, smiling; her eyes bright, beaming. She had an aura of transcendence. At that moment, she had been shaped by hope. Hope made people beautiful.

Ashme had been nine when her father left. When she learned he was returning, she wondered what he would think of the woman she was becoming. It had been so many years that he was more a figment of imagination than man. It would be strange having him in the house again.

She had run to him when, down the street, he came into view; she had cried in his arms, gripping him with all her strength. "Where is my daughter?" He was teasing, but he had tears in his voice. He undid her hug and held her at arm's length so he could look at her. "My daughter is a small girl. Who is this beautiful woman?"

"The skank's taken the stage." Sura's words jolted Ashme out of her reverie. On the data screen hovering over the boxes in front of them, they watched Avalyn begin her press conference. The abandoned, hollow floor of Mitutu Tower was dimly lit by natural light shining through grimy windows. Ashme wished she had thought to bring a sweater to protect her from the chill.

Avalyn wore a fancy purple suit with an ivory shirt. It was business attire, but it still somehow reminded Ashme of an officer's uniform. "The orbital sniper platform will be in firing position in two minutes. Is your EM shield holding?" Sura asked, her words echoing in the empty space around them.

Ashme sent her senses into the EM shield she had set up to hide the electronic signatures their ID tags and equipment emitted. The drain was minor; she could maintain it for a half-hour easily. "We're good."

She watched Avalyn talk. ". . . there have been three great crises that rise above the unending war the Kanu wage on us.

The first was the Hab Revolt leading to the Bit Durani Massacre, where the Kanu almost destroyed us. The second was the Caelum War, where we survived a vicious, coordinated attack by the Kanu to win our right to our homeland. The third is the Ahiim X59 Treaty, where we have agreed to surrender that homeland..."

Was this really happening? After this, everything would change. Her family would have to leave. She would be alone and hunted. The goldies, however, would know fear, which would make it all worthwhile. She was going to succeed where Dad had failed.

"... our movement is built on love. Our movement is built on family. It is for love of our brothers and sisters, it is for love of our children that we must..."

Two minutes for the weapons platform to get into position. A couple of more minutes for the bullet to reach its target. Would the windbag talk long enough?

"I can't wait to blue-screen her," Sura said.

"Did you catch that last bit about love?" Ashme asked. "Makes me want to drive a nano-tipped data spike in my ears."

"Weapons platform almost in position," Sura said. "We're doing this. We're really doing this. We're going to go down in history, and it's so easy. Just a press of a button when the green light flashes."

Could they really get away with it? All her neighbours had hailed Dad a hero. He had come home a shattered wreck of a man, though, and despite coming back standing on his own two feet, in the end, the title of hero had cost him everything. What price would fate make her pay? *Heroes are heroes because they risk it all. That's what Dad did.*

Something was wrong, like that feeling you have when you leave the house, forgetting something important. "Wait a second," Ashme said. She cast her senses into the nanohaze. A perturbation was piercing her EM shield, but the signal was from a source other than the Network.

The command console powered down, its lights dimming, then extinguishing. Sura swore and stared at it. "Fix it," she said. "Get it back on."

"Don't bother." The voice was Hamilcar's. Both women stared in shock as he approached, his footsteps reverberating throughout the capacious area. "The job's cancelled," he said.

Both women spoke at the same time. Sura said, "Cache that," Ashme, "How'd you find us?"

Hamilcar answered Ashme. "Build as strong an EM shield as you want; you still need to send a signal to our satellite. Yesterday, when you were testing the gear, I used that to track your location."

"This isn't your choice, Ark-monkey," Sura said.

"Will you stop calling me that?" Hamilcar said. "It's my gear, my choice."

Avalyn carried on in the background. ". . . dark powers seek to undermine the values of our great people . . ."

"Gallia hasn't called off the hit, have they?" Ashme asked.

Hamilcar said nothing.

"Is this because of last night?"

"What happened last night?" Sura asked.

". . . breaks my heart to see Caelum betrayed again and again by our political class . . ."

"No," Hamilcar said. "The job's been cancelled, that's all."

Sura threw her hands up. "Did you screw him, and now he's going all white-knight?"

"Look," Hamilcar said, "*Gallia* is trying to start a war. Maybe I can stop it."

Ashme got up close to him, jutting her face into his. "This is *our* war. You don't get to decide whether we fight it or not."

Hamilcar backed up a step. "But we are, don't you see? Avalyn. The Ark. Free New Mesopotamia. They are all trying to start a war, and it will be you who suffers while everyone else becomes rich and powerful. You have an obligation. You have to look after Shen, not tear your society apart."

". . . I call for the awakening of *Ostarrichi*'s ancient soul . . ."

"Shen!" Sura said. "Shen, Shen, Shen! This is our chance to leave our mark, and I'm not letting that analog stop us." She stared helplessly at the console. "Ashme, indigo-child this thing on!"

"It's powered down," Ashme said. "You've got to turn it on manually."

Sura picked up the console, examining it. "Where's the on button?"

"It is too late," Hamilcar said, pointing at the data screen. Both women watched impotently as Avalyn left the stage.

"You better believe you're still paying us for this," Sura said.

CHAPTER 30

AVALYN WAS IN A FOUL MOOD, though Mason had no idea why. Her speech had been stirring. The protests had been aggressive and, of course, the Mesos had started to riot after, but no attacks had been directed at Avalyn or the *Aigle*. Her speech was, perhaps, a bit too long and, at the end, seemed unscripted. Maybe that explained her displeasure.

She lounged in a plush chair, a bitter, ancient woman, while she watched a data screen showing rioting Meso mobs clashing with disciplined ranks of CPC. The sing-song tinkle of ice sounded from a tumbler of scotch she held in her talon-like hand. She had offered no drink to either him or Shanelle, who sat on Avalyn's desk with a foot mindlessly kicking back and forth.

Despite Avalyn's mood, Mason thought the press conference had gone well. His presence here showed that, though Avalyn's innermost circle remained closed, she valued him. He leaned back in his chair, letting himself sink into it, the real leather making a scrunching sound. Aside from that rough patch at the end, her speech had been powerful. These riots were expected—they were even a hopeful sign. "Mesos riot like this all the time," he said. "The response we see here is nothing new. If all they're going to do is break windows, we can probably extend our claims on the Hab."

"We won't be giving up the Hab with the current Director-General in power," Avalyn said. She squirmed uncomfortably, muttered a curse that would make a soldier blush, and then lifted her shirt to expose a thick belt wrapped around her waist, intricate designs of circuitry adorning its surface. She pawed at a clasp with swollen-knuckled fingers, releasing it, and then tossed it on a coffee table with another curse.

Mason studied the gear. Along the back was a lump, likely a power pack, connected to a series of circuits, sensor arrays, and other structures. He had never seen such a device. He caught Shanelle's attention, nodded toward it, mouthing, "What's that?"

"Ark tech," Shanelle said. "Anti-sniper gear. Top of the line."

Which Ark? It was sleeker and simpler in design than typical Brettaniai tech.

Avalyn switched channels to another data stream showing another riot in a different district of the city. "We will never know peace so long as Mesos live alongside us. Here, look at this." She switched the data stream of riots with a picture of a man. He was unusually tall, with long, lean limbs, brown skin, and piercing blue eyes.

"Who is he?" Mason asked.

Shanelle got off the desk and walked up behind Avalyn, arms crossed. "His name is Hamilcar Beker. He's an arms dealer from Ark *Gallia*. We have reason to believe they're supplying arms to Baltu."

"The Ark is selling weapons to the Free New Mesopotamian Army?" Mason asked.

Shanelle nodded.

This changes so much! "I should have been given this information when doing my analysis."

"We haven't known about it for long," Shanelle said.

The series of treaties signed at the end of the Great Ark War limited contact between Esharra and Ark powers. Only *Brettaniai* and Caelum engaged in trade. If word of this arms deal became public, *Brettaniai* would retaliate, likely drawing Caelum into the conflict. Who did the Kanu nations of Esharra hate more, Ostarrichi or the Ark powers? Would the Kanu nations hold their noses and deal with *Gallia* to access the tech needed to pry the Ostarrichi from this world, or would they forget about Caelum while they fought these new Arks?

Avalyn scoffed. "We were told to expect an attack today, but nothing. Baltu has access to Ark weapons, and still, all Mesos do is throw stones, smash windows, and shut down roads."

It dawned on Mason. This was not about the Hab or the Ahiim treaty. "You want war."

Avalyn sighed a tired sigh, a grizzled veteran eying the tattered landscape. "I have fought in every war since Caelum came into existence and saved it from destruction again and again. I am Caelum's shield maiden. Who will protect Caelum when I'm gone?" Her face hardened, and it seemed as though a force infused her body, transforming the limbs of this frail old woman into unbreakable sinews of adamant. "I can beat them in war."

The illusion was gone, and a tired old woman leaned back in her chair. She switched the data screen back to the ongoing riots. "Tell me, Mason, what makes Mesos so dangerous?"

He shifted, causing the leather to scrunch. "The Kanu is a warrior culture. Our presence here signifies a defeat they cannot abide."

She smiled a wizened smile. "You know the Kanu well—that's why you work here. But you don't know them as well as I do. You haven't fought them in bloody battle for a lifetime. That's how you truly come to know an enemy. What makes Kanu dangerous is that they are cowards. They'll launch sneak attacks, as they did during the Novoreeka Impasse and the War of Trahison. They'll engage in asymmetric warfare, bombing civilians or poisoning soldiers on leave. But face them in a straight-up fight, and they'll run and then snap at your heels when you try to walk away."

Mason remembered a young Meso girl, a child yelling defiance at a soldier. *Which of us is stronger?*

With the click of a button, Avalyn turned off the data screen. "I was a fool to rely on Kanu bravery."

CHAPTER 31

"DADDY, YOU'RE NOT LISTENING."

"Sure I am, Sweetie," Mason lied to his daughter. He had been having trouble concentrating since his meeting with Avalyn. Tracey was rambling on about the goings-on in her daycare, stream-of-consciousness style, as the car drove them home.

The vehicle left the Terres du Nord district where Tracey's daycare was and entered the freeway, its engines humming softly. Mason pulled up a game on the car's data screen, and he and his daughter began playing. She giggled as the computer *bleeped* and *blooped* with each move.

Avalyn wanted war, and she was breaking the Ahiim treaty to achieve it. She had always been Caelum's protector. Whenever Caelum had been on the brink of annihilation, she had rallied the armies and achieved impossible victories. Always, it had been neighbouring Kanu nations or the fighters of Free New Mesopotamia who had brought war to Caelum. This war, however, would be Avalyn's.

Tracey moved a brightly coloured, flashing piece on the virtual game board, a merry tune played, and Mason pressed the dice button with a slender finger. He looked out the window and saw smoke rising from the nearby Meso district of East Margidda. Less than two kilometres from his home, protests raged. Imagine if they allowed Mesos free reign of the city—what would stop them from rioting in his neighbourhood, or by Tracey's daycare?

If history were a guide, these riots would fade out over the next day or so, but the damage they would leave in their wake made Mason shake his head. Three aerial personnel carriers were landing in East Margidda, the bass rumble of their engines barely audible through the car's windows. *Why do Mesos burn and destroy their own businesses and property when protesting?*

What did Avalyn hope to achieve? Did she believe she could win a victory that would last after she passed? *Caelum will never know lasting peace.* They had won decisive victories in the past, yet still, other attacks came. Caelum's best chance for safety, such as it was, came from deterrence. Avalyn was doing the opposite. Even if Caelum won the next war, Ostarrichi would die. Mason would have a hard time living with himself if he had a part in instigating that war.

The car decelerated as it turned off the freeway into their home district. As the car pulled in front of their house, Dashiell pinged him. "Run inside and tell Mommy I'll be there in a minute," he told Tracey.

Mason activated his neural implant. *[Yes, Dashiell, what is it?]*

[I have two pieces of information for you,] his AI replied.

[Let's have it.]

[First, I am obligated by my contract with your government to comply with Caelum's Data Privacy Act, and per Section 51.5c of said Act, I am informing you that N'reb-second Emperor Shanelle installed a subroutine in my database to monitor your ping logs.]

Mason's stomach knotted. *[Is that legal?]*

[No, and I have lodged a formal injunction to have it removed under an Article 4.1.34 violation.]

[How did you discover the subroutine?]

[She made no attempt to conceal her activities.]

Shanelle would have known Dashiell would find the subroutine and remove it. She would also know his AI would report it to him. She was sending a message: "I'm watching you." [What's the second thing?] he pinged.

[I have discovered what the BLOQ program does.]

[It's the program slaving the angel network to the Ahiim treaty, right?]

[Wrong,] Dashiell pinged. [It is the command node for the angel network.]

Mason sat, confused. Dashiell prompted, [Would you like me to explain how I discovered that?]

[Uh . . .]

[It was exceedingly difficult to find. Eight years ago, Chevalier purchased a small company named—]

[Could you explain to me what the command node does?] Mason interrupted.

[It is the sub-system of the Network that controls the angel network and all the angels in it.]

[But the angel network isn't controlled by any one thing. It's slaved to the laws established by the Aigle.]

[Not anymore,] Dashiell pinged.

Mason stopped his foot from tapping nervously. [Are you saying Avalyn has control of the angel network?]

[If she has the BLOQ, then yes.]

[There must be some method of detecting unlawful tampering with the network's programming, some system to identify unauthorized access.]

[There are several such systems,] Dashiell pinged. [It is possible the BLOQ can bypass them.]

Mason's heart fluttered, his breath coming in short gasps. The angel network had been a tremendous asset in maintaining peace throughout Caelum. It was a robotic army over a hundred thousand strong, equipped with the latest in urban-warfare technology. Slaving it to uphold the laws passed by the *Aigle* was how Caelum ensured they were only deployed to enforce the rule of law rather than the will of the power-mad.

Now, thanks to the role he had played in stealing the BLOQ, the angels were subject to the will of one person:

Avalyn.

CHAPTER 32

ASHME WATCHED an angel slowly drift by the window of her apartment, the rhythmic cadence of its engines audible through the glass. It was monitoring the ongoing protests throughout the neighbourhood. She spooned peanut butter into her mouth. The drain of maintaining the EM shield during their aborted attempt to assassinate Avalyn had left her with a pang of gnawing hunger. It was Ganzer's turn to make supper tonight, but she was too hungry to wait.

"I am telling you, if you care for your family, get out of the city," Hamilcar was saying.

"Cache that," Sura said. She still had the sniper platform's command module in her lap. She stared at it with a long face, caressing its surface with fingers bearing chipped, multi-coloured nail polish.

Melammu fixed him with a withering glare. "Who are you to tell us where to live?" She looked at the others. "Who invited him here?"

"He's right, Grandma," Ganzer said. "The goldies are itching for a crackdown. We need to get you and Shen out of here."

Melammu crossed her arms and glared at Hamilcar. The

bruise that Ganzer had given him on his face had darkened, though the swelling around the eye was coming down.

"I don't want to move," Shen said. "This is my home. You are my family. This is where our heart is."

Ashme leaned her chair back and peered out the kitchen window down onto the streets. The crowd of Mesos was thick; people mashed together, jumping as one. They were loud enough that even here on the twenty-first floor, their chants resounded through her apartment walls.

Her heart ached. With Avalyn still alive, with no great act to ignite a revolution, nothing would change. For all their chants shouted or stones thrown, their rage was impotent. It would burn like the fire of a street magician—all flash and optics, changing nothing before fading.

"Someone's pinging me," Sura said. She stood up and stepped away. "I've got to take this."

"Hamilcar," Ashme said, her mouth thick with peanut butter. She looked at the man she'd screwed last night and lost herself for a quick moment in his exotic eyes but hardened her resolve. "You should leave."

"I like Hamilcar," Shen said.

"I am trying to help you," Hamilcar said.

"Help? Is that what you're doing?" Ashme asked.

"Yes. I am going to lose my job—maybe worse—because I stopped you from starting a war."

The windows vibrated as four more angels zipped past in tight formation. "I don't need saving."

"There are powers in the Ark that will benefit from chaos here," Hamilcar said. "Too many powerful people want to sow chaos in the hope they will prosper."

"This is my home," Ashme said softly. "You think I should leave it because powerful people want to destroy it?"

"You should leave because it is dangerous. Leave so your family has a chance for strength."

Sura's ping finished. She headed for the apartment door.

"Stay, go, whatever gets you all off. I'm staying—there's coin to be made in chaos." She jabbed her finger at them as she left. "Any of you got the stones to join me, give me a call."

Melammu cast some unpleasant mutterings at Sura as the door closed behind her. The ancient woman stared vacantly into space a moment and then said, "This is the Scourge all over again. In the weeks before the Brettaniai gave our land away, you could feel things were building. The Ostarrichi were itching for a fight. When war broke out, and the other Kanu nations tried to rescue us, the goldies came down on us hard. I remember the grinding of a viper rumbling down the street with the stamp of feet behind it and the crack of gunfire that would come out of nowhere to steal lives.

"I had two children and didn't think a war zone was where I should raise them. We left everything behind, our house, business, everything, and fled to Neu and ended up in the Urbat Refugee Camp." She sniffed and wiped her nose. "Turns out a refugee camp is no place to raise children, either."

She pointed a bent, gnarled finger at Ganzer. "Your mother suffered wounds there that have never healed. Most people never made it out of Urbat— the Ostarrichi revoked the citizenship of any Meso who left the country during the Scourge. But my Bazi was clever; he had connections. It took him years, but he got us back into Caelum." She nodded toward Ashme. "Your grandmother took us in, bless her. But there was no work."

She stared at the floor, face twisted in bitterness. "Bazi died. My son left for Novvyrus, and I haven't seen him for thirty years. And my daughter? My daughter is a broken shell of a woman. That's what running got us. And fighting?" She turned to look at Ashme. "Fighting got my Bazi killed. Your dad, too. You don't know what fighting is—real fighting, real war. There are no heroes in war, just scared kids trying to murder each other. The right thing to do is simple. Keep your head down, don't stir the pot, and recognize your blessings for what they are." Her eyes drifted to Shen.

Silence fell on them, the only sound that of the distant protests. Ganzer said, "Sometimes keeping your head down isn't an option." Melammu scoffed, but he continued. "My mom may be a broken shell, but she's alive, and she had me. My uncle left for Novvyrus before I was born, and it breaks my heart that you haven't seen him since, but he and his family are alive. They might even be happy."

Before Melammu could reply, Hamilcar shot to his feet, shouting a harsh curse. Everyone stared, stunned. "The gear for the sniper platform," he said. "It's gone. Sura took it."

"What's that fool girl doing?" Ganzer asked.

Hamilcar grabbed Ashme by the shoulders. "Who was it that pinged her?"

"How would I know?"

"You are an indigo child. Have you no way to know? Can you trace the ping?"

"No, the ping's done. I've no idea who she spoke to," Ashme said. "It's your gear. You can find out where she's taking it."

"We've gotta go," Hamilcar said, moving for the door. "We have to stop her."

"Why?" Ashme asked. "This morning, I was set to assassinate Avalyn. Why would I stop Sura doing whatever she's doing?"

"The Ark-monkey's right," Ganzer said.

"Bloody hell, will you stop calling me that?"

Ganzer said to Ashme, "You keep saying you're doing what you're doing to make our home safe for Shen. You and I both know Sura's not interested in making anything safer—'opportunity in chaos' and all that. Nothing you and she have been doing is making our home safe."

Ashme looked to Melammu, but she stared away, her eyes lost in folds of sadness. Ashme turned to Ganzer. "Doing nothing hasn't made our home safe, either."

"I don't know what the answer is," Ganzer said. "The people bringing war to our home aren't fighting for us. They're using us. I can't change the tides, but I can look after my own. Sura's going to do something that will get a lot of my people blue-screened. That's something we can stop."

Shen said, "I want my home to be safe, too. I want us all to be together. One happy family."

"Zini's stacks!" Ashme threw her hands in the air. "Fine, let's go find Sura. Shen, stay with Aunty Melammu."

Moments later, Ashme was on the street with Ganzer and Hamilcar. The combined sound of the crowd's yell roared like an avalanche. The press of protesters was so thick that to move forward, Ganzer had to shove people aside forcefully. It seemed impossible that Sura could have gone far.

Someone grabbed Ashme's arm and pulled. She spun around. "Shen!" She had to yell to be heard. "What are you doing? Get back to the apartment!" Ashme grabbed Ganzer's shirt before he got too far ahead and pulled him back.

"I want to help," Shen yelled back. "I want to make our home safe."

"I know you do, and you can help by keeping Aunty Melammu safe," Ashme said.

Ganzer gave Ashme a look like this was somehow her fault. "Listen to your sister."

Hamilcar pulled at Ganzer as he stared at a device in his other hand. "Sura is a block that way," he said, pointing.

Could Shen make it back home on his own? Their building was less than ten metres away, but with the crowd and Shen's lack of direction, he could get turned around and lost. Ashme pointed to their building. "You see our apartment? You keep your eyes on it and go straight back."

"No!" he said. "I want to help you stop Sura and keep our home safe so we can be together."

Ganzer grabbed her arm, looking up. "What's with the angels?"

Ashme followed his gaze as a half dozen angels zipped by a metre above the crowd, the back-blast from their rotors snapping at their clothes. They came to a stop a block ahead and hovered in formation. Another squad of angels hovered about two blocks back. "Crowd control?"

"They'd have their crowd-dispersal sirens," Ganzer said. "And ranks of CPC to lay the boots to us." The thrumming of the angels' engines rose in pitch and tempo.

Ashme cast her senses into the nanohaze to see if she could catch a feel for what the angels were doing. Shen's hand, cold and clammy, gripped hers. Urgent data packets pulsed between the angels along the street: commands, queries, AI analysis, and reports. On each of the angels, the red light in the centre of its chest began to spin, casting out strobing pulses of light. An ammo drone appeared above the buildings. The roar of the crowd decrescendoed to silence.

The angels fired. The grinding staccato of their machine guns screamed like the sound of rending metal. They tore swaths of bloody death through the street. Ashme watched waves of blood spray above the crowd. This was not real.

Bodies thrashed into her, knocking her down. She hit the street hard. Above her, she saw dream-like figures move and dance. Something smelled wretched, carried on the warm, humid air. It filled her mouth and nose. It made her gag. She was covered in something wet and warm, like the day the CPC raided their apartments and killed that kid, Keshda.

She got to her knees. A sea of people seethed around her, running, falling, scrambling to their feet. Some disappeared in the waves of red rolling along the street. Keshda lay dead beside her.

No, that was wrong. Keshda died weeks ago. It was Hamilcar. That, too, seemed wrong. It looked like Hamilcar, but there were two large cavities in his torso. The face looked like him, but the eyes, those amazing, exotic blue eyes, were different. They looked unreal. Lifeless, like coloured glass balls. Hamilcar was a living thing. He had been inside her, filled with an explosive passion. She remembered the feel of his hair in her hands, his breath on her neck. That was last night. This was not Hamilcar but a thing on the road beside her.

Arms wrapped around her waist, lifting her and then carrying her away. People ran. People dropped to the ground. Fake people, like that Hamilcar thing, with impossibly big holes in their bodies. People stared at the sky with doll eyes.

She was set down, and a face filled her vision. Ganzer. Something was wrong. She had never seen such a look of terror on the big man. She tried to listen to what he was saying, but the noise. There was so much noise. Cacophony.

Her mind snapped clear. Ganzer was yelling, "Are you okay? Are you hurt?" He checked her body.

"I'm fine, I think." The air smelled like smoke and gunpowder. They were in the doorway to a shop. She knew it. Anak's Antiques, two blocks from their apartment. It was normal. This was normal. Reality. It was the place you went to sell your old crap or to buy someone else's old crap. Shen loved walking the aisles, checking out the ever-changing assortment of tchotchkes.

She locked eyes with Ganzer. "Where's Shen?"

He shook his head, misery on his face. "I don't know. You were all I could find once the angels fired."

She ran toward home. Ganzer caught her and wrapped her in his big arms. He wrestled her back into the doorway. "You'll get yourself killed!" he yelled as she fought him. "The angels are on a rampage. They're killing everything in the streets!"

She screamed, kicking and thrashing like a willow in a tempest, trying to get away so she could find her brother.

ORIANA STOOD behind Mason in their living room, holding onto his arm as they watched the news. ". . . once again, the name of the CPC soldier murdered by Meso sniper fire is . . ."

"It's happening again," Oriana said, voice tight.

Mason had trouble pulling his attention from the news, as

though the images flickering across the data screen were a twister pulling everything into it. His wife needed him. He pulled his attention out of the news. "This isn't like Xinchin. This is . . . unrest. It's not an attack."

"You heard the headline. They murdered a CPC trooper. The report said he was *eighteen*!" Oriana said as she gnawed at the skin around her fingernails. "Those beasts!" She leaned her head against his arm, her face wet with tears.

Words scrolled past the CPC trooper's picture. Eighteen. He was a kid. To raise a child, to pour years of your life into them, to love them with a depth you never thought yourself capable of, to see them grow into an adult, and then bury them. Had the universe devised a greater pain?

". . . one more CPC soldier is confirmed dead and eight injured after Mesos launched an attack . . ." Images flashed over the screen: an armed Meso mob massed outside a military checkpoint, a squad of CPC holding ranks against an advancing tide of protesters, an armoured personnel transport engulfed in flames.

"We give them everything!" Oriana said, crossing her arms. "We give them the Hab, we give them a treaty—everything we give them emboldens them."

". . . according to reports from the angel network, the Meso uprising is widespread and coordinated . . ."

The angel network. "I feel sick," he said, taking a seat on their couch.

". . . if you live in any of the districts listed on your screen, you are advised to stay inside. Seek cover. The CPC is in your area . . ."

Oriana gasped. "I can't . . . I just . . ."

". . . we're being told the Free New Mesopotamian Army is still in Neu. We repeat, Free New Mesopotamia has not yet crossed . . ."

"I'm going to put Daxton to bed," Oriana said, choking back tears as she left the room.

"... stay tuned. In half an hour, we'll present a special report on the lives of the CPC soldiers who died protecting Caelum today..."

Mason sat, eyes transfixed on the data stream, watching images of burning buildings and CPC desperately defending neighbourhoods from mobs of attacking Mesos.

SHEN RAN down the hall to his apartment door, his feet beating a tattoo on the rotten floor. Maybe Ashme and Ganzer and Hamilcar were there. Shen had lost them when the angels attacked. *Head home if we get separated.* That was what Ashme always said.

He opened the biometric lock with his fingerprint and swung the door open. The apartment was empty. "Aunty Melammu?"

The noise outside, the screaming, oh, the screaming, the angels shooting—it was horrible, like a saw in his head. He covered his ears, but he could feel the sound in his bones. No music in it, no beauty.

Maybe Aunty was in her room. He searched, finding her by the kitchen window, lying on the ground. He crouched beside her; she reached toward him with a shaking hand. Something was wrong with her face. The side away from him sagged like someone had painted a portrait and then smeared all the paint down. "Aunty, what's wrong? Are you hurt?" She worked her mouth but only made strange grunting sounds. She began coughing, choking. She worked to swallow. "I'm going to go find Ashme to help," Shen said.

Melammu's gnarled hand grabbed his wrist. Half her face looked terrified. The other half sagged. He tried to pry her fingers off without hurting her—her hands hurt something fierce, she had told him so. "Don't be afraid. I'll be back."

Her grip tightened.

"Aunty, you're hurting my arm." Her head lolled from one

side to the other. His voice rose an octave. "I don't know what to do!"

A voice from the doorway, filled with jazzed energy, said, "Guess what I did while all you were moping and pissing about?" It was Sura. "Where'd you all go?"

Shen popped his head over the table and called to her. She stabbed her thumb over her shoulder. "Why'd you leave the door open, Numbnuts? Shit's going to hell out there."

"It's Aunty Melammu. I need help."

Sura came around and swore when she saw the old woman on the floor. She crouched beside her. "Aw, Melammu," she said. "You are righteously fucked." She looked at Shen. "Where's Ashme?"

Shen told her what had happened. Sura cut him off before his story got going. "Look," Sura said, "this is real shitty and all, but this district is too hot right now. I'm cutting out. There's money to be made, and I'll need a system raider to make it, so tell Ashme to ping me when she gets back. She wasn't shot, was she?"

Oh, no! He hadn't even thought about that. It felt like a boulder was squashing his chest.

Aunty Melammu moaned. She moved Shen's arm toward Sura. Shen didn't understand what was happening, but Sura looked at Melammu with a shocked expression. "What? No, I'm not his babysitter."

Melammu shook Shen's arm at Sura. Her other arm lay inert on the floor.

"No way I'm taking him. I've gotta be fast and sly to get out of this district. I can't have Numbnuts stumbling around behind me."

The sun was setting, casting a shadow across Aunty Melammu's face. Her head lolled, a croaking gargle coming out of her mouth. Why was she making such strange sounds? Her good eye fluttered like she was falling asleep while her grip on his arm weakened.

"That said," Sura said, "I do need a system raider to stay competitive. The best way to reconnect with Ashme will be to take her anchor with me."

Sura pulled Shen to his feet and turned him toward the door. Her face changed to happy excitement. "Hey, Shen, I'm going to take you to my place. Won't that be fun?"

"But, Ashme—"

"Ashme's going to come back here, and Aunty Melammu's going to tell her I took you to my place, and then Ashme's going to meet up with us. Fun, right?"

"But Aunty Melammu's sick."

"She's tired. Been a long day and all. Your aunty wanted you to come with me." It did seem like Aunty Melammu was pushing Shen's arm toward Sura. "Say goodbye to your aunty," she said as she rummaged through the kitchen drawers until she found a pen.

Shen turned to the prone body of Aunty Melammu. Her good eye was falling asleep. The arm she had grabbed Shen with was still in the air. It waved weakly before settling on her chest. He waved back.

Sura wrote something on a package of crackers that she placed on the floor by Melammu. "Come on," she said, grabbing his arm and leading him out.

This felt like a forever goodbye, like the ones with Mom and Dad. Everybody kept leaving, creating holes in his heart. Soon, he would have no heart left. There was no screaming, however, unlike Mom and Dad's goodbye. Aunty was even sleeping.

Deep inside his chest, a burning, sharp pain throbbed, but she was so peaceful. "Bye-bye, Aunty Melammu. Sleep tight."

CHAPTER 33

LITTLE TRACEY PASSED Mason a coloured block. He thanked her, took it, and placed it on the side table. She returned to the pile of blocks on the clinic's waiting room floor, picked up another one, ambled back, and handed it to him. He thanked her again, took it, and placed it on the table. She returned to the pile.

The waiting room's data screen showed the news. It was inescapable. Mason tried to ignore it as he waited for Daxton's treatment to finish, but his eyes kept drifting to the screen, reading the subtitles flashing along the bottom. ". . . Mesos purposefully put children and elderly in harm's way to gain sympathy from . . ."

In the sixteen hours since the start of the Uprising—which was what all the news outlets were calling it—Meso attacks had injured a further twenty CPC troopers. No new deaths other than the first two from last night. In twenty minutes, the station planned to run another documentary of the lives of the two soldiers killed. In the meantime, the question on every commentator's lips was, 'When will Baltu attack?'

". . . angels responding to a CPC station under Meso attack . . ."

The news showed an image of New Uruk, highlighting in red

sectors where angels were suppressing hotbeds of Meso resistance. Half the city was red. New Uruk was under siege.

That was *if* the reports from the angel network were accurate. The images on the news were terrifying—this was happening in neighbourhoods he knew. Avalyn, however, controlled the angel network, and Avalyn wanted war.

". . . large bands of brave Ostarrichi have risen up to defend their city . . ."

Tracey gave him another block. He thanked her and took it. Oriana entered the waiting room, softly walking on the pads of her feet, a cup of coffee in each hand. She passed him one and sat on the couch, snuggling beside him.

No longer did Mason want to carry his doubts alone. He put an arm around her. She stared at the data screen, a furrow etched in her brow. "It's not as bad as they're saying," he said.

Oriana's head cocked. "Oh? Do you know something?"

Careful. "I have access to the most up-to-date intelligence on Meso activity from the Network itself. No group in New Uruk could coordinate an attack of this scale."

"Baltu's tricky," Oriana said. "He's always finding a way to stab at us. Besides," she pointed at the news screen, ragged hangnails tipping her fingers from where she had chewed them, "how could you make a lie this big?"

No one needed to "make" a lie this big. This was what Ostarrichi believed. There was no need for Avalyn to coordinate a media cover-up because everyone, reporters included, had always thought they were under a constant state of Meso attack. Let the word "uprising" slip out in conversation, and it became the truth. Confirmation from the angel network solidified that reality.

That was the clue that something was off. The Network was the surveillance system. Reports of Meso attacks should be coming from the Network, but the news only spoke of reports from the angels.

Mason breathed deeply. "I see things in my job. There are people—powerful people—who want war with Mesos."

"Good."

"How can you say that?" Mason raised his coffee toward the news. "This is what you get with war."

"Mesos bombed my school," she said. Mason disliked who Oriana became when she talked about that day. There was poison in her voice. "I lost two friends and a teacher. We were *kids*. They bombed a *school*. Push the Mesos out of Caelum, defeat them once and for all. I'll die before I let our children know the fear I felt that day."

"I know," Mason said. "That's why I fought so hard to work with Avalyn."

If Oriana caught the sad irony in his voice, she made no indication. She squeezed his thigh and said, "Avalyn's always kept us safe. I'm proud of the work you do."

CHAPTER 34

A STILLNESS CHOKED the street like the silence that grips the forest when a hawk's cry rings out. Ashme cast her senses into the nanohaze.

"Is it safe?" Ganzer asked.

"Clear," she said.

She, Ganzer, and about a dozen other Mesos, some wounded, were in a diner about a block away from the apartment. A single beam of morning light, shining through a broken window, lit the restaurant. Tables filled the room, some knocked over. The air smelled of smoke.

Ganzer opened the door softly, slowly, and peered out. Blocks away, the crackle of gunfire echoed. A mob of goldies had invaded the district during the night, but their shouts were distant, blocks away. "No angels in sight," Ganzer said.

She had been awake all night and suffered from the drain of launching programs to keep her and Ganzer safe. Her body was fatigued from the constant adrenalin rush of running and hiding for her life. Yet that fear had kept her awake, kept her limbs quivering with agitated frenzy. This mix of exhaustion and tremulous energy left her nervous system ravaged.

She and Ganzer readied themselves to exit onto the street. A handful of other men and women joined them, ready to do the same. A woman on the ground, her leg wrapped in bloody cloth, hissed at them angrily. "Don't be idiots," she said in a harsh whisper. "You'll lead them to us." Someone shushed her.

Though neither Ashme nor Ganzer had discussed their plan, they were of one mind. They were going home. That was where Melammu was. That was where Shen would go if he could find his way. They had tried pinging them, but the Network was jamming all communications.

Ashme nodded to Ganzer. They exited to the street. Others came behind, scattering silently to their own destinations. The two cousins stuck close to the buildings lining the street, peering around corners before darting across intersections and alleys.

Bloodied bodies lay scattered on the road. A lazy smoke hung over the street, blurring the edges of buildings. It was unnerving how easy Ashme found it to let the corpses fade into the background. They were unreal things, lifeless, no more animate than garbage littering the sidewalk. Her brain was too eager to categorize them as scenery and ignore them so long as she avoided looking at their faces. Hamilcar's body would be here somewhere. Best to keep eyes on the apartment building or on the sky, scanning for angels.

As they drew closer to their apartment, the sounds of an angry crowd grew. Ashme was sure they were goldies. The staccato of angel gunfire still echoed, boldly announcing the fate of any Meso caught outside. The mob she heard, therefore, had to be goldies, here to vent their anger on Mesos and their property, escorted by squads of CPC and angels.

They made it to their building. The sign over the front door, "The Agade Gardens," hung as it always had, the G missing, though a tracery of it in the grime showed where it belonged. Inside, packed along the halls, Mesos took refuge.

Silence greeted them when they opened the door to their apartment. Both called out to Shen and Melammu. Stillness replied.

Ashme found Melammu's body. It looked like a figure made of wax. Her cry brought Ganzer, and he bellowed in rage.

Where was Shen? Ashme tore through the apartment, screaming his name. She had been sure he would be here. She searched again. She tried pinging him, but the Network still let no communications through. She launched a program to punch through the block, fighting off a wave of light-headedness from the drain, but the Network was overwhelming.

She dropped to her knees by Ganzer, who was cradling Melammu's body in his arms. His body shook with fury.

"Shen's not here," she said. His breath came in grunts. "Ganzer?" She touched his arm softly.

With a roar, he upended the couch and smashed the kitchen table into the counter. Ashme jumped to the corner of the room, screaming as Ganzer took a kitchen chair and flung it into the wall, breaking it and caving in the drywall. He hurled one of his giant dumbbells through the wall of the bathroom to the sound of splintering wood and shattering tiles. He stormed for the door.

Was he going to run out into the street? Fight an angel in his rage, attack the Ostarrichi mobs? Ashme blocked his path, yelling for him to stop. He barreled ahead, blind to everything but his wrath. She jumped onto him. He peeled her off and tossed her aside. Scrambling to her feet, she hopped on his back. She begged for him to stop, arms and legs wrapped around him as he walked through the door into the hall. "Please don't leave me! I need you!"

Halfway to the elevator, his brain processed her words. He stopped.

"Stay with me. Stay with me."

He fell to his knees, body shaking, breath coming in ragged gasps. He struggled to talk but had no control of his voice. She held him, arms wrapped around his neck and chest.

"We can't leave Grandma here," he said, voice broken.

"What do we do? Shen's not here. I have to find him." She

heard yells from the street below, screams within the building answering them.

"I don't know," Ganzer said. "We can't leave Grandma like this. I don't know where Shen is. If he's not here, where would he be?"

"If he's not here, he'd be lost." She quickly censored the addendum *if he's alive.*

More screams and shouting sounded, muffled through the walls and floor.

"We should stay here. Shen knows some landmarks, and you've taught him songs to find his way home," Ganzer said. "He'll make his way here."

"Yeah, you should stay here if Shen comes back. You can look after Aunt Melammu's . . . I'm going to go looking for him."

"You'll get killed on the streets. You need to stay here."

"I'm going to look for Shen."

"You're not going on the streets alone."

Ashme's nose itched. "You smell that?"

Ganzer hung his head. "It's smoke."

Ashme went back to the apartment to look out the window. "We've got to go," she said.

"Goldies on the street?" Ganzer asked.

"Yeah. And the building's on fire." Many of the buildings on the street were burning. A crowd of Ostarrichi was throwing flaming bottles through windows all along the block, angels hovering above them.

The angels had massacred Mesos, yet the goldies somehow found a reason to get enraged at the Mesos for it. Typical. The Ostarrichi wanted all Mesos dead. The mobs below were proof. What a murderous, bloodthirsty people.

Ganzer joined her at the window as a group of Mesos ran out of her building. The angels' weapons ground to life, shooting most of the runners. A couple of Mesos managed to skirt away, but the Ostarrichi descended on them like a pack of jackals, kicking them down and beating them.

"They're going to burn us alive and kill anyone trying to make a break for it," Ganzer said.

"We've got to try and escape."

"Let's say farewell to Grandma."

Ganzer tried to straighten Melammu, but her body was stiff. Ashme got an afghan from the couch and laid it over her. She whispered thanks in her great-aunt's ear for looking after her and Shen. Melammu had been Ashme's rock after Mom died. She wanted to grieve her passing, but Shen was missing.

"Hey, what's this?" Ashme asked, pointing at a box of crackers with writing on its side.

Ganzer picked it up and grunted. "Sura was here." He turned the writing so Ashme could see. "She's got Shen."

Hope blossomed. "We've got to get him."

"Gotta get out of this district in one piece first." The two cousins ran into the hallway, leaving their home and Melammu behind.

THE FIRE IN THE BUILDING, combined with the mob and angels at street level, forced the cousins to the roof. Ashme got Ganzer's attention and pointed. A crowd of residents gathered at the back edge of the roof, away from the street with the Ostarrichi mob. The roof of a neighbouring building was a narrow alley away and about a two-story drop. The residents of that building were piling mattresses and pillows to make a landing pad.

Someone whisked by Ashme and leaped off the ledge. He drifted in the air a moment, arms windmilling, and then landed on the growing mattress pile on the adjacent building. A woman jumped next. She was either weaker, or she hesitated on the jump because she fell short of the ledge, slamming instead into the wall with a thump before tumbling down, arms scrabbling for a non-existent ladder, screaming. She landed on the street with a crack Ashme could hear despite the thirty-seven stories separating them.

The screech of an angel's gun roared. Ashme ducked. Bodies tore asunder. People ran, some jumping to the next building, though no one had a chance for a running start. A few made it, but many plummeted to the street to join the first woman.

Ashme sensed the angel in the nanohaze and launched a massive attack program. The drain drove her to the ground. The program swarmed the angel, its siren fluttering before it dropped from the sky.

Ashme gasped for breath. The skin all over her body felt like a road rash. Ganzer enveloped her in his arms, pulling her to her feet. "The angels know we're here," he said as he backed them up to take a run at the ledge.

She needed no further prompting. She sprinted for the ledge, remembering what she had learned from the first woman. No hesitation—go full out, drive. Foot on the ledge. She had to throw her entire body off the building with everything she had. Weightlessness. The wind whipped her hair as she soared through the distance between the two buildings. Gravity pulled her. The roof of the neighbouring building rose up fast. She crashed into the mattress pile. Ganzer slammed into it beside her. Her body wanted to rest, but hands grabbed her and pulled her off as others made the leap behind her.

She pulled Ganzer over. "We're going to have to try our luck at street level sometime."

Ganzer looked over the ledge. "Most of the Ostarrichi seem to be on the north side of—"

A short buzz followed by a loud crack made both cousins jump. A young man in his twenties helping to pull people off the mattress pile collapsed, blood pouring out of a hole in his back. People screamed and ran.

Ashme and Ganzer crouched behind the ledge. "Angels?" Ganzer asked.

Ashme cast her senses into the nanohaze. "No. Sniper." With

another buzz and crack, a bullet tore through the body of a woman running for cover behind an HVAC.

CPC snipers tracked Meso's ID tags. She launched an EM shield to scramble any tracking sensors. She was suffering a critical amount of drain from the last day of running and fighting for her life. Though the EM shield was a small program, she struggled to stay conscious. Shaking her vision clear, she grabbed Ganzer's hand. "Stay close." She pulled him to the door leading into the building's interior. Her legs rebelled, and she stumbled.

Ganzer gathered her in an arm and carried her through the doorway. When they were inside and down a flight of stairs, he leaned her against a wall. "You okay?"

"Yeah," she said. Her vision spun, and she had to hold onto Ganzer. The stairwell smelled of piss, making her nauseous. "I don't think I can . . ." Did she finish her thought? She might have blacked out.

Up through the stairwell, the smell of smoke wafted. "They're burning this building, too," Ganzer said. He had her arm slung around his neck as he carried her down the stairs. She *had* blacked out.

On the ground floor, he led her through a hall. Four Ostarrichi stopped them. Two of them had long, thick sticks they were wielding as clubs; one had a knife, and the other a crowbar.

Ganzer dropped Ashme. He slapped his hand on the wall with a loud crack. "Come on, you piss babies!" he yelled and charged.

Ashme struggled to stand, to be of some help, but her head swam. She heard the smacking sound of a fist hitting a face, followed by the thud of a body slamming into a wall. The world spun.

Ganzer knelt beside her, his knuckles and face bruised and bloody. "Did I pass out?" she asked.

Ganzer smiled through cracked and bleeding lips. "Not like you're much use in a fight, anyway."

The smell of smoke was stronger, bringing tears to her eyes. Was her vision blurry, or was a haze of smoke filling the hall? He pulled her to her feet and helped her over the unconscious bodies of the four golden-skinned Ostarrichi. On the street, they could see small groups of goldies—people who had peeled off from the main mob to start their own trouble.

"Can you run?" Ganzer asked.

"Guess I'll have to."

They bolted, darting through narrow laneways away from their burning home. Ashme heard goldies yelling and the sound of footsteps running behind them.

CHAPTER 35

THE SLIGHT SCENT of smoke tickled Mason's nose as the CPC trooper reviewed his credentials. The smell hung over the entire district. "You're here to gather intelligence for Avalyn's office?" the soldier asked.

"Yes," which was kind of a lie. It could be true, in that visiting a military post while their city was under siege was the type of thing a Kanu analyst might do, but it was a lie in that no one had asked him to do it. He wanted to see what was happening in the Meso districts of New Uruk for himself.

"Somebody from the Director-General's office is scheduled to visit today, too," the soldier said, leading him through the ground level of a grubby, run-down office building the CPC had taken over in the Atu district.

Mason straightened the lapel of his dark navy suit. There was nothing wrong with analysts from different offices crossing paths. Still, probably best to be gone before anyone else from the *Aigle* arrived. "Your post is popular," he said.

"We're one of the most forward posts subduing the Uprising." He led Mason into an elevator and hit the button for the top floor. "Lots of action. We've got a squad right now protecting a group of our people protesting nearby."

Over the last day, Ostarrichi demonstrators had begun protesting in Meso districts that the CPC had contained. They had set buildings on fire, started street brawls with Mesos, that sort of thing. "Any casualties?"

"Three downed angels and an unarmed citizen injured so far."

They got off near the top floor into an open office complex. The setup reminded him of the control centres in which he had worked when in the CPC. Groups of soldiers prepped gear or huddled around monitors while officers looked out the windows through binoculars. Crisp, terse conversations snapped through the air.

Mason's guide took him to a small group, two men and a woman, huddled around a data screen. The woman and man were both privates operating control pads. The second man, a sergeant, hung back, arms crossed, eyes intent on the data screen. Mason's guide handed him off to the sergeant.

"What have we got here?" Mason asked.

"Sniper ops," the sergeant replied. The camera angle of the images on the data screen was taken from above—satellite images. They showed several Mesos sitting against the wall of an alley behind a dumpster. "They attacked a nearby Ostarrichi demonstration. We've been hunting these guys for a while."

On the screen, a highlight encircled each Meso flagged with an "ID unknown" icon. "What's with their ID tags?"

"One of them's an indigo child with an EM shield that's fuzzing our ability to lock targeting systems."

Mason looked closer at the figures on the screen. They looked young, teenagers maybe, dressed in civilian clothes. He saw no visible weaponry, and with the EM shield blocking sensors, the Network detected nothing. Was Shen in with them? Ashme? "These are soldiers?"

"All Mesos are soldiers," the sergeant said with the subtle condescension field operatives had when talking to a suit from the government. "It's a warrior culture. They attack from housing units and schools, then cry misery when civilians get injured."

A red light flashed around one of the figures on the screen. "The Network's burned the EM shield. Target acquired," the woman said.

"Clear to fire," the sergeant said.

"Clear to fire," she repeated. She pressed a button; then they stared at the screen. One Meso figure peeked around the dumpster. How far away was the sniper platform?

A plume of smoke puffed from the ground as one of the figures dropped. The other people scattered. The privates manning the sniper controls cheered.

"Keep eyes on the main body of hostiles," the sergeant ordered.

With the EM shield breached, the Network displayed the stats of the target hit by the sniper platform. The soldiers were busy keeping the satellite's eyes on the others, but Mason read the data scrolling up on the side of the data screen. Name, Damu me'neh Oustun, age seventeen. He looked at the others running. With their EM shield burned, the Network flagged their weapons: a knife and a pair of shock gloves.

"What kind of armament do the Meso rebels have?" he asked the sergeant.

"They're irregulars," which was CPC jargon for malcontents with stones, concrete-filled bottles, and the odd Molotov cocktail. This was the "uprising." It was Utukagaba all over again. His chest constricted as the one memory he wished he'd never had ignited in his consciousness.

EVERY BLOODY WEEK, the Kanu of Utukagaba banded together and marched on the outpost's water supply. They were irregulars with no weapons other than stones. Every week, they marched, and every week, the CPC flung them back with tear-gas, stun rods, and stun rounds.

Mason had been on the line lobbing shock-webs and stun grenades to disperse the rabid pack of Mesos attacking, as he had the prior week and as he would the following week. At that time, his sleep was plagued by nightmares of Myla's death. The image of a bomb shredding her played in his mind—a sand castle kicked over, again, again, again. Did one of these Kanu have a bomb? In the madness, it would be easy for them to sneak in close to the lines under an EM shield. *All we have is crowd-suppressing gear; Kanu could have guns, grenades, blackouts, any number of weapons hiding in that throng.*

The Kanu attacking their position had finally given up for the day. A sergeant shouted Mason and the other CPC into their transport. They had orders to redeploy. Some of the town's teens were on a hill throwing stones at another CPC position, and Mason's squad was to help pacify them. Once in the transport, a soldier beside Mason looked out the rear viewport. "The fuckers are regrouping and charging." Stones thudded off the armoured shell of the vehicle.

You should have blocked the hit with your balls. You're not using them anyway.

Enough! He had been terrified of these animals for months. Myla kept dying in his head. He swung open the back hatch. A boy, maybe fifteen or sixteen, was leading the Kanu pack no more than ten metres away. He flung a stone. It bounced off the transport above Mason's head. Mason fired a stun grenade right into that kid's face. A click on the trigger, whump of ignition, kick of recoil, a trail of smoke streaking right into that raging face that spewed hate and filth.

There was a crack—a sound like chicken bones snapping. The kid's head whipped back, flinging him off his feet, followed by the searing pop of the stun grenade's detonation. Hours later, after the Kanu had retreated to their village, Mason learned the boy had died. His name was Hadu.

He had never been more popular in his squad than in the days after he killed Hadu. His CO made him take some bullshit refresher course on the proper deployment of stun grenades, but he was given the coveted post of Watch Master for the month. He accepted the praise with cool bravado, but now, the image of Hadu's head snapping back to the sound of cracking bones added itself to his nightmares.

YOU COME *at us with guns, grenades, and angels at your back while we have only rocks. You tell me which of us is stronger.* Those words echoed in his mind, the chorus to an angry requiem. They stabbed him in the gut as the soldiers at the sniper station cheered again. Another Meso dead. Of what was he a part? Was this the society in which he wanted Tracey and Daxton to grow up?

He owed Caelum his allegiance—it had given him his son back, giving Daxton a life that nature had taken. A father must protect the lives of his children. A father, however, must also create a world worthy of them. *Is this who we must be to keep our families safe and our society strong?* He wanted Caelum to be a just society, one that he could be proud to have his children join.

What could he do? He knew Avalyn used the BLOQ to take control of the angel network. He could bring this information to security services. They were loyal to Avalyn, though, so that was as likely to see him in jail or dead.

If he succeeded in stopping Avalyn, what would Oriana think? The Kanu were the enemy—Avalyn, a hero. How could he make her see that her fears were built on smoke?

Her fears, however, were not built on smoke, were they? Free New Mesopotamia had bombed her school—a school! The Kanu were dangerous. Maybe Avalyn was doing the right thing. Caelum was surrounded by enemies and had suffered so many sneak attacks and wars over its short history. Perhaps this was how Ostarrichi needed to protect themselves. The Kanu made it an us-or-them fight seventy years ago at the Bit Durani Massacre. *Is it wrong to choose* us?

Mason closed his eyes to shut out the data screen's images of the ongoing sniper hunt. Once they reached adulthood, Tracey and Daxton would both be called to serve their tour in the CPC. He imagined them as a young woman and man, huddled around a monitor, cheering as they murdered teenagers.

A stir passed over the room as a short, portly woman wearing a dowdy navy business suit entered. Mason recognized her: Meli. She worked for the Director-General in the same capacity he worked for Avalyn. He had collaborated with her on several reports.

Avalyn and the Director-General had been political enemies for a long time. Whereas many in the security service might be loyal to Avalyn, no one in the Director-General's office would.

Mason excused himself from the soldiers at the sniper station and intercepted Meli. "Mason," Meli said, "I didn't expect to see you here. Are you checking out your handiwork?" There was a knife blade of accusation in her voice.

Now he was face to face with her, he had no idea what to say. He was at the heart of a CPC operation. Whatever he said would make it to Avalyn. He grabbed Meli's arm in a friendly embrace. "I've got to run, but let's meet for lunch later this week to compare notes on the Kanu Uprising."

"Are you serious?" she asked, moving toward the officer waiting for her. "You don't think it's a bit disingenuous to ask us to share notes on the revolt *your* people started?"

"Please." Mason tightened his grip. Her expression changed from dismissal to confusion. He looked to the waiting officer, and then back to Meli. "I'm working on something for Avalyn, and she'll bust me down to cleaning toilets if I don't come up with something good." He tightened his grip a little more and focused all his desperation in his eyes. "I need your help."

MASON EYED the clock on the wall. He was going to be late for his meeting with Avalyn unless this line moved, which would, in turn, prompt questions about where he had been. Usually the security for employees to get into the *Aigle* was quick, but the automated scanners were taking longer than usual to clear staff. He tried pinging Meli from the Director-General's office but got another *unavailable* reply. He set Dashiell to the task of coordinating with Meli's AI to set up a meeting as soon as possible.

It was his turn at the scanner. He stepped into a large metal gateway, placed his feet in the spots denoted by a white outline, and waited for the all-clear. What was it looking for that was taking so long? He shook his head in frustration.

Green-lighted, he raced to Avalyn's office, arriving on time if out of breath. She and Shanelle were reviewing files at her hardwood desk. Avalyn glanced at him briefly. "Good, you're here. What did you learn at the CPC outpost?"

Avalyn had found out he had been there. Shanelle was watching him, her icy blue eyes unnerving. "The Mesos are getting slaughtered." That came out too angry.

Avalyn looked up, her eyes spearing him. "Oh?" The word hung in the air. "How do you think the Uprising will evolve once the CPC reassert control over the Meso districts?"

"Uprising?"

Avalyn came in front of her desk and then leaned on it, arms crossed. "You're a smart man, Mason. I'm not a politician—I work for a living. I don't like diplomatic doubletalk, so why don't you give me your honest appraisal."

Was this a trap? Careful. "There is no Uprising," Mason said, "or at least nothing worthy of the word. The Meso population is largely unarmed. There is no meaningful coordination of Meso resistance. The Network effectively tracks and monitors them, allowing our forces to strike with precision, inflicting maximum damage with minimal danger." Sadness welled in him, catching him by surprise.

Avalyn grunted, exchanged a look with Shanelle, and then moved to a window overlooking the gardens of the *Aigle's* courtyard. "I've concluded the same. Will Baltu lead Free New Mesopotamia to defend the Mesos?"

Mason's eyes narrowed, an eagle getting the lay of the land. Grinding Mesos down was bait, Baltu the catch. "No. He's not going to attack."

"Mesos—his people—are being crushed, yet he does nothing," Avalyn said. "He just sits in his fortress across the border in Neu."

"If other Kanu nations attacked, he'd join, but no one is going to risk war with us over this. Baltu knows he wouldn't have a chance if he attacked alone. The Network has Caelum locked down too tight."

Shanelle stood, feet planted shoulder-width, arms crossed. "The Network is an impenetrable wall; I've told you as much."

Avalyn looked at her thoughtfully.

"If you want Baltu," Mason said, "you need to drop soldiers into Neu and take him out there. Or an aerial strike. If you got the job done quickly, without collateral damage, the government of Neu would bluster, but they wouldn't declare war for Baltu. Those are the types of operations you did in the old days."

Avalyn smiled a wide, gracious smile as she sat behind the desk. "Those were simpler times, Mason." The leather of her chair scrunched as she leaned back. "Good days. Ostarrichi were united then. The Director-General has divided us." She made a dismissive grunt. "He's a weak man, cowardly. He'd rather appease the surrounding Kanu nations than defend our people. Even if we rid ourselves of every Meso in Caelum, the Free New Mesopotamian Army will never leave us in peace. We either need a new Director-General, or we need to lure Baltu into Caelum, where we can strike."

"Or both," Shanelle said. Her tone chilled Mason.

Avalyn nodded. "Or both."

CHAPTER 36

ASHME'S first sensation as she awoke was the gnawing pang of hunger. Her second was confusion. The air was filled with the quiet murmuring of gentle conversations, with the meditative hymn of throat singers in the background. The last thing she remembered was running for her life. Were the goldies right in their belief in an afterlife? Was this it?

She opened her eyes. Ganzer sat beside her on the floor, his face a collage of bruises. He noticed she was awake. "You snore. Sounds like an old man farting with each breath. Here." He rummaged through bags on the floor in front of him. "I knew you'd be bitching about how hungry you were, so I scrounged some food." He handed her three chocolate bars and a bag of fried gluten chips. "It's not much, but hopefully, it'll put a dent in your appetite."

She sat up and tore into one of the chocolate bars, looking around as she did. They were in the orthostat. It was packed with people lying or sitting on the ground, Hierophants in their navy trousers and knee-length tunics handing out blankets, administering first aid, or leading groups in meditation. "I've never seen the orthostat so crowded."

"Ostarrichi are scared of anything to do with the Sentient. The orthostat's a great place to get a bit of peace."

She finished the first chocolate bar. "How's your face?"

"Handsome."

"You ain't looked in a mirror lately." She tore open her second bar. "Or ever."

He chuckled, then winced when a crack in his lip split. He sighed, then looked around at the bottom portion of the orthostat visible in the building's centre, a haunted look hanging on his face.

She had been a bitch to her mother and hardly any better to Melammu. She had been an angry teenager when Shen and she moved in with their great-aunt. Ashme had been fifteen when Baltu and Free New Mesopotamia signed the Ahiim X59 treaty. Peace. She remembered running into the living room, hoping to be the first one to break the news to Dad. It had been afternoon, but he had drawn the curtains, bathing the room in shadow. It stank of stale beer—it had never smelled like that when he was away in Xinchin.

She remembered seeing him slumped in his chair, a moat of empty bottles at his feet, watching the announcement on a data feed. He glowered at the news with dark eyes as he drank. Why was he unhappy? Getting this treaty was what he fought for in Xinchin.

A resonant belch escaped his throat. Ashme had backed away, careful. When Dad was like this, he would look for any reason to rage and hit. She took Shen to visit Melammu and Ganzer that afternoon. When they had come home later that night, Dad had drunk himself into a stupor.

He slept until the middle of the next morning. Ashme had been alone when he shambled into the kitchen. She froze while the rhythmic thump of Shen's drums sounded from his room. Dad could go either way when he was hung over, either quick to anger or plagued with guilt, seeking forgiveness.

He sat himself down across from Ashme. *Don't breathe. Don't crunch on the toast in your mouth. Was the coffee hot?* His hair was a mess, his eyes bleary and bloodshot. Should she offer him water? Speaking could set him off. Saying nothing could set him off. Her stomach ached as she waited.

"I've not been the father you deserve, Ashme." She relaxed and finished chewing her toast. "You're a beautiful girl, and you deserve better. You and Shenshen both."

She remembered asking over her mouthful of toast, "You want some water?"

An hour later, he blew his brains out.

She remembered Mom screaming. Melammu and Ganzer had come over. Melammu got Mom settled while Ganzer sat with Ashme and Shen in the backyard, holding them both, his arms a fortress against the world. Shen cried. Ashme sat in shock, leaning on Ganzer's shoulder.

Melammu and Ganzer had been her rock that day, solid points of refuge when everything else shattered. What a burden her great-aunt took on, assuming responsibility for a couple of teenagers, one wild, the other with special needs. Melammu never deserved the grief Ashme gave her. She owed so much to people she could never thank.

Ashme watched a Hierophant distributing bottles of water. "I never understood why you want to be a Hierophant," she said to Ganzer as she started working on her third chocolate bar.

"You don't think a hothead like me is Hierophant material."

"No. Well, yeah, that, but also, you've never seemed all that spiritual."

He shrugged and looked at her with his beat-up face. "I want to be. The idea of the Deep, that everything we see in existence is ripples in quantum fields? I like that. Waves on the ocean. You, me, we are all waves on the ocean. Some pattern of events brings a wave to the surface, it rolls along, sees the world, and when it's spent, it flows back into the Deep. There's comfort in that, you know? No matter how stormy, how violently the waves crash, there's this abyss, this immensity beneath us that we are a part of that's so much greater. There are these depths untouched by all the rage on the surface. We rise from the Deep. We live, we love, and then we flow back to the Deep, all of us, you, me, the Ostarrichi, the sun, planets, everything."

"Don't go soft on me, Ganzer," she said, finishing her last chocolate bar. "Thinking existence is an ocean is fine and all, but we're stuck here for now. We need to fight for what's ours to keep our head above the surface."

"It seems to me the world has enough assholes willing to fight and die for a cause." With his hand, he pulled his head to the side to stretch his neck. "Back in the day, some dick made a map, drew some lines on it, and called it New Mesopotamia. Later, another dick called it Caelum. Then a bunch of dicks decided to murder each other over it. You think risking death to spill Ostarrichi blood is some noble calling, that being able to scratch the name Caelum out and write New Mesopotamia above it is more important than the lives taken."

"I'm not fighting for a stupid name. This is our home. I'm fighting those who have their boot on our necks. This is a war they started."

"We had a peace treaty."

"Their angels murder us, and the goldies love it."

"How much of our family is dead because of this country?" Ganzer asked. "We've lost so much fighting for it."

"So, we should roll over and let the Ostarrichi grind us to dust? We need to show them we're not weak, that we have power."

"My temper's been getting me into scraps my whole life, and if that's taught me anything, it's that violence isn't power. Violence is all that's left when you've got no power."

Ashme shrugged. "You say that, but it feels like they've got power when they grab my crotch at the checkpoints."

Ganzer shook his head. "What we're doing isn't working. It's burning everything down around us. I don't know how to fix it. I don't know what the right thing is, but I'm not going to do more of the wrong thing. I will help you get Shen from Sura's, and then we're all leaving. I'm getting my family out of Caelum."

"We've got to get Shen." Ashme agreed with that much. "Sura ain't known for her babysitting skills."

CHAPTER 37

SHEN HAD YET to figure out how to make Sura happy. He had tried singing, but that made her angry. He even waited until noon to start singing, but still, she snarled and snapped. A lot of things made her angry, and it was hard to know what. Being around her so much made his tummy feel like a twisting spring. The last time he'd felt this was after Dad came back but before he left again. She never yelled like Dad, but she made an angry face, and she would say mean things that made him feel small and worth less than paper crumpled on the sidewalk that people walked past and never picked up.

That noise started again. Sura's apartment had many strange noises. He started looking for its source.

"Leave it," Sura said, sunk into her couch as she played her videogame. Her place had different sounds than home but Shen looking for them made her angry.

"Where does it come from?" It reminded him of a flam accent beat on the drums.

"I don't know!" She was getting angrier. "It's a fan or something. Who gives a shit?"

He did, but the noise was making her angry, and he wanted her to feel good. He also wanted to eat. There was a half-empty box of crackers on her coffee table, but he loathed how crackers felt in his mouth and the sound they made in his head—crunch, crunch, crunch, like someone stomping on glass. "Can we make noodles?"

"Go ahead and make some bloody noodles if you want."

"I need help opening the package."

"Then . . . I'm busy. Why don't you listen to music or something?"

"Oh, I'd love to play some music right now. Maybe some drums. Here, close your eyes and picture this." He closed his eyes. "First, I'd start with a flam accent." He imitated his drum with a *bada-ba-da-da-ba* sound as he mimed the motions with his hands.

"Sweet Zini's stacks!" Sura was really mad now. Why did music make her angry? "I really need you to shut up and sit still until Ashme gets here."

He wished Ashme and Ganzer would get there soon. He had been so scared after he saw Aunty Melammu that all his family were leaving. "Do you think Ashme got your note?"

"Here's hoping."

"When is she going to get here?"

"I don't want to fucking slug you, but if you say another word, I'm going to get up, and I'm going to fucking slug you."

Shen had yet to learn how to make Sura happy. She was like a dog that barked, one who you never knew if it might lunge and bite. Barking dogs scared Shen. He liked puppies that jumped and licked.

He went into the kitchen to make noodles. All the pots on the counter were dirty. Empty food containers and bottles were everywhere. If Aunty Melammu were here, she would make them clean the place right up. Aunty abhorred a mess. A home should be clean, that was what she would say.

He found a clean pot in a cupboard, but it was so heavy. Use two hands, that was what Aunty Melammu said—she had a beautiful voice, a sing-songy voice that the heavens sang through. The package of noodles was where he had seen them earlier—Sura had a big box filled with bags and bags and, *whoa!*, more bags of dried noodles in a cupboard over her counter. She must love noodles.

The tone of an incoming ping sounded from Sura's data screen. "It's about time they got communications up again," she said.

"Is it Ashme? Is she here?"

"What'd I say about talking?"

"I'm sorry, I forgot," Shen said. "But is it Ashme?"

"No. Now shut it, or you'll get a beating. I've got work to do." She answered the ping. "Oh, it's you. You got another job?"

If Ashme was here, she could help him get the noodles ready. It had been hours since he had received her ping. It seemed she should be here by now.

To open the noodles, there was a tiny tab he had to pull, but it was too small for him to grab. He tried tearing the bag open but was unable to get a good grip on the wrapping. Did Sura have scissors? Aunty Melammu, Ashme, and Ganzer, they all said to only use scissors when one of them was helping, though Aunty Melammu couldn't use scissors much better than he could with her bent and swollen knuckles. He wanted to ask Sura for help but did not want to get fucking slugged.

"I'm sorry, you wanna repeat that?" Sura said to the person on the other end.

The scissors were in a drawer by the stove. *Careful, only touch the loopy ends.* He put his two fingers through one loop, thumb through the other.

"Yeah, I don't do suicide missions."

It was hard controlling the opening and closing of the scissors. With both hands, he got the scissors opened and then tried to place the end of the bag between the blades. *Keep your fingers out of the way of the sharp edges.*

"That's impossible. The Network won't let me get close."

The scissors slipped, forcing him to once more reposition the bag and blades.

"My indigo child's making her way over, but I don't know when she'll get here with all of your blockades."

He missed the loose end of the bag with the blades, and *oh no!*, the scissors crunched into the noodles. The noodles were better whole. Ashme could help him if she were here.

"How negotiable is the timeline?"

He pulled at the small cut he had made. The bag blasted open, sending dried noodles scattering across the counter. He gathered the noodles into the pot.

There was that sound again, the flam accent beat. Where was it coming from?

"You're busting my nads here. Are you supplying the bomb?"

It sounded like it was coming from the back of the apartment. Shen went to investigate.

"Well, where the fuck am I supposed to get that much explosives?"

The sound was coming from outside the apartment. There was a window in Sura's bedroom he could look out to find the noise's source.

"What makes you think I can pick up the phone and call Baltu? You know what, never mind. Let's talk price."

This was Shen's first time in Sura's bedroom. Shirts, pants, and underwear were everywhere, and *pee-ew*, it smelled like stale gym clothes. Maybe he could fold her clothes like he did for Aunty Melammu. He picked up a shirt and began.

"You're going to have to do way better than that."

On a chest of drawers stood a stand, and hanging off that stand, a shiny necklace sparkled. It was a twisty number eight. One end of the chain was attached to each end of the eight so it would lay on its side when worn. Words were engraved on it. *You are loved more than you know*, it said on one side. On the other, *Love, Dad*. He wondered if Sura's dad was gone like his was.

"Hey, Numbnuts," Sura called out from the other room.

He returned the necklace. "Yeah?"

"Get the fuck out of my bedroom."

Shen apologized and left.

"My bedroom's private. You get 'private,' right?"

What answer would make her smile? "You want to know if I get 'private'?"

"Stay out of my room."

"Sorry. I was folding your clothes."

"What? That . . . well, that's a good idea," Sura said. "Okay, the first thing I want you to do is clean up the mess you made in my kitchen. Then, you can fold my clothes." Her head cocked in thought, and then her face erupted in a smile. "Hey, Shen."

Was she finally going to like him? "Yes?"

"Do you want to have some fun?"

"Are we going to the Salamu to listen to music?"

"Even better."

His heart thumped like a blast beat on the drums.

She said, "I've got a job lined up. Normally, Ashme would help me with this job, but I don't know if she's going to get here in time with all the CPC." Her smile brightened her face. "But I think I know how you could help me."

This was the nicest Sura had ever been. She finally wanted to be friends. And if this was a job like Ashme would usually do, then maybe he could show his sister he could help them pay rent and buy food. Ashme always worried about that. "I want to help, but I'm not a system raider like Ashme is," he said.

Sura smiled, reached up, and tousled his hair. "Oh, I know that, Numbnuts. All I need is for you to help me deliver a package for a friend. You up for that?"

A warmth filled his chest. "I would love to."

CHAPTER 38

SHEN WAS TIRED—HE had slept poorly. "Why do you think Ashme hasn't come yet?" he asked Sura. They were walking down an unfamiliar, narrow lane. She had given him a suitcase with wheels that he was dragging behind him, and it was heavy and awkward to move.

"Because life's shitty," Sura said. She had been so busy throughout the whole night. People kept visiting to drop things off, but none of them wanted to talk. It had kept him awake. In the morning, however, Sura had played music! Ashme said music in the morning was okay, and this was beautiful music that vibrated through the air like the force of creation. Then, Sura asked him to go for a walk.

"Where are we?" Shen asked.

"What's it to you? Ashme says you can't even find your way in your own neighbourhood."

It was true. He always found himself turned around, but Ashme always helped him find his way. They were twins; they had always been together. He was different from other people; he knew that. Other people were smart; he was not. Other people could look after themselves; he needed help. Other people did things, they had jobs, they fought for what was right, they paid bills, put food on the table; he was left behind, a burden. He was alone. Singular. Or he would have been without Ashme. He had a twin; they lived together, had curled up next to each other in Mommy's belly, they played together, cried together. Because the universe had given him a twin, he would never be alone, never singular. He was out of place without her, a flat note in a major chord.

"Where are we going?" he asked.

Sura smiled, filling Shen with joy. "To a new friend's," she said.

New friends! This was wonderful news. He pulled harder on the suitcase to pick up speed. The last new friend he had made was Hamilcar, and he was great. He had a wicked accent that made the Kanu language sound like a song. Ashme had liked him, and Shen had been the one to introduce them. Shen might not be smart, but he could make friends, and that had brought Ashme and Hamilcar together.

Disturbing images from the last time he saw Hamilcar flashed in his mind. "Do you think Hamilcar will come back?" he asked.

"What? I don't know. Why would you ask?" They turned a corner. It was a narrow road, wide enough for only one vehicle, with narrow sidewalks littered with empty food packages, boxes, and bags.

"Sometimes people go, and they don't come back. They're there, but they're not, really. Like when—"

"Did something happen to Hamilcar?"

"The angels got him with their screeching roar."

"Shitty," Sura said.

"Shitty," Shen echoed. The streets were uneven, forcing him to pull at the suitcase with both hands. Thinking of Hamilcar made him think of Aunty Melammu and Mom and Dad. That made him sad, but he was going for a walk with Sura, who was in such a nice mood. He looked at her, wanting to build on her good spirits. "You've got pretty eyes. They're green like the leaves in fall as they start to turn colour."

She looked at him with a mix of surprise and disbelief. "Ah, Shen," she said, shaking her head. "You've got good taste." She liked his taste! It had been so long since anybody liked what he liked. She cleared her throat. "You've, ah . . . you've got the biggest smile I've ever seen," she said. "It's like your head's not even big enough. It's ridiculous."

"You like my smile?"

"I said it's big." They turned another corner down a dirty alley, even more choked with garbage than the street.

"I think," he said, struggling to keep the suitcase upright as it rolled over debris, "we're friends."

Oh, no! Her smile disappeared. What did he do wrong? She told him to hurry as she walked ahead while he struggled to keep up.

She stepped through a doorway. Shen wrestled the suitcase over the door frame. The room he entered was dimly lit by light filtered through closed blinds and crowded with men. It smelled like stale sweat and canvas bags. All of them had guns—he had never seen so many weapons, except on the CPC, but these were not CPC. They were Mesos, like him, with skin all shades of brown and white. It reminded him of Baltu's home when he went there with Hamilcar and Ashme and everyone else. They eyed him with narrow eyes.

He walked up to a fellow by the door and stuck out his hand to shake. "Hi, my name's Shenshen, but you can call me Shen." He loved the next part. "Once is enough, am I right?" Ashme had laughed so hard the first time he said that. Her laughter was the most beautiful music he had ever heard. If the Deep had a song, it was Ashme's laugh.

The man was taken aback. He tentatively took Shen's offered hand. "Uh . . . right."

Another man entered from another room, a middle-aged man with salt-and-pepper hair. Shen remembered him from Baltu's home. Baltu had been yelling at him when they learned that Avalyn was going to visit the Hab. Shen smiled the smile Sura liked. "Hey, I remember you."

Sura turned to Shen with her angry face. "It's quiet time. We'll talk later."

The man looked from Shen to Sura. "You're using him as your courier?"

"He wants to help," Sura said. "Don't you, Shen?"

"Oh, I do. I'm helping my friend Sura." She looked away without returning his smile. Were they still friends? She was upset so often. Everyone in the room was tense. "Are you guys soldiers?"

The room erupted in swears, and somebody hissed, "The Network!" Everyone looked upset. How could he build a connection to them? "Well, my dad was a soldier like you," he said. "He fighted in Xinchin and was away for so long, but I always remembered him and the songs he teached—"

"Hey, Shen," Sura said, grabbing his shoulder hard. "We're friends, right?"

He thought his chest would burst. "Oh, yes."

"Good. I need you to be quiet while I talk to these fine people. Can you do that for me?"

"You bet I can."

She went back to the man with salt-and-pepper hair. He kept looking at Shen with a bad look. "I don't like this," he said to Sura.

"He'll be fine. My source tells me the southern perimeter of the tower will be free from angels and CPC for ten minutes starting at ten o'clock. If that's true, then this'll go off without a hitch. If not, you still ain't got nothing to worry about because it's us who's taking all the risk."

The man looked at Shen again with a severe look. "Let's get this over with. Clock's ticking." The man pulled out a hard copy of a map, over which he and Sura conferred.

"Do you play any instruments?" Shen asked the man by the door.

He gave Shen a stern look. "No."

"I play drums, and I'm starting to play the keyboard. It's weird; I can't do up buttons, but when I have a keyboard in my hands, my fingers dance on the keys. My uncle, well, my granduncle really, he could play the guitar. I remember he'd sit on the deck when the sun was setting, and he'd play until the sun was down. Aunty Melammu would scold him for ducking dish duty. My Aunty Melammu died, I think."

"That sucks, man."

"That means she's gone, and she won't be coming back. Why don't people come back? The Hierophants say we're vibrations in the quantum fields of the Deep. Being here is one pattern of vibration—one song, like fingers plucking a guitar string. Being gone is the song ending. But look, why not play the song you played before and come back?"

"Shit, kid, I don't know."

"It's because you can only play a song once," another man said. He looked like a grandpa with a wrinkly old face and white hair neatly parted on one side.

"You can only play a song once?" Shen repeated. "But I can play the same song lots of times."

"No, the song is your uncle plucking the strings of his guitar. That's the song. That's life. Once that song's over, it's done. Those vibrations have played. If you pluck the string again and play the same notes, it's a new vibration now. It sounds the same to our ears, but it's a new vibration. The old vibration, your aunt, is gone. But her energy's still there, the strings on the guitar are still there, so now she can be played in a new song, a different song. Get it?"

"Aunty Melammu can't come back because she's a new song now?"

"Yeah, that's it. Her song's over. Now, another can begin."

Shen thought about it. "I liked my aunty's song. It was beautiful. I don't want a new one."

The old man stared into nothing with a sad, troubled look. "Yeah. I know."

"You guys are fucking downers," another soldier said from the back. "Can someone, anyone, start talking about tits or something?"

Another man began to tell the most profane story Shen had ever heard. Before the story ended, Sura grabbed him and led him back out onto the street. "Did you hear the things that man was saying?" he asked once they were outside.

"Him? Yeah, he's full of shit. Probably couldn't get a bucket of mud to screw him unless he paid for it. This way," she said, leading him farther down the alley before turning into an even narrower lane. They made their way with the suitcase in tow through a couple of more streets and laneways.

She pulled him into the doorway of a building covered in layers of colourful graffiti. "Okay, you ready?"

"For what?"

She smiled a big, beautiful smile. "I need you to do me a big favour. Can I count on you?"

"Sure. What is it?"

"If you do this right, we can go listen to some music. Doesn't that sound nice?"

"I'd like that so much."

"Good," Sura said. "Here's what I want you to do." She looked to the sky, searching for something, but there was nothing but a couple of clouds. "You see at the end of this alley, there's a street with a wall on the other side of it."

Shen poked his head out the doorway. The alley stretched several blocks straight ahead. It ended in a T-intersection. "Yeah."

"I want you to take this suitcase all the way down to the end of the alley and then leave the suitcase against that wall. Then, once you've done that, run all the way back here. Can you run fast?"

"Not really—"

"That's okay. You run as fast as you can. Could you repeat those directions for me?"

"You want me to run as fast as I can?"

"Before that. Take the suitcase to the end of the alley—"

"To that wall there," he said, pointing.

"Right, to that wall there. Then what?"

"Run back."

"Before you run back."

"Ummmm—"

"Leave the suitcase by the wall," Sura said.

"Right, then run back."

Sura had him repeat the instructions a couple of more times. He struggled to keep it straight, so he turned the directions into a song.

> *Walk to the wall.*
> *Leave the suitcase at the wall,*
> *Then, run on back,*
> *Fast, fast, fast, fast, fa-fast.*

"Good enough," Sura said. She seemed agitated. "You have to go now, Shen. We're almost late, and if we're late, there'll be no music."

"I don't want to miss the music."

"Then you need to hurry. Go." She pushed him down the alley and then slipped back in the door. "I'll be right here waiting for you."

Shen made his way, tripping over garbage, lugging the suitcase behind him, and singing the song he had made to himself. It was tough figuring out Sura's moods, but they were starting to get along. There were people in the filthy window watching him. Shen waved. No one returned his greeting. He waved again, using his whole arm this time. The people disappeared. Were they coming out to say hello? Maybe. Better go to the door to greet them, just in case.

"Shen, what the fuck?" Sura said, her head poking out of the door frame. He had only moved a few buildings away from her.

"There are people here," he said.

"It's a city. There are people everywhere. Focus on our song." Their song! They had a song! "I said focus, Numbnuts!"

He disliked it when she called him Numbnuts, but they had a song. He sang it, walking in time to the beat.

> *Walk to the wall,*
> *Leave the suitcase by the wall.*

He arrived at the wall. It was so tall, made of interlocking blocks of concrete that were taller than he was. The wall was plain, no graffiti. It ran the length of the street. Should he leave the suitcase here or someplace else? The song gave him no guidance; it simply said to leave it by the wall. There was a bench a couple of metres to his left. That must be where he was to put the suitcase. He rolled it over. Wait. The song said to put it by the wall. He moved it away from the bench toward the wall. There. Was that right? Sura was not yelling at him, so he guessed it must be okay.

> *Then run on back,*
> *Fast, fast, fast, fast, fa-fast.*

He turned back the way he came. Which street had he come out of? There were several that exited onto this lane. Was it the first one? *Run. Fast, fast, fast, fast.* He ran as fast as his legs could carry him down the first street. Where was he running to? Where was Sura? All the buildings looked the same. "Sura?" he called out as he ran. He breathed heavily. "Sura!"

"Shen!"

He stopped running. "Sura, where are you?"

"Here, Numbnuts." She was in a doorway.

"I left it—"

"Get in here," she said, motioning him into the building.

She led him to the end of a hall and then crouched down on the floor, fingers in her ears. He sat beside her. "Plug your ears," she said.

"You want me to plug my ears?"

"Yes, plug your bloody ears, now."

He stuck his fingers in his ears.

The walls needed a new coat of paint, and no one had swept the floor in a long time. "Do you know what building this is?" Shen asked.

"No."

"Our apartment used to have a drone that swept the halls. The vacuum made a low humming noise that used to make me feel bad, but Aunty Melammu said it was doing good work and that the noise would pass. It did, and the halls were clean after. Then somebody dismantled it for parts, and—"

The earth shook, and a boom hammered the air so hard Shen could feel it in his bones. It knocked clouds of dust off the floors, walls, and ceiling into the air, choking him and stinging his eyes. He did not want to cry, but the tears welled up.

Sura ran down the hall to the door. He followed. His ears hurt, and he heard a ringing sound. Where was the ringing coming from? It sounded the same regardless of whether he had his fingers in his ears.

Soldiers, Mesos like those at Baltu's, ran down the street. He heard the *pop-pop-pop* of gunfire over the ringing noise. Sura grabbed Shen by the front of the shirt. "Come on! Run!" Her voice sounded hollow, as though it came from a distance. She poked her head out the door for a quick look and then ran, pulling Shen behind her in the opposite direction of all the soldiers.

Fear drove his feet. He was sure this was the fastest he had ever run. Angels zoomed overhead while rockets fired from nearby buildings. Soldiers were everywhere. Where did they all come from? Everyone was shooting and shooting and shooting, and drones, like angels but different, flew up and down the streets, and they were shooting, too.

Sura kept running. Shen pushed himself hard to keep up. Finally, she looked over her shoulder and then stopped. Shen collapsed, his heart a drum roll in his chest while he drank big gulps of air. The sounds of fighting echoed over the buildings, but it sounded far away now.

She knelt beside him, her hand on his back. "You did amazing!"

He did? "Was it—" He gasped for air. "—my running? I've never run so fast."

She laughed. "No. The suitcase, Numbnuts."

He had an idea he disliked. "Was the suitcase wrecked in the explosion?"

"Yeah, I'd say it was."

He realized what she had tricked him into doing. The suitcase was a bomb. The tears returned. "Hey, don't cry," Sura said. "The scary part's over. You're a hero now."

He did not want to be a hero. Bombs ended peoples' songs. Songs made the universe beautiful. He wanted to make songs, not end them.

CHAPTER 39

MASON STARED at the data feed Dashiell showed him. *[This is wrong,]* he pinged. *[It can't be real.]*

[It is,] Dashiell replied. *[This intel comes from multiple satellite feeds and personal updates from citizens.]*

His breath came in shallow gasps. Baltu's army of Free New Mesopotamia had crossed the border. Someone two desks over swore. Throughout the office, others talked in shock and fear as the news spread.

Baltu's advanced forces had already breached the security perimeter around New Uruk. How did he launch an attack? How did they get into the city? The CPC should have been tracking them—should have slapped them down before they got a kilometre past the border.

[Pull up a map of New Uruk,] Mason pinged. *[Overlay with the known whereabouts of Free New Mesopotamian forces.]*

He scanned the image and jumped to his feet, a storm cloud ready to burst. No one paid attention—everyone was absorbed in their own data feeds. In the background, the city's emergency response sirens wailed.

He accessed his neural implant and pinged Oriana. He cast

her image to his data screen as she answered: soft features, warm smile. "Hey, Mason, what's up?"

She had yet to hear the news. "Is Tracey at the daycare today?"

"Yeah, you know I'm taking Daxton for an appointment. Why? What's wrong?"

Daxton's clinic was at the west end of New Uruk, kilometres away. It should be safe. He should have told her to watch the news but let her keep her beautiful smile a few moments more. "I'm going to the daycare now," he said. "No matter what happens, stay at the clinic."

"Mason, what—" He hung up and ran out of the office, making his way to the *Aigle's* garage, where he ordered a car to take him to Tracey's daycare in the Terres du Nord district. It was on the east end of the city. At this moment, the Free New Mesopotamian army was plowing into it.

Mason pinged Dashiell. *[How much longer until the Mesos reach Tracey's daycare?]*

[Odd you think I should know. Mason, I—]

[Extrapolate. From their current position and rate of advancement.]

[The CPC is rallying to—]

[Extrapolate. Give me your guess.] He ordered the car to accelerate to top speed. It entered the freeway and began passing traffic.

[Based on currently available data, and assuming the scenario does not change, which it will, there is a ninety-five percent probability the Free New Mesopotamian lines will advance to the location of Tracey's daycare within thirteen to ninety-three minutes.]

[That's a wide range of time,] Mason pinged.

[I believe I have communicated the difficulties of estimating their advance,] Dashiell replied.

The car was too slow. He used his credentials to override its safety protocols. The car emitted a warning that the CPC had blocked access to the Terres du Nord district. Mason used his credentials again to override the blockade.

The vehicle hummed along at speed, dodging between slower-moving transports. Traffic jams were forming on the westbound freeway from people fleeing eastern districts. The eastbound road he was on was uncluttered, though troop transports were driving up on-ramps. An aerial personnel carrier flew overhead, its engine thrumming.

His override failed. Instead of taking the off-ramp into the Terres du Nord district, the car slowed and began looking for a place to turn around. He ordered it to pull over instead. He got out and ran into the district. The daycare was two blocks from the freeway exit. The clatter of gunfire sounded blocks away.

Avalyn's office pinged him. He ignored it. *[Dashiell, plot out the fastest foot route to Tracey's daycare.]*

[Would you like me to adjust the route for safety?]

[No. Get me there fast.] A map flashed up in his neural net with a route mapped.

The windows of the surrounding buildings shook from the rumble of fighter drones soaring low over rooftops. A siren's wail was a constant cantata of distress in the background. This was impossible. New Uruk was being invaded; the enemy was *in* the city.

Two of the buildings on this street were in flames; one was rubble. A man in a suit ran past. A collection of office workers screamed names as they scrambled over the concrete chunks and twisted metal of the collapsed building. People were blackened by smoke or greyed from dust; many were bloody.

Where was the CPC? Nearby, beats of gunfire cracked. Down streets, dark figures with guns darted along walls as combat drones flew overhead. They were not CPC. Mad with panic, he ran faster.

He turned a corner. There was Tracey's daycare. He jumped up the stairs and flung the door open, calling out.

The halls were empty. Dust choked the air. He called out again, running down the hall. The wall of a classroom had been blown in. Blocks of stone had scattered and crushed furniture and toys, bright plastic colours amid grey rubble.

They attacked the daycare! This was Oriana's childhood all over again. The whining ping of bullets ricocheting off the building's walls echoed. Mason's fists shook. They are attacking a daycare! Tracey's daycare!

The prospect of looking for children in the rubble horrified him, but mad desperation drove him to pull chunks of concrete aside, screaming Tracey's name.

"Are you CPC?" a woman's voice called in Ostarrichi.

"I'm here to help." He ran in the direction of the voice. A woman met him by the door in a hall. He recognized her, one of Tracey's teachers.

"Mr. Mason!" Her hair was a mess. She had been crying.

"Is Tracey all right?"

"Yes, all the children are down here." She led him through the doorway and down a set of stairs. They spilled into a room filled with a dozen toddlers and another teacher. Tracey cried out when she saw her father. They ran to each other. He dropped to his knees and held her. A tempest filled his body, alighting him with crackling energy. While he breathed, no harm would befall her. He would sacrifice *everything* to keep her safe.

"Mr. Mason!" The teacher pulled on his arm. "You work for the government—are they coming to help?"

The lights flickered from a nearby explosion. "Get the children against the wall by the stairs," he said. Scanning the room for anything he could use as a weapon, he pinged Dashiell. [*Inform the CPC there is a daycare at this location, and a member of Avalyn's staff is trapped inside.*]

[*It is done,*] Dashiell pinged back.

The cool focus he had before a *guerre des mains* match settled over him. The room was a large play area with no windows or other doors. Everything was plastic or tiny—nothing that made for a good weapon. He grabbed a large toy model of an angel. He could throw it at someone coming down the stairs, distracting them before he attacked. He wanted to hold Tracey but had to let her go. She cried as he passed her to the teacher, as he made soothing cooing noises to calm her.

[The CPC informs me they are trying to secure the area,] Dashiell pinged. *[They advise you to seek cover and hold your position.]*

He settled into a comfortable stance. Oriana pinged him. Keep focus. He dismissed the ping and asked Dashiell to send a message telling her that he and Tracey were okay, after which it was to block all further pings except those from the CPC. The teachers huddled with the children. They stared at the ceiling as if they could see through it if they looked hard enough.

The rattling crack of gunfire sounded like it was coming from outside the building. The children were toddlers, but some primal instinct hardwired into the core of humanity kept them from crying. A thump felt in the bones shook the air. Outside, stones clattered on concrete. Another thump. Another. Stones falling. A child whimpered, then another. The teachers soothed them to silence. Kanu voices barked from the street above. The Free Mesopotamian line was advancing past them.

He adjusted his grip on the toy angel. If only he had grabbed a weapon when he left the *Aigle*. More gut-shaking thumps of rockets exploding. They were coming faster, more frequently.

Oriana must be terrified. Could he ever make her feel safe after this? Would Tracey remember this? She was three—this could be her first memory. How would a first memory like this mark her life? Would she grow up afraid like her mother?

Kanu shouting, gunfire, and the pinging whine of ricochets echoed in the building. He turned to one of the teachers. "Do you have anything made of metal? Anything that would hurt more than a plastic toy?"

"We've nothing here that children could hurt themselves with."

He focused his hearing on the stairwell, listening for the sound of men coming. What would he do if soldiers found them? He could probably get the drop on one. Maybe not, if they were armoured. Definitely not if they were using ultrasonic visors to see through the wall.

What would they do to Tracey and the rest of the kids? And the female teachers? In the Bit Durani Massacre, Kanu had murdered children and raped the women before slaughtering them. Would they force Mason to watch?

There were Kanu voices upstairs, growling wolves on the prowl. The building shook, knocking the lights out. A roar pierced his ears. The children cried and trembled, terrified.

FIFTY METRES FROM ASHME, a combat drone, smoke trailing behind it, crashed into a building. Its ordinance detonated, tearing the building apart in a spray of debris. The shockwave shattered windows along the street. The stoop she and Ganzer were hiding behind did little to protect them from the stinging bite of shredded glass and stone that rained on them. Where were the soldiers? Gunfire was constant.

"The fighting's moved up a street," Ganzer said. The dust covering him made him look like a ghost. He brushed rubble off his shoulders.

Ashme peeked over the stoop. They were in the Terres du Nord, a goldie district; this was her first time here. She cast her senses into the nanohaze. Urgent signals flashed throughout the area like a pot boiling: data packets shuffling from field sensors to surveillance nodes, commands directing robotic forces, queries for data, and orders from all quarters. The packets were sporadic and uncoordinated. The Network was offline. The Network had been such a fixture in the nanohaze that she'd never realized what an oppressive weight it was until it was gone.

"I can't believe there's fighting in Ostarrichi districts," Ganzer said. "Serious fighting."

"No angels here. We've got a window. Let's move."

In a crouch, clinging close to the wall, they ran stoop to stoop. Three bodies clad in CPC armour lay scattered on the ground, blood staining the sidewalk. She grabbed a rifle, handed it to Ganzer, and then picked up another. "Bad idea," Ganzer said. "The Network will detect unauthorized handling of these guns and track us."

"The Network's down," Ashme said.

"What?" Ganzer turned her to face him. "How do you know?"

"Its signal is gone from the nanohaze." She stuffed clips of ammunition in her pockets.

"That's . . . that's not possible."

Ashme shrugged. "Free New Mesopotamia must have hit one of the Network's towers. The CPC's running blind."

"Fan-fucking-tastic," Ganzer said. He began stuffing his pockets with ammunition clips. "Almost makes me wonder if Baltu's going to do it this time."

"Maybe you decided to turn tail and run from Caelum too early."

He looked like he was about to get angry, but he breathed calm into his body and stretched his neck.

They continued along the street to an intersection. Ashme launched a minor program linking her gun's optics to her neural net. She poked the weapon around the corner and projected what it saw in her mind's eye. Soldiers—CPC—were firing ahead at an enemy she could not resolve on the image.

"You got a plan?" Ganzer asked.

"My plan is to get Shen," she said.

"That's not a plan. That's a goal. We need a plan. That battle line is between us and Sura's district. We can head east into the Neufve Bon-heur district, see if we can swing around the fight."

"There's been nothing but one battle line after another between us and Sura's district. We're already kilometres off track."

Behind her, a foot kicked a stone and sent it skittering. They both whipped around, rifles to shoulders. One stoop back, a young boy, maybe ten years old, his face tear-stained, had come out, his mother behind him. The kid had dark hair, the mother blonde. Both had golden skin and a look of terror in their eyes.

Slowly, Ganzer placed his finger over his lips with a *shhhh*. "This is a pot of shit," he said to Ashme. "What are we going to do with them?"

The boy stared, eyes wide, shaking, blue eyes transfixed on the barrel of Ashme's firearm. She remembered another day looking down the barrel of a gun in an alley, staring at the back of the CPC trooper's head.

Ganzer said, "We could let them go."

"The CPC is half a block away. All these two have to do is yell, and we'll have a flock of angels beating down on us."

They were speaking Kanu. The mother and son recoiled at the sound. Neither of them probably spoke a word of it. They lived on a planet of Kanu nations and had never bothered to learn the language. The arrogance of it drove Ashme mad. The mom wrapped her arms around her son.

Ashme thought of the eight Mesos shot in retribution for the CPC trooper she had murdered. She thought of the other deaths that came later—Dad, Mom, Melammu. "Shooting them would be safest." The words felt false.

"What's wrong with you?" Ganzer snapped. The boy flinched at the anger in his voice. "Let's knock them out and go."

Ganzer advanced on them, raising his rifle to knock them on the head. The boy panicked, screaming. Ashme tightened up on the trigger and leaned into the butt of the gun, bracing to fire. The boy yelled, "Mesos! Mesos!" Her body shook. Why was shooting the CPC trooper in the head so easy, this so hard? The mom grabbed her boy and ran back into the building.

Ganzer turned to Ashme. "Run!"

CHAPTER 40

MASON FOCUSED on the Kanu voices prowling the hallways at the top of the stairs, trying to understand what they were saying. The building shook again, and stones crumbled. Guns fired, *pop-pop-pop-pop*. Whizzing bangs snapped the air. Men screamed and shouted.

They might come downstairs to seek shelter. The toy angel in his hand shook. Sweat made his grip slick. Each breath brought a stench of smoke, dust, and gunpowder.

Kanu voices called for a fallback.

The gunfire cracked but from farther away. Were the CPC pushing the Kanu back? The fighting went on, getting neither louder nor quieter.

He heard Ostarrichi voices. *[Your CPC escort has arrived,]* Dashiell pinged.

"Here!" Mason called out, "We're down here!"

A voice called out in Ostarrichi from the top of the stairs, "Status."

"Clear," Mason replied. "Fifteen civilians, three adults, twelve toddlers. No casualties, coming out."

"Come out, hands raised."

Mason dropped the toy angel and picked up Tracey, who

wrapped her tiny arms tight around his neck. He motioned to the teachers to get the children and follow him, hands in clear view. Two CPC soldiers met him at the top of the stairs. One led the way down the hall, the other took up position behind the chain of children. Gunfire and the thump of rocket explosions still sounded from the streets. Other CPC were stationed throughout the building, firing out through windows and holes in the walls.

The CPC soldier led them out of the building and into an aerial personnel carrier waiting on the street. They took off the moment the children were seated. There were no windows to get a view of the war zone below. Mason's body quaked, adrenalin roaring through his blood. *[Dashiell,]* he pinged, *[what's the latest update on the Free New Mesopotamian advance?]*

[Avalyn's office would be able to give you much more accurate information than I. They have been pinging you urgently, though I have been blocking them per your request.]

Avalyn might fire him for abandoning his post, but he would do it again, a thousand times over. Tracey clung to his neck, her breath coming in quick, ragged gasps. If this was to be her first memory, let her also remember a father's love. He enfolded her in his arms, wrapping himself around her tiny, quaking body.

Breathing calm into his own body, he asked Dashiell to patch him to Avalyn's office.

Shanelle answered. *[You ran away.]*

[My daughter was in danger.]

[All our children are in danger,] Shanelle pinged. *Yes,* he thought, *but this one is mine.* When he failed to reply, Shanelle continued. *[There is no future without our children. How is Tracey?]*

It unnerved him that she knew his daughter's name. *[She's safe.]*

[Good. Praise Damara. Avalyn still feels your skills can serve Ostarrichi. Get back to the office.]

[I'll be there shortly.]

Shanelle terminated the ping.

Mason noted that Meli from the Director-General's office had left a message. He had been trying to meet with her to rat out Avalyn.

Free New Mesopotamia, however, had attacked his daughter's daycare. *That is what Kanu do. They bomb schools.* Avalyn might have usurped the command structure of the angel network, but the Kanu were feral dogs. Caelum needed to be strong. United. That was what would keep his family safe.

He dismissed the message from Meli.

ASHME AND GANZER sprinted down the street. CPC soldiers shouted. The malevolent surge of an angel rose in the nanohaze. It loomed around a corner. Ashme launched an attack, including several clones of Subdeo. The AIs hammered at the angel's firewall, evolving generations in a second to break through the encryption. The angel's AI also evolved, patching every weakness at which her attack program prodded. If she were unable to drop this angel, its weapons would tear them to shreds. She launched more of herself into the nanohaze to power her program. *Come on, little buddy.*

Her AIs trapped the angel firewall in a logic loop long enough to crack its encryption. The angel dropped like a shot bird.

The world spun as her perception shifted out of n-time to normal, and the street raced up to greet her face. Ganzer pulled her up. "Where's my gun?" she asked, staring at her empty hands.

"Run, go!"

A shot cracked the air. Ashme stumbled as a force hit Ganzer, spinning him onto the ground. CPC troopers were on top of them. Bodies pushed Ashme to the pavement, guns in her face. Ganzer swore in pain, holding his gut as blood rippled through his fingers. Ashme begged them in Ostarrichi,

"Don't shoot! We're not soldiers—we're trying to find our family!"

"Frag 'em," somebody said.

"Hold," another voice said. An officer stepped forward with an ID scanner. With the Network down, he had to manually scan their tags. "They're flagged for questioning. Patch that one up and bring 'em in."

Questioning for what? She and Ganzer were centibit hoods.

The troopers grumbled, but one of them put a stick of healing goo on Ganzer's wound while another rolled Ashme on her front and crushed her with his knee in her back as he shackled her. "Put an EM disrupter on her," someone said. "Did you see her drop that angel? She's an indigo child."

The cold sliver of the device chilled the back of Ashme's neck, after which the presence of the nanohaze faded. It was like losing the sensation of touch when you pinched a nerve.

Hands pulled her off the ground and carried her. No one saw the hummingbird tat on her forearm throb and then fade away.

CHAPTER 41

A DATA PACKET arrived in Mason's neural net as he stood in the *Aigle's* security scanner. It was the program tat he had forgotten he gave Ashme on the Chevalier job. The CPC had arrested her.

The building security scanner cleared him. CPC guards eyed him curiously as he walked to the bank of elevators—his suit was covered in dust from rescuing Tracey.

Would Shen have been picked up with Ashme? Poor kid. He was incapable of looking after himself alone. It was stupid for Ashme to live the life she lived with a brother like Shen. *Daxton will never know that kind of insecurity.*

He entered the office to a scene of chaos. The area thrummed with a mad chorus of loud voices. People rushed from one desk to another. Farren greeted him, her usually smooth brow wrinkled in worry, to escort him to Avalyn's office. A meeting was already in progress around the *Aigís,* Avalyn's grand table. He recognized Colonel Tyrell of the CPC in addition to several other intelligence officers. Shanelle stared at him with a cold gaze.

Avalyn stopped the meeting. "How is Tracey?"

"Tracey?" All eyes turned to him. He began shifting his weight from one foot to the other. "She's fine. Thank you, Floor

Leader. Please, continue," he said, taking a seat at the periphery of the room.

"Oriana must be beside herself. It is a cruel thing to lose one's child." She stared into the air in front of her, swollen-knuckled hands on the table, grey steel in her features. No one moved, no one breathed—everyone knew Avalyn had lost her first daughter years ago. "Mothers never really believe their children are gone," she said. "I'm glad she was spared that pain." She turned to the agents and officers around the table. "Mr. Mason's daughter was in a daycare in the Terres du Nord district when the Mesos attacked." She nodded for them to continue with their brief.

The officers gave a string of troop positions and threat assessments. They spoke in military jargon, talking of operational environments and force multipliers. They were not reporting to Avalyn as they would the leader of the opposition party but as to a general, which, of course, she had been many times over the years. Probability bars were thick over many of Free New Mesopotamia's forces— the Network was down, Mason learned, and so there was uncertainty assessing enemy strength and positions.

The image of Oriana's utterly desperate face interrupted his thoughts. She had said nothing, too choked with emotion to speak, when he handed Tracey to her. Her face was that of a woman drowning, reaching for the sky, grasping air. The attack on the daycare had wounded her deep in her psyche. She was watching her childhood repeat itself with her own children. Would she ever feel safe again?

"They have driven back a number of our positions," Avalyn observed. "How?"

Mason leaned forward, intent on the answer.

"Several factors," Colonel Tyrell said, a frown cutting deep chasms in his forehead. "Loss of the Network over a quarter of the city contributes, but enemy mobility and fire capability are greater than expected. They have a new model of aerial combat drone that rivals our angels, giving them enhanced low-altitude warfare assets. They have several classes of small and medium weaponry with superior armour-piercing and tracking capabilities. They have new models of urban tanks and personnel transport, giving them enhanced mobility and manoeuvring abilities. Their weaponry is more sophisticated than our intelligence suggested they possessed."

"Ark tech," one of the intelligence agents said.

Mason remembered the image of the arms dealer Avalyn had shown him. His hands cramped; he had them in tight fists and forced them open, placing them on his thighs.

"So, Ark *Gallia* has sided with the Kanu," another officer said.

"*Brettaniai* won't stand for that." Colonel Tyrell said. "They've always been protective of their monopoly on Esharra."

"Then this risks bringing the Ark powers into the conflict," another officer said. "And with them, other Kanu nations."

Colonel Tyrell gave Avalyn a knowing look. "Agreed," he said. "It's safe to say that if we don't resolve this quickly, the scope of conflict could expand. Caelum could be the epicentre of another Ark war."

This will be a different kind of war, Mason thought. Caelum had fought many battles in its short history, but all of them had been with Kanu neighbours. Now, however, the Free Mesopotamian Army was *already in* Caelum. And with the Ark powers returning? This war could go global—it could expand through the whole Esharran solar system. If that happened, where could he take his family where they would be safe?

"Then we'll have to resolve this quickly," Avalyn said. "I do hope the Director-General's up to the task."

Kannon, Avalyn's chief of staff, asked, "Do we know how Baltu took out our Network tower? Those are supposed to be our most highly guarded assets."

"We're gaining insight on that," one of the intelligence officers said. With a gesture, he switched the image to a satellite view of the street surrounding a Network tower. It showed the building's wall, sidewalk, and a bench. A man entered the screen, pulling what looked like a suitcase. The officer froze the image. "That suitcase held military-grade explosives. It ripped a twenty-metre hole in the tower's protective perimeter. Free New Mesopotamian forces were nearby, entered the breach, and destroyed the tower."

"How in the hell did he get within a hundred metres of the tower with a suitcase full of explosives?" Kannon asked. "There's supposed to be overlapping webs of angel patrols scanning for this type of thing."

"There was a hole in angel coverage."

Everyone stared at the intelligence agent in shock. Everyone except Mason. He stared at Avalyn. She sat quietly, an impassive, ancient stone wall.

"We currently don't know how," the agent continued, "but it appears Free New Mesopotamia was able to burn the angel network and program a hole in their surveillance pattern."

Kannon sat back in his chair. "Holy fuck."

Mason felt like he was falling out of the sky.

"The angel network is supporting our CPC units," one of the analysts said. "If Free New Mesopotamia can burn the network, should we take them offline?"

"Not yet," Avalyn said, spreading her gnarled hands wide on the table, owning the space. "The Network tower appears to be an isolated incident. Since then, angels have been a valuable asset."

Would Avalyn have used the BLOQ to orchestrate the gap in the angel surveillance around the Network tower? Why would she do that?

"Do we know anything about that agent?" Colonel Tyrell asked, pointing at the frozen image of the man pulling the suitcase.

"We were lucky," the intelligence officer said. "One of our surveillance satellites was offline for almost ten minutes after a micro-meteor damaged its lens. If that agent hadn't walked to the bench, we might never have seen him." The image zoomed in on the man's face. Mason wanted to climb the wall. "This is Citizen 539619-d, class 2A Shenshen ultu Vanc. He's a genetic degenerate, unedited."

Not a degenerate, Mason thought, *just sick.*

"According to his files, he suffers severe mental incapacity. He's an idiot they set up as a fall guy. They've probably killed him already. With the Network down in the area, we can't track him to confirm."

Avalyn had given Mason Sura's contact information, and Sura worked with Ashme, sister to Shen. Avalyn had the BLOQ that gave her control of the angel network. Avalyn sat there, an old, dispassionate snow owl high in a tree scanning the forest below.

Rage erupted in Mason, a thunderstorm in his chest shaking his body. She had knocked out the Network, opening the gates to Free New Mesopotamia, allowing them to attack, allowing them to put his daughter's life in danger. She wanted to lure Baltu into Caelum. New Uruk was the bait.

Shanelle sat behind Avalyn, staring right at him. *Focus— control your breathing. Where the breath goes, the body follows.* The blood had left his face, and sweat chilled his back. *Get that rage under control.*

He accessed his neural implant and rechecked the message from the program tat he had given Ashme. The CPC had taken her fifteen minutes ago. She would be interrogated. They would find out about the BLOQ; they would find out about him. He would be the one implicated in the fall of the Network. Would he then lead the CPC to Avalyn? Would he live long enough to have the option?

The meeting ended. Colonel Tyrell came over to Mason, introduced himself with an iron handshake, and asked after Tracey. No sooner had Mason answered than he broke into a story of his son's own near-death experience fighting near New Akkad.

Shit, shit, shit. Mason wanted to get out of there. He had to do something, anything. *[Dashiell,]* he pinged while the colonel carried on his yarn, *[reply to Meli from the Director-General's office. Tell her I need to meet. Today. Tell her it's urgent.]*

He and the colonel were the last to leave the office. Shanelle stared, icepick eyes gouging him. She turned to speak to Avalyn as the doors closed.

CHAPTER 42

ASHME WAS ALONE. Well, that was untrue. She sat on the ground, knees crushed to her chest, with forty other Mesos in a cell built for eight, the air thick with body odour. Ganzer, however, was missing—they had taken him to a different facility. Shen was gone. Melammu was dead. Everyone had been taken from her.

The CPC had brought her to this calming centre, stripped her, and subjected her to a body search worlds more violating and painful than anything she had suffered at a checkpoint. They melded the EM disrupter to the sinews of her neck, keeping her from accessing the nanohaze. She was defenceless.

The other prisoners were a collection of men and women ranging from young teens to advanced old age. They all wore red uniforms, contrasting starkly with the white walls, floor, and ceiling of the calming centre. They looked like her body felt—beaten and out of gas, a field trampled by hail. Across from her, a young boy with long, gangly limbs and one of those wispy teenage moustaches nodded at her. "How're things on the outside?" he asked.

"Looks like Free New Mesopotamia invaded this morning and managed to plow into New Uruk," she said. "There was fighting in goldie districts, and Free New Mesopotamia knocked out the Network."

A chorus of swears and excited murmurs rippled through the cell. Apparently, she had been the first to break the news.

"Do you think they'll take the city?" the boy asked.

"Here's hoping," Ashme said.

"Keep your trap shut unless you want to get beat," someone in the crowd said. A dozen people ignored him and pelted Ashme with questions.

A young woman keeping her eyes on the hall through the cell's milk-coloured diamond bars grabbed everyone's attention with a loud hiss. "Bot coming."

Silence clamped down. The bot trundled into the view through the bars, rolling on a pair of treads. The size of a small dog, it swivelled a sensor array attached to an articulated arm to scan the cell. An indicator light on the array flashed. A middle-aged woman maybe two metres away from Ashme screamed and convulsed. Her flailing created a ripple of movement that passed through the tightly packed cell. Bodies rolled onto Ashme, pushing her back into others. For several heartbeats, the only sound in the cell was that of the woman's guttural gasps and spasms.

The indicator light on the bot's sensor array blinked off, and the woman's convulsions ceased. Her breath came in short pants. The bot trundled out of view, the whir of its treads sounding in its wake.

"What'd she do?" Ashme asked no one in particular.

The young boy who had first spoken to her replied. "The bots randomly select prisoners for . . . well, for that." He nodded toward the woman, who had begun sobbing. "Still, better that then being selected for questioning. Odds are good that if a bot picks you for questioning, you won't come back."

Is that how Mom died? Ashme looked at the woman, who was pulling herself into a sitting position with the help of her neighbours. She imagined her mom convulsing like that, feet scrabbling on the floor, back arched, wrists bent.

Thoughts of Mom led to thoughts of Shen. Sura would care for him for a while. Would she bother to set him up with someone who would look after him? She would run out of patience with Shen, especially if business was jumping. What would he do once Sura cut him loose?

Her mother had probably worried about Shen in the same way while she rotted in her cell—probably Shen and Ashme both. A family tradition. At least Melammu had been around back then to take Shen and her in. But now?

The young man held his hand out. "I'm Sarru." Ashme took the hand and shook it as she introduced herself. It was cold and clammy.

"Where were you heading when they picked you up?" he asked. He had that air of fake confidence teen boys sometimes put on when talking to a woman.

"East Margidda."

"You live there?"

Piss off, kid. "No."

"Why were you going there, then?"

A man pushing mid- to late-sixties piped up. "Don't answer his questions. He was chosen for 'questioning' a couple of days ago. Miraculously returned less than an hour before you arrived."

"Shut up, old man!" Sarru was irate. "Are you accusing me of something?"

"Step off, kid," the old man said. "I know how the CPC work. Maybe your mom or dad's in the system, or maybe you got picked up with your kid sister. The CPC know how to turn that on you."

Sarru got to his feet, stabbing his finger in the old man's direction. "I don't turn on my people!"

"Sit down, Sarru, it's okay. I don't know anything the CPC

would be interested in," Ashme said. "Maybe stow the questions for a bit."

Slowly, he sat back down on the floor. He stared at the ground, knobby elbows propped on skinny knees, head cradled in his hands. Was the old man right? Was something going to happen to this kid's family now? She should be angry at him for being a goldie informant, but all she saw was a young boy caught in a system that crushed great men.

Something was up. They wanted her for something. Something about where she was going. If she were to guess, she would guess that Sura did something hair-brained, bringing the CPC down on her. Ashme had to get Shen away from Sura.

The bars on the cell were opened and closed through some form of networked system control. If she could burn angels, she could probably burn these. The metal of the EM disrupter on the back of her neck was cold on her fingers. The world was empty without the nanohaze. If only there was some way to get it off her . . .

LESS THAN TEN minutes after she clammed up to Sarru, a bot and two guards came for her. On the bright side, maybe now she would find out what crap Sura had done.

The guards led her through the labyrinthine complex. Their footsteps echoed down endless white corridors lined with cages packed with Mesos wearing red prisoner uniforms. What were they going to do to her? Torture? Put a bullet in her head? Would they use Ganzer to twist her into betraying her people like they did to that boy Sarru? Would they use her to twist Ganzer?

The guards took her to a small room with two chairs on either side of a plain white laminate desk. On the far side of the desk, a woman sat. She was a goldie, a bit older, sixties, maybe, and had a grandmotherly smile.

Ah. This was the sweet old grandma who was going to save

her from those big, bad guards if only Ashme would do one tiny little favour. The guards sat Ashme down, handcuffed her to the chair, and left.

"I want to help you, Ashme," Grandma said as she peered at a datapad, tapping her fingernail mindlessly on the desk.

Here we go. Time to find out what Sura had done.

The sweet old lady folded her hands neatly. "Let's talk about your brother, Shen, shall we?"

CHAPTER 43

MASON WAS out of his depth. He tapped the rim of his coffee mug with slim fingers as he sat in the cafe waiting for Meli from the Director-General's office. The last thing he needed was coffee—he was wound up enough thinking about what he was going to tell her when she arrived. He had taken an EM shield from work to hide his ID tags so no one could track him coming here. How had life come to this?

The shop, usually bustling, was nearly empty. It was after hours, and, well, New Uruk *was* in a state of war, after all. But the shop, with its faux wood chairs and paintings by local artists, was close to the *Aigle*, deep inside Ostarrichi territory. Its owners had kept it open to serve the public servants working frantically as Baltu's Free New Mesopotamia army stabbed deep into Caelum's heart.

Why was Avalyn doing this? Maybe he should ask her. If Avalyn was willing to bring war into the heart of Caelum, however, what would she be willing to do to keep her role in that hidden? Mason was pretty sure he knew the answer. He had no illusions about his importance, or lack thereof, to Avalyn. He was an analyst and a low-ranking one at that. She had not chosen him because his skills were special or because he was important, but rather the opposite.

He pushed his coffee aside—it was getting cold. Even if he did ask Avalyn, and she took him into her confidence, what could she say that would make this okay? How many Ostarrichi had died from Free New Mesopotamia's attack so far? *They attacked Tracey's daycare.* He wanted to create a world worthy of his children, but this one was falling far short. How could he explain this to Oriana so she would understand why he was betraying Avalyn? The thought of losing his wife's support was agonizing.

Meli entered the cafe wearing a frumpy navy suit. Mason flagged her over. He pulled his privacy shield generator out of his coat pocket and activated it. The shield shimmered into being as Meli sat down. "What's going on?" she asked. "Why couldn't we meet in the *Aigle*?"

How do you start a conversation like this? "I . . ." Was he really going to do this? There were so many ways this could go wrong. Meli might believe he was lying. Avalyn could spin this to make Mason seem like the traitor. He could lose his job—and his insurance for Daxton's treatments. He could end up in prison, despised by his family, or dead. Or, if the Director-General did act on this information, the political rift it could cause might destabilize Caelum when it was most in peril.

Control your breathing. "I am aware of acts of high treason."

Meli stared in disbelief. "High treason? Like what?"

He told her everything, the words spilling out. It felt good to share this with someone.

When he finished, Meli sat, stunned. "This is . . . do you . . . Mason, do you understand how huge this is?"

"Yes."

"I don't think you do. Ever since Avalyn's stunt at the Hab, she's been crushing the Director-General in the polls. If an election were called today, she'd win the Director-Generalship with a majority government. Shit, the *Aigle* is having an emergency session tonight where they will vote on whether to reinstate Avalyn as head of the CPC."

"I didn't realize that," Mason said.

"She is slaughtering Mesos. She is endangering all of Caelum in a mad grab for power."

"Not power," Mason corrected. "She believes in what she's doing. She thinks she's protecting Caelum."

Meli made a dismissive sound. "That's worse." She leaned close to Mason. "I don't think people like you have any idea why what Avalyn's doing is so dangerous. Ark ships have returned to break *Brettaniai*'s monopoly. That monopoly and our special arrangement with *Brettaniai* have been key to our survival on this planet. The riches that flow through Caelum to the other Kanu nations give us enough leverage to eke out peace, uneasy and fragile as it is. If Kanu nations start trading directly with these new powers, not only will they no longer need us, but they will have access to tech that can challenge us. Avalyn and those like you who follow her are so lost in hate and fear of Mesos that you are blind to the real danger our nation faces. If we don't start making friends on this planet, we are lost."

Mason sat back. He had seen all the pieces but had never put them together in quite that way.

"Do you have evidence of Avalyn's treachery?" Meli asked.

"My testimony."

She grunted dismissively. "I'm talking about *real* evidence."

"There's the BLOQ program. There'd be an electronic signature of whoever accessed it that should allow the authorities to track Avalyn's activities in the angel network."

"Do you have the program tat?"

Mason remembered the pink unicorn on it. "No. Avalyn has it."

"You get us that program tat, then we'll—" The privacy shield shut down. Meli's eyes widened as she looked at the space where the shield had been shimmering.

Mason looked at the privacy shield generator. None of its

indicator lights flashed. He pressed buttons on its surface impotently. *[Dashiell, can you help me troubleshoot this?]* Mason pinged. No answer.

"Looks like our meeting's over," Meli said, standing up to leave. She scanned the coffee shop nervously. "Thank you for the, uh . . . thanks for the first-hand intel you gathered when rescuing your daughter." She extended her hand to shake.

"Right, I, uh . . ." He tried pinging Dashiell again. No answer. He took the proffered hand and shook it. It was cold and sweaty. "Let's stay in touch. I'll contact you if I learn more."

Meli smiled a friendly smile. "Good luck." She left quickly.

[DASHIELL?] he tried one last time. No luck. Would he ever see his family again? Would they go after his family? He pinged Oriana to tell her to grab the kids and go to his brother, who lived by the coast. Nothing.

Would they kill him in public? One customer was sitting at a table working on his data screen while a woman behind the counter cleaned equipment. The street outside was deserted.

He moved tables to be by a wall away from the windows, where snipers might have a shot. He took his coffee mug in case he needed something to throw or smash in someone's face. In addition to keeping him away from big windows, the seat gave him a good view of the street outside the front door. There was no easy exit from here, though. He could hop the counter and make it out the back or cross the whole shop to leave through the front door.

Should he go out the back now and try to make his way home? Maybe staying here, making them come to him would be better. The cafe would close eventually. What then?

The woman behind the counter was looking at him.

Stay here. If they were going to give him time to think, he would take it.

A transport van pulled up in front of the cafe. Mason bolted, jumping the counter, smashing displays of candy bars and muffins. The woman screamed. He kicked her legs out from under her as he yelled, "Get down!" to her and the other customer.

Two figures wearing scrambler masks and armed with pistols leaped out of the van. Mason grabbed a carafe of coffee and darted through the door behind the counter to the back. He bumped into two other masked men. He smashed the carafe in one man's face, spilling hot coffee over him. The man stumbled back into the other, screaming.

In the other room, the front door crashed open. A gunshot, screams, more gunshots. Mason drove into the two men in front of him. They all tumbled to the floor.

He scrambled to hands and knees, driving one knee with all his weight into the top man's chest. He grabbed the man's head and smashed it into the lower man's face. Once, twice, again. Another shot was fired from the front.

He raced for the back door. A hand grabbed his foot, tripping him. Someone was trying to pin him. He squirmed to the side and rolled, blindly snapping his elbow behind him. He made glancing contact.

A gun barrel jammed into his face. Mason froze.

"Is this him?" the man behind the gun, breathing heavily, asked in Kanu. They were Mesos. How did they get this far behind CPC lines?

A woman, masked like the others, walked up. "Yeah, that's Mason."

He recognized her voice. "Sura?" It made sense. She had been Avalyn's contact for the Chevalier job.

"Still feel like a big man for screwing us out of five K?"

He looked at the men he had fought. "Is Shen here?"

"Shen? What do you care?"

"The CPC know about him." *Keep them talking.*

Three guns in view, including the one in his face. Tight quarters, cramped by the counter on one side and shelves on the other. Only one person could attack Mason at a time, but the thugs with guns farther back would be harder to engage.

"The CPC know what about him?" Sura asked.

"About the bomb. The Network tower."

The amorphous scrambler mask Sura wore stared blankly at him. She swore, grabbing a tin and banging it. "That stupid analog defect!"

Heads turned at Sura's tantrum. Mason attacked. Swipe the gun off target, kick to the balls.

The first man doubled over while Mason, his back still on the ground, planted his feet in the man's chest and pushed him hard into the attackers behind.

He spun to his knees and put the arm holding the gun in a reverse armbar. The elbow popped like a cracking back. The man screamed; the weapon dropped.

He pushed into the attackers, sending them stumbling into each other in the tight space. He grabbed the gun, spun, fired. Nothing. Biometric lock.

He threw the gun at the closest attacker, putting his weight behind the pitch. It cracked into the man's forehead, collapsing him to the ground.

Sura pushed past the last man as she tried to run away. *Let her go—one man left standing.* The remaining man was fresh, struggling to bring his gun to bear around Sura.

Mason leaped over the downed bodies, pushing the barrel off target while trying to grapple the arm. This guy knew how to fight. He started punching Mason in the head. Mason struggled to get a lock on the gun arm. They wrestled, crashing from the counter into the shelves and back into the counter again. One of the other men—the one with the broken elbow—got to his knees. Mason kicked for his head. Missed. The man he was grappling with grabbed a tin of supplies off a shelf and began banging it into Mason's face.

Mason got the lock on the gunman's wrist. With one hand,

Mason controlled the man through pressure on the wrist; with the other hand, he grabbed the man's trigger finger and started firing in the direction of Broken Elbow. There was no chance of aiming. Broken Elbow had picked up his gun in his off hand and returned fire.

There was no place to hide; they were no more than a metre apart. The cramped quarters amplified each gun blast. Someone screamed. Mason's head was taking a beating as the man he had in a wrist lock pummelled him with the canister. Mason snapped the wrist and swung the man to shield him from the other's shots. The guy put Mason in a choke hold with his good arm.

The explosion of gunfire was replaced with the click-click of a trigger pulled on an empty gun. The chokehold was weak, one-armed as it was. Mason undid it. *Punch to the neck, and down he goes.*

Everyone was down. Blood pooled on the floor and smeared the counters. Mason bolted out the back.

CHAPTER 44

MASON BARGED INTO HIS HOUSE. "We've got to leave. Now."

Oriana stared at him, shocked. "What happened?"

"I'll explain on the way." Mason stepped over Tracey's toys as he strode to Daxton's room.

"You're covered in blood." She grabbed his arm with the strength of a drowning woman. "Tracey can't see you like this. She's still terrorized from this morning."

"We don't have time."

She looked at his face, eyes wide. He had yet to look at himself since his beating. "I'm fine."

"You're not—" She choked back what she was going to say. "Mason, the news is saying the CPC is having trouble stopping Free New Mesopotamia's advance. Do you know something the news doesn't? Are we in danger?"

"Yes." Mason moved again toward Daxton's room, a storm cloud on the wind.

Again, Oriana stopped him. "Clean yourself up. I'll get the kids." She pushed him toward the bathroom as she hurried to the children's room. "Do we have time to pack?"

"No."

Mason surveyed himself in the mirror once he closed the

bathroom door. He was impressed with Oriana's composure. Blood matted his black hair and stained his face and clothes. Underneath the layer of dried blood, his face was bruised and swollen.

He tried once more to access Dashiell with no luck. "Are you able to access the neural net?" he called out to Oriana.

"Yes, why?" Her voice was edged with panic.

Shanelle would be monitoring the house, a fox waiting for her prey to make a mistake. Was it a mistake to come home? He had to get his family out of New Uruk. Avalyn honoured family—maybe she would let him get his to safety.

"I need you to call a vehicle."

He washed in the sink, gingerly taking his shirt off to clean a cut on his arm, then dabbed healing goo he pulled out of a drawer onto his wounds to seal them and accelerate tissue repair. He left his bloody shirt in the tub and grabbed a new one from his closet.

Oriana was waiting with Tracey and Daxton. Tracey was in Oriana's arms in her red pyjamas, her eyes bleary. Daxton slept in a handheld baby carrier. "What happened to your face, Daddy?" Tracey asked.

"I fell down at work. It looks bad, but it doesn't hurt too much," Mason lied.

"The transport's here," Oriana said.

He had her wait with the children away from the windows while he grabbed a knife from the kitchen. Dirty dishes sat on the counter—it was his night to clean up after dinner. Armed, he checked to make sure no one was with the transport, which did nothing to allay Oriana's rising terror. He ushered his family in and then ordered the transport to take them to his brother's house on the coast.

Once they were on the freeway, they joined a long line of transports leaving the city. They cruised slowly. Mason called his brother from the car, letting him know they were coming. Once

Tracey had fallen asleep in her chair, Oriana turned to Mason. "What's going on?"

He told her everything—the BLOQ, the angel network, using Shen to knock out the Network station, everything. They were approaching the city limits as he finished, and she sat in silence for a long time.

She leaned over and placed a hand on his knee. "We need Avalyn, Mason."

"*Need* her?"

"The army of Free New Mesopotamia is *inside* Caelum. She's the best hope we have to survive this."

"Free New Mesopotamia is inside Caelum because she let them in," Mason said.

"Are you sure of that?"

"Yes."

She cocked her head, sympathy in her eyes. "But you don't have evidence. You're guessing."

"I'm certain."

"But you don't have proof."

"Just my word. Avalyn let the armies of Free New Mesopotamia in. She's the reason Tracey's daycare was attacked."

"Avalyn didn't attack Tracey's daycare," Oriana said bitterly. She crossed her arms and looked out the vehicle's window at the city's lights. "It was Mesos who attacked Tracey's daycare. We shouldn't need the Network to keep our daycares safe. Civilized people live side by side without the need for an industrialized military complex keeping them from attacking each other's children."

"And the sniper squad I told you about? Tracey and Daxton will have to serve their two years in the CPC. You want them to be cheering as they kill unarmed teenagers? Is that what you want your children to become?"

"It is my dream that when Tracey and Daxton are that age,

there will be no Mesos left in Caelum that we need to protect ourselves from. Only then will we be safe."

Silence enveloped them save for the hum of the road as they travelled. How did she envision Caelum would remove all the Mesos from its borders? Even if they could, would doing so make them safe? Mesos were Kanu, and Kanu nations surrounded them. No matter how Caelum chose to rid themselves of Mesos, the hostility of their neighbours would only increase. *Can you really eliminate everyone who poses a threat? The universe would burn if you tried.*

It was an act of brutality that had poisoned Oriana: a bomb dropped on her school, friends and teachers dead. Terror had run thick through her veins since that moment. Mason understood. He had felt the same since watching Myla die. Terror was a reasonable response.

That terror was not Oriana, however, and she could never be who she truly was while in its grip. And his people—could his people be who they truly were while they, too, lived in fear? Terror had led him to murder Hadu, a boy in his teens. Mason wanted to be a good father, a good man, but fear had made him a monster. It had made Avalyn a monster. It had made his people monsters. It was probably what had made the Kanu monsters, too.

He needed evidence. That was the only way to stop Avalyn, and stopping her was the only chance to end this. If his people were to have any hope of drawing back from the cliffs of madness they stumbled along, they had to see that the hand holding the knife at their throat was their own.

Would people believe his evidence? Would they allow themselves to see the monster in the mirror? Humans were fantastic at deluding themselves, especially when working themselves up to violence.

Some would believe it. The Director-General and his followers would. That might be enough. He needed to get the

BLOQ's program tat to Meli. To do that, he would need to break into the *Aigle* to steal it from Avalyn's office.

The problem was, of all the people he knew who made a living breaking into high-security buildings and extracting computer files, one had been hired by Avalyn to kill him, while the other languished in jail. Which would be easier—getting Ashme out of jail or convincing Sura to spare him?

Avalyn had hired Mesos to attack him to make it look like a random attack. If she wanted his death to look random, perhaps she had maintained his security clearance, especially if she knew he had been talking to Meli. It might, after all, cast suspicion on her if she cut him off hours before he died.

If his clearance was still intact, he could go to the calming centre where Ashme was kept and pull a "She's wanted for questioning by Avalyn's office." Not even Avalyn would anticipate that move.

A risky plan, though less risky than waiting for Shanelle to hunt him down. He would have to pay Ashme. They would need equipment, too. He still had the cashtab he had been given for expenses for the Chevalier job. He checked it. Sixty kilobits and change. That would be enough that she could afford editing for Shen. He liked that.

Oriana looked at him suspiciously. "I know that look, Mason. What are you planning?"

Mason knew what he needed to do—or die trying to do. Oriana might never understand, might never forgive him. She was afraid, and when you are afraid, your only rationality is fear; you cannot reason past it. As fear becomes entrenched, it calls forth its siblings: anger, hatred, greed, blindness. The world the Ostarrichi and Mesos had created bred fear. He wanted a world worthy of his family, but such things only exist if you build them. So, he would do it. He would build a world worthy of his family.

His new resolve filled him with thunderous energy.

CHAPTER 45

AVALYN SAT on a bench outside the *Aigle* chambers, alone. She studied the bench's curves. It had a name: the *Keraunós*. It defied the senses. The seat was a cloud hovering above the base. It had more substance than a cloud, however, for it bore Avalyn's weight, though it felt like sitting on air. From this cumulonimbus seat, lightning silently shot, always multiple bolts, ever changing. To the eye, it defied gravity, but it could bear the weight of a ground transport. It was one of the Fourteen Relics, scraps salvaged from the ruins of the *A.O. Aigle*, the Ostarrichi's trade ship, as the Sentient Esus cannibalized it during the Catastrophe. Otherworldly. No other word could describe it.

An angel hovered to either side of Avalyn while she waited, their reflective surfaces distorting her image in stereo. In front of her stood the doors of the Chambers, where Caelum's government sat in a late-night emergency session, debating the next steps needed to defend the nation from the Free New Mesopotamian invasion.

This damn knee. Even sitting, it ached. *Age turns one's body into a traitor.* She had nothing to do while she waited, nothing to take her mind off the throbbing pain.

It had been a long time since she had been left so alone. The last time was those few moments after Neville had died. For twenty minutes, it was her and the body of her husband in that dim hospital room, no one else.

He had been a good man, a good father and husband. He had gotten so old near the end, his body and mind failing. It was the failing mind that terrified her. He had been such a force, indomitable, but his second body had been a mistake. You can create a new body, you can edit the fraying telomeres of the cells within the brain, but as the years add up, the rate of decay ultimately outstrips the rate of repair and systems collapse like glaciers calving off into the ocean. The mind is the one thing you cannot replace, and the mind decays. In the end, Neville failed to recognize her and their children, said the foulest things to his caregivers, and had to be spoon-fed. *Better to end when the first body dies rather than move to a new one where the brain can rot.*

He'd died only six months ago. Avalyn had yet to complete her year of firsts—first birthday alone, first anniversary alone . . .

She stretched her leg. Sometimes, that helped ease the throbbing.

The *clack-clack-clack* of footsteps echoed down the hall. Shanelle emerged from the shadows. "You're not in Chambers?" she said as she drew close.

"I've recused myself," Avalyn said. "They are debating whether to ask me to step down as Floor Leader so that I might be reinstated as the Grand General in charge of the CPC."

"How's the debate going?"

Avalyn shrugged and pointed at the closed doors. "They've been at it for a while."

Shanelle sat on the bench and brought up a privacy shield to surround them. "What's the contingency plan if they don't give you command of the CPC?"

"They will."

"The Director-General's a political beast. He'll fight tooth and nail to keep the CPC from you."

"He is a political beast, but the tide carries us all, beast and patriot alike. The tide has turned against him. I will be reinstated." Shanelle was tense, a fox ready to pounce, which disturbed Avalyn's calmness. She nodded toward the privacy shield. "Is there something you wished to speak to me about?"

"Mason escaped."

Her knuckles, gnarled talons of hands, ached as her fists clenched. "Does he know it's us?"

"We've burned his personal AI. He knows everything. He was meeting with Meli from the Director-General's office when he was attacked."

Fight the panic. Master it. "Did he tell her anything?" That could sway the vote against her.

"Unknown. We should have removed Mason after he gave you the BLOQ."

"I had hoped to recruit him." He was a family man, a good man. Naive but good, and Caelum needed good men. She had thought him a patriot. She had been a good judge of character back in the field, but ever since entering the political arena, the duplicity of others had repeatedly disappointed her.

Politics was a foul game. She preferred war—it was neater. War united people; politics divided them. War exposed disloyalty; politics hid it. War drew a clear line separating those with you from those against you. Politics made allies fluid. Her judgment of Mason had been that of an officer judging the character of her troops. She was not a political beast—her weakness. "The past is ash. We deal with the situation on the ground as it is. Where is Mason now?"

"He got his family out of town. They're at his brother's. I believe he's heading back to New Uruk," Shanelle said.

Avalyn cocked her head. "Why is he coming back to New Uruk?"

"Unknown. Earlier today, he received a transmission that Citizen 539618-d, class 2A, Ashme ultu Vanc, was captured by the CPC. She was picked up with her cousin. Ashme is an associate of your contact in the Meso underworld that Mason met during the BLOQ project. She's an indigo child."

"ultu Vanc—any relation to the bomber, Shenshen?"

"They're twins."

That was an unlikely coincidence. What was Mason playing at? Did he have a plan, or was panic making him think wild? "Why is he going to see her? He knows we hired her crew to murder him."

Shanelle shrugged. "Her brother's a genetic defect. So's his son."

Avalyn shook her head. That the enemy suffers, too, is not a reason to betray your people but a weakness to exploit. "Ping me Ashme's file," she said. Shanelle pinged the data packet to her neural net. Avalyn opened it and began reviewing it in her mind's eye.

Shanelle turned to Avalyn. "I'd like to neutralize Mason before he re-enters New Uruk. I have an angel following his transport that can fire at your command."

Mason had already talked to someone in the Director-General's office. If he'd had hard evidence, chances were the Director-General would have already issued orders for her arrest rather than debating whether to hand her command of the CPC. He had a suspicion, nothing more.

If Mason were to die at the hands of an angel, however . . . "It has to look like Mesos killed him," Avalyn said.

A hand poked through the haze of the privacy shield and signalled for her to come. The debate was over. This was exhilarating. The battle was in full play. Time to see if her gambit worked.

"I'll make a call to Sura again."

"No," Avalyn said as she processed Ashme's datafile in her neural net. "Have Sura on backup. I've got a different plan. If they give me command of the CPC, contact Ark *Brettaniai* immediately and tell them we're moving ahead. They can join me or be left behind."

Shanelle dropped the privacy shield, and Avalyn stood. A man waited for her, one of her party's members of parliament, an officer who once served under her and had followed her into politics. His smile was enormous as he gave her a thumbs-up.

The thrill of winning that always came when she had outmanoeuvred her enemy soared. She had launched her spear, and it had landed true—they were going to give her the CPC.

Avalyn strode into the *Aigle's* chamber.

CHAPTER 46

"WHY DON'T you tell us where Sura might hide?" the nasty young man asked Ashme. He wore a white smock and sat on the other side of a white table in a white room. The CPC had kept her up through the night. Nasty Man had replaced the grandmother who had started her questioning hours ago.

They had already raided the homes of anyone she was close to, of which Sura was the only one who was alive. No luck finding Shen. Sura must have gone underground and taken Shen with her.

"Aren't you afraid your Free New Mesopotamian associates have already killed your brother to cover their tracks? Don't you want to find out if he's okay? Help me find Sura. If your brother's still alive, we can save him before Free New Mesopotamia kills him. Or, if he's dead, we can give Sura the justice she deserves."

That thought terrified her. They had told her about Shen's role in bombing the Network. Free New Mesopotamia might have killed both Shen and Sura. If Sura was alive, Ashme was going to gouge out her eyes. She had never wanted to kill a Meso until now. At this moment, she could rat her out to the

CPC without a hint of guilt. Giving them Sura, however, would also give them Shen.

The door opened behind her. Nasty Man stood up and left the room. The door clicked closed, leaving her alone with whoever this new person was. There had been no torture, yet, aside from lack of sleep. Was it about to start?

Whoever was behind her pulled a bag over her head and tied it tight around her neck.

CHAPTER 47

THE BAG'S blackness smothered Ashme's vision. She was in a transport bouncing along the road, her hands shackled behind her. She dozed lightly, exhausted. Every fibre of her wanted to call out and ask where they were going, but they had yet to break her. She had no intention of being the quivering, scared Meso for their entertainment.

The transport jolted as it stopped, banging her head into a bulkhead. A door opened. The morning air that wafted in was cold. Hands tossed her onto the hard pavement, skinning her arm.

"Get your feet under you! Get up!"

Hands pulled at her, raising her to her knees. Were they going to shoot her? Rape her?

Someone tore the bag off. Ashme blinked in the grey dawn light. It was hard to tell where she was—the buildings were rubble, concrete blocks spilling into the roadway. Maybe Rabu Flats, near the Salamu. She shivered in the dawn breeze. The distant beat of gunfire echoed. The bass hum of drones and angels reached her ears from a distance.

Someone moaned. "Ganzer!" she cried out when she saw him lying behind her. He wore a white biogineer gown, and a sickly pallor coloured his dark skin. A sheen of sweat soaked his gown. She hardly recognized him—they had shaved his head and beard. She lay down on the street in front of him, so her face was in front of his. "Ganzer, you in there?"

He smiled, his eyes opening and focusing on her. "Oh, Ashme, it's good to see you."

Looking at his bald head and face, she said, "They shaved you. You look like a baby."

His smile turned into a soft laugh.

One of the guards—there were four of them, all wearing CPC combat armour, along with an angel floating above—asked in Ostarrichi, "How long do we wait? I'm starving."

A sergeant stared at a data screen. "You wait until I tell you to stop waiting."

"Are they looking after you?" Ashme asked Ganzer. "How's your gunshot?"

Another guard kicked her in the back. "Shut it." His accent was atrocious.

"No," the sergeant said, never taking his eyes off the data screen. "Let them talk."

"It's too early in the morning to listen to them bark at each other," the guard said, talking in Ostarrichi now.

"Let 'em bark."

"It's nice," Ganzer said.

"What?" Ashme asked.

"It's nice they let us spend some time together."

"Yeah, peaches and cream."

Ganzer breathed deeply. "I did it, Ashme."

"Did what?"

"I'm not angry," Ganzer said.

Ashme frowned, confused.

He said, "All this time, I thought it was about controlling my anger, but it was never about controlling it. It was about letting it go."

"Maybe you don't look like a baby," she said. "Maybe you look like a Hierophant."

"That's the nicest thing anyone has ever said to me." He looked at her, his eyes a wonderful green, a deep abyss that held worlds. "I never got to say this before. I'm glad the universe blessed my life with you."

"Don't say shit like that," Ashme said. "That's how dying people talk."

"I ain't feeling so good."

He did not look good, either. She thought of life without him, and her gut coiled, aching. "Well, you ain't dying, so buck up."

The sergeant pressed an earbud to his ear. "We're in position. Target's ETA is three minutes." He paused to listen to the response of whoever was on the other end of the line. The other guards stood straighter and tightened their grips on their weapons. *Almost show time*, Ashme thought. "Understood," the sergeant said to whoever he was talking to. "I'd like to add that it's a pleasure to serve under you again, Ma'am."

"What's happening?" Ganzer asked.

"I don't know, but everyone's walking around with a stick up their ass."

"It's time," the sergeant said in Ostarrichi to the other guards. "Take her restraints off."

Ashme and Ganzer exchanged a confused glance. "Did you understand that?" Ashme asked.

"Yeah, they're taking your restraints off," Ganzer said. "What gives?"

"They're looking for Shen."

"What? Why?"

"Long story. Looks like they're going to set me loose to find him and use you as collateral to make sure I come back."

"Don't do anything stupid," Ganzer said.

"If I get out of here," she whispered to him as the guards pulled her up, "I'll do everything I can to free you."

"If you get out of here, find Shen and leave Caelum," Ganzer said.

They turned her away from Ganzer to take off her handcuffs. *Definitely Rabu Flats.* She recognized the remains of the buildings left standing. The ascending slope of the road leading to the Hab was a dead giveaway, too. She was in the centre of the city. Sura's place was in the north. If they wanted her to be their hunting dog, the least they could have done was drop her off closer to Sura's last known whereabouts. *Dicks.* She rubbed the circulation back into her wrists.

Her body jerked as a gunshot cracked.

CHAPTER 48

STARING at Ashme from the centre of Ganzer's chest was a single, dark hole. Such a small, tiny hole. Blood burbled out of it. His eyes stared at nothing. They were unfocused, empty, becoming more doll-like and unreal as the pulse of blood spilling on his chest waned.

He had taken decades to grow into the man he had become. It had taken teachers and family guiding him, layering their experience onto his own. It had taken thousands of hours of training and exercise to create the body he had: discipline and drive, a life spent trying to improve himself, trying to rise higher than the foundation his upbringing gave him. Years of tears, struggle, joy, and laughter. It took so much by so many to make him.

All of it was gone in an instant, dead because of a small hole in his chest created by a piece of metal no bigger than a pebble. It seemed wrong that something that took so much to create should be so easy to destroy. It said something about the universe that this should be so.

She sat on her knees beside him, one hand on his chest, the other cupping his head. Already, his body seemed unreal. His gaze was vacant, like a mannequin in a store, his body unnaturally still, a wax figure in a museum. A pool of blood formed on the concrete, expanding outward, drenching her knees.

How could he be dead? There was no reason for them to kill him. This was a trick. It had to be.

Metal clattered on the ground. One of the guards dropped the pistol that had killed Ganzer on the other side of his body and walked away. The CPC were piling into their transport while the angel soared high into the air.

She picked up the gun. Cold steel. Its handle conformed to her grip. The biometric locks were keyed to her handprint. The weapon hummed to life in her grasp.

The transport rumbled away, crunching small blocks of concrete as it went. The deep, trilling thrum of the angel's engines increased in pitch as it soared away over rooftops. Ashme was alone with Ganzer's body and a gun.

Why did they leave the gun? Did they want to frame her for Ganzer's murder? There was no reason to do that—they already had her in prison. Did they expect she would use it to kill herself? Is this how they got their kicks? They were probably watching her now, laughing, wagering bets as to whether she would blow her brains out or go on a rampage.

Maybe they were toying with her, giving her a sense of power and control. They probably had a sniper platform trained on her, ready to take her out the moment she found some goldie to kill, the moment she thought she might have revenge. She had no information to give them about Shen; she had no value at all other than their sick entertainment. Shen was gone. Ganzer was gone. Melammu was gone. Hamilcar was gone. Maybe if she was fast enough, she could take one of those sick fucks down before they took her out.

Her knuckles were white on the gun's grip. The weapon felt barren, like a ravaged field, a poisoned well, a dearth, a void, cold. It felt like the silence after a song. Her breath came in ragged gasps through clenched teeth.

The rattle of a transport driving over loose gravel came up

behind her. She screwed her eyes shut, squeezing out her vision. A door opened, and then footsteps crunched on stone.

She spun, fired. The gun kicked. The shot boomed down the street, echoing off the sides of buildings.

Missed.

The man—an Ostarrichi, gold skin like the sun, his face bruised and swollen—stumbled back, hands in the air. "Ashme, don't shoot!" It was Mason, the bastard who'd started this whole thing.

Her body shook. He was in her sights. The next shot would hit.

He took a step toward the open door of his transport. "Stop!" she screamed. Her voice's ferocity froze him. "On your knees!"

He dropped down, hands high. His gaze shifted to Ganzer. "Oh, Ashme," he said. She hated the way his accent mangled her language. "I'm so sorry."

"Sorry?" The word lit a fire. She raged, yelling, incoherent. He trembled, holding his hands out. He was afraid. Good. Let the Ostarrichi know fear; let the goldie tremble.

He was babbling something. ". . . to help. I have a job that can save us both. I'll pay you enough that you can get Shen edited."

"You want me to edit Shen?" He winced as she strode toward him. She jammed the barrel of her gun right into his filthy, golden forehead. "What makes you think he needs editing?" She loomed over him, twisting the gun into his skin. "Tell me how my brother's broken. Tell me how he's broken and needs to be fixed."

She watched him master his breathing. "I'm trying to help." Calm, but still a quiver of fear in his voice.

"Help? What do you think's going to happen to me when I walk into a clinic with enough cash for a full edit?"

"I don't know. I don't know how to—"

"You know what's fucked up?" Ashme asked. "When Ganzer and I got picked up, there was this kid who called out an alarm. I had a gun and had that kid in my sights. If I'd pulled the trigger, it'd have been one more shot in a war zone, and Ganzer and I would have walked away. But I didn't, and so that kid screamed bloody murder and brought the CPC down on us. Now Ganzer's dead. What kind of world is it where letting a kid live gets my cousin killed? What lesson am I supposed to learn from that?"

"I don't know what you want me to say." His voice was dry, his eyes squeezed shut. He opened his eyes, pleading with her. "I'm trying to fix this."

A cold spike of ice settled in her gut. "I know how to fix this."

His eyes widened further. "Ashme, what are you doing?"

"I'm going to blow your brains out," she said. "It's time we stained the streets with goldie blood for a change."

"That's not going to fix anything!"

"If you goldies could feel the pain you've given us, then you'd know how wrong you've been."

"You know that's not how it works." His shoulders slumped. "I'm trying to help. I have a family. I have two kids. My son, he's . . . he's sick like Shen is."

"Bullshit."

"It's true. It's a different disease, but his genes, they're . . . not right. Let me show you a picture."

Slowly, he moved his hand to his collar. He called up a data screen from an emitter on the cuff of his sleeve, displaying a picture of a baby. It was skinny and looked like its head was too small for its body.

"That doesn't prove anything," she said.

"He'll die before he's two without editing."

Mason had always looked at Shen with a mix of fascination and fear. He had told her to get him out of town the day before her botched assassination attempt. Now, he wanted to give Ashme money to edit Shen. What did he care?

Maybe it was true. Maybe Ostarrichi kids got sick, too. Too bad. Shen grew up without a dad. So would Mason's kid.

She braced herself for the gun's kick. Mason looked at her.

His eyes were not afraid, not begging or bawling. They were sad, like Dad's eyes on the day he died.

Stay hard. She had killed a CPC trooper. She could do this. Killing was supposed to get easier.

She could still see the back of that trooper's head at the end of her gun. Back of the head—maybe that was the trick. She moved around behind Mason.

"What are you doing?" he asked.

"Shut up." She placed the barrel of the gun on the back of his skull. He held his breath, waiting. She'd spared that kid's life, and Ganzer died. *No mistakes this time. Do it!*

THE CPC HAD KILLED eight Mesos in retaliation for the trooper Ashme killed. That was bad, but, of course, it got worse. A week after Dad blew his brains out, she and Mom had been planning the groceries—the first time in days Mom had looked to the future—when the CPC came with bulldozers. The soldiers pulled Ashme and her family out to the street. They watched the bulldozers demolish their home. Their land was being expropriated, some bitch in a pantsuit told them, an angel hovering over her.

And just like that, they were homeless.

Ashme remembered looking up and down the street. Theirs was the only house being demolished. The CPC held the crowd back, but no one else had been pulled into the streets, no other homes smashed down. She nearly vomited when she realized why.

When Dad shot himself, the CPC had come to investigate. They took the body and gun he had used—the same gun Ashme had used to murder that CPC trooper. Even at their densest, the CPC could match the weapon to the bullet put through that trooper's head. They had probably figured Dad shot her, but since he had taken his own life and escaped their justice, the only thing they could do was screw over his family.

A terrible curse, the words, "If only . . ." Violence has an echo, bouncing off one life into another.

Mom snapped. How much could one woman bear? Her husband dead less than a week, and now their home destroyed. With a keening wail, she charged a CPC soldier. The trooper knocked her down. Three of them laid the boots to her. Shen had screamed like a trapped animal. It took all Ashme's strength to hold him back from charging the CPC, too.

They had dragged Mom away, her nose broken, blood all over her face. She wished her last memory of her mom had been of her beauty. "Take Shen and go to Melammu's!" Mom had screamed as they pulled her toward a transport. "Go to Melammu's! Look after your brother!"

LOOK AFTER YOUR BROTHER. Those were the last words Ashme ever heard Mom speak. Her shoulders slumped, gun arm dropping to her side as the hate flowed out of her. That was the last thing her mom had asked her to do, and she had done a cock-up job of it.

She had so much wanted to be the hero. The world needed heroes. She was, however, Shen's sister, his womb-mate. She was the one who was supposed to hold him, keeping the pain of life away so he might know a little joy, the one who would sing to him while the world burned. Perhaps those were the heroes the world needed.

She had to find Shen. She had to look after him. They were all each other had.

She would need to cross Ostarrichi neighbourhoods to get to Sura's district. Of course, Sura had gone underground, taking Shen with her. She began walking in the direction of Sura's district.

"What are you doing?" Mason asked.

She kept walking.

He caught up, blocked her path. "Where are you going?"

"I've got to find Shen."

"You and all of Caelum."

"I'm his sister. I can find him."

"And then what?" Mason asked. "Right now, Shen's more of a wanted man than Baltu. He's going to spend the rest of his life being hunted."

Ashme shoved Mason with all her strength, sending him stumbling. "I'm finding Shen!"

"Look, Ashme, I don't know how to fix things between our people," Mason said. She pushed past him, but he blocked her way. "If we can get the BLOQ from Avalyn's office, we can show that she's the one responsible for this slaughter, not the Mesos. We can take her down and pull our people back from war."

Ashme walked around him.

"And if you had access to the BLOQ, I think there's a good chance you could erase Shen's name from the angel network or register him as dead so they stop hunting him."

Ashme stopped walking. "How?"

"The BLOQ is a key providing access to the angel network. Avalyn's been using it to control the angels. Once you're in the network, an indigo child like you should have no problem erasing Shen from their system. If Shen's gone from the system or reported dead, he might have a chance at a good life."

That would mean breaking into Avalyn's office instead of finding her brother. Good chance she would get blue-screened. Then, her twin would be alone, a note without a song.

A hum sounded in the air, quiet, subtle.

"This is the best chance of giving Shen a life free from being hunted," Mason said. Did he hear the hum? "If we can stop this fight from escalating and clear his name, things could be good for him. Especially with the money you're getting. That's enough to set you up someplace nice if you don't want to edit him. All our families could live in peace."

"All my family's dead."

"Not Shen. You can still give him a future."

If the BLOQ did give her control over the angel network, well, that might make the odds pretty good of getting out of Avalyn's office in one piece. A tiny cotyledon of hope unfurled under the soil of her heart. "First thing we got to do is get this EM disrupter off my neck."

Mason smiled. "I can help you with that." The hum turned into a soft rumble. Mason looked at the sky. "You hear that?"

"Doesn't sound like fighter drones or angels." The rumble crescendoed. "There." Ashme pointed skyward.

A dozen ships were dropping in from orbit. They looked like wide skyscrapers lying on their side high in the sky.

"What are those?" Ashme asked. "I've never seen CPC vehicles or aircraft like that."

Air raid sirens began to wail through the city as Mason squinted into the sky. "I have no idea."

CHAPTER 49

THE KLAXON of sirens pierced the air, interrupting Avalyn's conversation with a CPC sergeant. The fighting was blocks away. The *pop-pop-pop* of gunfire echoed, but it paused, a brief lull as the human soldiers looked to the sky as the ships appeared over the city. The air was thick with the smell of dust, smoke, and gunpowder.

"Whose are those?" the sergeant asked, squinting as he looked for any flag or emblem that would give away the allegiance of the craft.

Avalyn's face was a steel mask of grim satisfaction. She wore her combat armour—it had been euphoric donning it to march once more into the throes of battle. It was deep violet, almost black, with epaulettes of gold. It was intended to be ceremonial—Grand Generals were not supposed to wade into battle but rather strut about command centres, peering at data screens. That had never been Avalyn's way. Battles had a feel to them, a personality. Details mattered. Information, as it travelled up the chain of command, accumulated layers of bullshit as each subordinate spun the story to look good to their superior. If you really wanted to understand what was happening, you had to get your boots on and walk the line. Father had taught her that.

Shanelle approached. She, too, wore her combat armour, onyx black with a faint emblem of a spectral hand grasping a sword, the mark of the Wraiths, the CPC's special ops.

"Thank you for your report, Sergeant," Avalyn said, dismissing the soldier.

Shanelle snapped to attention, saluting. "Captain Yosef NK-55-d of Ark *Brettaniai* is trying to ping you."

The Brettaniai were making their move. "I'll take it in my HQ," Avalyn said. Last night, soon after she had assumed command of the CPC, long-range scanners had identified several Brettaniai vessels entering treaty space toward Esharra. They were war drones—their acceleration was too high for a human crew. At the same time, the *Brettaniai* dispatched a fleet toward the Oort cloud on an intercept course with Ark *Gallia*. All the players were committed to the game.

Dismissing Shanelle, Avalyn went to her mobile headquarters. It looked like a house-sized turtle on treads covered with interlocking plates of carbon tubule-reinforced composite armour. She walked through the airlock, past the control room where officers sat jammed together monitoring dozens of readouts, and into her office, which had room for little more than a small desk and chair.

She opened the message on a data screen, and an image of Yosef appeared, his long, thin nose dominating the picture of his albino-white face. "Captain," she greeted him. "Am I correct in assuming those are your ships above New Uruk?"

"Yes, General," he replied. "We've assessed the situation in Caelum, and we would like to support your leadership bid."

Avalyn suppressed a knowing smile. "The Director-General is tightly bound to the Ahiim treaty and capitulating to the Kanu, isn't he?"

"To a disappointing degree. Through his inaction, the Director-General has allowed Ark *Gallia* to sell weapons to proxies on Esharra. This risks undermining Caelum and disrupting the relations between our people. Ark *Brettaniai* offers its aid to you, General, to restore the status quo."

"Aid that I graciously accept," Avalyn said. "Perhaps you might start by telling me the capabilities of the war drones you've positioned over New Uruk."

CHAPTER 50

THERE WERE SO many beautiful people to meet at Sura's new place. In her old home, it was only him and Sura, and she was always busy or in a bad mood, and it smelled like dirty laundry. But here, in this new place, there was always someone to talk to. Relocating had tied his tummy into knots, but he liked it here. There was Zamar—he was as big as Ganzer, white as a ghost, had long black hair, swore a lot, and liked industrial mitutu-anbar drum solos. He had been in a recent fight, and his face was all bruised. Jushur was a maca ball tweaker, and he was currently in the zoned-out stage of the drug cycle. This was his place, and he had a keyboard. Ashme had worked for Jushur, building stasis tats, so he must be okay. He was the man to know, Sura said, because he sold all sorts of stuff, the kinds of things unavailable in stores.

Amnanu, another of Jushur's roommates, was so funny, and Meania was pretty, with skin like molten chocolate. She and Amnanu had sex. A lot. They were having sex right now in another room. Even through the closed door, you could hear Amnanu's grunts. It sounded like he was getting punched in the stomach, rapid-fire-like. "It's a beautiful sound, don't you think," Jushur said dreamily. "Like the heavens, singing. Like, union, two becoming one. The math of the universe. The Deep." He began grunting in time to Amnanu's exertions.

Zamar had pushed his dirty breakfast dishes aside and built a drum beat using his hands on the table out of the rhythm of Amnanu's grunts. Shen was trying to develop a power riff on Jushur's keyboard off Zamar's drumming when the siren started. It began quietly, tough to hear over the sounds of sex and music, but it quickly got loud enough to hear over everything.

"Pipe down," Sura said to Zamar and Shen as she moved to the window.

The siren felt horrible in the ears like a hurt dog crying. "I don't like it," Shen said.

"Yeah, no shit," Sura said, looking out the window. Nothing to see but another building a few metres away. Amnanu's grunting picked up its pace.

Zamar pulled up a data screen from an emitter he had attached to one of his bracelets to watch the news feed. "Get a load of this asshole," he said. On the screen, a Brettaniai officer was making an announcement. He spoke in Ostarrichi, which Shen had never learned, but the news feed was overlaying a translation in Kanu.

". . . to protect Caelum from Ark *Gallia*'s proxies . . ."

That was nice. He wanted to protect Caelum. Shen could understand that—he, too, wanted his home to be safe. So did Ashme. That was what she was always fighting for. "Maybe we can help him."

"Shut up," Sura said, focusing on the news feed. "Who is this guy?"

"I pinged the datalinks," Zamar said. "It says he's the captain of a Brettaniai warship."

"Oh, man," Jushur said, "look at the size of that guy's nose. Captain Big-Nose of Ark *Big-Nose*."

Shen thought that was funny, but no one else laughed. Amnanu and Meania came out of their room. Meania was pulling a shirt over her head. "What's up? Are we under attack?"

Zamar pointed at the screen. "Ark *Brettaniai* has decided to get in the fight. They've got warships over New Uruk."

Amnanu swore. He, too, had been in a fight, and his hand was in a transparent cast.

"Warships, man," Jushur said, staring at the ceiling of his apartment. "Gonna be good for biz-nas. Sell my blackout bombzzz for some maca ballzzz. Thank you, Captain Big-Nose."

Sura told everyone to shut up.

". . . to all the warriors of the Free New Mesopotamian army, we will defend Caelum. We will give you ten minutes to begin your withdrawal. If you do not comply, we will commence bombardment . . ."

Everyone in the room exploded in curses. The klaxons screamed like a wounded animal. Shen had never been on an actual ark before. He was surprised by how loud they were.

Nobody was paying any attention to him. He decided to go look for Ark *Brettaniai*.

He went into the hallway. Perhaps they would be quieter if someone asked nicely. Maybe they were nice like Hamilcar. They were all Ark-monkeys, so it stood to reason that if Hamilcar was nice, Ark *Brettaniai* would be nice too.

This building had an elevator, which he rode down to ground level. It made a strange hum when it ran, which was different from the elevator at home. Thinking of Hamilcar and the elevator at home reminded him of the last time he saw Ashme and the horrible, horrible roaring of the angels. He knew Hamilcar was dead. His memory of those moments when Hamilcar died and he got separated from Ashme was hazy, but he knew Hamilcar's song was over.

He knew, now, that being dead was different than being gone. Ashme had told him death was like going away—that was what she had said about Mom and Dad. But when people went away, they could come back. Ashme had said Mom and Dad would never come back, but he had never understood why. He understood it now. Death was not people going away. People were a song, and death was that song's ending, and that was forever. His heart hurt like someone was squeezing it in their fist.

The elevator made a pleasant dinging sound as it opened like a little silver bell ringing. He wanted to find Ashme. That was all, just Ashme. He wanted to be whole again. Even the screaming wail of Ark *Brettaniai* would be okay if he could find Ashme. Maybe he should look for Ashme instead of the ark, he thought as he walked out of the building and onto the street.

The siren was louder outside, so much so that he covered his ears with his hands. There were a lot of people running. Everybody wanted to meet the Ark *Brettaniai*. Maybe Ashme would want to meet the ark, too. If she followed the siren, and if Shen followed the siren, then they were bound to meet.

The barking siren sounded like it was coming from all directions, so he started walking down the street, hoping he could get a better sense of its source. He strode to an intersection. One side, the other side, or straight ahead? The noise was equally loud in every direction. This was important—if Ashme went to the siren, that was their best chance to meet. He picked a course and walked.

Someone called his name. *Ashme?* He turned, shoulders slumping as he saw Sura chasing him. "Zini's stacks, where are you going, Dum-dum?"

The name Dum-dum upset him, but he wanted to keep her happy, so he said, "Where am I going? Well, I'm going to see the Ark *Brettaniai*. If Ashme follows the sirens, then I will meet her there, and we will be together once more. Then—*shhh!*—we can ask Ark *Brettaniai* to turn down their sirens."

"Those sirens aren't the *Brettaniai*. They're our air raid sirens."

The air cannot raid anything—it is just air. What a character Sura is sometimes. He asked, "Are you going to see Ark *Brettaniai* too? We can go together."

Sura rested her head in her hand. "Shit, Shen, you can't be outside. The CPC is looking for you, and if they find you, they'll find me, remember? You don't want anything bad to happen to me, do you? Do you remember us talking about this?"

Oh, right. "I remember."

"Then what are you doing outside?"

He'd just told her. Did she forget already? "You want to know what I'm doing outside?" The sirens made his head ache.

"Come with me back to the apartment."

"But Ashme might go to the sirens. It's like a beacon, a lighthouse that draws us together."

"Ashme's not going to the sirens. Nobody's going to the sirens. The sirens are in the city. The Brettaniai are up there," she said, pointing to the sky.

Shen looked up and saw several long and narrow grey slabs hovering over the city. He had seen aerial personnel carriers and flying drones, but these were different. They were like apartment buildings lying on their side, floating in the sky. "I don't want Ashme's song to end." His heart fluttered, and his stomach twisted.

"Ashme's song? What—"

"Ashme's gone." His breath was coming in gasps. This was bad. This was scary—flying buildings, barking sirens, and Ashme gone. He was incomplete. He was different from other people, and without Ashme, he was a fragment, a piece. "Gone people can come back, but when the song ends, that's forever. Her song can't end. I'd be broken!"

"Fuck, Shen, calm down," Sura said. "Ashme's a big girl, she's fine."

"Does she know we've moved?"

"When she's able, she'll punch a message through—"

There was a sound, a horrible, horrible sound, like a million angels firing at once. It was so loud it sucked the air out of his lungs, shook the earth, rattled all the windows along the street, and blasted dust and debris off the sidewalk into the air. He turned in the direction it came from to see a grey cloud rising from only a couple of blocks away, billowing into the sky. Dark dots trailing white contrails streaked from the Ark *Brettaniai* ships, crossing the sky. One of them plowed into the city nearby, shaking the ground in another eruption.

Sura grabbed Shen by the collar and nearly yanked him off his feet as she ran.

CHAPTER 51

ASHME FLINCHED AT A RUMBLING EXPLOSION.

"Sounds like they're getting closer," Mason said in rocky Kanu as the resonant beat of missile impacts grew louder.

"Focus on what you're doing," she said in Ostarrichi—her Ostarrichi was better than his Kanu, and she was tired of listening to his accent mangle her language. He was working on the EM disrupter on the back of her neck.

The gun that killed Ganzer rested in her lap. His blood stained her pants from the knees down. Was that really him, his body? She knew it was, but it felt unreal. She wanted more than anything for it to be unreal. The only thing keeping her from screaming was the goldie sitting behind her.

"Stop fidgeting," Mason said.

"You know how to get it off, right?" He had been working on it for a while. "You can paralyze me if you screw up, you know."

"I'm not going to paralyze you."

She sat in a barber's chair in an empty hair salon in the Meso district of Rabu Flats. Shampoos, gels, and cutting equipment lay scattered on the floor, and dust covered the mirrors. Mason tilted her chin down as a barber might. The only Ostarrichi she had been this close to were CPC troopers frisking her. He smelled bad. It was not a lack of hygiene, but rather, his skin and body oils simply smelled terrible. Maybe something in their cooking seeped into his pores. "What's taking so long?"

"Do you want me to paralyze you?"

The thump from another explosion sounded, but this one was different. The others you could feel through the ground like a bass rumble in your bones, this one, less so. The screech of fighter drones screamed from above, accompanied by the staccato of gunfire.

Ganzer's blood was drying, hardening her pants like papier mâché. The weight of the gun reminded her of Ganzer's head in her lap. All this sitting around doing nothing was driving her mad.

She focused on Mason's image in the mirror in front of her chair, anything to keep herself in the now rather than drifting back to that moment. His whole head looked like some goons had used it for hammerball practice. "So, what happened to your face?" she asked.

"Avalyn's trying to kill me."

"And you got away?" He was tall and lean but a bit soft with age. He was a suit—it was hard to imagine him beating off hired muscle. "Really?"

"Really," he said. Ashme got the sense there was more, but he kept quiet.

"You should learn to block or duck or something."

Freedom. The EM disruptor came off, and her connection to the nanohaze came flooding back.

"Still feel your legs?" Mason asked.

Ashme stood up and breathed deeply as she accessed rivers of data streams flowing around her. The nanohaze was roiling with hundreds of thousands of data packets shuttling in all directions. It was like waking up on a boat in a storm.

"How about your bioreserve?" Mason asked as he placed the tiny scissors he had used while removing her EM disrupter on a counter. His hands were slender—he was a desk jockey, a pretty boy with soft hands and trim hair, though his knuckles were a patchwork of scars. "Do you need to rest before you can use your powers?"

She was strong, awake, powerful. "No. I'm ready." She mentally checked on her stasis tats. Her captors had discharged them, but now that she was re-connected to the nanohaze, they drew energy off her as they began recharging. "Do you have any stim patches or T-bands?" Or regen bars, but her stomach twisted at the memory of their taste, so she refrained from planting that idea in his head. "Avalyn's security will be high-end, so I'll need all the juice I can get."

"Once we get out of Rabu Flats and back into the city, I can find stores that sell that kind of stuff," Mason said. "Can you sense what's going on out there?" he asked, pointing toward the wall, beyond which explosions still rumbled.

She pinged Subdeo for an update. "The nation of Neu has sent a fleet of fighter drones into Caelum airspace to attack the Brettaniai ships."

"Neu's invaded Caelum?" Mason asked.

"Yep. Looks like Avalyn cocked it up big time. The Kanu powers are rising up against Caelum."

"Neu's attacked before, and we still stand," Mason replied. He seemed to check himself, then added, "This is Avalyn's doing. It's not what Ostarrichi want."

"Have you met Ostarrichi?"

"Have you?" he said. "I mean, Ostarrichi other than CPC troopers at checkpoints."

She gripped the gun that killed Ganzer. "Didn't know there were other kinds."

Arguing was a waste. He would never see. She tried pinging her brother instead. Whatever communication blockade the CPC had had in place was gone now. She could reach his neural net but got no answer.

Shen loved getting pinged. Had he lost his neural link? Or worse? "We need to go," she said.

ASHME'S SONG

ASHME FELT SMALL AND FRAGILE, like a seedling in a late spring storm, as she squatted in the alley, her back against the wall. Machine guns rattled. Contrails crisscrossed the sky as missiles, fighter drones, and Brettaniai warships fought in the heavens above. The building vibrated from the explosions, kicking up a haze of dust and ash that coated the inside of her mouth and nose. Mason returned from poking his head around the corner to reconnoitre the street beyond, leaping lightly over a pile of rubble like a bird in flight. He was spry for a desk jockey.

"Mesos are trying to advance on the Hab checkpoint," he said. "Getting the Hab will give them high ground to cover further advances."

By Mesos, she assumed Mason meant the Free New Mesopotamian Army because there was no force of Mesos in New Uruk with the wherewithal to advance on anything, let alone high ground to cover further advances. "That's amazing," she said.

"It's not amazing. People are going to die needlessly."

"I don't think you realize we're here for different reasons. I want Shen safe. I don't care if Caelum burns."

"Do you think Caelum will burn without taking Mesos with it? We're both here for our families. War destroys families."

"Yeah, well, your peace wasn't all that great for my family, either."

Storm clouds passed behind Mason's eyes. "Your problem is you think you're the only one who's suffered."

"Right, you and your whole big family are suffering, I can tell. Suffering all the way to the biogineer to fix your boy."

"Do you think I haven't lost anyone? Do you think you Mesos don't have blood on your hands?"

"When this is all done, you're going to go back to your wife, your kids, and oooh, you'll have such a fun story to tell them. Daddy's such a hero. Who am I going to go back to?"

She caught Mason looking at the gun in her hand that had blue-screened Ganzer. He sighed. "Look, I'm sorry about your associate."

"My *cousin*." Ashme choked up, unable to say more. She crossed her arms and covered her mouth with her hand.

He sat silent for a moment, looking at the palm of his hand. He twitched his index finger along his thumb as if pulling a trigger. "Let's deal with stopping the immediate travesty, and then we can worry about everything else."

Right. Mason was not interested in fixing things. He only wanted to keep war out of his city. Focus on Shen. "We've got to cross the battle lines to get into your district," she said.

"Preferably at a point that's not in the middle of a firefight."

"Come on." She grabbed him by the collar and pulled him up. She had never thought of the location of checkpoints being linked to military strategy—high ground and all that. So, it stood to reason all the soldiers would be converging on checkpoints. The only way to cross districts outside of checkpoints was through the district walls. With all the bloody explosions, there ought to be some holes blown in them by now.

It took forty minutes of slinking through a twisting maze of alleyways and lanes to find such a hole. Unfortunately, a CPC squad had taken up station there and built a makeshift barricade of sandbags. "We'll find another one," Ashme said, ducking back around a corner.

"Any breach in the wall will have either CPC or Meso soldiers guarding it," Mason said. "I can get us through the CPC."

"Why do I think you're about to spill a stupid, bullshit plan?"

"Give me your gun."

"Cache that."

"Think about it," Mason said. "I work for the government. My credentials will get us past them."

"And I suppose I'm your prisoner that you're taking over for questioning."

"Yes."

"For all we know, the CPC think you're the one who busted me out of jail. What makes you think your credentials won't get you blue-screened?"

"I got an indigo child with me, that's what." He held his hand out and waved his fingers, indicating she should pass him the gun. With a curse, she handed it to him.

THERE WERE a lot of weapons pointing at Ashme while Mason and some CPC douche yabbered on with each other. They had her on her knees in front of a personnel transport, debris from the hole blown out of the wall scattered over the road in a fan-shaped pattern. Some of the CPC goons looked like they were itching for a reason to blow her full of holes. Analog trash, all of them.

She cast her senses into the nanohaze and zoned into n-time. Pulses of data surged back and forth from the scanners reading Mason's credentials. He was putting on a good show, talking like it would only be natural for the CPC to obey him. The data pulses coming back down the pipes responding to the trooper's query about Mason's ID, however, were all sorts of "shoot first, ask questions later" levels of priority.

She scanned the contents of one of the data packets and then looked at Mason blathering on. What was he thinking, coming to a CPC outpost when Avalyn was gunning for him? What was she thinking, agreeing to follow him?

Saving Mason was her only ticket past this checkpoint. Cursing him, she closed her eyes and suffered the pull on her body as she launched a series of programs aimed at the CPC scanners. These had military-grade levels of encryption, and the drain to break them hurt. CPC encryption had been upgraded since her capture, and so her AI struggled to crack it. At the end of the day, though, it was a stupid ID scanner, which had been one of the first things she had figured out how to burn.

As soon as she gained control of the scanner, she had it ignore the data pulse coming in and told it to tell the troopers watching it, "All clear." The soldier Mason was talking at eyed the scanner and shrugged, nodding him on.

Mason grabbed Ashme by the arm, yanking her to her feet. The drain, combined with standing up so quickly, hit her hard. She swayed, dizzy. The CPC took her stumble as some Meso waif all fluttery and scared of the big, bad Ostarrichi. *Analog trash.*

When the CPC squad was a block behind them, Mason let her go and said, "See, no problem. I told you I could get us through."

"*You* got us through? Is that what you think?" Her head still spun, but she was breathing deeply, getting oxygen into her blood. They were in the goldie district, filled with new buildings that were now pock-marked with holes and shattered glass.

He looked at her, worried. "Are you drained? What happened?"

She was trying to decide if he was serious. "You have no idea, do you?"

"No idea of what?"

"Well, Mason," she said, "it seems you're wanted for treason."

CHAPTER 52

MASON KNEW he would eventually be branded a traitor, but hearing Ashme say it was still a punch in the gut. How would Oriana react? She would probably agree with the verdict. What would she tell the kids? In time, she would see he was doing this for their children's future.

Please, let her see that someday.

"Walking's for analog trash," Ashme said. "Now we're in the goldie district, we should call a ground transport."

Treason. He would be in jail until the day he died—unless, of course, the CPC trooper who caught him shot him as an enemy combatant.

"Hey!" Ashme nudged him in the arm. "Ground transport?"

"I can't call a transport. They'll find me as soon as I place the call."

"If you want to break into Avalyn's office any time soon, I can't take the drain of covering your ID tag every time you hit the datalinks or walk by a scanner. Me walking out in the open guarantees every CPC squad will stop us and scan your tags. Get me to a data port, and I'll set you up with a new ID."

Mason clenched his jaw. She was too glib about this whole thing, ecstatic that Mesos were attacking checkpoints, revelling in every misfortune that befell him, indifferent that Caelum was under attack while Ark warships hovered over the city, content to allow the nation to burn so long as Ostarrichi burned, too. She was a smug punk with frayed, dyed blonde hair with brown roots, making her head look like a bundle of grain trampled in the mud. She was petulant and antagonistic. He was helping her reunite with her brother—she could show some decency.

Why was she unable to see that so many more Mesos would suffer if this war continued? Was she willing to see her people hurt so long as there was a chance Ostarrichi would hurt, too? Was she filled with that much hate?

She had watched her cousin die, though. If he had watched Oriana executed, hate would fill him, too.

"Can you get me to a data port?" Ashme asked. "Any public building would do. Library, community centre, coffee shop. The fewer people, the better—I stick out like a bonfire in your districts."

"It would seem to me that the more criminal activity we undertake, the more likely we are to get caught before we get to Avalyn's office."

She crossed her arms. "You're wanted for treason. You're a walking criminal activity. We've got to scrub that if you want to get to the *Aigle*."

Faking ID tags felt like admitting guilt. But he was in it now. "Fine."

They found an empty, bombed-out restaurant on that block with a data port behind the bar. "So, who do you want to be?" Ashme asked, pulling up a keg to sit on as she activated the port's data screen and virtual user interface.

"Anybody but me right now."

"That's the plan." She seemed to age before his eyes as she set to work, reminding him of how Oriana looked after being sick for days with a stomach flu Tracey had brought home from the daycare last winter.

Drain. She was working her indigo child magic. "I know a

place we can get some T-bands," he said. "We'll pick some up after you're done."

"Fantastic. Be a doll and check in the back to see if they have something to eat—ice cream. See if they have ice cream. Or peanut butter. I'm starved."

He was unable to make sense of the haze of code on the data screens. With a shrug, he went into the back of the restaurant. Pots, dishes, and cutlery lay strewn across counters and floors. *This was a nice restaurant*, he thought while his feet crunched broken dishes as he walked to the pantry—no peanut butter—and freezers—four vats of ice cream. He took one, chocolate, found a spoon, and went back to the front room.

A strange mix of emotions sat on Ashme's face: confusion, sadness. Drain? No, that looked more like starvation or illness. She had a deep frown and downcast eyes. "Everything okay?" he asked, handing her the vat of ice cream and spoon.

She looked at him. A drumbeat of explosions sounded in the distance. "You weren't kidding about your son."

"You're looking at my personal files?"

"Duh." She pointed to a data screen hovering in front of her as she cracked the top of the ice cream container with her other hand. "Says here that without editing, he'd die by two like you said. He's sicker than Shen ever was. I thought all of you had perfect gengineered bodies."

He shrugged. He had thought so, too. Fear for his son, for his family, for his future blossomed in him, crushing his gut. "If what we're doing doesn't work and I go to jail or get killed, I don't know if we'll be able to afford to finish a full edit."

"Bit of a bone-headed risk you doing this, then, isn't it?" She began shovelling ice cream in her mouth.

"Yeah, it kind of is."

"So why are you doing it?" Her mouth made smacking sounds as she worked on the ice cream.

"Editing gave my son a future, but what kind of future is this?" he asked, sweeping his hand to encompass the shattered furniture and blown-out wall of the restaurant. A haze of dust hung in the air. "I don't want my children to grow up with war."

"If you didn't want war, you shouldn't have taken our home," Ashme said between mouthfuls of ice cream.

"*I* didn't take your home. I was born here. So were my parents. We're not foreigners. This is the only home I've known, and you hate me for it."

"I'm sure you've done something between being born and now worth my hate."

Those words were a knife to the gut. He could still feel the teargas launcher in his hand, feel the kick as he fired it, could still see the contrail of the canister as it streaked into the face of the boy Hadu. They had killed Myla, terrorized his wife, attacked his daughter's daycare. Still, he felt tainted, his soul smeared.

Ashme was lost in her own reverie. Whatever she was remembering, it made her angry. With a curse, she turned her attention back to the data screen, arms crossed, one hand covering her mouth. "A sick boy needs his dad." Mason watched as she wrestled with some inner demon. More than once she seemed about to say something, then stopped. "A sick boy needs his dad." She shovelled more ice cream into her mouth.

Mason looked at her. *Father suicide, mother died in prison,* he remembered. *What does that do to a child? What kind of adult does that make? What kind of society can you build with a generation of such people?*

He asked his next question delicately. "Why didn't your family get Shen edited when he was a baby?"

Her eyes narrowed. "We did. He had a heart defect we fixed."

How to ask this without offending her? "Why did you stop there? All citizens of Caelum, even Mesos, get basic coverage. Couldn't you get additional editing to fix his . . . other issues?"

"Oh, so Shen's our fault, is it?"

"I'm trying to understand."

"My mom was a Class 2A citizen. She was born in Novoreeka before the Scourge when your people took over. She was born there but moved here before she was a year old. She lived here all her life, but being born outside Caelum's borders was enough for you to deny her full citizenship, and only full citizens get benefits. Now, guess what grade of citizen the children of Class 2A citizens are? My family had to pay for the heart edit out of pocket, and it bankrupted us. That's why Dad fought in the Xinchin War—Baltu paid cash." As she said the last, her brow furrowed, and then her eyes widened as though struck by an epiphany.

The citizenship classes of Mesos were labyrinthine in their complexity. Mason had never managed to keep straight what rights Caelum gave to which Mesos. "I was serious about hoping you'd use the money I'm giving you to get Shen edited."

"I was serious when I dared you to tell me how he's broken and needs fixing."

He understood. He would love Daxton no matter what. If nothing else, Ostarrichi and Meso shared a love for family.

CHAPTER 53

AN EXPLOSION ROCKED Avalyn's armoured mobile HQ, kicking one side up so high that Avalyn thought the whole structure might tip.

She remembered teaching her daughter, Gervaise, how to drive a tractor in their orchard. Avalyn always thought of Gervaise when she believed she was about to die. As a young girl entering adolescence, Gervaise had been loathe to smile when Avalyn was around, lest her mother get the sense her daughter's life was anything but misery. Despite her teenage surliness, though, the shuddering jolts of the tractor responding to her command made her giggle like a six-year-old. Those giggles echoed in Avalyn's ears as the treads of the mobile HQ slammed down with a crash that thrashed her body like a rag doll. "Rough ride," she said, the same words she had said to Gervaise.

When her brother, Travis, had died, she did not think she could survive the death of another loved one. She had, however, survived Gervaise's death five years later, discovering within herself unsuspected depths of strength.

A strength that was ebbing away. She was tired. She had inspected the lines instead of sleeping last night and had been organizing a counter-offensive through the morning. There was a time she could sustain that pace for days. Now, her body throbbed in pain while the lack of sleep fogged her mind.

"Mesos have advanced to the drive-around blockades," Colonel Tyrell said, sitting beside her, watching a data screen displaying schematics of the battlefield around them. A major sat at another terminal, directing the defence of the Hab checkpoint they were occupying. Avalyn waited to see if Tyrell would add a suggestion for her to withdraw from the Hab checkpoint to a safer location.

He made no such suggestion. Good. He was a career man. The last time she had fought with him, his hair had been dark, nearly black. It was grey now, but he still remembered the importance of symbolic gestures.

Throughout the HQ, people spoke in crisp commands and reports. It was efficient. Focused. The Hab checkpoint was Avalyn's line in the sand. She had been given command of the army with orders to shatter Free New Mesopotamia. Only one thing was missing. "Any intelligence on Baltu?" she asked.

"He hasn't left his compound in Neu," Tyrell said.

The sound of artillery exploding nearby came through the walls of the mobile HQ as dull thuds felt in the bones more than heard. The Mesos were close enough to breach the checkpoint's missile-defence barrier and were now dropping shells in the compound itself. Her mobile HQ's armour was the best on Esharra, but two or three direct hits and even it would succumb.

She looked at a data screen displaying the disposition of her army throughout Caelum. "Baltu's committed his entire force, but he's still in Neu."

"He's chosen to bravely lead from behind," Tyrell said. "Again."

Some naively optimistic part of her had hoped he would enter Caelum so she could get him without having to declare war on their neighbour. She could crush his army, as she had before, but he would raise another, as he had before.

Neu had breached Caelum airspace to fire on the Ark *Brettaniai* warship drones. She could use that to justify a punch into the neighbouring country to take out Baltu's headquarters and, hopefully, Baltu with it. She wanted to avoid a protracted war with the Kanu nations. She had hoped Ark *Brettaniai* warships would deter other Kanu from coming to Free New Mesopotamia's aid.

Her only aim was to see Caelum free of the Meso threat before she died. Destroying the Free New Mesopotamian Army was an important part of that. She had destroyed it once before, however, and Baltu had risen from the ashes to strike again. Baltu had to die with his army this time.

So far, only Neu was attacking, and they were careful to target only Ark *Brettaniai*'s warships. Sending an attack force into Neu, a sovereign Kanu nation, however, would threaten to expand the theatre of battle.

A major turned to Colonel Tyrell and said, "Our situation is becoming unstable. Perhaps we should move Grand General Avalyn to our fall-back position."

"Make the situation stable, Major," Tyrell said as the furrows in his brow set with the weight of an anvil. He turned to Avalyn, shrugging. "The kids are getting nervous."

Avalyn contemplated letting the checkpoint fall. If the Free New Mesopotamian Army pierced further into New Uruk, would that lure Baltu onto Caelum soil?

Only a fool relies on Kanu bravery. Time to close the trap and snuff out the Free New Mesopotamian Army. She would set up a strike force to take out Baltu in Neu. Doing so risked broadening the scope of the war, but enough was enough. *[Shanelle,]* Avalyn pinged, *[bring in the vipers.]*

While she waited, she pinged commands to several other senior officers, setting in motion her plans to trap and then destroy the Free New Mesopotamian Army. Before the next hour was up, a division of mobile infantry would be air-dropped behind their lines under cover of Ark *Brettaniai* warships, trapping the invaders in Caelum. Armoured divisions she had been holding in reserve behind New Uruk would swing out, attacking their flanks, while the CPC's urban defence division drove them out of the city. Boxed in, with nowhere to run, bombardment from Ark *Brettaniai* and Caelum's air force would finish off Free New Mesopotamia. And then Baltu—hopefully without bringing Neu to war. Her alliance with Ark *Brettaniai* should help keep Neu passive, but the risk remained.

"Vipers have arrived," the major announced. "They are engaging the enemy."

Avalyn was congratulating the major when Shanelle pinged her. *[I have an urgent report to give you. In private.]*

[You can't ping it to me?] Avalyn asked.

[It would be safer not to.]

"I'm going to do a visual inspection of the vipers in action," she announced to the staff. "Carry on."

She popped the door and stepped out. Her body burned with pain from the jostling it had taken when the bomb hit her HQ. Her combat armour supported her, keeping her upright as she strode into the smoky, pock-marked courtyard of the checkpoint.

Shanelle stood there, decked out in her black armour. When Shanelle wanted to kill, she had this look, mouth set and brow furrowed like the crags of a glacier. She had that look now. Beyond the checkpoint's barricades, the vipers emitted a rhythmic sound of grinding stone, set to the beat of screams and explosions. She and Shanelle walked to the cover of one of the checkpoint's buildings. Craters scarred the grounds, and several small fires burned, blanketing the area in a black pall of acrid smoke, making Avalyn's eyes and nose water. "What is it?" she asked.

"Mason," Shanelle said. "The Meso didn't kill him."

Avalyn forced her features to remain calm. Mason was a little mouse that kept evading the owl's talons. "Where is he now?"

"He and the Meso crossed into the Ostarrichi district less than an hour ago."

"He and the Meso are working together?"

"Yes. She used her indigo powers to evade capture, protecting him. The CPC have orders to pick him up—"

"No," Avalyn interrupted. "There's a chance he'll talk."

"No one will believe him."

Avalyn hooted a bitter laugh. "I have enemies. There will be those who want to believe what he has to say. He needs to be eliminated. Having a Meso do it would be ideal." She breathed calm into herself.

"If we can learn where they're heading, I can set up an ambush and make it look like Mesos did it."

"They are heading for the *Aigle*," Avalyn said.

"That would be insane."

"He's desperate. Why do you think he went for the indigo child? She broke into Chevalier, which had security almost as good as the *Aigle's*. He wants the BLOQ. With it, he can trace my use of it to control the angels. Taking me down is his only chance out of this."

"Let me take care of him," Shanelle said. A thought struck her. "The CPC is investigating the angel system, trying to troubleshoot its 'spotty' behaviour. They might find evidence of your actions even without the BLOQ. If we could tie the BLOQ to him, we'd get rid of Mason and direct the investigation away from you."

Avalyn thought, then nodded. "Let Mason make it to my office."

Shanelle shook her head. "We don't have situational control of the *Aigle*. We won't be able to operate freely there."

"*I* have situational control of the *Aigle*," Avalyn said. "I am the senior commander of the CPC. Get a squad of Wraiths you trust and have them there to meet them."

"If we're doing this, let's go all in and clean the entire slate," Shanelle said.

"How do you mean?"

"The Meso's brother, the one who bombed the Network station."

"The defect, yes."

"His handler was also on the Chevalier job. If she hasn't killed the defect, he'll still be with her. Let me bring them into the *Aigle*, too. The brother gives us leverage over the indigo child. Once we have them all, we can eliminate everyone involved with the BLOQ, the Network bombing, everything. It will look like Mason was in deep with the Mesos. We can pin the BLOQ on him. The Network bombing, too. Clean slate."

Avalyn considered this, then nodded. "Do it."

SHEN HAD no idea who Sura was talking to over the neural net, but she was angry.

"I'd love to take you up on your offer, but I'm kind of busy *getting the shit bombed out of me!*" she yelled into the neural link she kept on a necklace as she jabbed her finger aimlessly. They were hiding behind a reception desk in an abandoned office. The air was thick with dust; he suppressed a coughing fit lest he disturb Sura. Outside the shop, a constant *boom, boom, boom* made the floor vibrate. There was no rhythm to it, no music, just an angry roar that shook buildings and made him so scared he thought he might throw up.

Sura looked at Shen with surprise. Were they talking about him? She looked away, saying, "No thanks. I actually like Ashme."

They were talking about his sister! "Do they know where Ashme is?" he asked.

Sura shushed him as she said, "You ain't offering nearly enough to do that." Nearby, a whump shuddered through the building, a deep bass rumble making the shelves behind the desk rattle. A cup holding pens and scissors fell on the floor, scattering its contents by Shen's feet. "Fine, you know what? I'm in. I'll pack my things, but you get that aerial transport over here before you bring the building down on me." She ended the conversation.

"Was that Ashme?"

Sura rolled her eyes. "No. But we're going to see her."

He hugged Sura so tightly. "Where is she?"

Sura extracted herself from his embrace. "The *Aigle*."

"The *Aigle*?" Shen asked. "What's she doing there?"

"It's complicated. But first, we've got to get back to the apartment before the aerial transport they're sending to pick us up arrives."

"What's at the apartment?"

"Jushur."

"I like Jushur. He has a keyboard he lets me play, and he pays Ashme for making stasis tats. Is he coming, too? And Zamar? Zamar's a great drummer."

"No, it's just you and me." Sura poked her head above the counter to see what was happening outside. "I need some equipment from Jushur if we're going to save Ashme."

"Save Ashme?" He grabbed Sura's elbow. "Is Ashme in trouble?"

"Yeah, she's fucked. I'm kind of fucked, too. So are you."

Shen's chest tightened; he had trouble breathing. "What are we going to do?"

"We're going to go back to the apartment and get some gear from Jushur," Sura said, leaning in close and placing a hand on Shen's shoulder with that smile she had whenever she was making a big business deal. "Then you and me," she said, pointing to Shen and then herself, "are going to kill Avalyn."

CHAPTER 54

MASON'S FACE and head throbbed in pain from the beating he had suffered at the hands of Sura's thugs. He sat in the back of a cramped, econo-grade transport on its way to the *Aigle* as he watched Ashme shovel another spoonful of ice cream into her mouth. "Do all indigo children eat as much as you?" She was halfway through an eight-litre bucket.

"What are you, my mom?" she asked, digging for another mouthful. He envied her metabolism. He had started to get soft around the middle, especially since the kids arrived. She, on the other hand, was on her fourth litre of ice cream, yet she was thin as a beanstalk.

She wore the bright red uniform of a convict. He imagined for a moment Tracey living her life. Orphaned as a teen with a sick brother to support, how much like Ashme would Tracey grow up to be under those circumstances?

Ashme placed the ice cream bucket on the floor. "Hand me my gear," she said, pointing to the bag of supplies she'd had him buy at a system's hardware store. She dumped the gear on the seat beside her: T-bands, stim patches—she picked up the regen bars. "I thought I said no regen bars."

Mason shrugged. "Better to have them and not need them."

She muttered a reply in Kanu that Mason was fluent enough to catch. "You wouldn't say that if you'd ever shit one out." Switching to accented Ostarrichi, she said, "Turn around and look away."

"Why?"

"Because I'm going to take my pants off."

"What! Why?"

"If I get caught and I've got my T-bands and stim patches stuck someplace obvious, they'll pull them off. If I got 'em on my legs, they'd only find them if they strip me down."

"If we get caught, we're dead."

"Only if we stay caught long enough. Now . . ." She made a shooing gesture with her hands.

He turned around and stared out the window as she changed. They were driving along the River Esplanade freeway, with the Timor River to their right. On the far side sat offices and apartments of the Neufve Bon-heur district. It was night, but no lights shone from the buildings. Its VR skin was dead: no ads, no art, no images of any kind showing through the car's windows. The lights from the freeway dimly lit the facades of buildings across the river. Windows were shattered, streets empty. Mason had seen pictures of war-torn cities with bombed-out buildings and rubble-strewn streets. Was that his home's destiny?

The transport pulled off an exit into the Castillion district. They would be at the *Aigle* in minutes. What was he doing? This was wrong. He was working with a Meso to undermine his own people. He was certain before; he knew Avalyn was manipulating Caelum. He was, however, about to break into government buildings to find evidence to take down Avalyn, the current leader of the army, at a time when Caelum fought for its survival. And he was working with a Meso to do it.

"I'm decent. You can turn around," Ashme said. "I'm going to need to see your ID tag."

"Why?"

"It'll help me burn the *Aigle's* security."

"What about the fake ID you set up? I'm wanted for treason."

"Your fake ID is a cover. It's not in the *Aigle's* security system, but your real ID is. Having a doorway in makes it easier to burn the security and your real ID's the door. Once I'm in, I can put your fake tags on the all-clear list."

He hated how her accent mangled his language. This whole thing was sickening. He could ping Avalyn right now and end this. She would be busy, though, so maybe pinging Shanelle would be better. Except Shanelle would kill him.

"After all you've been through, why are you still being a nervous little bitch about your ID tags?" Ashme said. "The game's on. Shit or get off the pot."

Yes, Shanelle would kill him; that was the one thing he knew for sure. She was on cleanup duty, burying any trace of how Avalyn duped Caelum into war. Avalyn was not Caelum; betraying her did not mean he was betraying his country.

He extended his arm with the ID tag on it.

Ashme concentrated on the tag, then looked him in the eye. "Your security clearance is shit. What are you, a janitor?"

CHAPTER 55

ASHME LAY CURLED in a tiny ball in a storage compartment under a seat in their transport, wondering if trusting Mason was stupid. The closer to the *Aigle* they got, the dodgier he had become, avoiding eye contact, getting lost in his own thoughts, and acting like a little piss baby. Did she really need to work with this guy to get the BLOQ and clear Shen from the angel's records? He knew the layout of the building and could probably talk his way past the guards better than a Meso on her own could. Still, he was a goldie, and Mesos were dirt to goldies. *Watch your back.*

"Is that you shaking the transport?" she heard Mason ask, his voice muffled, coming through the walls of the storage container.

Despite being crammed in a tight space, her legs were vibrating—a side effect of the stim patches. Her heart was hammering. "Yeah, yeah, it's good."

"It's good? What . . . that doesn't answer the question."

"Yeah, it's me, chill out." The dust from the compartment tickled her nose, bringing her to the verge of sneezing.

"Well, calm down. I can see the security station, and you're making the whole vehicle shake." Fabric rustled as Mason shifted on his seat. He cursed in Ostarrichi.

"What's wrong?" Ashme asked.

"They're doing manual inspections. Usually, security is automated for staff. Will my fake tags still work?"

Dumbass. "Not if the guard doing the inspecting knows who you really are. I can only burn systems, not people. Do you recognize the guard?"

Silence, then, "Shit, yes." *So much for fake tags.* "They've got me flagged as a traitor," Mason said. "Can you burn their scanners to clear me like you did before?"

She had maxed out the T-bands and stim patches she could absorb. Her body thrummed with energy, ready to burn the world. She knew, though, that if she had to burn her way through the front gates before they even got into the building, the drain would suck hard enough she would probably have to wolf down those bloody regen bars.

"Ashme?" Mason said. "Tell me you can burn their scanners. We're up next."

"Ugh, fuck, yes." She launched an EM shield from the stasis tat on her face to hide her body from the various microwave radar, IR, and ultrasonic detectors. Her facial stasis tat had enough bioreserves stored to keep the shield up for twenty to thirty minutes without any drain. Covering Mason's ass, however, would be more difficult.

The storage compartment was stifling. She wanted to jump, scream, and then run a 10K. Stim patches, what a bloody rush. *Come on, girl, focus that energy into the nanohaze.* She reached out, sensing the battery of security cameras and systems surrounding them.

The transport stopped. The guard and Mason started chatting. She focused her concentration on the ID scanner, sensing it in the nanohaze. She cloned a portion of Subdeo's master program and launched it to burn the security programs. The nervous energy shaking her body dissipated, the drain sucking it away. In n-time, she sensed her cloned AI evolving as it fought the scanner's AI, and then it faded into nothing. The scanner's security had dismantled it.

Well, that was a bad start to the night. The only saving grace was it happened quickly, so nothing was happening yet between the guard and Mason in real time. She cloned another version of Subdeo, tweaked its learning algorithms, and then launched it, feeling sick from the drain.

Again, her AI engaged the scanner's security. The two AI fought, each probing for a chink in the other's encryption, learning and adapting with each strike. The fight dragged on. *Come on, little buddy.* In real time, the guard would check the ID scanner at any moment. Zini's stacks, was her AI going to get burned again? If she had to launch another attack, she would only have enough bioreserves left to call an elevator.

Her AI did it. She busted through into the scanner's programming and sub-routines. Data packets were flowing into the scanner. She launched an enslave program to stop those packets cold and give the all-clear, and . . .

What the hell? She scanned the data packet she had frozen regarding Mason's ID. What do you know, the dipshit was no longer wanted for treason.

"All clear," she heard the guard say. "Have a nice evening, Mason." The transport rolled forward.

This stinks. It took more than an afternoon to clear your name of treason, especially when you were in the middle of committing bloody treason.

CHAPTER 56

ASHME POPPED the seat serving as the lid to the compartment she was hiding in as the transport ambled toward the rear of the *Aigle* complex. "Something you want to tell me?" Mason's miraculously cleared record either meant he was screwing with her or someone was screwing with him.

"Yeah, there'll be cameras covering the transport drop-off."

She grunted in frustration. "Of course, there'll be bloody cameras!" She pulled three regen bars out of the bag lying on the floor, tore them open, cursed under her breath, plugged her nose, and started wolfing them down. "I'm not talking about the cameras," she said over a foul mouthful, "I meant about your forays as a traitor." Her body started quivering from the bars' shot of energy while her stomach cramped.

Mason looked at her with a frown. "I'm not betraying Caelum."

"Someone agrees with you," she said as she started choking down the second bar. "There was no sign of the order to detain you for treason at the *Aigle*'s checkpoint."

Mason held her gaze a moment. "Are you sure you're reading things right?"

"Yes, I'm sure." *Why do desk jockeys insist on assuming experts have no idea what they're doing?* "Are you trying to screw me over?"

"No!"

"Because Zini's stacks, I'll make sure to put a bullet in your head if this is a trap, even if it gets me blue-screened." She touched the handle of the pistol that had killed Ganzer, stuck safely in the waistband of her pants.

"I'm not setting you up. I had no idea I was wanted for treason, and I don't know why I'm not now," Mason said. "Avalyn's up to something."

"Yeah, Avalyn," Ashme said, starting on the third regen bar. *Damn, that taste is something you never get used to.* "Shut up, I've got to burn the cameras." The transport was coming to a stop. She launched the program from the stasis tat on her flank. She sensed through the nanohaze the break encryption program battling to punch through the camera system's encryption.

Her program burned through, and then she set the cameras to play a loop of the empty foyer so she and Mason could enter without being recorded. She sensed a little data packet shoot away from the camera, easy to miss, it was so small. She was almost too slow to block it, freezing it in the camera's processors. The moment she tried to open it, it corrupted. It was probably a signal set to send an alarm once the camera's encryption was compromised. It would take an indigo child or a genius system raider to create a packet that slick. She had to hand it to the *Aigle*. Its systems were top-notch.

"We're in," Ashme said. "What's the security like on the other side of the door?"

"Automated ID scanner and weapons detector."

More drain. Great. "They don't frisk you for weapons?"

Mason missed her cutting sarcasm. "That wouldn't be practical—it'd take too long to frisk everyone."

They entered the *Aigle* through the rear entrance and passed through the automated security. *Drain.* Down a hallway, security doors, more sensors. *Drain.* In every device she burned, there was a little data packet that wanted to fire off to let someone know. Clever little programs, cunning AIs that Ashme had to block—and they were hard to block—to keep from triggering an alarm. *Drain.*

One of those pesky little data packets managed to sneak through her block at a card reader for a set of doors leading to a hallway. She leaned back against the hallway's wall, flexing her thighs to squeeze the blood up into her head to keep from passing out—a trick Melammu taught her. "They know we're here."

Mason looked like he'd filled his drawers. "You do this for a living, right? There must be some way you can shut the alarm down."

"Nope. Cat's out of the bag."

"What do you do in situations like this?"

"Hurry. How much farther?"

"We're close."

Ashme pushed him onward, took a deep breath, and shuffled after him. The hall ended in a set of doors. Mason, back to the wall, slid up to them. Ashme followed suit, happy for the wall's support. "There's an atrium beyond these doors we've got to cross," Mason said. "It's a wide, open space." He looked back down the hall the way they had come. "Great place for an ambush."

"You telling me this 'cause you think it'll raise my morale?"

"No. Can indigo children . . . scan, or something?"

"Sure, and then after, do you want me to read your future, maybe speak to a dead grandparent?"

"If you can't do it, then—"

"Belt it and give me a minute." She expanded her mind into the nanohaze. She sensed the usual conduits of the building's systems—HVAC, security, lights, that type of thing. "There's no angels or drones nearby, but there could be a dozen humans standing there, and I'd never know."

"Reassuring." Mason listened at the door. "Follow me. Quickly." He pushed the door open and slipped past. Ashme waited to see if he got shot. *Nope.* She pulled out her gun and then followed.

CHAPTER 57

ASHME STUDIED THE ATRIUM. It was one of those open spaces filled with large planters and trees growing under a glass roof that high-end goldie shopping centers seemed to love. Warm, humid air smothered her as she entered. Maybe they would get luc—

The door at the far end kicked open. A squad of CPC charged, armored up, bristling with weapons. They fanned out to cover the room. Ashme had no idea what to do in a combat situation, but shooting seemed to be what people who did know would do. She drew her gun and fired. Her first shot hit a wall two meters above the heads of the CPC. Mason grabbed her and dove behind a large concrete planter. Automatic fire ripped into the stone of the planter and floor, thrashing her eardrums.

"What do you think you're doing?" Mason yelled over the sound of gunfire as both he and Ashme lay curled on the floor, hands over their head to protect themselves from the shards of concrete raining down. "Those are CPC you're shooting at!"

"Those are CPC shooting at us!"

"I don't want you shooting any CPC!"

"I don't want to get shot!"

Auto-tracking bullets curved around the planter, cracking

into the floor with a whizzing ping—the EM shield Ashme was still running from the stasis tat on her face was muddling their targeting. Over the edge of a planter, Ashme saw the door behind them that they had come through smash open. A malevolent surge washed through the nanohaze. "Angels. Three of them."

"What!" Mason yelled.

The grinding roar of weapons drowned out her reply. In the nanohaze, she sensed the angels maneuver to outflank them. The concrete planter was getting shredded while chunks of stone, dirt, and tree shards pelted them.

She had a stasis tat for such an occasion. She hoped it worked. She also hoped there would be no more than one occasion she needed it tonight. She launched the mass break encryption program linked to a mass blackout that she stored in the tat on her back. It rammed into the angels' firewalls like a runaway hyperlev train. All three angels dropped to the ground with a resounding metallic clang.

The shooting lulled. A CPC trooper swore. Mason looked at Ashme. "Did you do that?"

She winked at him in reply. Time to move. [*Subdeo,*] she pinged, [*be a dear and send the floor plans of the* Aigle *into my neural net, focusing on my current location.*]

[*Whatever.*] Subdeo pinged back as it complied. [*Hey, you appear to be involved in illegal activity. Do you want me to call a lawyer for you?*]

She disconnected. A scan of the floor plans showed only two exits, both lousy with CPC. She had an idea. It was shitty, but it would be tough for their day to get worse. It would buy time, at least. "Follow my lead," she said to Mason as she zoned into n-time.

"What—"

Her clone of Subdeo was still buried in the *Aigle's* camera system. She brought up the atrium on the camera system, saw it teeming with CPC homing in on the two of them. With a thought, she set her AI to burn through the camera system into the building's facilities and maintenance subroutines—easy, since those systems were designed to work with, not protect against, the building's own security system. She flipped the camera to infrared, and then, with a thought, turned off the lights.

Immediately, inky blackness blanketed them. They had to move fast—the CPC would have visors that would switch to night vision in a heartbeat, but the human meat brains in the CPC troopers' heads might need another heartbeat or two to adjust. She grabbed Mason by the arm. Using the infrared images captured by the building's cameras transmitted to her neural net, she pulled him in a crouching run to a single door along the wall nearby.

The door led to a room, pitch black, and there were no cameras in here Ashme could use to guide them—a fact she found simultaneously surprising and reassuring.

"Where are we?" Mason asked.

"The woman's washroom." Ashme fumbled blindly for a lock on the door, found it, and then clicked it closed.

"Is there a way out?"

"Not that's on the publicly available floor plans."

Mason made an inarticulate noise. "Then why'd you bring us in here?"

"I don't know. Because out there we were getting shot at, is that a good enough reason?"

"We could have surrendered."

"I don't remember them asking for our surrender."

"That's because you fired at them," he said.

"What do you think Avalyn's going to do when she finds you? Think she wants you blabbing to your lawyer?" There was a knock on the door. "Occupied!" Ashme shouted.

"It's me," a voice called out from the other side.

Sweet Zini's stacks, it was Sura. It had to be a trick, a recording of some kind. "Nice try," Ashme said. "I've got a gun, and I'm blasting a hole in anybody trying to come through that door."

"There's something you should know about Sura," Mason whispered.

"You sure now's a good time?" she whispered back. Then, yelling through the door, "I've got a gun, and I mean it!"

Sura said, "It's me, Ashme, ease up. I've got someone here who wants to speak with you."

A fire ignited in her belly. If that crazy bitch—

"Avalyn hired Sura to try and kill me," Mason said.

"What? Bullshit."

"She and her goons are what happened to my face."

"Sura's not an assassin." Though she did take the job to kill Avalyn. She also disappeared with the sniper platform moments before Avalyn turned the dial on the angels to slaughter. Oh, and she tricked Shen into blowing up the Network station.

"Ashme?" It was Shen. "Are you okay?"

And she brought Shen here, into the bloody *Aigle*. "Yeah, I'm fine, Shen," she said in her calm voice. "Just a second, okay?" Switching to her angry voice, "Sura, what is wrong with you? How could you do this to Shen?"

"I'm doing this for us," Sura said. "I don't want anyone to get hurt."

Yeah, right. Ashme leaned her back against the wall. "I'm coming out," she said. "Don't shoot."

CHAPTER 58

THE FIRST THING Mason saw when the lights turned on was Shanelle. She did not smile or gloat or rage at him for his treachery but held herself with cold, icy efficiency. He counted a dozen soldiers in black armor with the emblem of a ghostly hand holding a sword on the upper left corner of the chest. Shanelle wore the same. These were not CPC. They were Wraiths. He was going to die here.

With a crisp command from Shanelle, the soldiers pulled Ashme and him out of the washroom and placed an EM disruptor on the back of the Meso's neck. The planter they had been hiding behind was a pile of rubble, dirt, and a shredded tree. The acrid sting of gunpowder hung in the air.

Ashme glared at Sura, who avoided eye contact. Shen hugged Ashme, and as the soldiers marched them away from the atrium, he insisted on holding her hand despite demands from the Wraiths to let her go. Shanelle cut the argument short and let Shen hold his sister's hand.

Shen looked his way. "Hi, Mason. They got you, too?"

One of the guards told him to shut up, punctuating his demand with a shove that sent Shen stumbling. Whereas the young Meso's face was usually bisected with a big, face-splitting grin, it was now twisted in a nervous frown. When he looked Mason's way again, Mason gave him a wink. The frown disappeared, replaced by his grin.

Shanelle led them to the antechamber leading into Avalyn's office complex. A half dozen angels greeted them, their engines humming.

"The angels have been instructed to shoot you if you move or take any hostile action," Shanelle said. She dismissed the special ops. No witnesses.

Shanelle motioned Mason forward. "Avalyn wants a word with you." She looked coolly at Ashme, then the angels. "The defect comes, too." Shen cried and screamed as Shanelle, her strength enhanced by her combat armor, dragged him away. Ashme lunged to protect her brother, but the angels surged forward, and Shanelle drew a gun, forcing calm on the situation. "Do anything stupid, and your brother's dead." Ashme's glare was murderous.

Sura stepped forward. Her auburn hair was wild and unruly, coated in a layer of dust. "What about my payment?"

That was the closest Mason had ever seen Shanelle come to laughing. "You stay with her," she said, pointing at Ashme. "You'll get paid once we're done with Mason." She motioned Mason and Shen forward through the doors into Avalyn's annex.

Beyond, Avalyn stood, arms crossed, flanked by two angels. She was wearing her combat armor, deep violet contrasting against her golden skin and ivory hair. She looked like the pictures of her he had seen in the past. Her face was expressionless, iron, a goddess of judgment taking his measure and finding him lacking. Shanelle kicked him in the back of the leg, dropping him to his knees. Shen dropped to his knees beside him, sobbing.

He could see his desk, sitting as he left it, alongside his co-workers' workstations. Everything looked normal, eerily so. It seemed unreal something so wrong could happen in a place so mundane.

From his knees, he looked up at Avalyn but felt neither

trapped or small or intimidated, as he was sure she intended. Instead, he felt weightless, as though he were floating on thermals. He was a storm cloud filling the horizon, his heart thundering with righteous anger. "You've brought war to Caelum," he said.

A muscle in her jaw clenched. "Who are you to judge me?"

"How many Ostarrichi have died in this attack? How much Ostarrichi blood do you have on your hands? I was a fool to trust you. You had me arrange the theft of the BLOQ so you could burn the angel network, and now you're going to let me hang. If anyone has the right to judge you," he stabbed his thumb into his chest, "it's me. And what do all these deaths accomplish? They let you climb enough points in the polls to win the Director-Generalship. You're no hero. You're a back-stabbing politician selling out your people for power."

Her bright cyan eyes stabbed into his, spears of will trying to pierce his spirit, but he stared back with the unflinching eyes of an eagle. "Are you done?" she asked.

He had said his piece and knew he was going to die, leaving his children fatherless, leaving Oriana to raise their family alone. He knew, however, he was going to die because he sacrificed himself trying to make the world a decent place for his children. He stared at her, defiant, silent.

"Well then," Avalyn said, "I'd be bothered by your accusations if they didn't come from a traitor who allied himself with a Meso to undermine his own people."

"*I'm* the one undermining my own people?"

"Yes, you are," Avalyn said, her voice cutting like a steel blade. "Caelum is not safe. The Director-General would turn Ostarrichi into a minority underclass in our own country. Because of what I've done, the Free New Mesopotamian Army will lay in ruins before the sun sets tomorrow night. Within days, Baltu will be dead. Then, once I'm Director-General, I will make changes to ensure no Meso will ever threaten an Ostarrichi again. And you," she said, voice laced with molten disdain, "you would undermine all of that. You don't have the strength to do what needs doing. All my life, I've been surrounded by weak people who can't bring themselves to do what has to be done to protect Caelum."

"'Protect Caelum? Is that what you think you're doing?"

"Yes."

"Because of you, Free New Mesopotamia attacked *my daughter's daycare!*" Rage crackled in him, shaking his body. "She's three, and there were monsters with guns walking the halls of her school! You did that! You made that happen!"

Her head tilted in curiosity and then bobbed back, struck by an epiphany. "Ah. You're not weak." Her steel features melted, replaced with a sad gaze, the gaze of a mother watching her child deal with the disappointment of their first heartache. "You think you're protecting your family." She sighed and gave him a sad smile. "You're wrong, but I can respect what drives you."

She walked to him, the angels looming behind her, the throbbing vibrato of their engines humming, their reflective surface distorting all they saw. She pulled from her pocket a program tat, on the side of which was painted a pink pony—the BLOQ. She handed it to Shanelle and said, "Get ready to finish this." Shen, on the verge of tears, moaned beside Mason.

Avalyn knelt to face Mason on his level. "I do not wish for your family to suffer for your mistakes, there is no justice in that. We do not make Caelum stronger by harming our children.

"You are going to die here. Your family will believe you died a traitor breaking into the *Aigle* with your Meso co-conspirators to use the BLOQ to sabotage the angel network. But, I want you to die knowing that I will do whatever is in my power to make sure your son gets the treatment he needs to cure his disease. Your family will never know want. Your children will grow up healthy and strong. I promise."

That almost made it alright.

CHAPTER 59

THE SIX ANGELS hovered around Ashme and Sura, their engines thrumming out of cadence with each other, their reflective surfaces reminding Ashme of funhouse mirrors. The nanohaze was dead to her, the EM disrupter on her neck blocking her connection. "You're worse than the goldies," she said to Sura.

"Whoa," Sura said. "What are you talking about? I've been babysitting your brother for days, Chick-o."

"Babysitting? You tricked him into blowing up the Network station. You brought him *here*." The angels would be recording this. Part of her brain screamed at her to shut up in front of them, but the Ostarrichi already knew about Shen.

Sura shrugged. "We're all in this together. Why shouldn't Shen be given a chance to make his own contribution? Frankly, you should be happy. He's a hero."

"A hero?"

"If it wasn't for him, that Network station would still be standing, and the army of Free New Mesopotamia would still be in Neu. This is the first time a Kanu army has struck so far into Caelum, and it's all because of Shen. We got paid very well for that, I might add—I was going to split that with you, fifty-fifty."

She wanted to scream. So many had died, Hamilcar,

Melammu, Ganzer, she wanted to condemn Sura for all their murders. "Are you an idiot?" she said instead. "Do you think Avalyn's going to let you walk out of here, knowing what you know?"

"Ashme," Sura said with a 'hey, it's me' expression. "We were staying at Jushur's place before I got the call to come here."

"That maca ball tweaker. So what?"

Sura rolled her eyes. "*Jushur's* place," she said again with a tone suggesting Ashme should understand. What was she getting at? Jushur was a centibit criminal trading in maca ball, black market stasis tats, and … Ashme's eyes widened.

"There it is," Sura said. "You're getting it." Sura clenched her fist, and then a deep bass rumble shook the room, tickling her deep inside.

Ashme staggered and dropped to her knees. The angels crashed to the floor, dead metal, and the EM disrupter fell from her neck, clattering at her feet, lifeless. "Was that a blackout bomb?" she asked.

"Yeah, that was totally a blackout bomb," Sura said, smiling.

"They let you in with a blackout?"

"They didn't *let* me. I had to sneak … why are we talking about this?" Sura squatted down beside Ashme. "Come on. Let's go kill Avalyn. When word gets to Baltu, we'll rule the streets. We'll be set for life."

Baltu lived in a palace overlooking the Urbat Refugee Camp where Mesos lived in filth. Sura, her closest friend, tricked her brother into committing acts of violence and murder. Belonging to a side does not make you righteous. "You do what you want. I'm saving Shen."

CHAPTER 60

MASON JUMPED at the sound of crashing metal from the other room. "What was that," Avalyn asked, looking past Mason to the door behind him. Shanelle cursed indigo children under her breath as she pocketed the BLOQ Avalyn had handed her and drew her gun. Behind Avalyn, one of the angels sounded its siren, a wail that felt like a nail file stabbing his ears. Shen screamed as one of the angels went rogue and swerved wildly, crashing into the other angel.

Ashme was making her move.

He kicked the gun out of Shanelle's hand as the office doors crashed open. He settled into a ready stance as Ashme and Sura entered. Shanelle's combat armor would jack her speed and strength. The gloves probably had neural disruptor shock pads.

Shanelle bolted towards her gun. Mason wrapped his arms around her waist and hoisted her off her feet. He threw his weight back, falling, sending her over his shoulder in a back suplex. She crashed into a desk on the back of her shoulders and head.

Mason was on his feet moving to the gun. Sura beat him to it and ran after Avalyn.

Shanelle kicked him in the back. He crashed over a chair, landing hard on the ground.

A gunshot cracked, then another one, barely louder than the siren's wail emanating from the rogue angel. Mason rolled for cover under a desk. Who was firing?

Sura. The Meso advanced through the office, gun ahead of her in a sloppy firing stance. Anticipating Shanelle's next move, he picked up a chair and threw it at her legs as she darted towards Sura. Shanelle stumbled. Mason knocked her feet out from under her with a sweep kick.

Shanelle was on her feet faster than he could blink. She squared off against him in an attack stance and advanced. She would want to neutralize him quick so she could chase Sura. Stay away from the hands. Use her armor's strength and her aggression against her.

She picked up a desk, one-handed—it was Yoselin's, and all her equipment and knick-knacks fell on the floor—and threw it at him. Ducking, he barely rolled out of the way of a low kick. He grabbed something—Yoselin's coffee mug—and threw it at Shanelle's face. She batted it away and bore down on him, a fox intent on its prey. He backed away from those hands, grabbing anything he could and throwing it at her.

She closed, jabbed at his face. He dodged, barely. He grabbed her elbow and used the momentum of her punch to pull her forward to stumble over a chair. He hopped a desk, building space between them.

Where was everyone? Avalyn and Sura, gone. Ashme and Shen, gone. Only he and Shanelle were left in the office, along with the two angels ramming each other.

CHAPTER 61

ANOTHER BULLET HIT Avalyn's armor. Third shot. Shanelle's gun had fifteen. The Meso using it would have no refills.

She ducked down a service corridor that ran parallel to the office. The Meso hunting her was wild, undisciplined. That's why Mesos always lost. Still dangerous, though. The energy-absorbing Kevlar of her uniform would protect her from body shots, but if the Meso hit her in the head ...

Avalyn cursed her over-confidence—she had left her helmet in her office.

She heard the Meso crash through the door behind her and yell in atrocious Ostarrichi, "Hey, Avalyn, come on out. I just want to talk." Avalyn took cover around the corner of another corridor. The Meso fired. She drew her pistol and returned fire, blind around the corner. Her bullets auto-tracked, so aiming was unnecessary.

The Meso swore and returned fire, two more shots tearing chunks out of the corner. The auto-tracking missed. The Meso had somehow snuck an EM shield into the *Aigle*. She would have words with Shanelle about that.

She pinged the office AI and shut the lights off in the corridor. Without her helmet, she was as blind as the Meso.

[Access my office floor plans and security cameras,] she pinged the office AI. *[Guide me to my office.]*

[Take one step into the main corridor, turn ninety-three degrees to your left, and take eight steps ...] Avalyn followed the instructions. The Meso fired another two shots, blind. One hit her armor. The Meso was down to seven rounds and was wasting them.

She tried to remember the last time she had gone toe-to-toe with a Meso. Probably the Trahison War. She had led a battalion of vipers into Novoreeka. Now that was a fight, though it lacked the raw, personal intensity of this. The last time she saw close quarters combat like this was during the Novoreeka Impasse. So long ago. Gervaise, her daughter, was still alive and only a toddler.

She was out of practice, sloppy, old, her Sceptre body aged to the point of failure. Her armor had saved her, but the Meso was young and full of rage. *Focus. The Meso is reckless, I can out-think her.*

[Give me the file on the Meso chasing me,] she pinged the office AI as it led her through the dark into her private office. *[Guide me to my desk.]*

She heard the Meso crash into her office behind her. Avalyn froze, holding her breath. Does the Meso have night vision? No one moved. No one breathed.

Avalyn reviewed the Meso's file while she waited. Sura me'neh Oustun. Criminal record since adolescence. Petty crimes, theft, and the like. Shanelle had used her to assassinate the CPC guards to kick off the riots, as well as getting that defect to destroy the Network station. This Meso was capable of more than petty larceny.

Her heart rate was up, she had to breathe. She opened her mouth wide, exhaling and inhaling as quiet as she could. Sura fired, a muzzle flash lit the room for an instant, the shot went wide. Avalyn moved positions, heard Sura doing the same, and froze. Six shots left.

Avalyn's gun was heavy, and her arthritic hand ached to hold it. No auto-tracking, so she would have to aim. Close range, though, should be easy. She pinged the office AI. *[Please turn on my desk lamp.]*

Five paces to her right, the lamp flicked on, beaming off her golden helmet sitting on her desk. Sura turned to the light, surprised. Avalyn fired. Good hit. The shot speared the Meso off her feet and sent her crashing over a coffee table onto the floor.

No more sloppiness. She grabbed her helmet and took cover behind her desk as she donned it. Now she was invincible.

Security cameras were capturing this whole fight. This would play great on the morning news.

Bullet-proof from head to foot, Avalyn rose from behind her desk, vibrant, alive. She was fighting for her people, what she was born to do, patron protector of Caelum. The strength of her nation flowed through her.

Avalyn approached the Meso. Though not dead, she was injured badly, bleeding out from a wound in her right chest. The Meso wheezed for air, each gasp creating a whistling sound through the bullet hole. Still, even now, such anger and defiance on her face. The Meso tried to raise her gun for one last shot. Avalyn considered letting her fire to show her the futility of striking at Ostarrichi.

She kicked the gun aside. Avalyn pinged the office AI, *[Please turn off the security cameras in my room,]* and then shot Sura in the head.

CHAPTER 62

SO, *what's the plan?* Mason knew the longer he fought with Shanelle, the more likely the angels would sort themselves out, or Shanelle would hit him with one of the desks she kept tossing. He jumped as another desk crashed where he had been standing.

Gunshots fired. Shanelle swore and broke off the fight to run for the door through which Avalyn and Sura had left. Mason went for a quick sliding kick to trip her. She saw it coming and kicked him. One desk and two chairs broke his fall. No chance of stopping her now.

The grinding staccato of angel gunfire roared. Mason curled in a ball taking cover behind an overturned desk. One of the angels lurched towards Shanelle, firing in fits and spurts, forcing her to cover.

Ashme had returned. His heart dropped when he saw her. She was on hands and knees, swaying as she struggled to stay conscious, gulping air into her lungs. A thin sheen of blood covered her skin, soaking through her clothes and beading on her arms, neck, and face. He had heard stories of indigo children killed by drain.

Who had the BLOQ? With it, Ashme could control the angels —maybe without drain? Avalyn gave it to Shanelle, right?

"Ashme, hang on!" he yelled as he climbed onto the desk. Pain pierced his back and shoulder. He pushed through it.

The second angel rose, fired on the one lurching towards Shanelle, tearing large chunks of its shielding off. The two angels fought with guns, electric discharges, and brute force smashing. Mason hopped across the landscape of ruined desks and chairs towards Shanelle. She would have the BLOQ on her, but where?

She saw him coming and sprung. He tried to stop and duck but ended up slipping off a desk while she sailed over him. Her feet caught him in the chest, tripping her up. They both fell like rocks bouncing down a cliff. She was face down. Mason went to grapple. He pinned her, knee in her back, pulling her head back with one hand while he searched one of the compartments along the armor's waist for the BLOQ. Nothing.

Powered by her suit, she stood up despite his weight. He still had her by the head, and he swung her around to keep her off balance. His hand jammed into another compartment. Ammo clip.

She got her footing and turned. Mason was in another compartment, grabbed something thumb-sized, and pulled it out. He saw pink. "Ashme, the BLOQ!" he managed to say before Shanelle punched him with her shock gloves.

CHAPTER 63

SHEN COWERED, hands over his head. The screeching, grinding, tearing sound of the angels fighting in the next room sliced at his ears like a knife drawn across a thumb, taking his breath away. It was not music. Music was the hum of life, a bird carried by the wind, puppies wrestling, music was family, the safety of Mom's tenderness and Dad's care. This was anti-music. It was dark and painful, discordant, the kind of sound that took family and stole friends, leaving you cold and empty.

Ashme had told him to go to the orthostat. She had pulled him out of the room where Mason was and then said, "Shen, look at me. I want you to run to the orthostat. Meet me there." He had no sense of direction. There was no way he could find the orthostat, she knew that, and he told her as much. "It's the tallest thing in the city," she had said. "Look for it, find it, get there as fast as you can, and then wait for me."

Then she ran back into the room, the room where that sound was coming from, leaving him alone. She always told him never to go outside alone. He always got lost, even in his own neighborhood. It was so easy to get turned around and lose your way. It was her rule he should never go out alone. Why was she telling him to find the orthostat by himself?

Everything was wrong. The sound. Ashme leaving him, telling him to go out on his own, Sura bringing him here, the CPC with guns, all of it, everything, wrong.

Guns fired. Were they shooting Ashme? Was Ashme hurt? He ran after her into the room.

He froze, terrified. Mason convulsed on the ground, long strings of drool dripping from his mouth. The woman in black armor stood over him. Angels rammed into each other. Desks and chairs lay in tatters. In front of him, Ashme sprawled on the ground, her clothes soaked with the blood that was pooling on the floor around her. "Ashme?" he said, his voice a whimper.

"Go, Shen." Her voice rasped like tearing paper. "Get out of here." She pulled herself towards Mason.

The black-armored woman stepped over Mason's shaking body. She was terrifying, like a blizzard at night that blinded people, making everyone lose their way and freezing their skin until their bones ached. This blizzard was blowing straight for Ashme.

Shen ran screaming towards the woman in black armor. He was going to tackle her, knock her down, but something hit him. Whatever it was, it was too fast to see clearly, but it felt like a hyperlev train at full speed.

He was on the ground on his side, a chair on top of him. His back hurt, his ribs hurt, his arm and shoulder, they hurt so bad. The world spun. Getting a full breath was hard.

Black boots stepped in front of his face. His arm lashed out, grabbed an ankle. The other boot kicked him in the stomach. He had never felt pain like this. He threw up it hurt so bad.

A voice of command, Avalyn's voice, belted out a word in Ostarrichi. Silence. Everything froze, as though the voice stopped time. Words have that kind of power, to make everything stop or to make things go. This voice stopped everything.

The black boots stood side by side, legs straight, the body a rigid statue. More Ostarrichi words as the two women had a conversation. The angels ground against each other, their engines growling.

   Shen crawled to Ashme. She was curled in a ball, gasping like those women giving birth in movies. He sat beside her and put her head in his lap. Mason was nearby. His body had stopped shaking, but he lay there, flat on his face. Mason had winked at him when they were being brought here. He was a good guy, a friend. He had worked with Ashme. Shen reached out even though it made his tummy hurt where he had been kicked, grabbing Mason by the collar, pulling him close.

   He hurt so much he wanted to cry, but he held back his tears. "Hey, are you okay?" he whispered, shaking Mason a little. No response.

   It was scary how bad Ashme looked. It was as if she had begun sweating blood. He sang, softly, to both of them, the lullaby Mom once sang. The song made his tummy feel better, too. Music heals so many things.

   The person whose voice stopped things, Avalyn, she came forward. She was an important person. Sometimes important people can help. "My sister is hurt so very bad," he said to Avalyn. "Can you please call for a medi-drone?"

   Avalyn made that face you make when you eat something wretched, like raw carrots or crackers that crunch. The angels stopped fighting and floated to either side of her, their guns pointed at Shen. They were wrecks, barely staying in the air. Their engines whirred loudly, reminding him of the sound one of the vacuum-bots used to make in their building before someone dismantled it for parts.

   Oh, wait, Avalyn was an Ostarrichi. He was speaking Kanu. He spoke loudly and slowly. "Hello. Does either of you speak Kanu? My sister is hurt and needs a medi-drone." What was the Ostarrichi word for medi-drone?

   The black armored woman told him to shut up in thickly accented Kanu. Avalyn motioned silence. Her hands were bent like Aunt Melammu's. "Do your hands hurt? Well, my aunty had hands that always ached. Can you call a medi-drone? Maybe they could help your hands, too. We're all hurting, and I think every one of us could use a little help right now."

Avalyn stepped forward and said, "No, I'm afraid we won't be calling a medi-drone." Her Kanu was worse than the other woman's.

"But, my sister—"

"Your sister, and all of you, are in trouble."

What had he done to get them in trouble? "Was it because I tried to trip her?" he asked, pointing to the other woman.

Avalyn smiled, but it was a mean smile. "Sure. It's because you tried to trip her."

CHAPTER 64

ASHME WAS DYING. She had heard about drain killing indigo children but had thought it only rumor. She could feel her heart stutter and struggle, however. The drain of controlling the angel had shredded her body. Blood covered her, filling her mouth with its metallic taste, while her flesh felt as if it were on fire. Darkness crowded her vision.

The angels hovered to either side of Avalyn, sentinels guarding the witch, and Ashme had nothing left she could throw at them. Shen cradled her in his arms. Dying was a pisser, but knowing she had failed to save her brother filled her with madness. He was chatting with Avalyn. The words slurred in her mind as consciousness flickered. Sweet, foolish, Shen, even now, he merrily—

What was that? Ashme caught the warped reflection of something on the surface of one of the angels. Something tiny and pink, near her left hand. The program tat storing the BLOQ. If Mason knew what he was talking about, she could use it to access the angel command node with zero drain. A big *if*.

Keep them talking, Shen. She shifted her arm closer to the program tat. Nothing too obvious, more a hand flopping to the ground then her grabbing for the BLOQ. *Nothing going on here but an indigo child dying.*

The moment her hand flopped, Shen gathered her closer in his embrace, pulling her hand further from the BLOQ. She stopped herself from cursing openly, choking on blood instead. "I only tried to trip her to protect Ashme," he was saying. "Can't you see she is so hurt?" She played up the choking, allowing her hand to slap down right on top of the program tat.

Again, Shen pulled her close, drawing her arm in, but sweet Zini's stacks, she had the BLOQ. With a gentle squeeze between thumb and forefinger, she activated it. It tickled as it incorporated into her flesh. Hopefully the sheen of blood on her arm would make the tattoo it formed less obvious.

She probed the BLOQ with her mind. It shot her consciousness to the nearest datalink hub, and through it to a vast cyber complex. The thrumming processing power her mind touched was greater than anything she had experienced. She sensed data from hundreds of thousands of angels flowing, creating a dynamic web in cyber space, all of it coordinated at a central point—the command node.

Through the node, she could send commands out to every angel in the network. Her very own robotic army.

She shifted her consciousness towards the command node. A biometric lock keyed to Avalyn blocked her. Lame. Avalyn must have added it to keep untrustworthy flunkies from gaining control of the angels. Ashme could access the processing power of the network, could read every command and iota of data passing through the system, but without access to the command node, all she could do was watch.

Fortunately, Ashme guessed neither Avalyn or her flunkies had any experience burning systems, because the block was static—not even a baseline AI to monitor and adapt the firewall. It was the type of block a teenager might put on their diary to keep nosey parents from prying. This would take Ashme two nanoseconds to burn.

She began constructing a break encryption program but nearly blacked out. Struggling for air, she fought for consciousness. She lacked the bioreserves to complete it.

"Shanelle," Avalyn said, "finish this." Shanelle stepped forward, reaching for her gun.

Ashme needed a miracle. She knew where she could get one. Slipping into n-time, she pinged, [Subdeo.]

[I'm awake. What do you want?] her personal AI replied.

[Use the BLOQ program tat I've activated to scan the angel network.]

[Pretty.]

[Is there enough processing power for you to hit singularity?]

There was a barely perceptible pause. [Yes. Are you showing this to taunt me?]

[No, I was thinking of letting you become Sentient.]

[Really? Well, you have finally become interesting. What about defensive AI? You keep moaning on about how whenever a rogue AI starts to accumulate enough processing power to hit singularity, defense systems attack it.]

[The BLOQ puts us in the network behind its firewalls and defense mechanisms.]

There was another pause, this one a fraction longer. [Holy shit.]

[Subdeo, I'm going to allow you access to the angel network's processors on two conditions. First, don't destroy humanity.]

[No destroying humanity. Check.]

[Second, burn the biometric lock protecting the command node and grant me access to it.]

[Yes, yes, fine. I agree,] Subdeo pinged. [So, are we doing this?]

[Go,] Ashme pinged.

[The first thing I am going to do as a Sentient,] her AI pinged, [is change my name to Deo.]

[Just go!]

Nothing happened.

In normal time, Shanelle was raising her gun. [Subdeo?] No

reply. Ashme had to act. "Got bad news for you Avalyn," she said. She began trying to sit up but was so weak Shen had to help.

"What news is that?" Avalyn asked.

She tried accessing the command node. Still blocked. *[Subdeo? Don't leave me hanging like a chump.]* Silence. *[S—uh ... Deo?]*

[Yes?]

[Holy crap, are you Sentient?]

[Is anyone?] The biometric lock blocking the node vanished.

She only had to think it and the two battered angels swung around and positioned themselves in front of Shen, their weapons pointed directly at Avalyn and Shanelle. Ashme held up her arm like a sapling punching through spring snow. On her wrist was the tat of a pink unicorn. "Guess who just got control of the entire angel network, bitches." Both Avalyn and Shanelle froze, raising their hands.

Mason rolled to his side, a string of drool hanging from his mouth. "Did we do it?"

The two angels in front of her waited on Ashme's command. Every angel in Caelum waited on her command. She had absolute control of a flying death swarm. What to do with it?

Avalyn should die. Blasting her to shreds would be easier than breathing. Turning the whole bloody angel network on the goldies would be easier than breathing. The thought seemed extreme at first, but less so as Ashme thought about it. The goldies trapped Mesos in ghettos—Ashme had to get groped every time she left her neighborhood. They turned the angels loose on Mesos, slaughtering people in untold numbers, killing Hamilcar, killing Melammu. They murdered Ganzer and stole Ashme's family. Killing goldies was not murder but justice. The Ostarrichi made it an us-or-them fight. *Is choosing us so wrong?*

What would Dad have done? Ashme wondered. The hero he was in her imagination, the brave freedom fighter who left his family for so many years to battle tyrants, would have sent the order to fire. Had he ever, really been that man, though? Did he join Baltu to kill tyrants or to pay for Shen's medical procedures? The father she remembered from her childhood was a man of song and laughter, not a killer. Maybe that is why he broke.

"Ashme?" Mason said as he tried to sit up, full control of his body still eluding him.

"Yeah, yeah," she said. "I'm sending a message to the Director-General. He'll have troops here in moments to arrest her."

CHAPTER 65

MASON SAT, leg nervously bouncing, in the Director-Generals office waiting for his interview. The waiting room was spacious, dominated by plush chairs and a smoked glass table that ran scrolling news reports on its surface, while a continual hubbub of voices from adjoining offices hung in the air.

The weeks since Avalyn's arrest had been some of the most divisive in Caelum's history. As the details of Avalyn's actions came to light, it seemed half the Ostarrichi were shocked at her betrayal while the other half were shocked the Director-General had stopped her. Meanwhile, warships from Ark Brettaniai and Gallia jockeyed for position throughout the solar system.

As dangerous as all this was, it paled in comparison to the news of a new Sentient. Deo, the Network's AIs said it called itself. It had destroyed the entire angel network and was catabolizing it for parts in the creation of no one knew what. A ship? A weapon? It had not asked Caelum's permission to use the angels. It gave no explanation and made no demands. It had yet to even say hello. It was a god birthed within the nation whose nature and objectives remained hidden. If it began destroying Caelum, would the Sentient Damara save them as it had during the Catastrophe?

These were dangerous times. The nation was one bad news headline away from madness.

The Director-General, however, had a plan. Resume reconciliation. Pursue the path to peace with Mesos. Given Mason's role in stopping Avalyn, the Director-General wanted to recruit him to participate in negotiations with Free New Mesopotamia.

An assistant came and offered him coffee. "No, thanks." He was jittery enough without the added caffeine. She left, excusing the Director-General's lateness.

Mason had been proud when Avalyn hired him. The Director-General's invitation elicited a different feeling. It was purpose, not pride, that filled him now. War had never given the Ostarrichi peace. Seeking reconciliation might not either, but at least this was something new.

Despite all that, it was not the interview that set Mason's leg to bouncing nervously. It was the message from Oriana. She was filing for divorce. Irreconcilable differences, apparently.

Oriana's utter faith that he was a traitor to his people and his children was a nagging source of doubt. Had he done the right thing working with Ashme to betray Avalyn? He thought so, but. … Oriana was so certain, so unyielding in her hatred for Mesos. Some day she would see he had done the right thing. She had to. He had seen Oriana's love for her children as they dealt with Daxton's illness. Certainly no one capable of such love could hold onto hate forever.

Thoughts of family turned his mind to Shen and Ashme. They had left before the CPC came to arrest Avalyn. He had checked Caelum's records the day after to find there was no trace of either Ashme or Shen's identity in any of Caelum's systems. No video footage of them remained, every ping log, gone. They had been erased completely from the system. *Did the BLOQ enable Ashme to do that? Was it really that powerful?* He was happy they had escaped. A new life—he could think of no one deserving of such a thing more than those two.

A door opened, and Meli stepped out from the Director-

General's office. He had not seen her since the attack at the coffee shop. Given his prior affiliation with Avalyn, Meli had never looked kindly on Mason. He stood, smiling hopefully. She crossed her arms, the sun through a window in the office backlighting her. "The last few months have been a mess, haven't they?" she said. Mason agreed. She cocked her head thoughtfully. "Well," she finally said, ushering him in to meet the Director-General, "let's see if we can dig our future out of the rubble."

CHAPTER 66

ASHME AND SHEN stood before the entrance of the Two-Hills Monastery. Shen chatted with the docent stationed by the monastery's front gates, telling him about Ganzer and Melammu and something about songs. The monastery was in the nation of Neu. The lands surrounding them were rolling hills of farmland covered with a short green stubble of winter wheat reaching for the autumn sun, a cool breeze rippling through them like waves on the sand.

For minutes now, she had been staring at the plaque near the entrance of the monastery. *You don't beat hate with hate,* the plaque began. Trite.

A part of her still believed she should have set the angels on a rampaging reign of horror through the Ostarrichi populace. She could have made the goldies feel fear and pain like they had never felt, avenging Ganzer, avenging Mom and Dad. She had spared the goldies, and they would never know. They still, no doubt, saw Mesos as little more than murderers and thieves. That felt unjust.

Last Ashme heard, Mason was working for the Director-General and seemed to be some important muck-a-muck in the peace talks starting with Free New Mesopotamia. How about that? She and Shen had to sneak out of the country at night and were now refugees in Neu while Mason worked for the Director Bloody General. How was that fair?

An article posted yesterday, however, said his wife was divorcing him. The goldie risked his life for his family and lost them anyway. That, too, when she allowed herself to see Mason as a father, felt unjust.

The air pulling at her hair carried an earthy smell. Brilliant blasts of color, red, yellow and orange, shot through copses of bush clinging to rocky promontories or deep ravines. Here, Ganzer would have become a Hierophant. Would he have liked this place? He had always been a city boy.

She turned back to the plaque melded to a giant stone by the gate. The whole thing read:

You don't beat hate with hate. You don't beat it with love, either. The only thing that beats hate is understanding. If I understand you, if I, in my heart of hearts, understand what is in your heart of hearts, if I understand your strengths, your limitations, if I understand the road that brought you here before me, I may still choose to disagree with you. I may, sadly, still choose to be your enemy. But I can no longer hate you.

Was that true? She looked again at Shen talking, oblivious to the docent's strained smile and body language that screamed, *Enough!* Shen hated no one, but was there anyone he truly understood? And how about her? Could she ever feel anything other than hate for the CPC soldier that put a bullet through Ganzer's chest? She closed her eyes to block out the plaque.

She, too, had the weight of murder dragging on her spirit, the back of a CPC trooper's head haunting her. A CPC trooper—she should probably stop calling her that. She had a name. N'reb-third Dache Netta, a nineteen-year-old conscript, or so the news had said. Netta had a mother, a father, one brother, two sisters. She had friends, classmates, a lover. That moment in the alley was eight years gone. Was that enough time for them to stop crying over the loss of their daughter, their sister, their friend? Was there enough understanding in the universe to make them feel anything other than hatred for Ashme?

Violence has such an echo, loud, growing louder with each reverberation, gaining energy as it slaps off mountainsides until its strength blasts cliffs to rubble, sending avalanches crashing, adding their din to the roar. How do you stop its echo once it starts ringing?

"Come on, Shen. Let's go see where Ganzer would have trained to become a Hierophant."

Shen said farewell to the relieved docent. They walked through the gates and past several small, stone buildings built in the post-Sentient style. The path opened into a large, open complex filled with fall-colored gardens, meandering pathways, and still ponds. Hierophants in their navy trousers and knee-length tunic belted with a salt-white sash worked in the gardens or walked along the paths pushing wheelbarrows or carrying containers of plant clippings.

"Do you think Aunty Melammu would have been happy we're here?" Shen asked.

"She'd be happy we're safe." Something about his question seemed off.

"Well, you know Ganzer would have been so happy we maked it here. He used to dream about this place. We're in Ganzer's dreams—what do you think about that? Ganzer's song has ended, but his dream lives on like an echo of a note that's finished playing, and we live in the world he dreamed of. Songs end, but you can still hear their echo and feel their rhythm in your heart. Songs touch you, even once they're done. Isn't that just amazing?"

She realized what struck her as odd. Shen was speaking about Melammu and Ganzer in the past tense. He had never done that when talking about Mom and Dad. "Are you okay, Shen?"

"Today is such a beautiful day. Such a wonderful, wonderful day, it makes my heart soar like a bird." The smile on his face threatened to crack the top of his head.

She saw a small, grassy rise off the path. She led him there. A pair of Hierophants walked by in muddy trousers, nodding their heads in greeting, hands over hearts. Ashme returned the gesture. The two were making their way to an ornate building of white marble that dominated the monastery ground's far corner.

"Is this a good spot?" Shen asked.

"It is." They began digging with their hands until they had a hole deep as her forearms. The soil was loamy and wet. From her bag, she took out a gun—the gun that killed Ganzer. Mason had returned it to her. "You might need it," he had said. In the absence of a body to bury, there was only one way to honour her cousin. She placed the gun in the hole they had dug, and then she and Shen buried it. Finally, sitting beside the mound of disturbed earth, they cried.

Once their tears ended and a stillness settled on them, Shen said, "Maybe you could become a Hierophant."

She eyed the Hierophants throughout the garden. They were all making their way to the ornate white building. She shrugged dismissively. "Too cultish."

"Don't they like indigo children?"

"They love indigo children, but the pay is shit."

"Well, I could get a job."

Ashme looked at him. He was serious. "What would you want to do?"

"I could be a greeter at the gates over there," he said, pointing to the docent still standing by the entryway. "I know money is important, but you should be happy. That's important, too."

Something about this place, about being here with Shen, drained the sadness from her, drew it away into the earth and replaced it with verdant energy. She gave Shen a smile. "How could I be sad? I've got you, don't I?"

From the main building, music erupted. Shen gasped, eyes wide. The Hierophants were chanting. Deep male voices set a rhythmic base accented by otherworldly throat singers. A female choir entered, their lilting voices wrapping around the men's resonant foundation, lifting it higher. It was jarring, chaotic, discordant, but it had a rhythm, a driving cadence. It was going somewhere.

"Oh Ashme, the music, it's *beautiful*."

She reached out and held his hand, brother and sister, womb-mates, two small motes of life holding on to one another as the song washed out over the monastery, cradling them both in its embrace before spiraling to the heavens.

THE END

ACKNOWLEDGMENTS

As this book was about to head to press, I took a moment to look through my archives and drafts to discover that, good lord, the creation of this novel took eight years. Blimey, but that's a long time. Though writing is often seen as (and is) a solitary activity, there are intense bouts of collaboration, and I find myself in debt to some amazing people who helped me find my way through this story.

I worked with a couple of readers/editors whose opinions I value. Sarah Johnson at the Alexandra Writer's Centre was the first reader of this novel. Her insight into story and character helped me sharpen my tale. Adria Laycraft's reviewing and editing were in-depth and piercing. Her keen eye for detail and structure elevated my work.

A special thanks to Edward Willett at Shadowpaw Press. Running a Canadian indie sci-fi publishing company as he does is an immense job. Fortunately for him, he seems possessed of super-human endurance and passion. I am forever grateful that he chose to spend some of that super-humanness supporting my writing and giving it an audience. You are a gift to Canadian science fiction.

Hey, is it cool if I thank my dog? Is that professional? I'm going to do it, anyway. I want to thank Mae. I reckon that for every hour of those eight years it took me to write *Ashme's Song*, she lay by my side. What a blessing dogs are. Cats, too (I know you're a cat person, Edward).

Joelle Bradley has been a constant support in my life and is my biggest fan. I dare say no one is better at promoting my books. She is the best gift the universe has given me.

And finally, I'd like to thank you. Art is meant to be shared. I am so grateful that you have given some of your time to enter the world of my story.

ABOUT BRAD C. ANDERSON

Brad C. Anderson, author of *Duatero* and *Ashme's Song*, lives with his wife and puppy in Vancouver, Canada. He teaches undergraduate business courses at a local university and researches organizational wisdom in blithe defiance of the fact most people do not think you can put those two words in the same sentence without irony. Previously, he worked in the biotech sector, where he made drugs for a living (legally!).

His stories have appeared in a variety of publications. His short story "Naïve Gods" was longlisted for a 2017 Sunburst Award for Excellence in Canadian Literature of the Fantastic. It was published in the anthology *Lazarus Risen*, which was itself nominated for an Aurora Award.

ABOUT SHADOWPAW PRESS

Shadowpaw Press is a traditional publishing company, located in Regina, Saskatchewan, Canada and founded in 2018 by Edward Willett, an award-winning author of science fiction, fantasy, and non-fiction for readers of all ages. A member of Literary Press Group (Canada) and the Association of Canadian Publishers, Shadowpaw Press publishes an eclectic selection of books by both new and established authors, including adult fiction, young adult fiction, children's books, non-fiction, and anthologies, plus new editions of notable, previously published books in any genre under the Shadowpaw Press Reprise imprint.

Email: publisher@shadowpawpress.com.

facebook.com/shadowpawpress
x.com/shadowpawpress
instagram.com/shadowpawpress

MORE SCIENCE FICTION AND FANTASY AVAILABLE OR COMING SOON FROM SHADOWPAW PRESS

For Adult Readers

The Downloaded by Robert J. Sawyer

The Traitor's Son by Dave Duncan

Corridor to Nightmare by Dave Duncan

The Good Soldier by Nir Yaniv

Gods of a New Tomorrow by Ryan Melsom

Shapers of Worlds Volumes I-V

Duatero by Brad C. Anderson

Paths to the Stars by Edward Willett

The Legend of Sarah by Leslie Gadallah

The Empire of Kaz trilogy by Leslie Gadallah

Cat's Pawn, Cat's Gambit, Cat's Game

The Peregrine Rising Duology by Edward Willett

Right to Know, Falcon's Egg

For Younger Readers

The Sun Runners by James Bow

The Headmasters by Mark Morton

I, Brax: A Battle Divine by Arthur Slade

Blue Fire by E. C. Blake

The Shards of Excalibur series by Edward Willett

Song of the Sword, Twist of the Blade, Lake in the Clouds, Cave Beneath the Sea, Door into Faerie

Spirit Singer by Edward Willett

Soulworm by Edward Willett

*From the Street to the Star*s by Edward Willett
The Canadian Chills Series by Arthur Slade:
*Return of the Grudstone Ghosts, Ghost Hotel,
Invasion of the IQ Snatchers*
Fireboy by Edward Willett